I0681555

CLASSIC WEIRD

Selected by
David A. Riley

Parallel Universe Publications

First Published in 2015 by Parallel Universe Publications 2015

ISBN: 978-0-9574535-3-1
Parallel Universe Publications, 130 Union Road, Oswaldtwistle, Lancashire, BB5 3DR, UK

CONTENTS

THE MONSTER-MAKER
By W. C. Morrow

A young man of refined appearance, but evidently suffering great mental distress, presented himself one morning at the residence of a singular old man, who was known as a surgeon of remarkable skill. The house was a queer and primitive brick affair, entirely out of date, and tolerable only in the decayed part of the city in which it stood. It was large, gloomy, and dark, and had long corridors and dismal rooms; and it was absurdly large for the small family - man and wife - that occupied it. The house described, the man is portrayed - but not the woman. He could be agreeable on occasion, but, for all that, he was but animated mystery. His wife was weak, wan, reticent, evidently miserable, and possibly living a life of dread or horror - perhaps witness of repulsive things, subject of anxieties, and victim of fear and tyranny; but there is a great deal of guessing in these assumptions. He was about sixty-five years of age and she about forty. He was lean, tall, and bald, with thin, smooth-shaven face, and very keen eyes; kept always at home, and was slovenly. The man was strong, the woman weak; he dominated, she suffered.

Although he was a surgeon of rare skill, his practice was almost nothing, for it was a rare occurrence that the few who knew of his great ability were brave enough to penetrate the gloom of his house, and when they did so it was with deaf ear turned to sundry ghoulish stories that were whispered concerning him. These were, in great part, but exaggerations of his experiments in vivisection; he was devoted to the science of surgery.

The young man who presented himself on the morning just mentioned was a handsome fellow, yet of evident weak character and unhealthy temperament - sensitive, and easily exalted or depressed. A single glance convinced the surgeon that his visitor was seriously affected in mind, for there was never bolder skull-grin of melancholia, fixed and irremediable.

A stranger would not have suspected any occupancy of the house. The street door - old, warped, and blistered by the sun -

was locked, and the small, faded-green window-blinds were closed. The young man rapped at the door. No answer. He rapped again. Still no sign. He examined a slip of paper, glanced at the number on the house, and then, with the impatience of a child, he furiously kicked the door. There were signs of numerous other such kicks. A response came in the shape of a shuffling footstep in the hall, a turning of the rusty key, and a sharp face that peered through a cautious opening in the door.

"Are you the doctor?" asked the young man.

"Yes, yes! Come in," briskly replied the master of the house.

The young man entered. The old surgeon closed the door and carefully locked it. "This way," he said, advancing to a rickety flight of stairs. The young man followed. The surgeon led the way up the stairs, turned into a narrow, musty-smelling corridor at the left, traversed it, rattling the loose boards under his feet, at the farther end opened a door at the right, and beckoned his visitor to enter. The young man found himself in a pleasant room, furnished in antique fashion and with hard simplicity.

"Sit down," said the old man, placing a chair so that its occupant should face a window that looked out upon a dead wall about six feet from the house. He threw open the blind, and a pale light entered. He then seated himself near his visitor and directly facing him, and with a searching look, that had all the power of a microscope, he proceeded to diagnosticate the case.

"Well?" he presently asked.

The young man shifted uneasily in his seat.

"I - I have come to see you," he finally stammered, "because I'm in trouble."

"Ah!"

"Yes; you see, I - that is - I have given it up."

"Ah!" There was pity added to sympathy in the ejaculation.

"That's it. Given it up," added the visitor. He took from his pocket a roll of banknotes, and with the utmost deliberation he counted them out upon his knee. "Five thousand dollars," he calmly remarked. "That is for you. It's all I have; but I presume - I imagine - no; that is not the word – assume - yes; that's the word - assume that five thousand - is it really that much? Let me count." He counted again. "That five thousand dollars is a sufficient fee for what I want you to do."

The surgeon's lips curled pityingly - perhaps disdainfully also. "What do you want me to do?" he carelessly inquired.

The young man rose, looked around with a mysterious air, approached the surgeon, and laid the money across his knee. Then he stooped and whispered two words in the surgeon's ear.

These words produced an electric effect. The old man started violently; then, springing to his feet, he caught his visitor angrily, and transfixed him with a look that was as sharp as a knife. His eyes flashed, and he opened his mouth to give utterance to some harsh imprecation, when he suddenly checked himself. The anger left his face, and only pity remained. He relinquished his grasp, picked up the scattered notes, and, offering them to the visitor, slowly said:

"I do not want your money. You are simply foolish. You think you are in trouble. Well, you do not know what trouble is. Your only trouble is that you have not a trace of manhood in your nature. You are merely insane - I shall not say pusillanimous. You should surrender yourself to the authorities, and be sent to a lunatic asylum for proper treatment."

The young man keenly felt the intended insult, and his eyes flashed dangerously.

"You old dog - you insult me thus!" he cried. "Grand airs, these, you give yourself! Virtuously indignant, old murderer, you! Don't want my money, eh? When a man comes to you himself and wants it done, you fly into a passion and spurn his money; but let an enemy of his come and pay you, and you are only too willing. How many such jobs have you done in this miserable old hole? It is a good thing for you that the police have not run you down, and brought spade and shovel with them. Do you know what is said of you? Do you think you have kept your windows so closely shut that no sound has ever penetrated beyond them? Where do you keep your infernal implements?"

He had worked himself into a high passion. His voice was hoarse, loud, and rasping. His eyes, bloodshot, started from their sockets. His whole frame twitched, and his fingers writhed. But he was in the presence of a man infinitely his superior. Two eyes, like those of a snake, burned two holes through him. An overmastering, inflexible presence confronted one weak and passionate. The result came

"Sit down," commanded the stern voice of the surgeon.

It was the voice of father to child, of master to slave. The fury left the visitor, who, weak and overcome, fell upon a chair.

Meanwhile, a peculiar light had appeared in the old surgeon's face, the dawn of a strange idea; a gloomy ray, strayed from the fires of the bottomless pit; the baleful light that illumines the way of the enthusiast. The old man remained a moment in profound abstraction, gleams of eager intelligence bursting momentarily through the cloud of sombre meditation that covered his face. Then broke the broad light of a deep, impenetrable determination. There was something sinister in it, suggesting the sacrifice of something held sacred. After a struggle, mind had vanquished conscience.

Taking a piece of paper and a pencil, the surgeon carefully wrote answers to questions which he peremptorily addressed to his visitor, such as his name, age, place of residence, occupation, and the like, and the same inquiries concerning his parents, together with other particular matters.

"Does any one know you came to this house?" he asked.

"No."

"You swear it?"

"Yes."

"But your prolonged absence will cause alarm and lead to search."

"I have provided against that."

"How?"

"By depositing a note in the post, as I came along, announcing my intention to drown myself."

"The river will be dragged."

"What then?" asked the young man, shrugging his shoulders with careless indifference. "Rapid undercurrent, you know. A good many are never found."

There was a pause.

"Are you ready?" finally asked the surgeon.

"Perfectly." The answer was cool and determined.

The manner of the surgeon, however, showed much perturbation. The pallor that had come into his face at the moment his decision was formed became intense. A nervous tremulousness came over his frame. Above it all shone the light of enthusiasm.

"Have you a choice in the method?" he asked.

"Yes; extreme anæsthesia."

"With what agent?"

"The surest and quickest."

"Do you desire any - any subsequent disposition?"

"No; only nullification; simply a blowing out, as of a candle in the wind; a puff - then darkness, without a trace. A sense of your own safety may suggest the method. I leave it to you."

"No delivery to your friends?"

"None whatever."

Another pause.

"Did you say you are quite ready?" asked the surgeon.

"Quite ready."

"And perfectly willing?"

"Anxious."

"Then wait a moment."

With this request the old surgeon rose to his feet and stretched himself. Then with the stealthiness of a cat he opened the door and peered into the hall, listening intently. There was no sound. He softly closed the door and locked it. Then he closed the window-blinds and locked them. This done, he opened a door leading into an adjoining room, which, though it had no window, was lighted by means of a small skylight. The young man watched closely. A strange change had come over him. While his determination had not one whit lessened, a look of great relief came into his face, displacing the haggard, despairing look of a half-hour before. Melancholic then, he was ecstatic now.

The opening of the second door disclosed a curious sight. In the centre of the room, directly under the skylight, was an operating-table, such as is used by demonstrators of anatomy. A glass case against the wall held surgical instruments of every kind. Hanging in another case were human skeletons of various sizes. In sealed jars, arranged on shelves, were monstrosities of divers kinds preserved in alcohol. There were also, among innumerable other articles scattered about the room, a manikin, a stuffed cat, a desiccated human heart, plaster casts of various parts of the body, numerous charts, and a large assortment of drugs and chemicals. There was also a lounge, which could be opened to form a couch. The surgeon opened it and moved the operating-table aside, giving its place to the lounge.

"Come in," he called to his visitor.

The young man obeyed without the least hesitation.

"Take off your coat."

He complied.

"Lie down on that lounge."

In a moment the young man was stretched at full length, eyeing the surgeon. The latter undoubtedly was suffering under great excitement, but he did not waver; his movements were sure and quick. Selecting a bottle containing a liquid, he carefully measured out a certain quantity. While doing this he asked:

"Have you ever had any irregularity of the heart?"

"No."

The answer was prompt, but it was immediately followed by a quizzical look in the speaker's face.

"I presume," he added, "you mean by your question that it might be dangerous to give me a certain drug. Under the circumstances, however, I fail to see any relevancy in your question."

This took the surgeon aback; but he hastened to explain that he did not wish to inflict unnecessary pain, and hence his question.

He placed the glass on a stand, approached his visitor, and carefully examined his pulse.

"Wonderful!" he exclaimed.

"Why?"

"It is perfectly normal."

"Because I am wholly resigned. Indeed, it has been long since I knew such happiness. It is not active, but infinitely sweet."

"You have no lingering desire to retract?"

"None whatever."

The surgeon went to the stand and returned with the draught.

"Take this," he said, kindly.

The young man partially raised himself and took the glass in his hand. He did not show the vibration of a single nerve. He drank the liquid, draining the last drop. Then he returned the glass with a smile.

"Thank you," he said; "you are the noblest man that lives. May you always prosper and be happy! You are my benefactor, my liberator. Bless you, bless you! You reach down from your seat with the gods and lift me up into glorious peace and rest. I love you - I love you with all my heart!"

These words, spoken earnestly, in a musical, low voice, and accompanied with a smile of ineffable tenderness, pierced the old man's heart. A suppressed convulsion swept over him; intense anguish wrung his vitals; perspiration trickled down his face. The young man continued to smile.

"Ah, it does me good!" said he.

The surgeon, with a strong effort to control himself, sat down upon the edge of the lounge and took his visitor's wrist, counting the pulse.

"How long will it take?" the young man asked.

"Ten minutes. Two have passed." The voice was hoarse.

"Ah, only eight minutes more!... Delicious, delicious! I feel it coming... What was that?... Ah, I understand. Music... Beautiful! ... Coming, coming... Is that – that - water?... Trickling? Dripping? Doctor!"

"Well?"

"Thank you... thank you... Noble man... my saviour... my bene... bene... factor... Trickling... trickling... Dripping, dripping... Doctor!"

"Well?"

"Doctor!"

"Past hearing," muttered the surgeon.

"Doctor!"

"And blind."

Response was made by a firm grasp of the hand.

"Doctor!"

"And numb."

"Doctor!"

The old man watched and waited.

"Dripping... dripping."

The last drop had run. There was a sigh, and nothing more.

The surgeon laid down the hand.

"The first step," he groaned, rising to his feet; then his whole frame dilated. "The first step - the most difficult, yet the simplest. A providential delivery into my hands of that for which I have hungered for forty years. No withdrawal now! It is possible, because scientific; rational, but perilous. If I succeed - if? I shall succeed. I will succeed... And after success - what?... Yes; what?

Publish the plan and the result? The gallows... So long as it shall exist... and I exist, the gallows. That much... But how account for its presence? Ah, that pinches hard! I must trust to the future."

He tore himself from the reverie and started.

"I wonder if she heard or saw anything."

With that reflection he cast a glance upon the form on the lounge, and then left the room, locked the door, locked also the door of the outer room, walked down two or three corridors, penetrated to a remote part of the house, and rapped at a door. It was opened by his wife. He, by this time, had regained complete mastery over himself.

"I thought I heard someone in the house just now," he said, "but I can find no one."

"I heard nothing."

He was greatly relieved.

"I did hear someone knock at the door less than an hour ago," she resumed, "and heard you speak, I think. Did he come in?"

"No."

The woman glanced at his feet and seemed perplexed.

"I am almost certain," she said, "that I heard footfalls in the house, and yet I see that you are wearing slippers."

"Oh, I had on my shoes then!"

"That explains it," said the woman, satisfied; "I think the sound you heard must have been caused by rats."

"Ah, that was it!" exclaimed the surgeon. Leaving, he closed the door, reopened it, and said, "I do not wish to be disturbed to-day." He said to himself, as he went down the hall, "All is clear there."

He returned to the room in which his visitor lay, and made a careful examination.

"Splendid specimen!" he softly exclaimed; "every organ sound, every function perfect; fine, large frame; well-shaped muscles, strong and sinewy; capable of wonderful development - if given opportunity... I have no doubt it can be done. Already I have succeeded with a dog, - a task less difficult than this, for in a man the cerebrum overlaps the cerebellum, which is not the case with a dog. This gives a wide range for accident, with but one opportunity in a lifetime! In the cerebrum, the intellect and the affections; in the cerebellum, the senses and the motor forces; in the medulla oblongata, control of the diaphragm. In these two latter lie all the essentials of simple existence. The cerebrum is merely an adornment; that is to say, reason and the affections are almost purely ornamental. I have already proved it. My dog, with its cerebrum removed, was idiotic, but it retained its physical senses to a certain degree."

While thus ruminating he made careful preparations. He moved the couch, replaced the operating-table under the skylight, selected a number of surgical instruments, prepared certain drug-mixtures, and arranged water, towels, and all the accessories of a tedious surgical operation. Suddenly he burst into laughter.

"Poor fool!" he exclaimed. "Paid me five thousand dollars to kill him! Didn't have the courage to snuff his own candle! Singular, singular, the queer freaks these madmen have! You thought you were dying, poor idiot! Allow me to inform you, sir, that you are as much alive at this moment as ever you were in your life. But it will be all the same to you. You shall never be more conscious than you are now; and for all practical purposes, so far as they concern you, you are dead henceforth, though you shall live. By the way, how should you feel without a head? Ha, ha, ha!... But that's a sorry joke."

He lifted the unconscious form from the lounge and laid it upon the operating-table.

About three years afterwards the following conversation was held between a captain of police and a detective:

"She may be insane," suggested the captain.

"I think she is."

"And yet you credit her story!"

"I do."

"Singular!"

"Not at all. I myself have learned something."

"What!"

"Much, in one sense; little, in another. You have heard those queer stories of her husband. Well, they are all nonsensical - probably with one exception. He is generally a harmless old fellow, but peculiar. He has performed some wonderful surgical operations. The people in his neighbourhood are ignorant, and they fear him and wish to be rid of him; hence they tell a great many lies about him, and they come to believe their own stories. The one important thing that I have learned is that he is almost insanely enthusiastic on the subject of surgery - especially experimental surgery; and with an enthusiast there is hardly such a thing as a scruple. It is this that gives me confidence in the woman's story."

"You say she appeared to be frightened?"

"Doubly so - first, she feared that her husband would learn of her betrayal of him; second, the discovery itself had terrified her."

"But her report of this discovery is very vague," argued the captain. "He conceals everything from her. She is merely guessing."

"In part - yes; in other part - no. She heard the sounds distinctly, though she did not see clearly. Horror closed her eyes. What she thinks she saw is, I admit, preposterous; but she undoubtedly saw something extremely frightful. There are many peculiar little circumstances. He has eaten with her but few times during the last three years, and nearly always carries his food to his private rooms. She says that he either consumes an enormous quantity, throws much away, or is feeding something that eats prodigiously. He explains this to her by saying that he has animals with which he experiments. This is not true. Again, he always keeps the door to these rooms carefully locked; and not only that, but he has had the doors doubled and otherwise strengthened, and has heavily barred a window that looks from one of the rooms upon a dead wall a few feet distant."

"What does it mean?" asked the captain.

"A prison."

"For animals, perhaps."

"Certainly not."

"Why!"

"Because, in the first place, cages would have been better; in the second place, the security that he has provided is infinitely greater than that required for the confinement of ordinary animals."

"All this is easily explained: he has a violent lunatic under treatment."

"I had thought of that, but such is not the fact."

"How do you know?"

"By reasoning thus: He has always refused to treat cases of lunacy; he confines himself to surgery; the walls are not padded, for the woman has heard sharp blows upon them; no human strength, however morbid, could possibly require such resisting strength as has been provided; he would not be likely to conceal a lunatic's confinement from the woman; no lunatic could consume all the food that he provides; so extremely violent mania as these precautions indicate could not continue three years; if there is a lunatic in the case it is very probable that there should have been communication with some one outside concerning the patient, and there has been none; the woman has listened at the keyhole and has heard no human voice within; and last, we have heard the woman's vague description of what she saw."

"You have destroyed every possible theory," said the captain, deeply interested, "and have suggested nothing new."

"Unfortunately, I cannot; but the truth may be very simple, after all. The old surgeon is so peculiar that I am prepared to discover something remarkable."

"Have you suspicions?"

"I have."

"Of what?"

"A crime. The woman suspects it."

"And betrays it?"

"Certainly, because it is so horrible that her humanity revolts; so terrible that her whole nature demands of her that she hand over the criminal to the law; so frightful that she is in mortal terror; so awful that it has shaken her mind."

"What do you propose to do?" asked the captain.

"Secure evidence. I may need help."

"You shall have all the men you require. Go ahead, but be careful. You are on dangerous ground. You would be a mere plaything in the hands of that man."

Two days afterwards the detective again sought the captain.

"I have a queer document," he said, exhibiting torn fragments of paper, on which there was writing. "The woman stole it and brought it to me. She snatched a handful out of a book, getting only a part of each of a few leaves."

These fragments, which the men arranged as best they could, were (the detective explained) torn by the surgeon's wife from the first volume of a number of manuscript books which her husband had written on one subject, - the very one that was the cause of her excitement. "About the time that he began a certain experiment three years ago," continued the detective, "he removed everything from the suite of two rooms containing his study and his operating-room. In one of the bookcases that he removed to a room across the passage was a drawer, which he kept locked, but which he opened from time to time. As is quite common with such pieces of furniture, the lock of the drawer is a very poor one; and so the woman, while making a thorough search yesterday, found a key on her bunch that fitted this lock. She opened the drawer, drew out the bottom book of a pile (so that its mutilation would more likely escape discovery), saw that it might contain a clue, and tore out a handful of the leaves. She had barely replaced the book, locked the drawer, and made her escape when her husband appeared. He hardly ever allows her to be out of his sight when she is in that part of the house."

The fragments read as follows: "... the motory nerves. I had hardly dared to hope for such a result, although inductive reasoning had convinced me of its possibility, my only doubt having been on the score of my lack of skill. Their operation has been only slightly impaired, and even this would not have been the case had the operation been performed in infancy, before the intellect had sought and obtained recognition as an essential part of the whole. Therefore I state, as a proved fact, that the cells of the motory nerves have inherent forces sufficient to the purposes of those nerves. But hardly so with the sensory nerves. These latter are, in fact, an offshoot of the former, evolved from them by natural (though not essential) heterogeneity, and to a certain extent are dependent on the evolution and expansion of a contemporaneous tendency, that developed into mentality, or mental function. Both of these latter tendencies, these evolvements, are merely refinements of the motory system, and not independent entities; that is to say, they are the blossoms of a plant that propagates from its roots. The motory system is the first... nor am I surprised that such prodigious muscular energy is developing. It promises yet to surpass the wildest dreams of human strength. I account for it thus: The powers of assimilation had reached their full development. They had formed the habit of doing a certain amount of work. They sent their products to all parts of the system. As a result of my operation the consumption of these products was reduced fully one-half; that is to say, about one-half of the demand for them was withdrawn. But force of habit required the production to proceed. This production was strength, vitality, energy. Thus double the usual quantity of this strength, this energy, was stored in the remaining... developed a tendency that did surprise me. Nature, no longer suffering the distraction of extraneous interferences, and at the same time being cut in two (as it were), with reference to this case, did not fully adjust herself to the new situation, as does a magnet, which, when divided at the point of equilibrium, renews itself in its two fragments by investing each with opposite poles; but, on the contrary, being severed from laws that theretofore had controlled her, and possessing still that mysterious tendency to develop into something more potential and complex, she blindly (having lost her lantern) pushed her demands for material that would secure this development, and as blindly used it when it was given her. Hence this marvellous voracity, this insatiable hunger, this wonderful ravenousness; and hence also (there being nothing but the physical part to receive this vast storing of energy) this strength that is becoming almost hourly Herculean, almost daily appalling. It is becoming a serious... narrow escape to-day. By some means, while I was absent, it unscrewed the stopper of the silver feeding-pipe (which I have already herein termed 'the artificial mouth'), and, in one of its curious antics, allowed all the chyle to escape from its stomach through the tube. Its hunger then became intense - I may say furious. I placed my hands upon it to push it into a chair, when, feeling my touch, it caught me, clasped me around the neck, and would have crushed me to death instantly had I not slipped from its powerful grasp. Thus I always had to be on my guard. I have provided the screw stopper with a spring catch, and... usually docile when not hungry; slow and heavy in its movements, which are, of course, purely unconscious; any apparent excitement in movement being due to local irregularities in the blood-supply of the cerebellum, which, if I did not have it enclosed in a silver case that is immovable, I should expose and..."

The captain looked at the detective with a puzzled air.

"I don't understand it at all," said he.

"Nor I," agreed the detective.

"What do you propose to do?"

"Make a raid."

"Do you want a man?"

"Three. The strongest men in your district."

"Why, the surgeon is old and weak!"

"Nevertheless, I want three strong men; and for that matter, prudence really advises me to take twenty."

At one o'clock the next morning a cautious, scratching sound might have been heard in the ceiling of the surgeon's operating-room. Shortly afterwards the skylight sash was carefully raised and laid aside. A man peered into the opening. Nothing could be heard.

"That is singular," thought the detective.

He cautiously lowered himself to the floor by a rope, and then stood for some moments listening intently. There was a dead silence. He shot the slide of a dark-lantern, and rapidly swept the room with the light. It was bare, with the exception of a strong iron staple and ring, screwed to the floor in the centre of the room, with a heavy chain attached. The detective then turned his attention to the outer room; it was perfectly bare. He was deeply perplexed. Returning to the inner room, he called softly to the men to descend. While they were thus occupied he re-entered the outer room and examined the door. A glance sufficed. It was kept closed by a spring attachment, and was locked with a strong spring-lock that could be drawn from the inside.

"The bird has just flown," mused the detective. "A singular accident! The discovery and proper use of this thumb-bolt might not have happened once in fifty years, if my theory is correct."

By this time the men were behind him. He noiselessly drew the spring-bolt, opened the door, and looked out into the hall. He heard a peculiar sound. It was as though a gigantic lobster was floundering and scrambling in some distant part of the old house. Accompanying this sound was a loud, whistling breathing, and frequent rasping gasps.

These sounds were heard by still another person - the surgeon's wife; for they originated very near her rooms, which were a considerable distance from her husband's. She had been sleeping lightly, tortured by fear and harassed by frightful dreams. The conspiracy into which she had recently entered, for the destruction of her husband, was a source of great anxiety. She constantly suffered from the most gloomy forebodings, and lived in an atmosphere of terror. Added to the natural horror of her situation were those countless sources of fear which a fright-shaken mind creates and then magnifies. She was, indeed, in a pitiable state, having been driven first by terror to desperation, and then to madness.

Startled thus out of fitful slumber by the noise at her door, she sprang from her bed to the floor, every terror that lurked in her acutely tense mind and diseased imagination starting up and almost overwhelming her. The idea of flight - one of the strongest of all instincts - seized upon her, and she ran to the door, beyond all control of reason. She drew the bolt and flung the door wide open, and then fled wildly down the passage, the appalling hissing and rasping gurgle ringing in her ears apparently with a thousand fold intensity. But the passage was in absolute darkness, and she had not taken a half-dozen steps when she tripped upon an unseen object on the floor. She fell headlong upon it, encountering in it a large, soft, warm substance that writhed and squirmed, and from which came the sounds that had awakened her. Instantly realizing her situation, she uttered a shriek such as only an unnameable terror can inspire. But hardly had her cry started the echoes in the empty corridor when it was suddenly stifled. Two prodigious arms had closed upon her and crushed the life out of her.

The cry performed the office of directing the detective and his assistants, and it also aroused the old surgeon, who occupied rooms between the officers and the object of their search. The cry of agony pierced him to the marrow, and a realization of the cause of it burst upon him with frightful force.

"It has come at last!" he gasped, springing from his bed.

Snatching from a table a dimly-burning lamp and a long knife which he had kept at hand for three years, he dashed into the corridor. The four officers had already started forward, but when they saw him emerge they halted in silence. In that moment of stillness the surgeon paused to listen. He heard the hissing sound and the clumsy floundering of a bulky, living object in the direction of his wife's apartments. It evidently was advancing towards him. A turn in the corridor shut out the view. He turned up the light, which revealed a ghastly pallor in his face.

"Wife!" he called.

There was no response. He hurriedly advanced, the four men following quietly. He turned the angle of the corridor, and ran so rapidly that by the time the officers had come in sight of him again he was twenty steps away. He ran past a huge, shapeless object, sprawling, crawling, and floundering along, and arrived at the body of his wife.

He gave one horrified glance at her face, and staggered away. Then a fury seized him. Clutching the knife firmly, and holding the lamp aloft, he sprang toward the ungainly object in the corridor. It was then that the officers, still advancing cautiously, saw a little more clearly, though still indistinctly, the object of the surgeon's fury, and the cause of the look of unutterable anguish in his face. The hideous sight caused them to pause. They saw what appeared to be a man, yet evidently was not a man; huge, awkward, shapeless; a squirming, lurching, stumbling mass, completely naked. It raised its broad shoulders. It had no head, but instead of it a small metallic ball surmounting its massive neck.

"Devil!" exclaimed the surgeon, raising the knife.

"Hold, there!" commanded a stern voice.

The surgeon quickly raised his eyes and saw the four officers, and for a moment fear paralysed his arm.

"The police!" he gasped.

Then, with a look of redoubled fury, he sent the knife to the hilt into the squirming mass before him. The wounded monster sprang to its feet and wildly threw its arms about, meanwhile emitting fearful sounds from a silver tube through which it breathed. The surgeon aimed another blow, but never gave it. In his blind fury he lost his caution, and was caught in an iron grasp. The struggling threw the lamp some feet toward the officers, and it fell to the floor, shattered to pieces. Simultaneously with the crash the oil took fire, and the corridor was filled with flame. The officers could not approach. Before them was the spreading blaze, and secure behind it were two forms struggling in a fearful embrace. They heard cries and gasps, and saw the gleaming of a knife.

The wood in the house was old and dry. It took fire at once, and the flames spread with great rapidity. The four officers turned and fled, barely escaping with their lives. In an hour nothing remained of the mysterious old house and its inmates but a blackened ruin.

THE MAN WHO WENT TOO FAR

By E.F. Benson

The little village of St. Faith's nestles in a hollow of wooded hill up on the north bank of the river Fawn in the county of Hampshire, huddling close round its grey Norman church as if for spiritual protection against the fays and fairies, the trolls and "little people," who might be supposed still to linger in the vast empty spaces of the New Forest, and to come after dusk and do their doubtful businesses. Once outside the hamlet you may walk in any direction (so long as you avoid the high road which leads to Brockenhurst) for the length of a summer afternoon without seeing sign of human habitation, or possibly even catching sight of another human being. Shaggy wild ponies may stop their feeding for a moment as you pass, the white scuts of rabbits will vanish into their burrows, a brown viper perhaps will glide from your path into a clump of heather, and unseen birds will chuckle in the bushes, but it may easily happen that for a long day you will see nothing human. But you will not feel in the least lonely; in summer, at any rate, the sunlight will be gay with butterflies, and the air thick with all those woodland sounds which like instruments in an orchestra combine to play the great symphony of the yearly festival of June. Winds whisper in the birches, and sigh among the firs; bees are busy with their redolent labour among the heather, a myriad birds chirp in the green temples of the forest trees, and the voice of the river prattling over stony places, bubbling into pools, chuckling and gulping round corners, gives you the sense that many presences and companions are near at hand.

Yet, oddly enough, though one would have thought that these benign and cheerful influences of wholesome air and spaciousness of forest were very healthful comrades for a man, in so far as nature can really influence this wonderful human genus which has in these centuries learned to defy her most violent storms in its well-established houses, to bridle her torrents and make them light its streets, to tunnel her mountains and plough her seas, the inhabitants of St. Faith's will not willingly venture into the forest after dark. For in spite of the silence and loneliness of the hooded night it seems that a man is not sure in what company he may suddenly find himself, and though it is difficult to get from these villagers any very clear story of occult appearances, the feeling is widespread. One story indeed I have heard with some definiteness, the tale of a monstrous goat that has been seen to skip with hellish glee about the woods and shady places, and this perhaps is connected with the story which I have here attempted to piece together. It too is well-known to them; for all remember the young artist who died here not long ago, a young man, or so he struck the beholder, of great personal beauty, with something about him that made men's faces to smile and brighten when they looked on him. His ghost they will tell you "walks" constantly by the stream and through the woods which he loved so, and in especial it haunts a certain house, the last of the village, where he lived, and its garden in which he was done to death. For my part I am inclined to think that the terror of the Forest dates chiefly from that day. So, such as the story is, I have set it forth in connected form. It is based partly on the accounts of the villagers, but mainly on that of Darcy, a friend of mine and a friend of the man with whom these events were chiefly concerned.

The day had been one of untarnished midsummer splendour, and as the sun drew near to its setting, the glory of the evening grew every moment more crystalline, more miraculous. Westward from St. Faith's the beechwood which stretched for some miles toward the heathery upland beyond already cast its veil of clear shadow over the red roofs of the village, but the spire of the grey church, over-topping all, still pointed a flaming orange finger into the sky. The river Fawn, which runs below, lay in sheets of sky-reflected blue, and wound its dreamy devious course round the edge of this wood, where a rough two-planked bridge crossed from the bottom of the garden of the last house in the village, and communicated by means of a little wicker gate with the wood itself. Then once out of the shadow of the wood the stream lay in flaming pools of the molten crimson of the sunset, and lost itself in the haze of woodland distances.

This house at the end of the village stood outside the shadow, and the lawn which sloped down to the river was still flecked with sunlight. Garden-beds of dazzling colour lined its gravel walks, and down the middle of it ran a brick pergola, half-hidden in clusters of rambler-rose and purple with starry clematis. At the bottom end of it, between two of its pillars, was slung a hammock containing a shirt-sleeved figure.

The house itself lay somewhat remote from the rest of the village, and a footpath leading across two fields, now tall and fragrant with hay, was its only communication with the high road. It was low-built, only two stories in height, and like the garden, its walls were a mass of flowering roses. A narrow stone terrace ran along the garden front, over which was stretched an awning, and on the terrace a young silent-footed man-servant was busied with the laying of the table for dinner. He was neat-handed and quick with his job, and having finished it he went back into the house, and reappeared again with a large rough bath-towel on his arm. With this he went to the hammock in the pergola.

"Nearly eight, sir," he said.

"Has Mr. Darcy come yet?" asked a voice from the hammock.

"No, sir."

"If I'm not back when he comes, tell him that I'm just having a bathe before dinner."

The servant went back to the house, and after a moment or two Frank Halton struggled to a sitting posture, and slipped out on to the grass. He was of medium height and rather slender in build, but the supple ease and grace of his movements gave the impression of great physical strength: even his descent from the hammock was not an awkward performance. His face and hands were of very dark complexion, either from constant exposure to wind and sun, or, as his black hair and dark eyes tended to show, from some strain of southern blood. His head was small, his face of an exquisite beauty of modelling, while the smoothness of its contour would have led you to believe that he was a beardless lad still in his teens. But something, some look which living and experience alone can give, seemed to contradict that, and finding yourself completely puzzled as to his age, you would next moment probably cease to think about that, and only look at this glorious specimen of young manhood with wondering satisfaction.

He was dressed as became the season and the heat, and wore only a shirt open at the neck, and a pair of flannel trousers. His head, covered very thickly with a somewhat rebellious crop of short curly hair, was bare as he strolled across the lawn to the bathing-place that lay below. Then for a moment there was silence, then the sound of splashed and divided waters, and presently after, a great shout of ecstatic joy, as he swam up-stream with the foamed water standing in a frill round his neck. Then after some five minutes of limb-stretching struggle with the flood, he turned over on his back, and with arms thrown wide, floated down-stream, ripple-cradled and inert. His eyes were shut, and between half-parted lips he talked gently to himself.

"I am one with it," he said to himself, "the river and I, I and the river. The coolness and splash of it is I, and the water-herbs that wave in it are I also. And my strength and my limbs are not mine but the river's. It is all one, all one, dear Fawn."

A quarter of an hour later he appeared again at the bottom of the lawn, dressed as before, his wet hair already drying into its crisp short curls again. There he paused a moment, looking back at the stream with the smile with which men look on the face of a friend, then turned towards the house. Simultaneously his servant came to the door leading on to the terrace, followed by a man who appeared to be some half-way through the fourth decade of his years. Frank and he saw each other across the bushes and garden-beds, and each quickening his step, they met suddenly face to face round an angle of the garden walk, in the fragrance of syringa.

"My dear Darcy," cried Frank, "I am charmed to see you."

But the other stared at him in amazement.

"Frank!" he exclaimed.

"Yes, that is my name," he said laughing, "what is the matter?"

Darcy took his hand.

"What have you done to yourself?" he asked. "You are a boy again."

"Ah, I have a lot to tell you," said Frank. "Lots that you will hardly believe, but I shall convince you -"

He broke off suddenly, and held up his hand.

"Hush, there is my nightingale," he said.

The smile of recognition and welcome with which he had greeted his friend faded from his face, and a look of rapt wonder took its place, as of a lover listening to the voice of his beloved. His mouth parted slightly, showing the white line of teeth, and his eyes looked out and out till they seemed to Darcy to be focused on things beyond the vision of man. Then something perhaps startled the bird, for the song ceased.

"Yes, lots to tell you," he said. "Really I am delighted to see you. But you look rather white and pulled down; no wonder after that fever. And there is to be no nonsense about this visit. It is June now, you stop here till you are fit to begin work again. Two months at least."

"Ah, I can't trespass quite to that extent."

Frank took his arm and walked him down the grass.

"Trespass? Who talks of trespass? I shall tell you quite openly when I am tired of you, but you know when we had the studio together, we used not to bore each other. However, it is ill talking of going away on the moment of your arrival. Just a stroll to the river, and then it will be dinner-time."

Darcy took out his cigarette case, and offered it to the other.

Frank laughed.

"No, not for me. Dear me, I suppose I used to smoke once. How very odd!"

"Given it up?"

"I don't know. I suppose I must have. Anyhow I don't do it now. I would as soon think of eating meat."

"Another victim on the smoking altar of vegetarianism?"

"Victim?" asked Frank. "Do I strike you as such?"

He paused on the margin of the stream and whistled softly. Next moment a moor-hen made its splashing flight across the river, and ran up the bank. Frank took it very gently in his hands and stroked its head, as the creature lay against his shirt.

"And is the house among the reeds still secure?" he half-crooned to it. "And is the missus quite well, and are the neighbours flourishing? There, dear, home with you," and he flung it into the air.

"That bird's very tame," said Darcy, slightly bewildered.
"It is rather," said Frank, following its flight.

During dinner Frank chiefly occupied himself in bringing himself up-to-date in the movements and achievements of this old friend whom he had not seen for six years. Those six years, it now appeared, had been full of incident and success for Darcy; he had made a name for himself as a portrait painter which bade fair to outlast the vogue of a couple of seasons, and his leisure time had been brief. Then some four months previously he had been through a severe attack of typhoid, the result of which as concerns this story was that he had come down to this sequestered place to recruit.

"Yes, you've got on," said Frank at the end. "I always knew you would. A.R.A. with more in prospect. Money? You roll in it, I suppose, and, O Darcy, how much happiness have you had all these years? That is the only imperishable possession. And how much have you learned? Oh, I don't mean in Art. Even I could have done well in that."

Darcy laughed.

"Done well? My dear fellow, all I have learned in these six years you knew, so to speak, in your cradle. Your old pictures fetch huge prices. Do you never paint now?"

Frank shook his head.

"No, I'm too busy," he said.

"Doing what? Please tell me. That is what every one is for ever asking me."

"Doing? I suppose you would say I do nothing."

Darcy glanced up at the brilliant young face opposite him.

"It seems to suit you, that way of being busy," he said. "Now, it's your turn. Do you read? Do you study? I remember you saying that it would do us all - all us artists, I mean - a great deal of good if we would study any one human face carefully for a year, without recording a line. Have you been doing that?"

Frank shook his head again.

"I mean exactly what I say," he said, "I have been doing nothing. And I have never been so occupied. Look at me; have I not done something to myself to begin with?"

"You are two years younger than I," said Darcy, "at least you used to be. You therefore are thirty-five. But had I never seen you before I should say you were just twenty. But was it worth while to spend six years of greatly-occupied life in order to look twenty? Seems rather like a woman of fashion."

Frank laughed boisterously.

"First time I've ever been compared to that particular bird of prey," he said. "No, that has not been my occupation - in fact I am only very rarely conscious that one effect of my occupation has been that. Of course, it must have been if one comes to think of it. It is not very important. Quite true my body has become young. But that is very little; I have become young."

Darcy pushed back his chair and sat sideways to the table looking at the other.

"Has that been your occupation then?" he asked.

"Yes, that anyhow is one aspect of it. Think what youth means! It is the capacity for growth, mind, body, spirit, all grow, all get stronger, all have a fuller, firmer life every day. That is something, considering that every day that passes after the ordinary man reaches the full-blown flower of his strength, weakens his hold on life. A man reaches his prime, and remains, we say, in his prime, for ten years, or perhaps twenty. But after his primest prime is reached, he slowly, insensibly weakens. These are the signs of age in you, in your body, in your art probably, in your mind. You are less electric than you were. But I, when I reach my prime - I am nearing it - ah, you shall see."

The stars had begun to appear in the blue velvet of the sky, and to the east the horizon seen above the black silhouette of the village was growing dove-coloured with the approach of moonrise. White moths hovered dimly over the garden-beds, and the footsteps of night tip-toed through the bushes. Suddenly Frank rose.

"Ah, it is the supreme moment," he said softly. "Now more than at any other time the current of life, the eternal imperishable current runs so close to me that I am almost enveloped in it. Be silent a minute."

He advanced to the edge of the terrace and looked out standing stretched with arms outspread. Darcy heard him draw a long breath into his lungs, and after many seconds expel it again. Six or eight times he did this, then turned back into the lamplight.

"It will sound to you quite mad, I expect," he said, "but if you want to hear the soberest truth I have ever spoken and shall ever speak, I will tell you about myself. But come into the garden if it is not too damp for you. I have never told any one yet, but I shall like to tell you. It is long, in fact, since I have even tried to classify what I have learned."

They wandered into the fragrant dimness of the pergola, and sat down. Then Frank began:

"Years ago, do you remember," he said, "we used often to talk about the decay of joy in the world. Many impulses, we settled, had contributed to this decay, some of which were good in themselves, others that were quite completely bad. Among the good things, I put what we may call certain Christian virtues, renunciation, resignation, sympathy with suffering, and the desire to relieve sufferers. But out of those things spring very bad ones, useless renunciations, asceticism for its own sake, mortification of the flesh with nothing to follow, no corresponding gain that is, and that awful and terrible disease which devastated England some centuries ago, and from which by heredity of spirit we suffer now, Puritanism. That was a dreadful plague, the brutes held and taught that joy and laughter and merriment were evil: it was a doctrine the most profane and wicked. Why, what is the commonest crime one sees? A sullen face. That is the truth of the matter.

"Now all my life I have believed that we are intended to be happy, that joy is of all gifts the most divine. And when I left London, abandoned my career, such as it was, I did so because I intended to devote my life to the cultivation of joy, and, by continuous and unsparing effort, to be happy. Among people, and in constant intercourse with others, I did not find it possible; there were too many distractions in towns and work-rooms, and also too much suffering. So I took one step backwards or forwards, as you may choose to put it, and went straight to Nature, to trees, birds, animals, to all those things which quite clearly pursue one aim only, which blindly follow the great native instinct to be happy without any care at all for morality, or human law or divine law. I wanted, you understand, to get all joy first-hand and unadulterated, and I think it scarcely exists among men; it is obsolete."

Darcy turned in his chair.

"Ah, but what makes birds and animals happy?" he asked. "Food, food and mating."

Frank laughed gently in the stillness.

"Do not think I became a sensualist," he said. "I did not make that mistake. For the sensualist carries his miseries pick-a-back, and round his feet is wound the shroud that shall soon enwrap him. I may be mad, it is true, but I am not so stupid anyhow as to have tried that. No, what is it that makes puppies play with their own tails, that sends cats on their prowling ecstatic errands at night?"

He paused a moment.

"So I went to Nature," he said. "I sat down here in this New Forest, sat down fair and square, and looked. That was my first difficulty, to sit here quiet without being bored, to wait without being impatient, to be receptive and very alert, though for a long time nothing particular happened. The change in fact was slow in those early stages."

"Nothing happened?" asked Darcy rather impatiently, with the sturdy revolt against any new idea which to the English mind is synonymous with nonsense. "Why, what in the world should happen?"

Now Frank as he had known him was the most generous but most quick-tempered of mortal men; in other words his anger would flare to a prodigious beacon, under almost no provocation, only to be quenched again under a gust of no less impulsive kindliness. Thus the moment Darcy had spoken, an apology for his hasty question was half-way up his tongue. But there was no need for it to have travelled even so far, for Frank laughed again with kindly, genuine mirth.

"Oh, how I should have resented that a few years ago," he said. "Thank goodness that resentment is one of the things I have got rid of. I certainly wish that you should believe my story - in fact, you are going to - but that you at this moment should imply that you do not, does not concern me."

"Ah, your solitary sojournings have made you inhuman," said Darcy, still very English.

"No, human," said Frank. "Rather more human, at least rather less of an ape."

"Well, that was my first quest," he continued, after a moment, "the deliberate and unswerving pursuit of joy, and my method, the eager contemplation of Nature. As far as motive went, I daresay it was purely selfish, but as far as effect goes, it seems to me about the best thing one can do for one's fellow-creatures, for happiness is more infectious than small-pox. So, as I said, I sat down and waited; I looked at happy things, zealously avoided the sight of anything unhappy, and by degrees a little trickle of the happiness of this blissful world began to filter into me. The trickle grew more abundant, and now, my dear fellow, if I could for a moment divert from me into you one half of the torrent of joy that pours through me day and night, you would throw the world, art, everything aside, and just live, exist. When a man's body dies, it passes into trees and flowers. Well, that is what I have been trying to do with my soul before death."

The servant had brought into the pergola a table with syphons and spirits, and had set a lamp upon it. As Frank spoke he leaned forward towards the other, and Darcy for all his matter-of-fact commonsense could have sworn that his companion's face shone, was luminous in itself. His dark brown eyes glowed from within, the unconscious smile of a child irradiated and transformed his face. Darcy felt suddenly excited, exhilarated.

"Go on," he said. "Go on. I can feel you are somehow telling me sober truth. I daresay you are mad; but I don't see that matters."

Frank laughed again.

"Mad?" he said. "Yes, certainly, if you wish. But I prefer to call it sane. However, nothing matters less than what anybody chooses to call things. God never labels his gifts; He just puts them into our hands; just as he put animals in the Garden of Eden, for Adam to name if he felt disposed."

"So by the continual observance and study of things that were happy," continued he, "I got happiness, I got joy. But seeking it, as I did, from Nature, I got much more which I did not seek, but stumbled upon originally by accident. It is difficult to explain, but I will try.

"About three years ago I was sitting one morning in a place I will show you to-morrow. It is down by the river brink, very green, dappled with shade and sun, and the river passes there through some little clumps of reeds. Well, as I sat there, doing nothing, but just looking and listening, I heard the sound quite distinctly of some flute-like instrument playing a strange unending melody. I thought at first it was some musical yokel on the highway and did not pay much attention. But before long the strangeness and indescribable beauty of the tune struck me. It never repeated itself, but it never came to an end, phrase after phrase ran its sweet course, it worked gradually and inevitably up to a climax, and having attained it, it went on; another climax was reached and another and another. Then with a sudden gasp of wonder I localized where it came from. It came from the reeds and from the sky and from the trees. It was everywhere, it was the sound of life. It was, my dear Darcy, as the Greeks would have said, it was Pan playing on his pipes, the voice of Nature. It was the life-melody, the world-melody."

Darcy was far too interested to interrupt, though there was a question he would have liked to ask, and Frank went on:

"Well, for the moment I was terrified, terrified with the impotent horror of nightmare, and I stopped my ears and just ran from the place and got back to the house panting, trembling, literally in a panic. Unknowingly, for at that time I only pursued joy, I had begun, since I drew my joy from Nature, to get in touch with Nature. Nature, force, God, call it what you will, had drawn across my face a little gossamer web of essential life. I saw that when I emerged from my terror, and I went very humbly back to where I had heard the Pan-pipes. But it was nearly six months before I heard them again."

"Why was that?" asked Darcy.

"Surely because I had revolted, rebelled, and worst of all been frightened. For I believe that just as there is nothing in the world which so injures one's body as fear, so there is nothing that so much shuts up the soul. I was afraid, you see, of the one thing in the world which has real existence. No wonder its manifestation was withdrawn."

"And after six months?"

"After six months one blessed morning I heard the piping again. I wasn't afraid that time. And since then it has grown louder, it has become more constant. I now hear it often, and I can put myself into such an attitude towards Nature that the pipes will almost certainly sound. And never yet have they played the same tune, it is always something new, something fuller, richer, more complete than before."

"What do you mean by 'such an attitude towards Nature'?" asked Darcy.

"I can't explain that; but by translating it into a bodily attitude it is this."

Frank sat up for a moment quite straight in his chair, then slowly sunk back with arms outspread and head drooped.

"That," he said, "an effortless attitude, but open, resting, receptive. It is just that which you must do with your soul."

Then he sat up again.

"One word more," he said, "and I will bore you no further. Nor unless you ask me questions shall I talk about it again. You will find me, in fact, quite sane in my mode of life. Birds and beasts you will see behaving somewhat intimately to me, like that moor-hen, but that is all. I will walk with you, ride with you, play golf with you, and talk with you on any subject you like. But I wanted you on the threshold to know what has happened to me. And one thing more will happen."

He paused again, and a slight look of fear crossed his eyes.

"There will be a final revelation," he said, "a complete and blinding stroke which will throw open to me, once and for all, the full knowledge, the full realization and comprehension that I am one, just as you are, with life. In reality there is no 'me,' no 'you,' no 'it.' Everything is part of the one and only thing which is life. I know that that is so, but the realization of it is not yet mine. But it will be, and on that day, so I take it, I shall see Pan. It may mean death, the death of my body, that is, but I don't care. It may mean immortal, eternal life lived here and now and for ever. Then having gained that, ah, my dear Darcy, I shall preach such a gospel of joy, showing myself as the living proof of the truth, that Puritanism, the dismal religion of sour faces, shall vanish like a breath of smoke, and be dispersed and disappear in the sunlit air. But first the full knowledge must be mine."

Darcy watched his face narrowly.

"You are afraid of that moment," he said.

Frank smiled at him.

"Quite true; you are quick to have seen that. But when it comes I hope I shall not be afraid."

For some little time there was silence; then Darcy rose.

"You have bewitched me, you extraordinary boy," he said. "You have been telling me a fairy-story, and I find myself saying,

'Promise me it is true.'"

"I promise you that," said the other.

"And I know I shan't sleep," added Darcy.

Frank looked at him with a sort of mild wonder as if he scarcely understood.

"Well, what does that matter?" he said.

"I assure you it does. I am wretched unless I sleep."

"Of course I can make you sleep if I want," said Frank in a rather bored voice.

"Well, do."

"Very good: go to bed. I'll come upstairs in ten minutes."

Frank busied himself for a little after the other had gone, moving the table back under the awning of the veranda and quenching the lamp. Then he went with his quick silent tread upstairs and into Darcy's room. The latter was already in bed, but very wide-eyed and wakeful, and Frank with an amused smile of indulgence, as for a fretful child, sat down on the edge of the bed.

"Look at me," he said, and Darcy looked.

"The birds are sleeping in the brake," said Frank softly, "and the winds are asleep. The sea sleeps, and the tides are but the heaving of its breast. The stars swing slow, rocked in the great cradle of the Heavens, and -"

He stopped suddenly, gently blew out Darcy's candle, and left him sleeping.

Morning brought to Darcy a flood of hard commonsense, as clear and crisp as the sunshine that filled his room. Slowly as he woke he gathered together the broken threads of the memories of the evening which had ended, so he told himself, in a trick of common hypnotism. That accounted for it all; the whole strange talk he had had was under a spell of suggestion from the extraordinary vivid boy who had once been a man; all his own excitement, his acceptance of the incredible had been merely the effect of a stronger, more potent will imposed on his own. How strong that will was, he guessed from his own instantaneous obedience to Frank's suggestion of sleep. And armed with impenetrable commonsense he came down to breakfast. Frank had already begun, and was consuming a large plateful of porridge and milk with the most prosaic and healthy appetite.

"Slept well?" he asked.

"Yes, of course. Where did you learn hypnotism?"

"By the side of the river."

"You talked an amazing quantity of nonsense last night," remarked Darcy, in a voice prickly with reason.

"Rather. I felt quite giddy. Look, I remembered to order a dreadful daily paper for you. You can read about money markets or politics or cricket matches."

Darcy looked at him closely. In the morning light Frank looked even fresher, younger, more vital than he had done the night before, and the sight of him somehow dinted Darcy's armour of commonsense.

"You are the most extraordinary fellow I ever saw," he said. "I want to ask you some more questions."

"Ask away," said Frank.

For the next day or two Darcy plied his friend with many questions, objections and criticisms on the theory of life and gradually got out of him a coherent and complete account of his experience. In brief then, Frank believed that "by lying naked," as he put it, to the force which controls the passage of the stars, the breaking of a wave, the budding of a tree, the love of a youth and maiden, he had succeeded in a way hitherto undreamed of in possessing himself of the essential principle of life. Day by day, so he thought, he was getting nearer to, and in closer union with the great power itself which caused all life to be, the spirit of nature, of force, or the spirit of God. For himself, he confessed to what others would call paganism; it was sufficient for him that there existed a principle of life. He did not worship it, he did not pray to it, he did not praise it. Some of it existed in all human beings, just as it existed in trees and animals; to realize and make living to himself the fact that it was all one, was his sole aim and object.

Here perhaps Darcy would put in a word of warning. "Take care," he said. "To see Pan meant death, did it not?"

Frank's eyebrows would rise at this.

"What does that matter?" he said. "True, the Greeks were always right, and they said so, but there is another possibility. For the nearer I get to it, the more living, the more vital and young I become."

"What then do you expect the final revelation will do for you?"

"I have told you," said he. "It will make me immortal."

But it was not so much from speech and argument that Darcy grew to grasp his friend's conception, as from the ordinary conduct of his life. They were passing, for instance, one morning down the village street, when an old woman, very bent and decrepit, but with an extraordinary cheerfulness of face, hobbled out from her cottage. Frank instantly stopped when he saw her.

"You old darling! How goes it all?" he said.

But she did not answer, her dim old eyes were riveted on his face; she seemed to drink in like a thirsty creature the beautiful radiance which shone there. Suddenly she put her two withered old hands on his shoulders.

"You're just the sunshine itself," she said, and he kissed her and passed on.

But scarcely a hundred yards further a strange contradiction of such tenderness occurred. A child running along the path towards them fell on its face, and set up a dismal cry of fright and pain. A look of horror came into Frank's eyes, and, putting his fingers in his ears, he fled at full speed down the street, and did not pause till he was out of hearing. Darcy, having ascertained that the child was not really hurt, followed him in bewilderment.

"Are you without pity then?" he asked.

Frank shook his head impatiently.

"Can't you see?" he asked. "Can't you understand that that sort of thing, pain, anger, anything unlovely throws me back, retards the coming of the great hour! Perhaps when it comes I shall be able to piece that side of life on to the other, on to the true religion of joy. At present I can't."

"But the old woman. Was she not ugly?"

Frank's radiance gradually returned.

"Ah, no. She was like me. She longed for joy, and knew it when she saw it, the old darling."

Another question suggested itself.

"Then what about Christianity?" asked Darcy.

"I can't accept it. I can't believe in any creed of which the central doctrine is that God who is Joy should have had to suffer. Perhaps it was so; in some inscrutable way I believe it may have been so, but I don't understand how it was possible. So I leave it alone; my affair is joy."

They had come to the weir above the village, and the thunder of riotous cool water was heavy in the air. Trees dipped into the translucent stream with slender trailing branches, and the meadow where they stood was starred with midsummer blossomings. Larks shot up carolling into the crystal dome of blue, and a thousand voices of June sang round them. Frank, bare-headed as was his wont, with his coat slung over his arm and his shirt sleeves rolled up above the elbow, stood there like some beautiful wild animal with eyes half-shut and mouth half-open, drinking in the scented warmth of the air. Then suddenly he flung himself face downwards on the grass at the edge of the stream, burying his face in the daisies and cowslips, and lay stretched there in wide-armed ecstasy, with his long fingers pressing and stroking the dewy herbs of the field. Never before had Darcy seen him thus fully possessed by his idea; his caressing fingers, his half-buried face pressed close to the grass, even the clothed lines of his figure were instinct with a vitality that somehow was different from that of other men. And some faint glow from it reached Darcy, some thrill, some vibration from that charged recumbent body passed to him, and for a moment he understood as he had not understood before, despite his persistent questions and the candid answers they received, how real, and how realized by Frank, his idea was.

Then suddenly the muscles in Frank's neck became stiff and alert, and he half-raised his head, whispering, "The Pan-pipes, the Pan-pipes. Close, oh, so close."

Very slowly, as if a sudden movement might interrupt the melody, he raised himself and leaned on the elbow of his bent arm. His eyes opened wider, the lower lids drooped as if he focused his eyes on something very far away, and the smile on his face broadened and quivered like sunlight on still water, till the exultance of its happiness was scarcely human. So he remained motionless and rapt for some minutes, then the look of listening died from his face, and he bowed his head satisfied.

"Ah, that was good," he said. "How is it possible you did not hear? Oh, you poor fellow! Did you really hear nothing?"

A week of this outdoor and stimulating life did wonders in restoring to Darcy the vigour and health which his weeks of fever had filched from him, and as his normal activity and higher pressure of vitality returned, he seemed to himself to fall even more under the spell which the miracle of Frank's youth cast over him. Twenty times a day he found himself saying to himself suddenly at the end of some ten minutes' silent resistance to the absurdity of Frank's idea: "But it isn't possible; it can't be possible," and from the fact of his having to assure himself so frequently of this, he knew that he was struggling and arguing with a conclusion which already had taken root in his mind. For in any case a visible living miracle confronted him, since it was equally impossible that this youth, this boy, trembling on the verge of manhood, was thirty-five. Yet such was the fact.

July was ushered in by a couple of days of blustering and fretful rain, and Darcy, unwilling to risk a chill, kept to the house. But to Frank this weeping change of weather seemed to have no bearing on the behaviour of man, and he spent his days exactly as he did under the suns of June, lying in his hammock, stretched on the dripping grass, or making huge rambling excursions into the forest, the birds hopping from tree to tree after him, to return in the evening, drenched and soaked, but with the same unquenchable flame of joy burning within him.

"Catch cold?" he would ask, "I've forgotten how to do it, I think. I suppose it makes one's body more sensible always to sleep out-of-doors. People who live indoors always remind me of something peeled and skinless."

"Do you mean to say you slept out-of-doors last night in that deluge?" asked Darcy. "And where, may I ask?"

Frank thought a moment.

"I slept in the hammock till nearly dawn," he said. "For I remember the light blinked in the east when I awoke. Then I went - where did I go? - oh, yes, to the meadow where the Pan-pipes sounded so close a week ago. You were with me, do you remember? But I always have a rug if it is wet."

And he went whistling upstairs.

Somehow that little touch, his obvious effort to recall where he had slept, brought strangely home to Darcy the wonderful romance of which he was the still half-incredulous beholder. Sleep till close on dawn in a hammock, then the tramp - or probably scamper - underneath the windy and weeping heavens to the remote and lonely meadow by the weir! The picture of other such nights rose before him; Frank sleeping perhaps by the bathing-place under the filtered twilight of the stars, or the white blaze of moon-shine, a stir and awakening at some dead hour, perhaps a space of silent wide-eyed thought, and then a wandering through the hushed woods to some other dormitory, alone with his happiness, alone with the joy and the life that suffused and enveloped him, without other thought or desire or aim except the hourly and never-ceasing communion with the joy of nature.

They were in the middle of dinner that night, talking on indifferent subjects, when Darcy suddenly broke off in the middle of a sentence.

"I've got it," he said. "At last I've got it."

"Congratulate you," said Frank. "But what?"

"The radical unsoundness of your idea. It is this: All nature from highest to lowest is full, crammed full of suffering; every living organism in nature preys on another, yet in your aim to get close to, to be one with nature, you leave suffering altogether out; you run away from it, you refuse to recognize it. And you are waiting, you say, for the final revelation."

Frank's brow clouded slightly.

"Well?" he asked, rather wearily.

"Cannot you guess then when the final revelation will be? In joy you are supreme, I grant you that; I did not know a man could be so master of it. You have learned perhaps practically all that nature can teach. And if, as you think, the final revelation is coming to you, it will be the revelation of horror, suffering, death, pain in all its hideous forms. Suffering does exist: you hate it and fear it."

Frank held up his hand.

"Stop; let me think," he said.

There was silence for a long minute.

"That never struck me," he said at length. "It is possible that what you suggest is true. Does the sight of Pan mean that, do you think? Is it that nature, take it altogether, suffers horribly, suffers to a hideous inconceivable extent? Shall I be shown all the suffering?"

He got up and came round to where Darcy sat.

"If it is so, so be it," he said. "Because, my dear fellow, I am near, so splendidly near to the final revelation. To-day the pipes have sounded almost without pause. I have even heard the rustle in the bushes, I believe, of Pan's coming. I have seen, yes, I saw to-day, the bushes pushed aside as if by a hand, and piece of a face, not human, peered through. But I was not frightened, at least I did not run away this time."

He took a turn up to the window and back again.

"Yes, there is suffering all through," he said, "and I have left it all out of my search. Perhaps, as you say, the revelation will be that. And in that case, it will be good-bye. I have gone on one line. I shall have gone too far along one road, without having explored the other. But I can't go back now. I wouldn't if I could; not a step would I retrace! In any case, whatever the revelation is, it will be God. I'm sure of that."

The rainy weather soon passed, and with the return of the sun Darcy again joined Frank in long rambling days. It grew extraordinarily hotter, and with the fresh bursting of life, after the rain, Frank's vitality seemed to blaze higher and higher. Then, as is the habit of the English weather, one evening clouds began to bank themselves up in the west, the sun went down in a glare of coppery thunder-rack, and the whole earth broiling under an unspeakable oppression and sultriness paused and panted for the storm. After sunset the remote fires of lightning began to wink and flicker on the horizon, but when bed-time came the storm seemed to have moved no nearer, though a very low unceasing noise of thunder was audible. Weary and oppressed by the stress of the day, Darcy fell at once into a heavy uncomforting sleep.

He woke suddenly into full consciousness, with the din of some appalling explosion of thunder in his ears, and sat up in bed with racing heart. Then for a moment, as he recovered himself from the panic-land which lies between sleeping and waking, there was silence, except for the steady hissing of rain on the shrubs outside his window. But suddenly that silence was shattered and shredded into fragments by a scream from somewhere close at hand outside in the black garden, a scream of supreme and despairing terror. Again, and once again it shrilled up, and then a babble of awful words was interjected. A quivering sobbing voice that he knew, said:

"My God, oh, my God; oh, Christ!"

And then followed a little mocking, bleating laugh. Then was silence again; only the rain hissed on the shrubs.

All this was but the affair of a moment, and without pause either to put on clothes or light a candle, Darcy was already fumbling at his door-handle. Even as he opened it he met a terror-stricken face outside, that of the man-servant who carried a light.

"Did you hear?" he asked.

The man's face was bleached to a dull shining whiteness.

"Yes, sir," he said. "It was the master's voice."

Together they hurried down the stairs, and through the dining-room where an orderly table for breakfast had already been laid, and out on to the terrace. The rain for the moment had been utterly stayed, as if the tap of the heavens had been turned off, and under the lowering black sky, not quite dark, since the moon rode somewhere serene behind the conglomerated thunder-clouds, Darcy stumbled into the garden, followed by the servant with the candle. The monstrous leaping shadow of himself was cast before him on the lawn; lost and wandering odours of rose and lily and damp earth were thick about him, but more pungent was some sharp and acrid smell that suddenly reminded him of a certain châlet in which he had once taken refuge in the Alps. In the blackness of the hazy light from the sky, and the vague tossing of the candle behind him, he saw that the hammock in which Frank so often lay was tenanted. A gleam of white shirt was there, as if a man sitting up in it, but across that there was an obscure dark shadow, and as he approached the acrid odour grew more intense.

He was now only some few yards away, when suddenly the black shadow seemed to jump into the air, then came down with tappings of hard hoofs on the brick path that ran down the pergola, and with frolicsome skippings galloped off into the bushes. When that was gone Darcy could see quite clearly that a shirted figure sat up in the hammock. For one moment, from sheer terror of the unseen, he hung on his step, and the servant joining him they walked together to the hammock.

It was Frank. He was in shirt and trousers only, and he sat up with braced arms. For one half-second he stared at them, his face a mask of horrible contorted terror. His upper lip was drawn back so that the gums of the teeth appeared, and his eyes were focused not on the two who approached him but on something quite close to him; his nostrils were widely expanded, as if he panted for breath, and terror incarnate and repulsion and deathly anguish ruled dreadful lines on his smooth cheeks and forehead. Then even as they looked the body sank backwards, and the ropes of the hammock wheezed and strained.

Darcy lifted him out and carried him indoors. Once he thought there was a faint convulsive stir of the limbs that lay with so dead a weight in his arms, but when they got inside, there was no trace of life. But the look of supreme terror and agony of fear had gone from his face, a boy tired with play but still smiling in his sleep was the burden he laid on the floor. His eyes had closed, and the beautiful mouth lay in smiling curves, even as when a few mornings ago, in the meadow by the weir, it had quivered to the music of the unheard melody of Pan's pipes. Then they looked further.

Frank had come back from his bath before dinner that night in his usual costume of shirt and trousers only. He had not dressed, and during dinner, so Darcy remembered, he had rolled up the sleeves of his shirt to above the elbow. Later, as they sat and talked after dinner on the close sultriness of the evening, he had unbuttoned the front of his shirt to let what little breath of wind there was play on his skin. The sleeves were rolled up now, the front of the shirt was unbuttoned, and on his arms and on the brown skin of his chest were strange discolorations which grew momently more clear and defined, till they saw that the marks were pointed prints, as if caused by the hoofs of some monstrous goat that had leaped and stamped upon him.

THE INTERVAL
By Vincent O'Sullivan

Mrs. Wilton passed through a little alley leading from one of the gates which are around Regent's Park, and came out on the wide and quiet street. She walked along slowly, peering anxiously from side to side so as not to overlook the number. She pulled her furs closer round her; after her years in India this London damp seemed very harsh. Still, it was not a fog to-day. A dense haze, grey and tinged ruddy, lay between the houses, sometimes blowing with a little wet kiss against the face. Mrs. Wilton's hair and eyelashes and her furs were powdered with tiny drops. But there was nothing in the weather to blur the sight; she could see the faces of people some distance off and read the signs on the shops.

Before the door of a dealer in antiques and second-hand furniture she paused and looked through the shabby uncleaned window at an unassorted heap of things, many of them of great value. She read the Polish name fastened on the pane in white letters.

"Yes; this is the place."

She opened the door, which met her entrance with an ill-tempered jangle. From somewhere in the black depths of the shop the dealer came forward. He had a clammy white face, with a sparse black beard, and wore a skull cap and spectacles. Mrs. Wilton spoke to him in a low voice.

A look of complicity, of cunning, perhaps of irony, passed through the dealer's cynical and sad eyes. But he bowed gravely and respectfully.

"Yes, she is here, madam. Whether she will see you or not I do not know. She is not always well; she has her moods. And then, we have to be so careful. The police - Not that they would touch a lady like you. But the poor alien has not much chance these days."

Mrs. Wilton followed him to the back of the shop, where there was a winding staircase. She knocked over a few things in her passage and stooped to pick them up, but the dealer kept muttering, "It does not matter - surely it does not matter." He lit a candle.

"You must go up these stairs. They are very dark; be careful. When you come to a door, open it and go straight in."

He stood at the foot of the stairs holding the light high above his head and she ascended.

The room was not very large, and it seemed very ordinary. There were some flimsy, uncomfortable chairs in gilt and red. Two large palms were in corners. Under a glass cover on the table was a view of Rome. The room had not a business-like look, thought Mrs. Wilton; there was no suggestion of the office or waiting-room where people came and went all day; yet you would not say that it was a private room which was lived in. There were no books or papers about; every chair was in the place it had been placed when the room was last swept; there was no fire and it was very cold.

To the right of the window was a door covered with a plush curtain. Mrs. Wilton sat down near the table and watched this door. She thought it must be through it that the soothsayer would come forth. She laid her hands listlessly one on top of the other on the table. This must be the tenth seer she had consulted since Hugh had been killed. She thought them over. No, this must be the eleventh. She had forgotten that frightening man in Paris who said he had been a priest. Yet of them all it was only he who had told her anything definite. But even he could do no more than tell the past. He told of her marriage; he even had the duration of it right - twenty-one months. He told too of their time in India - at least, he knew that her husband had been a soldier, and said he had been on service in the "colonies." On the whole, though, he had been as unsatisfactory as the others. None of them had given her the consolation she sought. She did not want to be told of the past. If Hugh was gone forever, then with him had gone all her love of living, her courage, all her better self. She wanted to be lifted out of the despair, the dazed aimless drifting from day to day, longing at night for the morning, and in the morning for the fall of night, which had been her life since his death. If somebody could assure her that it was not all over, that he was somewhere, not too far away, unchanged from what he had been here, with his crisp hair and rather slow smile and lean brown face, that he saw her sometimes, that he had not forgotten her…

"Oh, Hugh, darling!"

When she looked up again the woman was sitting there before her. Mrs. Wilton had not heard her come in. With her experience, wide enough now, of seers and fortune-tellers of all kinds, she saw at once that this woman was different from the others. She was used to the quick appraising look, the attempts, sometimes clumsy, but often cleverly disguised, to collect some fragments of information whereupon to erect a plausible vision. But this woman looked as if she took it out of herself.

Not that her appearance suggested intercourse with the spiritual world more than the others had done; it suggested that, in fact, considerably less. Some of the others were frail, yearning, evaporated creatures, and the ex-priest in Paris had something terrible and condemned in his look. He might well sup with the devil, that man, and probably did in some way or other.

But this was a little fat, weary-faced woman about fifty, who only did not look like a cook because she looked more like a seamstress. Her black dress was all covered with white threads. Mrs. Wilton looked at her with some embarrassment. It seemed more reasonable to be asking a woman like this about altering a gown than about intercourse with the dead. That seemed even absurd in such a very commonplace presence. The woman seemed timid and oppressed: she breathed heavily and kept rubbing her dingy hands, which looked moist, one over the other; she was always wetting her lips, and coughed with a little dry cough. But in her these signs of nervous exhaustion suggested overwork in a close atmosphere, bending too close over the sewing-machine. Her uninteresting hair, like a rat's pelt, was eked out with a false addition of another colour. Some threads had got into her hair too.

Her harried, uneasy look caused Mrs. Wilton to ask compassionately: "Are you much worried by the police?"

"Oh, the police! Why don't they leave us alone? You never know who comes to see you. Why don't they leave me alone? I'm a good woman. I only think. What I do is no harm to any one," she continued in an uneven querulous voice, always rubbing her hands together nervously. She seemed to the visitor to be talking at random, just gabbling, like children do sometimes before they fall asleep.

"I wanted to explain -" hesitated Mrs. Wilton.

But the woman, with her head pressed close against the back of the chair, was staring beyond her at the wall. Her face had lost whatever little expression it had; it was blank and stupid. When she spoke it was very slowly and her voice was guttural.

"Can't you see him? It seems strange to me that you can't see him. He is so near you. He is passing his arm round your shoulders."

This was a frequent gesture of Hugh's. And indeed at that moment she felt that somebody was very near her, bending over her. She was enveloped in tenderness. Only a very thin veil, she felt, prevented her from seeing. But the woman saw. She was describing Hugh minutely, even the little things like the burn on his right hand.

"Is he happy? Oh, ask him does he love me?"

The result was so far beyond anything she had hoped for that she was stunned. She could only stammer the first thing that came into her head. "Does he love me?"

"He loves you. He won't answer, but he loves you. He wants me to make you see him; he is disappointed, I think, because I can't. But I can't unless you do it yourself."

After a while she said:

"I think you will see him again. You think of nothing else. He is very close to us now."

Then she collapsed, and fell into a heavy sleep and lay there motionless, hardly breathing. Mrs. Wilton put some notes on the table and stole out on tip-toe.

She seemed to remember that downstairs in the dark shop the dealer with the waxen face detained her to show some old silver and jewellery and such like. But she did not come to herself, she had no precise recollection of anything, till she found herself entering a church near Portland Place. It was an unlikely act in her normal moments. Why did she go in there? She acted like one walking in her sleep.

The church was old and dim, with high black pews. There was nobody there. Mrs. Wilton sat down in one of the pews and bent forward with her face in her hands.

After a few minutes she saw that a soldier had come in

noiselessly and placed himself about half-a-dozen rows ahead of her. He never turned round; but presently she was struck by something familiar in the figure. First she thought vaguely that the soldier looked like her Hugh. Then, when he put up his hand, she saw who it was.

She hurried out of the pew and ran towards him. "Oh, Hugh, Hugh, have you come back?"

He looked round with a smile. He had not been killed. It was all a mistake. He was going to speak...

Footsteps sounded hollow in the empty church. She turned and glanced down the dim aisle.

It was an old sexton or verger who approached. "I thought I heard you call," he said.

"I was speaking to my husband." But Hugh was nowhere to be seen.

"He was here a moment ago." She looked about in anguish. "He must have gone to the door."

"There's nobody here," said the old man gently. "Only you and me. Ladies are often taken funny since the war. There was one in here yesterday afternoon said she was married in this church and her husband had promised to meet her here. Perhaps you were married here?"

"No," said Mrs. Wilton, desolately. "I was married in India."

It might have been two or three days after that, when she went into a small Italian restaurant in the Bayswater district. She often went out for her meals now: she had developed an exhausting cough, and she found that it somehow became less troublesome when she was in a public place looking at strange faces. In her flat there were all the things that Hugh had used; the trunks and bags still had his name on them with the labels of places where they had been together. They were like stabs. In the restaurant, people came and went, many soldiers too among them, just glancing at her in her corner.

This day, as it chanced, she was rather late and there was nobody there. She was very tired. She nibbled at the food they brought her. She could almost have cried from tiredness and loneliness and the ache in her heart.

Then suddenly he was before her, sitting there opposite at

the table. It was as it was in the days of their engagement, when they used sometimes to lunch at restaurants. He was not in uniform. He smiled at her and urged her to eat, just as he used in those days...

I met her that afternoon as she was crossing Kensington Gardens, and she told me about it.

"I have been with Hugh." She seemed most happy.

"Did he say anything?"

"N-no. Yes. I think he did, but I could not quite hear. My head was so very tired. The next time -"

I did not see her for some time after that. She found, I think, that by going to places where she had once seen him - the old church, the little restaurant - she was more certain to see him again. She never saw him at home. But in the street or the park he would often walk along beside her. Once he saved her from being run over. She said she actually felt his hand grabbing her arm, suddenly, when the car was nearly upon her.

She had given me the address of the clairvoyant; and it is through that strange woman that I know - or seem to know - what followed.

Mrs. Wilton was not exactly ill last winter, not so ill, at least, as to keep to her bedroom. But she was very thin, and her great handsome eyes always seemed to be staring at some point beyond, searching. There was a look in them that seamen's eyes sometimes have when they are drawing on a coast of which they are not very certain. She lived almost in solitude: she hardly ever saw anybody except when they sought her out. To those who were anxious about her she laughed and said she was very well.

One sunny morning she was lying awake, waiting for the maid to bring her tea. The shy London sunlight peeped through the blinds. The room had a fresh and happy look.

When she heard the door open she thought that the maid had come in. Then she saw that Hugh was standing at the foot of the bed. He was in uniform this time, and looked as he had looked the day he went away.

"Oh, Hugh, speak to me! Will you not say just one word?"

He smiled and threw back his head, just as he used to in the old days at her mother's house when he wanted to call her out of the room without attracting the attention of the others. He moved towards the door, still signing to her to follow him. He picked up her slippers on his way and held them out to her as if he wanted her to put them on. She slipped out of bed hastily…

It is strange that when they came to look through her things after her death the slippers could never be found.

THE DOLL'S GHOST
By F Marion Crawford

It was a terrible accident, and for one moment the splendid machinery of Cranston House got out of gear and stood still. The butler emerged from the retirement in which he spent his elegant leisure, two grooms of the chambers appeared simultaneously from opposite directions, there were actually housemaids on the grand staircase, and those who remember the facts most exactly assert that Mrs. Pringle herself positively stood upon the landing. Mrs. Pringle was the housekeeper. As for the head nurse, the under nurse, and the nursery maid, their feelings cannot be described. The head nurse laid one hand upon the polished marble balustrade and stared stupidly before her, the under nurse stood rigid and pale, leaning against the polished marble wall, and the nursery-maid collapsed and sat down upon the polished marble step, just beyond the limits of the velvet carpet, and frankly burst into tears.

The Lady Gwendolen Lancaster-Douglas-Scroop, youngest daughter of the ninth Duke of Cranston, and aged six years and three months, picked herself up quite alone, and sat down on the third step from the foot of the grand staircase in Cranston House.

"Oh!" ejaculated the butler, and he disappeared again.

"Ah!" responded the grooms of the chambers, as they also went away.

"It's only that doll," Mrs. Pringle was distinctly heard to say, in a tone of contempt.

The under nurse heard her say it. Then the three nurses gathered round Lady Gwendolen and patted her, and gave her unhealthy things out of their pockets, and hurried her out of Cranston House as fast as they could, lest it should be found out upstairs that they had allowed the Lady Gwendolen Lancaster-Douglas-Scroop to tumble down the grand staircase with her doll in her arms. And as the doll was badly broken, the nursery-maid carried it, with the pieces, wrapped up in Lady Gwendolen's little cloak. It was not far to Hyde Park, and when they had reached a quiet place they took means to find out that

Lady Gwendolen had no bruises. For the carpet was very thick and soft, and there was thick stuff under it to make it softer.

Lady Gwendolen Douglas-Scroop sometimes yelled, but she never cried. It was because she had yelled that the nurse had allowed her to go downstairs alone with Nina, the doll, under one arm, while she steadied herself with her other hand on the balustrade, and trod upon the polished marble steps beyond the edge of the carpet. So she had fallen, and Nina had come to grief.

When the nurses were quite sure that she was not hurt, they unwrapped the doll and looked at her in her turn. She had been a very beautiful doll, very large, and fair, and healthy, with real yellow hair, and eyelids that would open and shut over very grown-up dark eyes. Moreover, when you moved her right arm up and down she said "Pa-pa," and when you moved the left she said "Ma-ma," very distinctly.

"I heard her say 'Pa' when she fell," said the under nurse, who heard everything. "But she ought to have said 'Pa-pa.'"

"That's because her arm went up when she hit the step," said the head nurse. "She'll say the other 'Pa' when I put it down again."

"Pa," said Nina, as her right arm was pushed down, and speaking through her broken face. It was cracked right across, from the upper corner of the forehead, with a hideous gash, through the nose and down to the little frilled collar of the pale green silk Mother Hubbard frock, and two little three-cornered pieces of porcelain had fallen out.

"I'm sure it's a wonder she can speak at all, being all smashed," said the under nurse.

"You'll have to take her to Mr. Puckler," said her superior. "It's not far, and you'd better go at once."

Lady Gwendolen was occupied in digging a hole in the ground with a little spade, and paid no attention to the nurses.

"What are you doing?" enquired the nursery-maid, looking on.

"Nina's dead, and I'm diggin' her a grave," replied her ladyship thoughtfully.

"Oh, she'll come to life again all right," said the nursery-maid.

The under nurse wrapped Nina up again and departed. Fortunately a kind soldier, with very long legs and a very small cap, happened to be there; and as he had nothing to do, he offered to see the under nurse safely to Mr. Puckler's and back.

Mr. Bernard Puckler and his little daughter lived in a little house in a little alley, which led out off a quiet little street not very far from Belgrave Square. He was the great doll doctor, and his extensive practice lay in the most aristocratic quarter. He mended dolls of all sizes and ages, boy dolls and girl dolls, baby dolls in long clothes, and grown-up dolls in fashionable gowns, talking dolls and dumb dolls, those that shut their eyes when they lay down, and those whose eyes had to be shut for them by means of a mysterious wire. His daughter Else was only just over twelve years old, but she was already very clever at mending dolls' clothes, and at doing their hair, which is harder than you might think, though the dolls sit quite still while it is being done.

Mr. Puckler had originally been a German, but he had dissolved his nationality in the ocean of London many years ago, like a great many foreigners. He still had one or two German friends, however, who came on Saturday evenings, and smoked with him and played picquet or "skat" with him for farthing points, and called him "Herr Doctor," which seemed to please Mr. Puckler very much.

He looked older than he was, for his beard was rather long and ragged, his hair was grizzled and thin, and he wore horn-rimmed spectacles. As for Else, she was a thin, pale child, very quiet and neat, with dark eyes and brown hair that was plaited down her back and tied with a bit of black ribbon. She mended the dolls' clothes and took the dolls back to their homes when they were quite strong again.

The house was a little one, but too big for the two people who lived in it. There was a small sitting-room on the street, and the workshop was at the back, and there were three rooms upstairs. But the father and daughter lived most of their time in the workshop, because they were generally at work, even in the evenings.

Mr. Puckler laid Nina on the table and looked at her a long time, till the tears began to fill his eyes behind the horn-rimmed spectacles. He was a very susceptible man, and he often fell in love with the dolls he mended, and found it hard to part with them when they had smiled at him for a few days. They were real little people to him, with characters and thoughts and feelings of their own, and he was very tender with them all. But some attracted him especially from the first, and when they were brought to him maimed and injured, their state seemed so pitiful to him that the tears came easily. You must remember that he had lived among dolls during a great part of his life, and understood them.

"How do you know that they feel nothing?" he went on to say to Else. "You must be gentle with them. It costs nothing to be kind to the little beings, and perhaps it makes a difference to them."

And Else understood him, because she was a child, and she knew that she was more to him than all the dolls.

He fell in love with Nina at first sight, perhaps because her beautiful brown glass eyes were something like Else's own, and he loved Else first and best, with all his heart. And, besides, it was a very sorrowful case. Nina had evidently not been long in the world, for her complexion was perfect, her hair was smooth where it should be smooth, and curly where it should be curly, and her silk clothes were perfectly new. But across her face was that frightful gash, like a sabre-cut, deep and shadowy within, but clean and sharp at the edges. When he tenderly pressed her head to close the gaping wound, the edges made a fine grating sound, that was painful to hear, and the lids of the dark eyes quivered and trembled as though Nina were suffering dreadfully.

"Poor Nina!" he exclaimed sorrowfully. "But I shall not hurt you much, though you will take a long time to get strong."

He always asked the names of the broken dolls when they were brought to him, and sometimes the people knew what the children called them, and told him. He liked "Nina" for a name. Altogether and in every way she pleased him more than any doll he had seen for many years, and he felt drawn to her, and made up his mind to make her perfectly strong and sound, no matter how much labour it might cost him.

Mr. Puckler worked patiently a little at a time, and Else watched him. She could do nothing for poor Nina, whose clothes needed no mending. The longer the doll doctor worked, the more fond he became of the yellow hair and the beautiful brown glass eyes. He sometimes forgot all the other dolls that were waiting to be mended, lying side by side on a shelf, and sat for an hour gazing at Nina's face, while he racked his ingenuity for some new invention by which to hide even the smallest trace of the terrible accident.

She was wonderfully mended. Even he was obliged to admit that; but the scar was still visible to his keen eyes, a very fine line right across the face, downwards from right to left. Yet all the conditions had been most favourable for a cure, since the cement had set quite hard at the first attempt and the weather had been fine and dry, which makes a great difference in a dolls' hospital.

At last he knew that he could do no more, and the under nurse had already come twice to see whether the job was finished, as she coarsely expressed it.

"Nina is not quite strong yet," Mr. Puckler had answered each time, for he could not make up his mind to face the parting.

And now he sat before the square deal table at which he worked, and Nina lay before him for the last time with a big brown paper box beside her. It stood there like her coffin, waiting for her, he thought. He must put her into it, and lay tissue paper over her dear face, and then put on the lid, and at the thought of tying the string his sight was dim with tears again. He was never to look into the glassy depths of the beautiful brown eyes any more, nor to hear the little wooden voice say "Pa-pa" and "Ma-ma." It was a very painful moment.

In the vain hope of gaining time before the separation, he took up the little sticky bottles of cement and glue and gum and colour, looking at each one in turn, and then at Nina's face. And all his small tools lay there, neatly arranged in a row, but he knew that he could not use them again for Nina. She was quite strong at last, and in a country where there should be no cruel children to hurt her she might live a hundred years, with only that almost imperceptible line across her face to tell of the fearful thing that had befallen her on the marble steps of Cranston House.

Suddenly Mr. Puckler's heart was quite full, and he rose abruptly from his seat and turned away.

"Else," he said unsteadily, "you must do it for me. I cannot bear to see her go into the box."

So he went and stood at the window with his back turned,

while Else did what he had not the heart to do.

"Is it done?" he asked, not turning round. "Then take her away, my dear. Put on your hat, and take her to Cranston House quickly, and when you are gone I will turn round."

Else was used to her father's queer ways with the dolls, and though she had never seen him so much moved by a parting, she was not much surprised.

"Come back quickly," he said, when he heard her hand on the latch. "It is growing late, and I should not send you at this hour. But I cannot bear to look forward to it any more."

When Else was gone, he left the window and sat down in his place before the table again, to wait for the child to come back. He touched the place where Nina had lain, very gently, and he recalled the softly tinted pink face, and the glass eyes, and the ringlets of yellow hair, till he could almost see them.

The evenings were long, for it was late in the spring. But it began to grow dark soon, and Mr. Puckler wondered why Else did not come back. She had been gone an hour and a half, and that was much longer than he had expected, for it was barely half a mile from Belgrave Square to Cranston House. He reflected that the child might have been kept waiting, but as the twilight deepened he grew anxious, and walked up and down in the dim workshop, no longer thinking of Nina, but of Else, his own living child, whom he loved.

An undefinable, disquieting sensation came upon him by fine degrees, a chilliness and a faint stirring of his thin hair, joined with a wish to be in any company rather than to be alone much longer. It was the beginning of fear.

He told himself in strong German-English that he was a foolish old man, and he began to feel about for the matches in the dusk. He knew just where they should be, for he always kept them in the same place, close to the little tin box that held bits of sealing-wax of various colours, for some kinds of mending. But somehow he could not find the matches in the gloom.

Something had happened to Else, he was sure, and as his fear increased, he felt as though it might be allayed if he could get a light and see what time it was. Then he called himself a foolish old man again, and the sound of his own voice startled him in the dark. He could not find the matches.

The window was grey still; he might see what time it was if

he went close to it, and he could go and get matches out of the cupboard afterwards. He stood back from the table, to get out of the way of the chair, and began to cross the board floor.

Something was following him in the dark. There was a small pattering, as of tiny feet upon the boards. He stopped and listened, and the roots of his hair tingled. It was nothing, and he was a foolish old man. He made two steps more, and he was sure that he heard the little pattering again. He turned his back to the window, leaning against the sash so that the panes began to crack, and he faced the dark. Everything was quite still, and it smelt of paste and cement and wood-filings as usual.

"Is that you, Else?" he asked, and he was surprised by the fear in his voice.

There was no answer in the room, and he held up his watch and tried to make out what time it was by the grey dusk that was just not darkness. So far as he could see, it was within two or three minutes of ten o'clock. He had been a long time alone. He was shocked, and frightened for Else, out in London, so late, and he almost ran across the room to the door. As he fumbled for the latch, he distinctly heard the running of the little feet after him.

"Mice!" he exclaimed feebly, just as he got the door open.

He shut it quickly behind him, and felt as though some cold thing had settled on his back and were writhing upon him. The passage was quite dark, but he found his hat and was out in the alley in a moment, breathing more freely, and surprised to find how much light there still was in the open air. He could see the pavement clearly under his feet, and far off in the street to which the alley led he could hear the laughter and calls of children, playing some game out of doors. He wondered how he could have been so nervous, and for an instant he thought of going back into the house to wait quietly for Else. But instantly he felt that nervous fright of something stealing over him again. In any case it was better to walk up to Cranston House and ask the servants about the child. One of the women had perhaps taken a fancy to her, and was even now giving her tea and cake.

He walked quickly to Belgrave Square, and then up the broad streets, listening as he went, whenever there was no other sound, for the tiny footsteps. But he heard nothing, and was laughing at himself when he rang the servants' bell at the big house. Of course, the child must be there.

The person who opened the door was quite an inferior person, for it was a back door, but affected the manners of the front, and stared at Mr. Puckler superciliously under the strong light.

No little girl had been seen, and he knew "nothing about no dolls."

"She is my little girl," said Mr. Puckler tremulously, for all his anxiety was returning tenfold, "and I am afraid something has happened."

The inferior person said rudely that "nothing could have happened to her in that house, because she had not been there, which was a jolly good reason why;" and Mr. Puckler was obliged to admit that the man ought to know, as it was his business to keep the door and let people in. He wished to be allowed to speak to the under nurse, who knew him; but the man was ruder than ever, and finally shut the door in his face.

When the doll doctor was alone in the street, he steadied himself by the railing, for he felt as though he were breaking in two, just as some dolls break, in the middle of the backbone.

Presently he knew that he must be doing something to find Else, and that gave him strength. He began to walk as quickly as he could through the streets, following every highway and byway which his little girl might have taken on her errand. He also asked several policemen in vain if they had seen her, and most of them answered him kindly, for they saw that he was a sober man and in his right senses, and some of them had little girls of their own.

It was one o'clock in the morning when he went up to his own door again, worn out and hopeless and broken-hearted. As he turned the key in the lock, his heart stood still, for he knew that he was awake and not dreaming, and that he really heard those tiny footsteps pattering to meet him inside the house along the passage.

But he was too unhappy to be much frightened any more, and his heart went on again with a dull regular pain, that found its way all through him with every pulse. So he went in, and hung up his hat in the dark, and found the matches in the cupboard and the candlestick in its place in the corner.

Mr. Puckler was so much overcome and so completely worn out that he sat down in his chair before the work-table and almost fainted, as his face dropped forward upon his folded hands. Beside him the solitary candle burned steadily with a low flame in the still warm air.

"Else! Else!" he moaned against his yellow knuckles. And that was all he could say, and it was no relief to him. On the contrary, the very sound of the name was a new and sharp pain that pierced his ears and his head and his very soul. For every time he repeated the name it meant that little Else was dead, somewhere out in the streets of London in the dark.

He was so terribly hurt that he did not even feel something pulling gently at the skirt of his old coat, so gently that it was like the nibbling of a tiny mouse. He might have thought that it was really a mouse if he had noticed it.

"Else! Else!" he groaned right against his hands.

Then a cool breath stirred his thin hair, and the low flame of the one candle dropped down almost to a mere spark, not flickering as though a draught were going to blow it out, but just dropping down as if it were tired out. Mr. Puckler felt his hands stiffening with fright under his face; and there was a faint rustling sound, like some small silk thing blown in a gentle breeze. He sat up straight, stark and scared, and a small wooden voice spoke in the stillness.

"Pa-pa," it said, with a break between the syllables.

Mr. Puckler stood up in a single jump, and his chair fell over backwards with a smashing noise upon the wooden floor. The candle had almost gone out.

It was Nina's doll voice that had spoken, and he should have known it among the voices of a hundred other dolls. And yet there was something more in it, a little human ring, with a pitiful cry and a call for help, and the wail of a hurt child. Mr. Puckler stood up, stark and stiff, and tried to look round, but at first he could not, for he seemed to be frozen from head to foot.

Then he made a great effort, and he raised one hand to each of his temples, and pressed his own head round as he would have turned a doll's. The candle was burning so low that it might as well have been out altogether, for any light it gave, and the room seemed quite dark at first. Then he saw something. He would not have believed that he could be more frightened than he had been just before that. But he was, and his knees shook, for he saw the doll standing in the middle of the floor, shining with a faint and ghostly radiance, her beautiful glassy brown eyes fixed on his. And across her face the very thin line of the break he had mended shone as though it were drawn in light with a fine point of white flame.

Yet there was something more in the eyes, too; there was something human, like Else's own, but as if only the doll saw him through them, and not Else. And there was enough of Else to bring back all his pain and to make him forget his fear.

"Else! my little Else!" he cried aloud.

The small ghost moved, and its doll-arm slowly rose and fell with a stiff, mechanical motion.

"Pa-pa," it said.

It seemed this time that there was even more of Else's tone echoing somewhere between the wooden notes that reached his ears so distinctly, and yet so far away. Else was calling him, he was sure.

His face was perfectly white in the gloom, but his knees did not shake any more, and he felt that he was less frightened.

"Yes, child! But where? Where?" he asked. "Where are you, Else?"

"Pa-pa!"

The syllables died away in the quiet room. There was a low rustling of silk, the glassy brown eyes turned slowly away, and Mr. Puckler heard the pitter-patter of the small feet in the bronze kid slippers as the figure ran straight to the door. Then the candle burned high again, the room was full of light, and he was alone.

Mr. Puckler passed his hand over his eyes and looked about him. He could see everything quite clearly, and he felt that he must have been dreaming, though he was standing instead of sitting down, as he should have been if he had just waked up. The candle burned brightly now. There were the dolls to be mended, lying in a row with their toes up. The third one had lost her right shoe, and Else was making one. He knew that, and he was certainly not dreaming now. He had not been dreaming when he had come in from his fruitless search and had heard the doll's footsteps running to the door. He had not fallen asleep in his chair. How could he possibly have fallen asleep when his heart was breaking? He had been awake all the time.

He steadied himself, set the fallen chair upon its legs, and said to himself again very emphatically that he was a foolish old man. He ought to be out in the streets looking for his child, asking questions, and enquiring at the police stations, where all accidents were reported as soon as they were known, or at the hospitals.

"Pa-pa!"

The longing, wailing, pitiful little wooden cry rang from the passage, outside the door, and Mr. Puckler stood for an instant with white face, transfixed and rooted to the spot. A moment later his hand was on the latch. Then he was in the passage, with the light streaming from the open door behind him.

Quite at the other end he saw the little phantom shining clearly in the shadow, and the right hand seemed to beckon to him as the arm rose and fell once more. He knew all at once that it had not come to frighten him but to lead him, and when it disappeared, and he walked boldly towards the door, he knew that it was in the street outside, waiting for him. He forgot that he was tired and had eaten no supper, and had walked many miles, for a sudden hope ran through and through him, like a golden stream of life.

And sure enough, at the corner of the alley, and at the corner of the street, and out in Belgrave Square, he saw the small ghost flitting before him. Sometimes it was only a shadow, where there was other light, but then the glare of the lamps made a pale green sheen on its little Mother Hubbard frock of silk; and sometimes, where the streets were dark and silent, the whole figure shone out brightly, with its yellow curls and rosy neck. It seemed to trot along like a tiny child, and Mr. Puckler could almost hear the pattering of the bronze kid slippers on the pavement as it ran. But it went very fast, and he could only just keep up with it, tearing along with his hat on the back of his head and his thin hair blown by the night breeze, and his horn-rimmed spectacles firmly set upon his broad nose.

On and on he went, and he had no idea where he was. He did not even care, for he knew certainly that he was going the right way.

Then at last, in a wide, quiet street, he was standing before a big, sober-looking door that had two lamps on each side of it, and a polished brass bell-handle, which he pulled.

And just inside, when the door was opened, in the bright

light, there was the little shadow, and the pale green sheen of the little silk dress, and once more the small cry came to his ears, less pitiful, more longing.

"Pa-pa!"

The shadow turned suddenly bright, and out of the brightness the beautiful brown glass eyes were turned up happily to his, while the rosy mouth smiled so divinely that the phantom doll looked almost like a little angel just then.

"A little girl was brought in soon after ten o'clock," said the quiet voice of the hospital doorkeeper. "I think they thought she was only stunned. She was holding a big brown-paper box against her, and they could not get it out of her arms. She had a long plait of brown hair that hung down as they carried her."

"She is my little girl," said Mr. Puckler, but he hardly heard his own voice.

He leaned over Else's face in the gentle light of the children's ward, and when he had stood there a minute the beautiful brown eyes opened and looked up to his.

"Pa-pa!" cried Else, softly, "I knew you would come!"

Then Mr. Puckler did not know what he did or said for a moment, and what he felt was worth all the fear and terror and despair that had almost killed him that night. But by and by Else was telling her story, and the nurse let her speak, for there were only two other children in the room, who were getting well and were sound asleep.

"They were big boys with bad faces," said Else, "and they tried to get Nina away from me, but I held on and fought as well as I could till one of them hit me with something, and I don't remember any more, for I tumbled down, and I suppose the boys ran away, and somebody found me there. But I'm afraid Nina is all smashed."

"Here is the box," said the nurse. "We could not take it out of her arms till she came to herself. Should you like to see if the doll is broken?"

And she undid the string cleverly, but Nina was all smashed to pieces. Only the gentle light of the children's ward made a pale green sheen in the folds of the little Mother Hubbard frock.

THE DEAD SMILE
BY F. Marion Crawford

CHAPTER I

Sir Hugh Ockram smiled as he sat by the open window of his study, in the late August afternoon; and just then a curiously yellow cloud obscured the low sun, and the clear summer light turned lurid, as if it had been suddenly poisoned and polluted by the foul vapours of a plague. Sir Hugh's face seemed, at best, to be made of fine parchment drawn skin-tight over a wooden mask, in which two eyes were sunk out of sight, and peered from far within through crevices under the slanting, wrinkled lids, alive and watchful like two toads in their holes, side by side and exactly alike. But as the light changed, then a little yellow glare flashed in each. Nurse Macdonald said once that when Sir Hugh smiled he saw the faces of two women in hell - two dead women he had betrayed. (Nurse Macdonald was a hundred years old.) And the smile widened, stretching the pale lips across the discoloured teeth in an expression of profound self-satisfaction, blended with the most unforgiving hatred and contempt for the human doll. The hideous disease of which he was dying had touched his brain. His son stood beside him, tall, white and delicate as an angel in a primitive picture; and though there was deep distress in his violet eyes as he looked at his father's face, he felt the shadow of that sickening smile stealing across his own lips and parting them and drawing them against his will. And it was like a bad dream, for he tried not to smile and smiled the more. Beside him, strangely like him in her wan, angelic beauty, with the same shadowy golden hair, the same sad violet eyes, the same luminously pale face, Evelyn Warburton rested one hand upon his arm. And as she looked into her uncle's eyes, and could not turn her own away, she knew that the deathly smile was hovering on her own red lips, drawing them tightly across her little teeth, while two bright tears ran down her cheeks to her mouth, and dropped from the upper to the lower lip while she smiled - and the smile was like the shadow of death and the seal of damnation upon her pure, young face.

"Of course," said Sir Hugh very slowly, and still looking out at the trees, "if you have made up your mind to be married, I cannot hinder you, and I don't suppose you attach the smallest importance to my consent -"

"Father!" exclaimed Gabriel reproachfully.

"No; I do not deceive myself," continued the old man, smiling terribly. "You will marry when I am dead, though there is a very good reason why you had better not - why you had better not," he repeated very emphatically, and he slowly turned his toad eyes upon the lovers.

"What reason?" asked Evelyn in a frightened voice.

"Never mind the reason, my dear. You will marry just as if it did not exist." There was a long pause. "Two gone," he said, his voice lowering strangely, "and two more will be four - all together - for ever and ever, burning, burning, burning bright."

At the last words his head sank slowly back, and the little glare of the toad eyes disappeared under the swollen lids; and the lurid cloud passed from the westering sun, so that the earth was green again and the light pure. Sir Hugh had fallen asleep, as he often did in his last illness, even while speaking.

Gabriel Ockram drew Evelyn away, and from the study they went out into the dim hall, softly closing the door behind them, and each audibly drew breath, as though some sudden danger had been passed. They laid their hands each in the other's, and their strangely-like eyes met in a long look, in which love and perfect understanding were darkened by the secret terror of an unknown thing. Their pale faces reflected each other's fear.

"It is his secret," said Evelyn at last. "He will never tell us what it is."

"If he dies with it," answered Gabriel, "let it be on his own head!"

"On his head!" echoed the dim hall. It was a strange echo, and some were frightened by it, for they said that if it were a real echo it should repeat everything and not give back a phrase here and there, now speaking, now silent. But Nurse Macdonald said that the great hall would never echo a prayer when an Ockram was to die, though it would give back curses ten for one.

"On his head!" it repeated quite softly, and Evelyn started and looked round.

"It is only the echo," said Gabriel, leading her away.

They went out into the late afternoon light, and sat upon a stone seat behind the chapel, which was built across the end of the east wing. It was very still, not a breath stirred, and there was no sound near them. Only far off in the park a song-bird was whistling the high prelude to the evening chorus.

"It is very lonely here," said Evelyn, taking Gabriel's hand nervously, and speaking as if she dreaded to disturb the silence. "If it were dark, I should be afraid."

"Of what? Of me?" Gabriel's sad eyes turned to her.

"Oh no! How could I be afraid of you? But of the old Ockrams - they say they are just under our feet here in the north vault outside the chapel, all in their shrouds, with no coffins, as they used to bury them."

"As they always will - as they will bury my father, and me. They say an Ockram will not lie in a coffin."

"But it cannot be true - these are fairy tales - ghost stories!" Evelyn nestled nearer to her companion, grasping his hand more tightly, and the sun began to go down.

"Of course. But there is the story of old Sir Vernon, who was beheaded for treason under James II. The family brought his body back from the scaffold in an iron coffin with heavy locks, and they put it in the north vault. But ever afterwards, whenever the vault was opened to bury another of the family, they found the coffin wide open, and the body standing upright against the wall, and the head rolled away in a corner, smiling at it."

"As Uncle Hugh smiles?" Evelyn shivered.

"Yes, I suppose so," answered Gabriel, thoughtfully. "Of course I never saw it, and the vault has not been opened for thirty years - none of us have died since then."

"And if - if Uncle Hugh dies - shall you -" Evelyn stopped, and her beautiful thin face was quite white.

"Yes. I shall see him laid there too - with his secret, whatever it is." Gabriel sighed and pressed the girl's little hand.

"I do not like to think of it," she said unsteadily. "O Gabriel, what can the secret be? He said we had better not marry - not that he forbade it - but he said it so strangely, and he smiled - ugh!" Her small white teeth chattered with fear, and she looked over her shoulder while drawing still closer to Gabriel. "And, somehow, I felt it in my own face -"

"So did I," answered Gabriel in a low, nervous voice. "Nurse Macdonald -" He stopped abruptly.

"What? What did she say?"

"Oh - nothing. She has told me things - they would frighten you, dear. Come, it is growing chilly." He rose, but Evelyn held his hand in both of hers, still sitting and looking up into his face.

"But we shall be married, just the same - Gabriel! Say that we shall!"

"Of course, darling - of course. But while my father is so very ill, it is impossible -"

"O Gabriel, Gabriel, dear! I wish we were married now!" cried Evelyn in sudden distress. "I know that something will prevent it and keep us apart."

"Nothing shall!"

"Nothing?"

"Nothing human," said Gabriel Ockram, as she drew him down to her.

And their faces, that were so strangely alike, met and touched - and Gabriel knew that the kiss had a marvellous savour of evil, but on Evelyn's lips it was like the cool breath of a sweet and mortal fear. And neither of them understood, for they were innocent and young. Yet she drew him to her by her lightest touch, as a sensitive plant shivers and waves its thin leaves, and bends and closes softly upon what it wants; and he let himself be drawn to her willingly, as he would if her touch had been deadly and poisonous; for she strangely loved that half voluptuous breath of fear, and he passionately desired the nameless evil something that lurked in her maiden lips.

"It is as if we loved in a strange dream," she said.

"I fear the waking," he murmured.

"We shall not wake, dear - when the dream is over it will have already turned into death, so softly that we shall not know it. But until then -"

She paused, and her eyes sought his, and their faces slowly came nearer. It was as if they had thoughts in their red lips that foresaw and foreknew the deep kiss of each other.

"Until then -" she said again, very low, and her mouth was nearer to his.

"Dream - till then," murmured his breath.

CHAPTER II

Nurse Macdonald was a hundred years old. She used to sleep sitting all bent together in a great old leathern arm-chair with wings, her feet in a bag footstool lined with sheepskin, and many warm blankets wrapped about her, even in summer. Beside her a little lamp always burned at night by an old silver cup, in which there was something to drink.

Her face was very wrinkled, but the wrinkles were so small and fine and near together that they made shadows instead of lines. Two thin locks of hair, that was turning from white to a smoky yellow again, were drawn over her temples from under her starched white cap. Every now and then she woke, and her eyelids were drawn up in tiny folds like little pink silk curtains, and her queer blue eyes looked straight before her through doors and walls and worlds to a far place beyond. Then she slept again, and her hands lay one upon the other on the edge of the blanket; the thumbs had grown longer than the fingers with age, and the joints shone in the low lamplight like polished crab-apples.

It was nearly one o'clock in the night, and the summer breeze was blowing the ivy branch against the panes of the window with a hushing caress. In the small room beyond, with the door ajar, the girl-maid who took care of Nurse Macdonald was fast asleep. All was very quiet. The old woman breathed regularly, and her indrawn lips trembled each time as the breath went out, and her eyes were shut.

But outside the closed window there was a face, and violet eyes were looking steadily at the ancient sleeper, for it was like the face of Evelyn Warburton, though there were eighty feet from the sill of the window to the foot of the tower. Yet the cheeks were thinner than Evelyn's, and as white as a gleam, and the eyes stared, and the lips were not red with life; they were dead, and painted with new blood.

Slowly Nurse Macdonald's wrinkled eyelids folded themselves back, and she looked straight at the face at the window while one might count ten.

"Is it time?" she asked in her little old, faraway voice.

While she looked the face at the window changed, for the

eyes opened wider and wider till the white glared all round the bright violet, and the bloody lips opened over gleaming teeth, and stretched and widened and stretched again, and the shadowy golden hair rose and streamed against the window in the night breeze. And in answer to Nurse Macdonald's question came the sound that freezes the living flesh.

That low-moaning voice that rises suddenly, like the scream of storm, from a moan to a wail, from a wail to a howl, from a howl to the fear-shriek of the tortured dead - he who has heard knows, and he can bear witness that the cry of the banshee is an evil cry to hear alone in the deep night. When it was over and the face was gone, Nurse Macdonald shook a little in her great chair, and still she looked at the black square of the window, but there was nothing more there, nothing but the night, and the whispering ivy branch. She turned her head to the door that was ajar, and there stood the girl in her white gown, her teeth chattering with fright.

"It is time, child," said Nurse Macdonald. "I must go to him, for it is the end."

She rose slowly, leaning her withered hands upon the arms of the chair, and the girl brought her a woollen gown and a great mantle, and her crutch-stick, and made her ready. But very often the girl looked at the window and was unjointed with fear, and often Nurse Macdonald shook her head and said words which the maid could not understand.

"It was like the face of Miss Evelyn," said the girl at last, trembling.

But the ancient woman looked up sharply and angrily, and her queer blue eyes glared. She held herself by the arm of the great chair with her left hand, and lifted up her crutch-stick to strike the maid with all her might. But she did not.

"You are a good girl," she said, "but you are a fool. Pray for wit, child, pray for wit - or else find service in another house than Ockram Hall. Bring the lamp and help me under my left arm."

The crutch-stick clacked on the wooden floor, and the low heels of the woman's slippers clappered after her in slow triplets, as Nurse Macdonald got toward the door. And down the stairs each step she took was a labour in itself, and by the clacking noise the waking servants knew that she was coming, very long before they saw her.

No one was sleeping now, and there were lights, and whisperings, and pale faces in the corridors near Sir Hugh's bedroom, and now some one went in, and now some one came out, but every one made way for Nurse Macdonald, who had nursed Sir Hugh's father more than eighty years ago.

The light was soft and clear in the room. There stood Gabriel Ockram by his father's bedside, and there knelt Evelyn Warburton, her hair lying like a golden shadow down her shoulders, and her hands clasped nervously together. And opposite Gabriel, a nurse was trying to make Sir Hugh drink. But he would not, and though his lips were parted, his teeth were set. He was very, very thin and yellow now, and his eyes caught the light sideways and were as yellow coals.

"Do not torment him," said Nurse Macdonald to the woman who held the cup. "Let me speak to him, for his hour is come."

"Let her speak to him," said Gabriel in a dull voice.

So the ancient woman leaned to the pillow and laid the feather-weight of her withered hand, that was like a brown moth, upon Sir Hugh's yellow fingers, and she spoke to him earnestly, while only Gabriel and Evelyn were left in the room to hear.

"Hugh Ockram," she said, "this is the end of your life; and as I saw you born, and saw your father born before you, I am come to see you die. Hugh Ockram, will you tell me the truth?"

The dying man recognised the little faraway voice he had known all his life, and he very slowly turned his yellow face to Nurse Macdonald; but he said nothing. Then she spoke again.

"Hugh Ockram, you will never see the daylight again. Will you tell the truth?"

His toad-like eyes were not yet dull. They fastened themselves on her face.

"What do you want of me?" he asked, and each word struck hollow upon the last. "I have no secrets. I have lived a good life."

Nurse Macdonald laughed - a tiny, cracked laugh, that made her old head bob and tremble a little, as if her neck were on a steel spring. But Sir Hugh's eyes grew red, and his pale lips began to twist.

"Let me die in peace," he said slowly.

But Nurse Macdonald shook her head, and her brown, moth-like hand left his and fluttered to his forehead.

"By the mother that bore you and died of grief for the sins you did, tell me the truth!"

Sir Hugh's lips tightened on his discoloured teeth.

"Not on earth," he answered slowly.

"By the wife who bore your son and died heartbroken, tell me the truth!"

"Neither to you in life, nor to her in eternal death."

His lips writhed, as if the words were coals between them, and a great drop of sweat rolled across the parchment of his forehead. Gabriel Ockram bit his hand as he watched his father die. But Nurse Macdonald spoke a third time.

"By the woman whom you betrayed, and who waits for you this night, Hugh Ockram, tell me the truth!"

"It is too late. Let me die in peace."

The writhing lips began to smile across the set yellow teeth, and the toad eyes glowed like evil jewels in his head.

"There is time," said the ancient woman. "Tell me the name of Evelyn Warburton's father. Then I will let you die in peace."

Evelyn started back, kneeling as she was, and stared at Nurse Macdonald, and then at her uncle.

"The name of Evelyn's father?" he repeated slowly, while the awful smile spread upon his dying face.

The light was growing strangely dim in the great room. As Evelyn looked, Nurse Macdonald's crooked shadow on the wall grew gigantic. Sir Hugh's breath came thick, rattling in his throat, as death crept in like a snake and choked it back. Evelyn prayed aloud, high and clear.

Then something rapped at the window, and she felt her hair rise upon her head in a cool breeze, as she looked around in spite of herself. And when she saw her own white face looking in at the window, and her own eyes staring at her through the glass, wide and fearful, and her own hair streaming against the pane, and her own lips dashed with blood, she rose slowly from the floor and stood rigid for one moment, till she screamed once and fell straight back into Gabriel's arms. But the shriek that answered hers was the fear-shriek of the tormented corpse, out of which the soul cannot pass for shame of deadly sins, though the devils fight in it with corruption, each for their due share.

Sir Hugh Ockram sat upright in his deathbed, and saw and

cried aloud:

"Evelyn!" His harsh voice broke and rattled in his chest as he sank down. But still Nurse Macdonald tortured him, for there was a little life left in him still.

"You have seen the mother as she waits for you, Hugh Ockram. Who was this girl Evelyn's father? What was his name?"

For the last time the dreadful smile came upon the twisted lips, very slowly, very surely now, and the toad eyes glared red, and the parchment face glowed a little in the flickering light. For the last time words came.

"They know it in hell."

Then the glowing eyes went out quickly, the yellow face turned waxen pale, and a great shiver ran through the thin body as Hugh Ockram died.

But in death he still smiled, for he knew his secret and kept it still, on the other side, and he would take it with him, to lie with him for ever in the north vault of the chapel where the Ockrams lie uncoffined in their shrouds - all but one. Though he was dead, he smiled, for he had kept his treasure of evil truth to the end, and there was none left to tell the name he had spoken, but there was all the evil he had not undone left to bear fruit.

As they watched - Nurse Macdonald and Gabriel, who held Evelyn still unconscious in his arms while he looked at the father - they felt the dead smile crawling along their own lips - the ancient crone and the youth with the angel's face. Then they shivered a little, and both looked at Evelyn as she lay with her head on his shoulder, and, though she was very beautiful, the same sickening smile was twisting her young mouth too, and it was like the foreshadowing of a great evil which they could not understand.

But by and by they carried Evelyn out, and she opened her eyes and the smile was gone. From far away in the great house the sound of weeping and crooning came up the stairs and echoed along the dismal corridors, for the women had begun to mourn the dead master, after the Irish fashion, and the hall had echoes of its own all that night, like the far-off wail of the banshee among forest trees.

When the time was come they took Sir Hugh in his winding-sheet on a trestle bier, and bore him to the chapel and through the iron door and down the long descent to the north vault, with tapers, to lay him by his father. And two men went in first to prepare the place, and came back staggering like drunken men, and white, leaving their lights behind them.

But Gabriel Ockram was not afraid, for he knew. And he went in alone and saw that the body of Sir Vernon Ockram was leaning upright against the stone wall, and that its head lay on the ground near by with the face turned up, and the dried leathern lips smiled horribly at the dried-up corpse, while the iron coffin, lined with black velvet, stood open on the floor.

Then Gabriel took the thing in his hands, for it was very light, being quite dried by the air of the vault, and those who peeped in from the door saw him lay it in the coffin again, and it rustled a little, like a bundle of reeds, and sounded hollow as it touched the sides and the bottom. He also placed the head upon the shoulders and shut down the lid, which fell to with a rusty spring that snapped.

After that they laid Sir Hugh beside his father, with the trestle bier on which they had brought him, and they went back to the chapel.

But when they saw one another's faces, master and men, they were all smiling with the dead smile of the corpse they had left in the vault, so that they could not bear to look at one another until it had faded away.

CHAPTER III

Gabriel Ockram became Sir Gabriel, inheriting the baronetcy with the half-ruined fortune left by his father, and still Evelyn Warburton lived at Ockram Hall, in the south room that had been hers ever since she could remember anything. She could not go away, for there were no relatives to whom she could have gone, and, besides, there seemed to be no reason why she should not stay. The world would never trouble itself to care what the Ockrams did on their Irish estates, and it was long since the Ockrams had asked anything of the world.

So Sir Gabriel took his father's place at the dark old table in the dining-room, and Evelyn sat opposite to him, until such time as their mourning should be over, and they might be married at last. And meanwhile their lives went on as before, since Sir Hugh had been a hopeless invalid during the last year of his life, and they had seen him but once a day for a little while, spending most of their time together in a strangely perfect companionship.

But though the late summer saddened into autumn, and autumn darkened into winter, and storm followed storm, and rain poured on rain through the short days and the long nights, yet Ockram Hall seemed less gloomy since Sir Hugh had been laid in the north vault beside his father. And at Christmastide Evelyn decked the great hall with holly and green boughs, and huge fires blazed on every hearth. Then the tenants were all bidden to a New Year's dinner, and they ate and drank well, while Sir Gabriel sat at the head of the table. Evelyn came in when the port wine was brought, and the most respected of the tenants made a speech to propose her health.

It was long, he said, since there had been a Lady Ockram. Sir Gabriel shaded his eyes with his hand and looked down at the table, but a faint colour came into Evelyn's transparent cheeks. But, said the grey-haired farmer, it was longer still since there had been a Lady Ockram so fair as the next was to be, and he gave the health of Evelyn Warburton.

Then the tenants all stood up and shouted for her, and Sir Gabriel stood up likewise, beside Evelyn. And when the men gave the last and loudest cheer of all there was a voice not theirs, above them all, higher, fiercer, louder - a scream not earthly, shrieking for the bride of Ockram Hall. And the holly and the green boughs over the great chimney-piece shook and slowly waved as if a cool breeze were blowing over them. But the men turned very pale, and many of them set down their glasses, but others let them fall upon the floor for fear. And looking into one another's faces, they were all smiling strangely, a dead smile, like dead Sir Hugh's. One cried out words in Irish, and the fear of death was suddenly upon them all, so that they fled in panic, falling over one another like wild beasts in the burning forest, when the thick smoke runs along before the flame; and the tables were over-set, and drinking glasses and bottles were broken in heaps, and the dark red wine crawled like blood upon the polished floor.

Sir Gabriel and Evelyn stood alone at the head of the table before the wreck of the feast, not daring to turn to see each other, for each knew that the other smiled. But his right arm held her and his left hand clasped her right as they stared before them;

and but for the shadows of her hair one might not have told their two faces apart. They listened long, but the cry came not again, and the dead smile faded from their lips, while each remembered that Sir Hugh Ockram lay in the north vault, smiling in his winding-sheet, in the dark, because he had died with his secret.

So ended the tenants' New Year's dinner. But from that time on Sir Gabriel grew more and more silent, and his face grew even paler and thinner than before. Often, without warning and without words, he would rise from his seat, as if something moved him against his will, and he would go out into the rain or the sunshine to the north side of the chapel, and sit on the stone bench, staring at the ground as if he could see through it, and through the vault below, and through the white winding-sheet in the dark, to the dead smile that would not die.

Always when he went out in that way Evelyn came out presently and sat beside him. Once, too, as in summer, their beautiful faces came suddenly near, and their lids drooped, and their red lips were almost joined together. But as their eyes met, they grew wide and wild, so that the white showed in a ring all round the deep violet, and their teeth chattered, and their hands were like the hands of corpses, each in the other's, for the terror of what was under their feet, and of what they knew but could not see.

Once, also, Evelyn found Sir Gabriel in the chapel alone, standing before the iron door that led down to the place of death, and in his hand there was the key to the door; but he had not put it into the lock. Evelyn drew him away, shivering, for she had also been driven in waking dreams to see that terrible thing again, and to find out whether it had changed since it had lain there.

"I'm going mad," said Sir Gabriel, covering his eyes with his hand as he went with her. "I see it in my sleep, I see it when I am awake—it draws me to it, day and night—and unless I see it I shall die!"

"I know," answered Evelyn, "I know. It is as if threads were spun from it, like a spider's, drawing us down to it." She was silent for a moment, and then she started violently and grasped his arm with a man's strength, and almost screamed the words she spoke. "But we must not go there!" she cried. "We must not go!"

Sir Gabriel's eyes were half shut, and he was not moved by the agony of her face.

"I shall die, unless I see it again," he said, in a quiet voice not like his own. And all that day and that evening he scarcely spoke, thinking of it, always thinking, while Evelyn Warburton quivered from head to foot with a terror she had never known.

She went alone, on a grey winter's morning, to Nurse Macdonald's room in the tower, and sat down beside the great leathern easy-chair, laying her thin white hand upon the withered fingers.

"Nurse," she said, "what was it that Uncle Hugh should have told you, that night before he died? It must have been an awful secret - and yet, though you asked him, I feel somehow that you know it, and that you know why he used to smile so dreadfully."

The old woman's head moved slowly from side to side.

"I only guess - I shall never know," she answered slowly in her cracked little voice.

"But what do you guess? Who am I? Why did you ask who my father was? You know I am Colonel Warburton's daughter, and my mother was Lady Ockram's sister, so that Gabriel and I are cousins. My father was killed in Afghanistan. What secret can there be?"

"I do not know. I can only guess."

"Guess what?" asked Evelyn imploringly, and pressing the soft withered hands, as she leaned forward. But Nurse Macdonald's wrinkled lids dropped suddenly over her queer blue eyes, and her lips shook a little with her breath, as if she were asleep.

Evelyn waited. By the fire the Irish maid was knitting fast, and the needles clicked like three or four clocks ticking against each other. And the real clock on the wall solemnly ticked alone, checking off the seconds of the woman who was a hundred years old, and had not many days left. Outside the ivy branch beat the window in the wintry blast, as it had beaten against the glass a hundred years ago.

Then as Evelyn sat there she felt again the waking of a horrible desire - the sickening wish to go down, down to the thing in the north vault, and to open the winding-sheet, and see whether it had changed; and she held Nurse Macdonald's hands as if to keep herself in her place and fight against the appalling attraction of the evil dead.

But the old cat that kept Nurse Macdonald's feet warm, lying always on the bag footstool, got up and stretched itself, and looked up into Evelyn's eyes, while its back arched, and its tail thickened and bristled, and its ugly pink lips drew back in a devilish grin, showing its sharp teeth. Evelyn stared at it, half fascinated by its ugliness. Then the creature suddenly put out one paw with all its claws spread, and spat at the girl, and all at once the grinning cat was like the smiling corpse far down below, so that Evelyn shivered down to her small feet, and covered her face with her free hand, lest Nurse Macdonald should wake and see the dead smile there, for she could feel it.

The old woman had already opened her eyes again, and she touched her cat with the end of her crutch-stick, whereupon its back went down and its tail shrunk, and it sidled back to its place on the bag footstool. But its yellow eyes looked up sideways at Evelyn, between the slits of its lids.

"What is it that you guess, nurse?" asked the young girl again.

"A bad thing - a wicked thing. But I dare not tell you, lest it might not be true, and the very thought should blast your life. For if I guess right, he meant that you should not know, and that you two should marry, and pay for his old sin with your souls."

"He used to tell us that we ought not to marry -"

"Yes - he told you that, perhaps - but it was as if a man put poisoned meat before a starving beast, and said 'do not eat,' but never raised his hand to take the meat away. And if he told you that you should not marry, it was because he hoped you would; for of all men living or dead, Hugh Ockram was the falsest man that ever told a cowardly lie, and the cruellest that ever hurt a weak woman, and the worst that ever loved a sin."

"But Gabriel and I love each other," said Evelyn very sadly.

Nurse Macdonald's old eyes looked far away, at sights seen long ago, and that rose in the grey winter air amid the mists of an ancient youth.

"If you love, you can die together," she said, very slowly. "Why should you live, if it is true? I am a hundred years old. What has life given me? The beginning is fire; the end is a heap of ashes; and between the end and the beginning lies all the pain of the world. Let me sleep, since I cannot die."

Then the old woman's eyes closed again, and her head sank a little lower upon her breast.

So Evelyn went away and left her asleep, with the cat asleep on the bag footstool; and the young girl tried to forget Nurse Macdonald's words, but she could not, for she heard them over and over again in the wind, and behind her on the stairs. And as she grew sick with fear of the frightful unknown evil to which her soul was bound, she felt a bodily something pressing her, and pushing her, and forcing her on, and from the other side she felt the threads that drew her mysteriously: and when she shut her eyes, she saw in the chapel behind the altar, the low iron door through which she must pass to go to the thing.

And as she lay awake at night, she drew the sheet over her face, lest she should see shadows on the wall beckoning to her; and the sound of her own warm breath made whisperings in her ears, while she held the mattress with her hands, to keep from getting up and going to the chapel. It would have been easier if there had not been a way thither through the library, by a door which was never locked. It would be fearfully easy to take her candle and go softly through the sleeping house. And the key of the vault lay under the altar behind a stone that turned. She knew the little secret. She could go alone and see.

But when she thought of it, she felt her hair rise on her head, and first she shivered so that the bed shook, and then the horror went through her in a cold thrill that was agony again, like myriads of icy needles boring into her nerves.

CHAPTER IV

The old clock in Nurse Macdonald's tower struck midnight. From her room she could hear the creaking chains and weights in their box in the corner of the staircase, and overhead the jarring of the rusty lever that lifted the hammer. She had heard it all her life. It struck eleven strokes clearly, and then came the twelfth, with a dull half stroke, as though the hammer were too weary to go on, and had fallen asleep against the bell.

The old cat got up from the bag footstool and stretched itself, and Nurse Macdonald opened her ancient eyes and looked slowly round the room by the dim light of the night lamp. She touched the cat with her crutch-stick, and it lay down upon her feet. She drank a few drops from her cup and went to sleep again.

But downstairs Sir Gabriel sat straight up as the clock struck, for he had dreamed a fearful dream of horror, and his heart stood still, till he awoke at its stopping, and it beat again furiously with his breath, like a wild thing set free. No Ockram had ever known fear waking, but sometimes it came to Sir Gabriel in his sleep.

He pressed his hands to his temples as he sat up in bed, and his hands were icy cold, but his head was hot. The dream faded far, and in its place there came the master thought that racked his life; with the thought also came the sick twisting of his lips in the dark that would have been a smile. Far off, Evelyn Warburton dreamed that the dead smile was on her mouth, and awoke, starting with a little moan, her face in her hands, shivering.

But Sir Gabriel struck a light and got up and began to walk up and down his great room. It was midnight, and he had barely slept an hour, and in the north of Ireland the winter nights are long.

"I shall go mad," he said to himself, holding his forehead. He knew that it was true. For weeks and months the possession of the thing had grown upon him like a disease, till he could think of nothing without thinking first of that. And now all at once it outgrew his strength, and he knew that he must be its instrument or lose his mind - that he must do the deed he hated and feared, if he could fear anything, or that something would snap in his brain and divide him from life while he was yet alive. He took the candlestick in his hand, the old-fashioned heavy candlestick that had always been used by the head of the house. He did not think of dressing, but went as he was, in his silk night clothes and his slippers, and he opened the door. Everything was very still in the great old house. He shut the door behind him and walked noiselessly on the carpet through the long corridor. A cool breeze blew over his shoulder and blew the flame of his candle straight out from him. Instinctively he stopped and looked round, but all was still, and the upright flame burned steadily. He walked on, and instantly a strong draught was behind him, almost extinguishing the light. It seemed to blow him on his way, ceasing whenever he turned, coming again when he went on - invisible, icy.

Down the great staircase to the echoing hall he went, seeing nothing but the flaring flame of the candle standing away from him over the guttering wax, while the cold wind blew over his shoulder and through his hair. On he passed through the open door into the library, dark with old books and carved bookcases; on through the door in the shelves, with painted shelves on it, and the imitated backs of books, so that one needed to know where to find it - and it shut itself after him with a soft click. He entered the low-arched passage, and though the door was shut behind him and fitted tightly in its frame, still the cold breeze blew the flame forward as he walked. And he was not afraid; but his face was very pale, and his eyes were wide and bright, looking before him, seeing already in the dark air the picture of the thing beyond. But in the chapel he stood still, his hand on the little turning stone tablet in the back of the stone altar. On the tablet were engraved words: "*Clavis sepulchri Clarissimorum Dominorum De Ockram*" - ("the key to the vault of the most illustrious lords of Ockram"). Sir Gabriel paused and listened. He fancied that he heard a sound far off in the great house where all had been so still, but it did not come again. Yet he waited at the last, and looked at the low iron door. Beyond it, down the long descent, lay his father uncoffined, six months dead, corrupt, terrible in his clinging shroud. The strangely preserving air of the vault could not yet have done its work completely. But on the thing's ghastly features, with their half-dried, open eyes, there would still be the frightful smile with which the man had died - the smile that haunted -

As the thought crossed Sir Gabriel's mind, he felt his lips writhing, and he struck his own mouth in wrath with the back of his hand so fiercely that a drop of blood ran down his chin, and another, and more, falling back in the gloom upon the chapel pavement. But still his bruised lips twisted themselves. He turned the tablet by the simple secret. It needed no safer fastening, for had each Ockram been coffined in pure gold, and had the door been open wide, there was not a man in Tyrone brave enough to go down to that place, saving Gabriel Ockram himself, with his angel's face and his thin, white hands, and his sad unflinching eyes. He took the great old key and set it into the lock of the iron door; and the heavy, rattling noise echoed down the descent beyond like footsteps, as if a watcher had stood behind the iron and were running away within, with heavy dead feet. And though he was standing still, the cool wind was from behind him, and blew the flame of the candle against the iron panel. He turned the key.

Sir Gabriel saw that his candle was short. There were new ones on the altar, with long candlesticks, and he lit one, and left his own burning on the floor. As he set it down on the pavement his lip began to bleed again, and another drop fell upon the stones.

He drew the iron door open and pushed it back against the chapel wall, so that it should not shut of itself, while he was within; and the horrible draught of the sepulchre came up out of the depths in his face, foul and dark. He went in, but though the fetid air met him, yet the flame of the tall candle was blown straight from him against the wind while he walked down the easy incline with steady steps, his loose slippers slapping the pavement as he trod.

He shaded the candle with his hand, and his fingers seemed to be made of wax and blood as the light shone through them. And in spite of him the unearthly draught forced the flame forward, till it was blue over the black wick, and it seemed as if it must go out. But he went straight on, with shining eyes.

The downward passage was wide, and he could not always see the walls by the struggling light, but he knew when he was in the place of death by the larger, drearier echo of his steps in the greater space, and by the sensation of a distant blank wall. He stood still, almost enclosing the flame of the candle in the hollow of his hand. He could see a little, for his eyes were growing used to the gloom. Shadowy forms were outlined in the dimness, where the biers of the Ockrams stood crowded together, side by side, each with its straight, shrouded corpse, strangely preserved by the dry air, like the empty shell that the locust sheds in summer. And a few steps before him he saw clearly the dark shape of headless Sir Vernon's iron coffin, and he knew that nearest to it lay the thing he sought.

He was as brave as any of those dead men had been, and they were his fathers, and he knew that sooner or later he should lie there himself, beside Sir Hugh, slowly drying to a parchment shell. But he was still alive, and he closed his eyes a moment, and three great drops stood on his forehead.

Then he looked again, and by the whiteness of the winding-sheet he knew his father's corpse, for all the others were brown with age; and, moreover, the flame of the candle was blown toward it. He made four steps till he reached it, and suddenly the light burned straight and high, shedding a dazzling yellow glare upon the fine linen that was all white, save over the face, and where the joined hands were laid on the breast. And at those places ugly stains had spread, darkened with outlines of the features and of the tight-clasped fingers. There was a frightful stench of drying death.

As Sir Gabriel looked down, something stirred behind him, softly at first, then more noisily, and something fell to the stone floor with a dull thud and rolled up to his feet; he started back and saw a withered head lying almost face upward on the pavement, grinning at him. He felt the cold sweat standing on his face, and his heart beat painfully.

For the first time in all his life that evil thing which men call fear was getting hold of him, checking his heart-strings as a cruel driver checks a quivering horse, clawing at his backbone with icy hands, lifting his hair with freezing breath, climbing up and gathering in his midriff with leaden weight.

Yet presently he bit his lip and bent down, holding the candle in one hand, to lift the shroud back from the head of the corpse with the other. Slowly he lifted it. Then it clove to the half-dried skin of the face, and his hand shook as if some one had struck him on the elbow, but half in fear and half in anger at himself, he pulled it, so that it came away with a little ripping sound. He caught his breath as he held it, not yet throwing it back, and not yet looking. The horror was working in him, and he felt that old Vernon Ockram was standing up in his iron coffin, headless, yet watching him with the stump of his severed neck.

While he held his breath he felt the dead smile twisting his lips. In sudden wrath at his own misery, he tossed the death-stained linen backward, and looked at last. He ground his teeth lest he should shriek aloud.

There it was, the thing that haunted him, that haunted Evelyn Warburton, that was like a blight on all that came near him.

The dead face was blotched with dark stains, and the thin, grey hair was matted about the discoloured forehead. The sunken lids were half open, and the candle light gleamed on something foul where the toad eyes had lived.

But yet the dead thing smiled, as it had smiled in life; the ghastly lips were parted and drawn wide and tight upon the wolfish teeth, cursing still, and still defying hell to do its worst - defying, cursing, and always and for ever smiling alone in the dark.

Sir Gabriel opened the winding-sheet where the hands were, and the blackened, withered fingers were closed upon something stained and mottled. Shivering from head to foot, but fighting like a man in agony for his life, he tried to take the package from the dead man's hold. But as he pulled at it the claw-like fingers seemed to close more tightly, and when he pulled harder the shrunken hands and arms rose from the corpse with a horrible look of life following his motion - then as he wrenched the sealed packet loose at last, the hands fell back into their place still folded.

He set down the candle on the edge of the bier to break the seals from the stout paper. And, kneeling on one knee, to get a better light, he read what was within, written long ago in Sir Hugh's queer hand.

He was no longer afraid.

He read how Sir Hugh had written it all down that it might perchance be a witness of evil and of his hatred; how he had loved Evelyn Warburton, his wife's sister; and how his wife had died of a broken heart with his curse upon her, and how Warburton and he had fought side by side in Afghanistan, and Warburton had fallen; but Ockram had brought his comrade's wife back a full year later, and little Evelyn, her child, had been born in Ockram Hall. And next, how he had wearied of the mother, and she had died like her sister with his curse on her. And then, how Evelyn had been brought up as his niece, and how he had trusted that his son Gabriel and his daughter, innocent and unknowing, might love and marry, and the souls of the women he had betrayed might suffer another anguish before eternity was out. And, last of all, he hoped that some day, when nothing could be undone, the two might find his writing and live on, not daring to tell the truth for their children's sake and the world's word, man and wife.

This he read, kneeling beside the corpse in the north vault, by the light of the altar candle; and when he had read it all, he thanked God aloud that he had found the secret in time. But when he rose to his feet and looked down at the dead face it was changed, and the smile was gone from it for ever, and the jaw had fallen a little, and the tired, dead lips were relaxed. And then there was a breath behind him and close to him, not cold like that which had blown the flame of the candle as he came, but warm and human. He turned suddenly.

There she stood, all in white, with her shadowy golden hair - for she had risen from her bed and had followed him noiselessly, and had found him reading, and had herself read over his shoulder. He started violently when he saw her, for his nerves were unstrung - and then he cried out her name in the still place of death:

"Evelyn!"

"My brother!" she answered softly and tenderly, putting out both hands to meet his.

THE GHOST-SHIP
By Richard Middleton

Fairfield is a little village lying near the Portsmouth Road about half-way between London and the sea. Strangers who find it by accident now and then, call it a pretty, old-fashioned place; we who live in it and call it home don't find anything very pretty about it, but we should be sorry to live anywhere else. Our minds have taken the shape of the inn and the church and the green, I suppose. At all events we never feel comfortable out of Fairfield.

Of course the Cockneys, with their vasty houses and noise-ridden streets, can call us rustics if they choose, but for all that Fairfield is a better place to live in than London. Doctor says that when he goes to London his mind is bruised with the weight of the houses, and he was a Cockney born. He had to live there himself when he was a little chap, but he knows better now. You gentlemen may laugh - perhaps some of you come from London way - but it seems to me that a witness like that is worth a gallon of arguments.

Dull? Well, you might find it dull, but I assure you that I've listened to all the London yarns you have spun tonight, and they're absolutely nothing to the things that happen at Fairfield. It's because of our way of thinking and minding our own business. If one of your Londoners were set down on the green of a Saturday night when the ghosts of the lads who died in the war keep tryst with the lasses who lie in the church-yard, he couldn't help being curious and interfering, and then the ghosts would go somewhere where it was quieter. But we just let them come and go and don't make any fuss, and in consequence Fairfield is the ghostliest place in all England. Why, I've seen a headless man sitting on the edge of the well in broad daylight, and the children playing about his feet as if he were their father. Take my word for it, spirits know when they are well off as much as human beings.

Still, I must admit that the thing I'm going to tell you about was queer even for our part of the world, where three packs of ghost-hounds hunt regularly during the season, and blacksmith's great-grandfather is busy all night shoeing the dead gentlemen's horses. Now that's a thing that wouldn't happen in London, because of their interfering ways, but blacksmith he lies up aloft and sleeps as quiet as a lamb. Once when he had a bad head he shouted down to them not to make so much noise, and in the morning he found an old guinea left on the anvil as an apology. He wears it on his watch-chain now. But I must get on with my story; if I start telling you about the queer happenings at Fairfield I'll never stop.

It all came of the great storm in the spring of '97, the year that we had two great storms. This was the first one, and I remember it very well, because I found in the morning that it had lifted the thatch of my pigsty into the widow's garden as clean as a boy's kite. When I looked over the hedge, widow - Tom Lamport's widow that was - was prodding for her nasturtiums with a daisy-grubber. After I had watched her for a little I went down to the Fox and Grapes to tell landlord what she had said to me. Landlord he laughed, being a married man and at ease with the sex. "Come to that," he said, "the tempest has blowed something into my field. A kind of a ship I think it would be."

I was surprised at that until he explained that it was only a ghost-ship and would do no hurt to the turnips. We argued that it had been blown up from the sea at Portsmouth, and then we talked of something else. There were two slates down at the parsonage and a big tree in Lumley's meadow. It was a rare storm.

I reckon the wind had blown our ghosts all over England. They were coming back for days afterwards with foundered horses and as footsore as possible, and they were so glad to get back to Fairfield that some of them walked up the street crying like little children. Squire said that his great-grandfather's great-grandfather hadn't looked so dead-beat since the battle of Naseby, and he's an educated man.

What with one thing and another, I should think it was a week before we got straight again, and then one afternoon I met the landlord on the green and he had a worried face. "I wish you'd come and have a look at that ship in my field," he said to me; "it seems to me it's leaning real hard on the turnips. I can't bear thinking what the missus will say when she sees it."

I walked down the lane with him, and sure enough there was a ship in the middle of his field, but such a ship as no man had seen on the water for three hundred years, let alone in the middle of a turnip-field. It was all painted black and covered with carvings, and there was a great bay window in the stern for all the world like the Squire's drawing-room. There was a crowd of little black cannon on deck and looking out of her port-holes, and she was anchored at each end to the hard ground. I have seen the wonders of the world on picture-postcards, but I have never seen anything to equal that.

"She seems very solid for a ghost-ship," I said, seeing the landlord was bothered.

"I should say it's a betwixt and between," he answered, puzzling it over, "but it's going to spoil a matter of fifty turnips, and missus she'll want it moved." We went up to her and touched the side, and it was as hard as a real ship. "Now there's folks in England would call that very curious," he said.

Now I don't know much about ships, but I should think that that ghost-ship weighed a solid two hundred tons, and it seemed to me that she had come to stay, so that I felt sorry for landlord, who was a married man. "All the horses in Fairfield won't move her out of my turnips," he said, frowning at her.

Just then we heard a noise on her deck, and we looked up and saw that a man had come out of her front cabin and was looking down at us very peaceably. He was dressed in a black uniform set out with rusty gold lace, and he had a great cutlass by his side in a brass sheath. "I'm Captain Bartholomew Roberts," he said, in a gentleman's voice, "put in for recruits. I seem to have brought her rather far up the harbour."

"Harbour!" cried landlord; "why, you're fifty miles from the sea."

Captain Roberts didn't turn a hair. "So much as that, is it?" he said coolly. "Well, it's of no consequence."

Landlord was a bit upset at this. "I don't want to be unneighbourly," he said, "but I wish you hadn't brought your ship into my field. You see, my wife sets great store on these turnips."

The captain took a pinch of snuff out of a fine gold box that he pulled out of his pocket, and dusted his fingers with a silk handkerchief in a very genteel fashion. "I'm only here for a few months," he said; "but if a testimony of my esteem would pacify your good lady I should be content," and with the words he loosed a great gold brooch from the neck of his coat and tossed it down to landlord.

Landlord blushed as red as a strawberry. "I'm not denying she's fond of jewellery," he said, "but it's too much for half a sackful of turnips." And indeed it was a handsome brooch.

The captain laughed. "Tut, man," he said, "it's a forced sale, and you deserve a good price. Say no more about it;" and nodding good-day to us, he turned on his heel and went into the cabin. Landlord walked back up the lane like a man with a weight off his mind. "That tempest has blowed me a bit of luck," he said; "the missus will be much pleased with that brooch. It's better than blacksmith's guinea, any day."

Ninety-seven was Jubilee year, the year of the second Jubilee, you remember, and we had great doings at Fairfield, so that we hadn't much time to bother about the ghost-ship though anyhow it isn't our way to meddle in things that don't concern us. Landlord, he saw his tenant once or twice when he was hoeing his turnips and passed the time of day, and landlord's wife wore her new brooch to church every Sunday. But we didn't mix much with the ghosts at any time, all except an idiot lad there was in the village, and he didn't know the difference between a man and a ghost, poor innocent! On Jubilee Day, however, somebody told Captain Roberts why the church bells were ringing, and he hoisted a flag and fired off his guns like a loyal Englishman. 'Tis true the guns were shotted, and one of the round shot knocked a hole in Farmer Johnstone's barn, but nobody thought much of that in such a season of rejoicing.

It wasn't till our celebrations were over that we noticed that anything was wrong in Fairfield. 'Twas shoemaker who told me first about it one morning at the Fox and Grapes. "You know my great great-uncle?" he said to me.

"You mean Joshua, the quiet lad," I answered, knowing him well.

"Quiet!" said shoemaker indignantly. "Quiet you call him, coming home at three o'clock every morning as drunk as a magistrate and waking up the whole house with his noise."

"Why, it can't be Joshua!" I said, for I knew him for one of the most respectable young ghosts in the village.

"Joshua it is," said shoemaker; "and one of these nights he'll find himself out in the street if he isn't careful."

This kind of talk shocked me, I can tell you, for I don't like to hear a man abusing his own family, and I could hardly believe that a steady youngster like Joshua had taken to drink. But just then in came butcher Aylwin in such a temper that he could hardly drink his beer. "The young puppy! the young puppy!" he kept on saying; and it was some time before shoemaker and I found out that he was talking about his ancestor that fell at Senlac.

"Drink?" said shoemaker hopefully, for we all like company in our misfortunes, and butcher nodded grimly.

"The young noodle," he said, emptying his tankard.

Well, after that I kept my ears open, and it was the same story all over the village. There was hardly a young man among all the ghosts of Fairfield who didn't roll home in the small hours of the morning the worse for liquor. I used to wake up in the night and hear them stumble past my house, singing outrageous songs. The worst of it was that we couldn't keep the scandal to ourselves and the folk at Greenhill began to talk of "sodden Fairfield" and taught their children to sing a song about us:

"Sodden Fairfield, sodden Fairfield, has no use for bread-and-butter,
Rum for breakfast, rum for dinner, rum for tea, and rum for supper!"

We are easy-going in our village, but we didn't like that.

Of course we soon found out where the young fellows went to get the drink, and landlord was terribly cut up that his tenant should have turned out so badly, but his wife wouldn't hear of parting with the brooch, so that he couldn't give the Captain notice to quit. But as time went on, things grew from bad to worse, and at all hours of the day you would see those young reprobates sleeping it off on the village green. Nearly every afternoon a ghost-wagon used to jolt down to the ship with a lading of rum, and though the older ghosts seemed inclined to give the Captain's hospitality the go-by, the youngsters were neither to hold nor to bind.

So one afternoon when I was taking my nap I heard a knock

at the door, and there was parson looking very serious, like a man with a job before him that he didn't altogether relish. "I'm going down to talk to the Captain about all this drunkenness in the village, and I want you to come with me," he said straight out.

I can't say that I fancied the visit much, myself, and I tried to hint to parson that as, after all, they were only a lot of ghosts it didn't very much matter.

"Dead or alive, I'm responsible for the good conduct," he said, "and I'm going to do my duty and put a stop to this continued disorder. And you are coming with me, John Simmons."

So I went, parson being a persuasive kind of man.

We went down to the ship, and as we approached her I could see the Captain tasting the air on deck. When he saw parson he took off his hat very politely and I can tell you that I was relieved to find that he had a proper respect for the cloth. Parson acknowledged his salute and spoke out stoutly enough. "Sir, I should be glad to have a word with you."

"Come on board, sir; come on board," said the Captain, and I could tell by his voice that he knew why we were there. Parson and I climbed up an uneasy kind of ladder, and the Captain took us into the great cabin at the back of the ship, where the bay-window was. It was the most wonderful place you ever saw in your life, all full of gold and silver plate, swords with jewelled scabbards, carved oak chairs, and great chests that look as though they were bursting with guineas. Even parson was surprised, and he did not shake his head very hard when the Captain took down some silver cups and poured us out a drink of rum. I tasted mine, and I don't mind saying that it changed my view of things entirely. There was nothing betwixt and between about that rum, and I felt that it was ridiculous to blame the lads for drinking too much of stuff like that. It seemed to fill my veins with honey and fire.

Parson put the case squarely to the Captain, but I didn't listen much to what he said; I was busy sipping my drink and looking through the window at the fishes swimming to and fro over landlord's turnips. Just then it seemed the most natural thing in the world that they should be there, though afterwards, of course, I could see that that proved it was a ghost-ship.

But even then I thought it was queer when I saw a drowned sailor float by in the thin air with his hair and beard all full of bubbles. It was the first time I had seen anything quite like that at Fairfield.

All the time I was regarding the wonders of the deep parson was telling Captain Roberts how there was no peace or rest in the village owing to the curse of drunkenness, and what a bad example the youngsters were setting to the older ghosts. The Captain listened very attentively, and only put in a word now and then about boys being boys and young men sowing their wild oats. But when parson had finished his speech he filled up our silver cups and said to parson, with a flourish, "I should be sorry to cause trouble anywhere where I have been made welcome, and you will be glad to hear that I put to sea tomorrow night. And now you must drink me a prosperous voyage." So we all stood up and drank the toast with honour, and that noble rum was like hot oil in my veins.

After that Captain showed us some of the curiosities he had brought back from foreign parts, and we were greatly amazed, though afterwards I couldn't clearly remember what they were. And then I found myself walking across the turnips with parson, and I was telling him of the glories of the deep that I had seen through the window of the ship. He turned on me severely. "If I were you, John Simmons," he said, "I should go straight home to bed." He has a way of putting things that wouldn't occur to an ordinary man, has parson, and I did as he told me.

Well, next day it came on to blow, and it blew harder and harder, till about eight o'clock at night I heard a noise and looked out into the garden. I dare say you won't believe me, it seems a bit tall even to me, but the wind had lifted the thatch of my pigsty into the widow's garden a second time. I thought I wouldn't wait to hear what widow had to say about it, so I went across the green to the Fox and Grapes, and the wind was so strong that I danced along on tiptoe like a girl at the fair. When I got to the inn landlord had to help me shut the door; it seemed as though a dozen goats were pushing against it to come in out of the storm.

"It's a powerful tempest," he said, drawing the beer. "I hear there's a chimney down at Dickory End."

"It's a funny thing how these sailors know about the

weather," I answered. "When Captain said he was going tonight, I was thinking it would take a capful of wind to carry the ship back to sea, but now here's more than a capful."

"Ah, yes," said landlord, "it's tonight he goes true enough, and, mind you, though he treated me handsome over the rent, I'm not sure it's a loss to the village. I don't hold with gentrice who fetch their drink from London instead of helping local traders to get their living."

"But you haven't got any rum like his," I said, to draw him out.

His neck grew red above his collar, and I was afraid I'd gone too far; but after a while he got his breath with a grunt.

"John Simmons," he said, "if you've come down here this windy night to talk a lot of fool's talk, you've wasted a journey."

Well, of course, then I had to smooth him down with praising his rum, and Heaven forgive me for swearing it was better than Captain's. For the like of that rum no living lips have tasted save mine and parson's. But somehow or other I brought landlord round, and presently we must have a glass of his best to prove its quality.

"Beat that if you can!" he cried, and we both raised our glasses to our mouths, only to stop half-way and look at each other in amaze. For the wind that had been howling outside like an outrageous dog had all of a sudden turned as melodious as the carol-boys of a Christmas Eve.

"Surely that's not my Martha," whispered landlord; Martha being his great-aunt that lived in the loft overhead.

We went to the door, and the wind burst it open so that the handle was driven clean into the plaster of the wall. But we didn't think about that at the time; for over our heads, sailing very comfortably through the windy stars, was the ship that had passed the summer in landlord's field. Her portholes and her bay-window were blazing with lights, and there was a noise of singing and fiddling on her decks. "He's gone," shouted landlord above the storm, "and he's taken half the village with him!" I could only nod in answer, not having lungs like bellows of leather.

In the morning we were able to measure the strength of the storm, and over and above my pigsty there was damage enough wrought in the village to keep us busy. True it is that the children had to break down no branches for the firing that autumn, since the wind had strewn the woods with more than they could carry away. Many of our ghosts were scattered abroad, but this time very few came back, all the young men having sailed with Captain; and not only ghosts, for a poor half-witted lad was missing, and we reckoned that he had stowed himself away or perhaps shipped as cabin-boy, not knowing any better.

What with the lamentations of the ghost-girls and the grumbling of families who had lost an ancestor, the village was upset for a while, and the funny thing was that it was the folk who had complained most of the carryings-on of the youngsters, who made most noise now that they were gone. I hadn't any sympathy with shoemaker or butcher, who ran about saying how much they missed their lads, but it made me grieve to hear the poor bereaved girls calling their lovers by name on the village green at nightfall. It didn't seem fair to me that they should have lost their men a second time, after giving up life in order to join them, as like as not. Still, not even a spirit can be sorry for ever, and after a few months we made up our mind that the folk who had sailed in the ship were never coming back, and we didn't talk about it any more.

And then one day, I dare say it would be a couple of years after, when the whole business was quite forgotten, who should come trapesing along the road from Portsmouth but the daft lad who had gone away with the ship, without waiting till he was dead to become a ghost. You never saw such a boy as that in all your life. He had a great rusty cutlass hanging to a string at his waist, and he was tattooed all over in fine colours, so that even his face looked like a girl's sampler. He had a handkerchief in his hand full of foreign shells and old-fashioned pieces of small money, very curious, and he walked up to the well outside his mother's house and drew himself a drink as if he had been nowhere in particular.

The worst of it was that he had come back as soft-headed as he went, and try as we might we couldn't get anything reasonable out of him. He talked a lot of gibberish about keel-hauling and walking the plank and crimson murders - things which a decent sailor should know nothing about, so that it seemed to me that for all his manners Captain had been more of a pirate than a gentleman mariner. But to draw sense out of that boy was as hard as picking cherries off a crab-tree. One silly tale he had that he kept on drifting back to, and to hear him you would have thought that it was the only thing that happened to him in his life. "We was at anchor," he would say, "off an island called the Basket of Flowers, and the sailors had caught a lot of parrots and we were teaching them to swear. Up and down the decks, up and down the decks, and the language they used was dreadful. Then we looked up and saw the masts of the Spanish ship outside the harbour. Outside the harbour they were, so we threw the parrots into the sea and sailed out to fight. And all the parrots were drownded in the sea and the language they used was dreadful." That's the sort of boy he was, nothing but silly talk of parrots when we asked him about the fighting. And we never had a chance of teaching him better, for two days after he ran away again, and hasn't been seen since.

That's my story, and I assure you that things like that are happening at Fairfield all the time. The ship has never come back, but somehow as people grow older they seem to think that one of these windy nights she'll come sailing in over the hedges with all the lost ghosts on board. Well, when she comes, she'll be welcome. There's one ghost-lass that has never grown tired of waiting for her lad to return. Every night you'll see her out on the green, straining her poor eyes with looking for the mast-lights among the stars. A faithful lass you'd call her, and I'm thinking you'd be right.

Landlord's field wasn't a penny the worse for the visit, but they do say that since then the turnips that have been grown in it have tasted of rum.

THE NEW CATACOMB
By Sir Arthur Conan Doyle

"Look here, Burger," said Kennedy, "I do wish that you would confide in me."

The two famous students of Roman remains sat together in Kennedy's comfortable room overlooking the Corso. The night was cold, and they had both pulled up their chairs to the unsatisfactory Italian stove which threw out a zone of stuffiness rather than of warmth. Outside under the bright winter stars lay the modern Rome, the long, double chain of the electric lamps, the brilliantly lighted cafes, the rushing carriages, and the dense throng upon the footpaths. But inside, in the sumptuous chamber of the rich young English archaeologist, there was only old Rome to be seen. Cracked and timeworn friezes hung upon the walls, grey old busts of senators and soldiers with their fighting heads and their hard, cruel faces peered out from the corners. On the centre table, amidst a litter of inscriptions, fragments, and ornaments, there stood the famous reconstruction by Kennedy of the Baths of Caracalla, which excited such interest and admiration when it was exhibited in Berlin. Amphorae hung from the ceiling, and a litter of curiosities strewed the rich red Turkey carpet. And of them all there was not one which was not of the most unimpeachable authenticity, and of the utmost rarity and value; for Kennedy, though little more than thirty, had a European reputation in this particular branch of research, and was, moreover, provided with that long purse which either proves to be a fatal handicap to the student's energies, or, if his mind is still true to its purpose, gives him an enormous advantage in the race for fame. Kennedy had often been seduced by whim and pleasure from his studies, but his mind was an incisive one, capable of long and concentrated efforts which ended in sharp reactions of sensuous languor. His handsome face, with its high, white forehead, its aggressive nose, and its somewhat loose and sensual mouth, was a fair index of the compromise between strength and weakness in his nature.

Of a very different type was his companion, Julius Burger. He came of a curious blend, a German father and an Italian mother, with the robust qualities of the North mingling strangely with the softer graces of the South. Blue Teutonic eyes lightened his sun-browned face, and above them rose a square, massive forehead, with a fringe of close yellow curls lying round it. His strong, firm jaw was clean-shaven, and his companion had frequently remarked how much it suggested those old Roman busts which peered out from the shadows in the corners of his chamber. Under its bluff German strength there lay always a suggestion of Italian subtlety, but the smile was so honest, and the eyes so frank, that one understood that this was only an indication of his ancestry, with no actual bearing upon his character. In age and in reputation, he was on the same level as his English companion, but his life and his work had both been far more arduous. Twelve years before, he had come as a poor student to Rome, and had lived ever since upon some small endowment for research which had been awarded to him by the University of Bonn. Painfully, slowly, and doggedly, with extraordinary tenacity and single-mindedness, he had climbed from rung to rung of the ladder of fame, until now he was a member of the Berlin Academy, and there was every reason to believe that he would shortly be promoted to the Chair of the greatest of German Universities. But the singleness of purpose which had brought him to the same high level as the rich and brilliant Englishman, had caused him in everything outside their work to stand infinitely below him. He had never found a pause in his studies in which to cultivate the social graces. It was only when he spoke of his own subject that his face was filled with life and soul. At other times he was silent and embarrassed, too conscious of his own limitations in larger subjects, and impatient of that small talk which is the conventional refuge of those who have no thoughts to express.

And yet for some years there had been an acquaintanceship which appeared to be slowly ripening into a friendship between these two very different rivals. The base and origin of this lay in the fact that in their own studies each was the only one of the younger men who had knowledge and enthusiasm enough to properly appreciate the other. Their common interests and pursuits had brought them together, and each had been attracted by the other's knowledge. And then gradually something had been added to this. Kennedy had been amused by the frankness and simplicity of his rival, while Burger in turn had been fascinated by the brilliancy and vivacity which had made Kennedy such a favourite in Roman society. I say "had," because just at the moment the young Englishman was somewhat under a cloud. A love-affair, the details of which had never quite come out, had indicated a heartlessness and callousness upon his part which shocked many of his friends. But in the bachelor circles of students and artists in which he preferred to move there is no very rigid code of honour in such matters, and though a head might be shaken or a pair of shoulders shrugged over the flight of two and the return of one, the general sentiment was probably one of curiosity and perhaps of envy rather than of reprobation.

"Look here, Burger," said Kennedy, looking hard at the placid face of his companion, "I do wish that you would confide in me."

As he spoke he waved his hand in the direction of a rug which lay upon the floor. On the rug stood a long, shallow fruit-basket of the light wicker-work which is used in the Campagna, and this was heaped with a litter of objects, inscribed tiles, broken inscriptions, cracked mosaics, torn papyri, rusty metal ornaments, which to the uninitiated might have seemed to have come straight from a dustman's bin, but which a specialist would have speedily recognized as unique of their kind. The pile of odds and ends in the flat wicker-work basket supplied exactly one of those missing links of social development which are of such interest to the student. It was the German who had brought them in, and the Englishman's eyes were hungry as he looked at them.

"I won't interfere with your treasure-trove, but I should very much like to hear about it," he continued, while Burger very deliberately lit a cigar. "It is evidently a discovery of the first importance. These inscriptions will make a sensation throughout Europe."

"For every one here there are a million there!" said the German. "There are so many that a dozen savants might spend a lifetime over them, and build up a reputation as solid as the Castle of St. Angelo."

Kennedy sat thinking with his fine forehead wrinkled and his fingers playing with his long, fair moustache.

"You have given yourself away, Burger!" said he at last. "Your words can only apply to one thing. You have discovered a new catacomb."

"I had no doubt that you had already come to that conclusion from an examination of these objects."

"Well, they certainly appeared to indicate it, but your last remarks make it certain. There is no place except a catacomb which could contain so vast a store of relics as you describe."

"Quite so. There is no mystery about that. I HAVE discovered a new catacomb."

"Where?"

"Ah, that is my secret, my dear Kennedy. Suffice it that it is so situated that there is not one chance in a million of anyone else coming upon it. Its date is different from that of any known catacomb, and it has been reserved for the burial of the highest Christians, so that the remains and the relics are quite different from anything which has ever been seen before. If I was not aware of your knowledge and of your energy, my friend, I would not hesitate, under the pledge of secrecy, to tell you everything about it. But as it is I think that I must certainly prepare my own report of the matter before I expose myself to such formidable competition."

Kennedy loved his subject with a love which was almost a mania - a love which held him true to it, amidst all the distractions which come to a wealthy and dissipated young man. He had ambition, but his ambition was secondary to his mere abstract joy and interest in everything which concerned the old life and history of the city. He yearned to see this new underworld which his companion had discovered.

"Look here, Burger," said he, earnestly, "I assure you that you can trust me most implicitly in the matter. Nothing would induce me to put pen to paper about anything which I see until I have your express permission. I quite understand your feeling and I think it is most natural, but you have really nothing whatever to fear from me. On the other hand, if you don't tell me I shall make a systematic search, and I shall most certainly discover it. In that case, of course, I should make what use I liked of it, since I should be under no obligation to you."

Burger smiled thoughtfully over his cigar.

"I have noticed, friend Kennedy," said he, "that when I want information over any point you are not always so ready to supply it."

"When did you ever ask me anything that I did not tell you? You remember, for example, my giving you the material for your paper about the temple of the Vestals."

"Ah, well, that was not a matter of much importance. If I were to question you upon some intimate thing would you give me an answer, I wonder! This new catacomb is a very intimate thing to me, and I should certainly expect some sign of confidence in return."

"What you are driving at I cannot imagine," said the Englishman, "but if you mean that you will answer my question about the catacomb if I answer any question which you may put to me I can assure you that I will certainly do so."

"Well, then," said Burger, leaning luxuriously back in his settee, and puffing a blue tree of cigar-smoke into the air, "tell me all about your relations with Miss Mary Saunderson."

Kennedy sprang up in his chair and glared angrily at his impassive companion.

"What the devil do you mean?" he cried. "What sort of a question is this? You may mean it as a joke, but you never made a worse one."

"No, I don't mean it as a joke," said Burger, simply. "I am really rather interested in the details of the matter. I don't know much about the world and women and social life and that sort of thing, and such an incident has the fascination of the unknown for me. I know you, and I knew her by sight - I had even spoken to her once or twice. I should very much like to hear from your own lips exactly what it was which occurred between you."

"I won't tell you a word."

"That's all right. It was only my whim to see if you would give up a secret as easily as you expected me to give up my secret of the new catacomb. You wouldn't, and I didn't expect you to. But why should you expect otherwise of me? There's Saint John's clock striking ten. It is quite time that I was going home."

"No; wait a bit, Burger," said Kennedy; "this is really a ridiculous caprice of yours to wish to know about an old love-affair which has burned out months ago. You know we look upon a man who kisses and tells as the greatest coward and villain possible."

"Certainly," said the German, gathering up his basket of curiosities, "when he tells anything about a girl which is previously unknown he must be so. But in this case, as you must be aware, it was a public matter which was the common talk of Rome, so that you are not really doing Miss Mary Saunderson any injury by discussing her case with me. But still, I respect your scruples; and so good night!"

"Wait a bit, Burger," said Kennedy, laying his hand upon the other's arm; "I am very keen upon this catacomb business, and I can't let it drop quite so easily. Would you mind asking me something else in return - something not quite so eccentric this time?"

"No, no; you have refused, and there is an end of it," said Burger, with his basket on his arm. "No doubt you are quite right not to answer, and no doubt I am quite right also - and so again, my dear Kennedy, good night!"

The Englishman watched Burger cross the room, and he had his hand on the handle of the door before his host sprang up with the air of a man who is making the best of that which cannot be helped.

"Hold on, old fellow," said he; "I think you are behaving in a most ridiculous fashion; but still; if this is your condition, I suppose that I must submit to it. I hate saying anything about a girl, but, as you say, it is all over Rome, and I don't suppose I can tell you anything which you do not know already. What was it you wanted to know?"

The German came back to the stove, and, laying down his basket, he sank into his chair once more.

"May I have another cigar?" said he. "Thank you very much! I never smoke when I work, but I enjoy a chat much more when I am under the influence of tobacco. Now, as regards this young lady, with whom you had this little adventure. What in the world has become of her?"

"She is at home with her own people."

"Oh, really - in England?"

"Yes."

"What part of England - London?"

"No, Twickenham."

"You must excuse my curiosity, my dear Kennedy, and you

must put it down to my ignorance of the world. No doubt it is quite a simple thing to persuade a young lady to go off with you for three weeks or so, and then to hand her over to her own family at - what did you call the place?"

"Twickenham."

"Quite so - at Twickenham. But it is something so entirely outside my own experience that I cannot even imagine how you set about it. For example, if you had loved this girl your love could hardly disappear in three weeks, so I presume that you could not have loved her at all. But if you did not love her why should you make this great scandal which has damaged you and ruined her?"

Kennedy looked moodily into the red eye of the stove.

"That's a logical way of looking at it, certainly," said he. "Love is a big word, and it represents a good many different shades of feeling. I liked her, and - well, you say you've seen her - you know how charming she could look. But still I am willing to admit, looking back, that I could never have really loved her."

"Then, my dear Kennedy, why did you do it?"

"The adventure of the thing had a great deal to do with it."

"What! You are so fond of adventures!"

"Where would the variety of life be without them? It was for an adventure that I first began to pay my attentions to her. I've chased a good deal of game in my time, but there's no chase like that of a pretty woman. There was the piquant difficulty of it also, for, as she was the companion of Lady Emily Rood, it was almost impossible to see her alone. On the top of all the other obstacles which attracted me, I learned from her own lips very early in the proceedings that she was engaged."

"*Mein Gott!* To whom?"

"She mentioned no names."

"I do not think that anyone knows that. So that made the adventure more alluring, did it?"

"Well, it did certainly give a spice to it. Don't you think so?"

"I tell you that I am very ignorant about these things."

"My dear fellow, you can remember that the apple you stole from your neighbour's tree was always sweeter than that which fell from your own. And then I found that she cared for me."

"What - at once?"

"Oh, no, it took about three months of sapping and mining.

But at last I won her over. She understood that my judicial separation from my wife made it impossible for me to do the right thing by her - but she came all the same, and we had a delightful time, as long as it lasted."

"But how about the other man?"

Kennedy shrugged his shoulders.

"I suppose it is the survival of the fittest," said he. "If he had been the better man she would not have deserted him. Let's drop the subject, for I have had enough of it!"

"Only one other thing. How did you get rid of her in three weeks?"

"Well, we had both cooled down a bit, you understand. She absolutely refused, under any circumstances, to come back to face the people she had known in Rome. Now, of course, Rome is necessary to me, and I was already pining to be back at my work - so there was one obvious cause of separation. Then, again, her old father turned up at the hotel in London, and there was a scene, and the whole thing became so unpleasant that really - though I missed her dreadfully at first - I was very glad to slip out of it. Now, I rely upon you not to repeat anything of what I have said."

"My dear Kennedy, I should not dream of repeating it. But all that you say interests me very much, for it gives me an insight into your way of looking at things, which is entirely different from mine, for I have seen so little of life. And now you want to know about my new catacomb. There's no use my trying to describe it, for you would never find it by that. There is only one thing, and that is for me to take you there."

"That would be splendid."

"When would you like to come?"

"The sooner the better. I am all impatience to see it."

"Well, it is a beautiful night - though a trifle cold. Suppose we start in an hour. We must be very careful to keep the matter to ourselves. If anyone saw us hunting in couples they would suspect that there was something going on."

"We can't be too cautious," said Kennedy. "Is it far?"

"Some miles."

"Not too far to walk?"

"Oh, no, we could walk there easily."

"We had better do so, then. A cabman's suspicions would be

aroused if he dropped us both at some lonely spot in the dead of the night."

"Quite so. I think it would be best for us to meet at the Gate of the Appian Way at midnight. I must go back to my lodgings for the matches and candles and things."

"All right, Burger! I think it is very kind of you to let me into this secret, and I promise you that I will write nothing about it until you have published your report. Good-bye for the present! You will find me at the Gate at twelve."

The cold, clear air was filled with the musical chimes from that city of clocks as Burger, wrapped in an Italian overcoat, with a lantern hanging from his hand, walked up to the rendezvous. Kennedy stepped out of the shadow to meet him.

"You are ardent in work as well as in love!" said the German, laughing.

"Yes; I have been waiting here for nearly half an hour."

"I hope you left no clue as to where we were going."

"Not such a fool! By Jove, I am chilled to the bone! Come on, Burger, let us warm ourselves by a spurt of hard walking."

Their footsteps sounded loud and crisp upon the rough stone paving of the disappointing road which is all that is left of the most famous highway of the world. A peasant or two going home from the wine-shop, and a few carts of country produce coming up to Rome, were the only things which they met. They swung along, with the huge tombs looming up through the darkness upon each side of them, until they had come as far as the Catacombs of St. Calistus, and saw against a rising moon the great circular bastion of Cecilia Metella in front of them. Then Burger stopped with his hand to his side.

"Your legs are longer than mine, and you are more accustomed to walking," said he, laughing. "I think that the place where we turn off is somewhere here. Yes, this is it, round the corner of the trattoria. Now, it is a very narrow path, so perhaps I had better go in front and you can follow."

He had lit his lantern, and by its light they were enabled to follow a narrow and devious track which wound across the marshes of the Campagna. The great Aqueduct of old Rome lay like a monstrous caterpillar across the moonlit landscape, and their road led them under one of its huge arches, and past the circle of crumbling bricks which marks the old arena. At last

Burger stopped at a solitary wooden cow-house, and he drew a key from his pocket. "Surely your catacomb is not inside a house!" cried Kennedy.

"The entrance to it is. That is just the safeguard which we have against anyone else discovering it."

"Does the proprietor know of it?"

"Not he. He had found one or two objects which made me almost certain that his house was built on the entrance to such a place. So I rented it from him, and did my excavations for myself. Come in, and shut the door behind you."

It was a long, empty building, with the mangers of the cows along one wall. Burger put his lantern down on the ground, and shaded its light in all directions save one by draping his overcoat round it.

"It might excite remark if anyone saw a light in this lonely place," said he. "Just help me to move this boarding."

The flooring was loose in the corner, and plank by plank the two savants raised it and leaned it against the wall. Below there was a square aperture and a stair of old stone steps which led away down into the bowels of the earth.

"Be careful!" cried Burger, as Kennedy, in his impatience, hurried down them. "It is a perfect rabbits'-warren below, and if you were once to lose your way there the chances would be a hundred to one against your ever coming out again. Wait until I bring the light."

"How do you find your own way if it is so complicated?"

"I had some very narrow escapes at first, but I have gradually learned to go about. There is a certain system to it, but it is one which a lost man, if he were in the dark, could not possibly find out. Even now I always spin out a ball of string behind me when I am going far into the catacomb. You can see for yourself that it is difficult, but every one of these passages divides and subdivides a dozen times before you go a hundred yards."

They had descended some twenty feet from the level of the byre, and they were standing now in a square chamber cut out of the soft tufa. The lantern cast a flickering light, bright below and dim above, over the cracked brown walls. In every direction were the black openings of passages which radiated from this common centre.

"I want you to follow me closely, my friend," said Burger.

"Do not loiter to look at anything upon the way, for the place to which I will take you contains all that you can see, and more. It will save time for us to go there direct."

He led the way down one of the corridors, and the Englishman followed closely at his heels. Every now and then the passage bifurcated, but Burger was evidently following some secret marks of his own, for he neither stopped nor hesitated. Everywhere along the walls, packed like the berths upon an emigrant ship, lay the Christians of old Rome. The yellow light flickered over the shrivelled features of the mummies, and gleamed upon rounded skulls and long, white armbones crossed over fleshless chests. And everywhere as he passed Kennedy looked with wistful eyes upon inscriptions, funeral vessels, pictures, vestments, utensils, all lying as pious hands had placed them so many centuries ago. It was apparent to him, even in those hurried, passing glances, that this was the earliest and finest of the catacombs, containing such a storehouse of Roman remains as had never before come at one time under the observation of the student.

"What would happen if the light went out?" he asked, as they hurried onwards.

"I have a spare candle and a box of matches in my pocket. By the way, Kennedy, have you any matches?"

"No; you had better give me some."

"Oh, that is all right. There is no chance of our separating."

"How far are we going? It seems to me that we have walked at least a quarter of a mile."

"More than that, I think. There is really no limit to the tombs - at least, I have never been able to find any. This is a very difficult place, so I think that I will use our ball of string."

He fastened one end of it to a projecting stone and he carried the coil in the breast of his coat, paying it out as he advanced. Kennedy saw that it was no unnecessary precaution, for the passages had become more complex and tortuous than ever, with a perfect network of intersecting corridors. But these all ended in one large circular hall with a square pedestal of tufa topped with a slab of marble at one end of it.

"*By Jove!*" cried Kennedy in an ecstasy, as Burger swung his lantern over the marble. "It is a Christian altar - probably the first one in existence. Here is the little consecration cross cut upon the corner of it. No doubt this circular space was used as a church."

"Precisely," said Burger. "If I had more time I should like to show you all the bodies which are buried in these niches upon the walls, for they are the early popes and bishops of the Church, with their mitres, their croziers, and full canonicals. Go over to that one and look at it!"

Kennedy went across, and stared at the ghastly head which lay loosely on the shredded and mouldering mitre.

"This is most interesting," said he, and his voice seemed to boom against the concave vault. "As far as my experience goes, it is unique. Bring the lantern over, Burger, for I want to see them all."

But the German had strolled away, and was standing in the middle of a yellow circle of light at the other side of the hall.

"Do you know how many wrong turnings there are between this and the stairs?" he asked. "There are over two thousand. No doubt it was one of the means of protection which the Christians adopted. The odds are two thousand to one against a man getting out, even if he had a light; but if he were in the dark it would, of course, be far more difficult."

"So I should think."

"And the darkness is something dreadful. I tried it once for an experiment. Let us try it again!" He stooped to the lantern, and in an instant it was as if an invisible hand was squeezed tightly over each of Kennedy's eyes. Never had he known what such darkness was. It seemed to press upon him and to smother him. It was a solid obstacle against which the body shrank from advancing. He put his hands out to push it back from him.

"That will do, Burger," said he, "let's have the light again."

But his companion began to laugh, and in that circular room the sound seemed to come from every side at once.

"You seem uneasy, friend Kennedy," said he.

"Go on, man, light the candle!" said Kennedy impatiently.

"It's very strange, Kennedy, but I could not in the least tell by the sound in which direction you stand. Could you tell where I am?"

"No; you seem to be on every side of me."

"If it were not for this string which I hold in my hand I should not have a notion which way to go."

"I dare say not. Strike a light, man, and have an end of this nonsense."

"Well, Kennedy, there are two things which I understand that you are very fond of. The one is an adventure, and the other is an obstacle to surmount. The adventure must be the finding of your way out of this catacomb. The obstacle will be the darkness and the two thousand wrong turns which make the way a little difficult to find. But you need not hurry, for you have plenty of time, and when you halt for a rest now and then, I should like you just to think of Miss Mary Saunderson, and whether you treated her quite fairly."

"You devil, what do you mean?" roared Kennedy. He was running about in little circles and clasping at the solid blackness with both hands.

"Good-bye," said the mocking voice, and it was already at some distance. "I really do not think, Kennedy, even by your own showing that you did the right thing by that girl. There was only one little thing which you appeared not to know, and I can supply it. Miss Saunderson was engaged to a poor ungainly devil of a student, and his name was Julius Burger."

There was a rustle somewhere, the vague sound of a foot striking a stone, and then there fell silence upon that old Christian church - a stagnant, heavy silence which closed round Kennedy and shut him in like water round a drowning man.

Some two months afterwards the following paragraph made the round of the European Press:

"One of the most interesting discoveries of recent years is that of the new catacomb in Rome, which lies some distance to the east of the well-known vaults of St. Calixtus. The finding of this important burial-place, which is exceeding rich in most interesting early Christian remains, is due to the energy and sagacity of Dr. Julius Burger, the young German specialist, who is rapidly taking the first place as an authority upon ancient Rome. Although the first to publish his discovery, it appears that a less fortunate adventurer had anticipated Dr. Burger. Some months ago Mr. Kennedy, the well-known English student, disappeared suddenly from his rooms in the Corso, and it was conjectured that his association with a recent scandal had driven him to leave Rome. It appears now that he had in reality fallen a victim to that fervid love of archaeology which had raised him to a distinguished place among living scholars. His body was discovered in the heart of the new catacomb, and it was evident from the condition of his feet and boots that he had tramped for days through the tortuous corridors which make these subterranean tombs so dangerous to explorers. The deceased gentleman had, with inexplicable rashness, made his way into this labyrinth without, as far as can be discovered, taking with him either candles or matches, so that his sad fate was the natural result of his own temerity. What makes the matter more painful is that Dr. Julius Burger was an intimate friend of the deceased. His joy at the extraordinary find which he has been so fortunate as to make has been greatly marred by the terrible fate of his comrade and fellow-worker."

THE LOST STRADIVARIUS
By John Meade Falkner

Letter from MISS SOPHIA MALTRAVERS to her Nephew, SIR EDWARD MALTRAVERS, then a Student at Christ Church, Oxford.
13 Pauncefort Buildings, Bath, Oct. 21, 1867.

MY DEAR EDWARD,

It was your late father's dying request that certain events which occurred in his last years should be communicated to you on your coming of age. I have reduced them to writing, partly from my own recollection, which is, alas! still too vivid, and partly with the aid of notes taken at the time of my brother's death. As you are now of full age, I submit the narrative to you. Much of it has necessarily been exceedingly painful to me to write, but at the same time I feel it is better that you should hear the truth from me than garbled stories from others who did not love your father as I did.

Your loving Aunt,
SOPHIA MALTRAVERS
To Sir Edward Maltravers, Bart.

"A tale out of season is as music in mourning."
ECCLESIASTICUS xxii. 6.

MISS SOPHIA MALTRAVERS' STORY

CHAPTER I

Your father, John Maltravers, was born in 1820 at Worth, and succeeded his father and mine, who died when we were still young children. John was sent to Eton in due course, and in 1839, when he was nineteen years of age, it was determined that he should go to Oxford. It was intended at first to enter him at Christ Church; but Dr. Sarsdell, who visited us at Worth in the summer of 1839, persuaded Mr. Thoresby, our guardian, to send him instead to Magdalen Hall. Dr. Sarsdell was himself Principal of that institution, and represented that John, who then exhibited some symptoms of delicacy, would meet with more personal attention under his care than he could hope to do in so large a college as Christ Church. Mr. Thoresby, ever solicitous for his ward's welfare, readily waived other considerations in favour of an arrangement which he considered conducive to John's health, and he was accordingly matriculated at Magdalen Hall in the autumn of 1839.

Dr. Sarsdell had not been unmindful of his promise to look after my brother, and had secured him an excellent first-floor sitting-room, with a bedroom adjoining, having an aspect towards New College Lane.

I shall pass over the first two years of my brother's residence at Oxford, because they have nothing to do with the present story. They were spent, no doubt, in the ordinary routine of work and recreation common in Oxford at that period.

From his earliest boyhood he had been passionately devoted to music, and had attained a considerable proficiency on the violin. In the autumn term of 1841 he made the acquaintance of Mr. William Gaskell, a very talented student at New College, and also a more than tolerable musician. The practice of music was then very much less common at Oxford than it has since become, and there were none of those societies existing which now do so much to promote its study among undergraduates. It was therefore a cause of much gratification to the two young men, and it afterwards became a strong bond of friendship, to discover that one was as devoted to the pianoforte as was the other to the violin. Mr. Gaskell, though in easy circumstances, had not a pianoforte in his rooms, and was pleased to use a fine instrument by D'Almaine that John had that term received as a birthday present from his guardian.

From that time the two students were thrown much together, and in the autumn term of 1841 and Easter term of 1842 practised a variety of music in John's rooms, he taking the violin part and Mr. Gaskell that for the pianoforte.

It was, I think, in March 1842 that John purchased for his rooms a piece of furniture which was destined afterwards to play no unimportant part in the story I am narrating. This was a very large and low wicker chair of a form then coming into fashion in Oxford, and since, I am told, become a familiar object of most college rooms. It was cushioned with a gaudy pattern of chintz, and bought for new of an upholsterer at the bottom of the High Street.

Mr. Gaskell was taken by his uncle to spend Easter in Rome, and obtaining special leave from his college to prolong his travels; did not return to Oxford till three weeks of the summer term were passed and May was well advanced. So impatient was he to see his friend that he would not let even the first evening of his return pass without coming round to John's rooms. The two young men sat without lights until the night was late; and Mr. Gaskell had much to narrate of his travels, and spoke specially of the beautiful music which he had heard at Easter in the Roman churches. He had also had lessons on the piano from a celebrated professor of the Italian style, but seemed to have been particularly delighted with the music of the seventeenth-century composers, of whose works he had brought back some specimens set for piano and violin.

It was past eleven o'clock when Mr. Gaskell left to return to New College; but the night was unusually warm, with a moon near the full, and John sat for some time in a cushioned window-seat before the open sash thinking over what he had heard about the music of Italy. Feeling still disinclined for sleep, he lit a single candle and began to turn over some of the musical works which Mr. Gaskell had left on the table. His attention was especially attracted to an oblong book, bound in soiled vellum, with a coat of arms stamped in gilt upon the side. It was a manuscript copy of some early suites by Graziani for violin and harpsichord, and was apparently written at Naples in the year 1744, many years after the death of that composer. Though the ink was yellow and faded, the transcript had been accurately made, and could be read with tolerable comfort by an advanced musician in spite of the antiquated notation.

Perhaps by accident, or perhaps by some mysterious direction which our minds are incapable of appreciating, his eye was arrested by a suite of four movements with a basso continuo, or figured bass, for the harpsichord. The other suites in the book were only distinguished by numbers, but this one the composer had dignified with the name of "l'Areopagita." Almost mechanically John put the book on his music-stand, took his violin from its case, and after a moment's tuning stood up and played the first movement, a lively Coranto. The light of the single candle burning on the table was scarcely sufficient to illumine the page; the shadows hung in the creases of the leaves, which had grown into those wavy folds sometimes observable in books made of thick paper and remaining long shut; and it was with difficulty that he could read what he was playing. But he felt the strange impulse of the old-world music urging him forward, and did not even pause to light the candles which stood ready in their sconces on either side of the desk. The Coranto was followed by a Sarabanda, and the Sarabanda by a Gagliarda. My brother stood playing, with his face turned to the window, with the room and the large wicker chair of which I have spoken behind him. The Gagliarda began with a bold and lively air, and as he played the opening bars, he heard behind him a creaking of the wicker chair. The sound was a perfectly familiar one - as of some person placing a hand on either arm of the chair preparatory to lowering himself into it, followed by another as of the same person being leisurely seated. But for the tones of the violin, all was silent, and the creaking of the chair was strangely distinct. The illusion was so complete that my brother stopped playing suddenly, and turned round expecting that some late friend of his had slipped in unawares, being attracted by the sound of the violin, or that Mr. Gaskell himself had returned. With the cessation of the music an absolute stillness fell upon all; the light of the single candle scarcely reached the darker corners of the room, but fell directly on the wicker chair and showed it to be perfectly empty. Half amused, half vexed with himself at having without reason interrupted his music, my brother returned to the Gagliarda; but some impulse induced him to light the candles in the sconces, which gave an illumination more adequate to the occasion. The Gagliarda and the last movement, a Minuetto, were finished, and John closed the book, intending, as it was now late, to seek his bed. As he shut the pages a creaking of the wicker chair again attracted his attention, and he heard distinctly sounds such as would be made by a person raising himself from a sitting posture. This time, being less surprised, he could more aptly consider the probable causes of such a circumstance, and easily arrived at the conclusion that there must be in the wicker chair osiers responsive to certain notes of the violin, as panes of glass in church windows are observed to vibrate in sympathy with certain tones of the organ. But while this argument approved itself to his reason, his imagination was but half convinced; and he could not but be impressed with the fact that the second creaking of the chair had been coincident with his shutting the music-book; and, unconsciously, pictured to himself some strange visitor waiting until the termination of the music, and then taking his departure.

His conjectures did not, however, either rob him of sleep or even disturb it with dreams, and he woke the next morning with a cooler mind and one less inclined to fantastic imagination. If the strange episode of the previous evening had not entirely vanished from his mind, it seemed at least fully accounted for by the acoustic explanation to which I have alluded above. Although he saw Mr. Gaskell in the course of the morning, he did not think it necessary to mention to him so trivial a circumstance, but made with him an appointment to sup together in his own rooms that evening, and to amuse themselves afterwards by essaying some of the Italian music.

It was shortly after nine that night when, supper being finished, Mr. Gaskell seated himself at the piano and John tuned his violin. The evening was closing in; there had been heavy thunder-rain in the afternoon, and the moist air hung now heavy and steaming, while across it there throbbed the distant vibrations of the tenor bell at Christ Church. It was tolling the customary 101 strokes, which are rung every night in term-time as a signal for closing the college gates. The two young men enjoyed themselves for some while, playing first a suite by Cesti, and then two early sonatas by Buononcini. Both of them were sufficiently expert musicians to make reading at sight a pleasure rather than an effort; and Mr. Gaskell especially was well versed in the theory of music, and in the correct rendering of the basso continuo. After the Buononcini Mr. Gaskell took up the oblong copy of Graziani, and turning over its leaves, proposed that they should play the same suite which John had performed by himself the previous evening. His selection was apparently perfectly fortuitous, as my brother had purposely refrained from directing his attention in any way to that piece of music. They played the Coranto and the Sarabanda, and in the singular fascination of the music John had entirely forgotten the episode of the previous evening, when, as the bold air of the Gagliarda commenced, he suddenly became aware of the same strange creaking of the wicker chair that he had noticed on the first occasion. The sound was identical, and so exact was its resemblance to that of a person sitting down that he stared at the chair, almost wondering that it still appeared empty. Beyond turning his head sharply for a moment to look round, Mr. Gaskell took no notice of the sound; and my brother, ashamed to betray any foolish interest or excitement, continued the Gagliarda, with its repeat. At its conclusion Mr. Gaskell stopped before proceeding to the minuet, and turning the stool on which he was sitting round towards the room, observed, "How very strange, Johnnie," - for these young men were on terms of sufficient intimacy to address each other in a familiar style, - "How very strange! I thought I heard some one sit down in that chair when we began the Gagliarda. I looked round quite expecting to see some one had come in. Did you hear nothing?"

"It was only the chair creaking," my brother answered, feigning an indifference which he scarcely felt. "Certain parts of the wicker-work seem to be in accord with musical notes and respond to them; let us continue with the Minuetto."

Thus they finished the suite, Mr. Gaskell demanding a repetition of the Gagliarda, with the air of which he was much pleased. As the clocks had already struck eleven, they determined not to play more that night; and Mr. Gaskell rose, blew out the sconces, shut the piano, and put the music aside. My brother has often assured me that he was quite prepared for what followed, and had been almost expecting it; for as the books were put away, a creaking of the wicker chair was audible, exactly similar to that which he had heard when he stopped playing on the previous night. There was a moment's silence; the young men looked involuntarily at one another, and then Mr. Gaskell said, "I cannot understand the creaking of that chair; it has never done so before, with all the music we have played. I am perhaps imaginative and excited with the fine airs we have heard to-night, but I have an impression that I cannot dispel that something has been sitting listening to us all this time, and that now when the concert is ended it has got up and gone." There was a spirit of raillery in his words, but his tone was not so light as it would ordinarily have been, and he was evidently ill at ease.

"Let us try the Gagliarda again," said my brother; "it is the vibration of the opening notes which affects the wicker-work, and we shall see if the noise is repeated." But Mr. Gaskell excused himself from trying the experiment, and after some desultory conversation, to which it was evident that neither was giving any serious attention, he took his leave and returned to New College.

CHAPTER II

I shall not weary you, my dear Edward, by recounting similar experiences which occurred on nearly every occasion that the young men met in the evenings for music. The repetition of the phenomenon had accustomed them to expect it. Both professed to be quite satisfied that it was to be attributed to acoustical affinities of vibration between the wicker-work and certain of the piano wires, and indeed this seemed the only explanation possible. But, at the same time, the resemblance of the noises to those caused by a person sitting down in or rising from a chair was so marked, that even their frequent recurrence never failed to make a strange impression on them. They felt a reluctance to mention the matter to their friends, partly from a fear of being themselves laughed at, and partly to spare from ridicule a circumstance to which each perhaps, in spite of himself, attached some degree of importance. Experience soon convinced them that the first noise as of one sitting down never occurred unless the Gagliarda of the "Areopagita" was played, and that this noise being once heard, the second only followed it when they ceased playing for the evening. They met every night, sitting later with the lengthening summer evenings, and every night, as by some tacit understanding, played the "Areopagita" suite before parting. At the opening bars of the Gagliarda the creaking of the chair occurred spontaneously with the utmost regularity. They seldom spoke even to one another of the subject; but one night, when John was putting away his violin after a long evening's music without having played the "Areopagita," Mr. Gaskell, who had risen from the pianoforte, sat down again as by a sudden impulse and said:

"Johnnie, do not put away your violin yet. It is near twelve o'clock and I shall get shut out, but I cannot stop to-night without playing the Gagliarda. Suppose that all our theories of vibration and affinity are wrong, suppose that there really comes here night by night some strange visitant to hear us, some poor creature whose heart is bound up in that tune; would it not be unkind to send him away without the hearing of that piece which he seems most to relish? Let us not be ill-mannered, but humour his whim; let us play the Gagliarda."

They played it with more vigour and precision than usual, and the now customary sound of one taking his seat at once ensued. It was that night that my brother, looking steadfastly at the chair, saw, or thought he saw, there some slight obscuration, some penumbra, mist, or subtle vapour which, as he gazed, seemed to struggle to take human form. He ceased playing for a moment and rubbed his eyes, but as he did so all dimness vanished and he saw the chair perfectly empty. The pianist stopped also at the cessation of the violin, and asked what ailed him.

"It is only that my eyes were dim," he answered.

"We have had enough for to-night," said Mr. Gaskell; "let us stop. I shall be locked out." He shut the piano, and as he did so the clock in New College tower struck twelve. He left the room running, but was late enough at his college door to be reported, admonished with a fine against such late hours, and confined for a week to college; for being out after midnight was considered, at that time at least, a somewhat serious offence.

Thus for some days the musical practice was compulsorily intermitted, but resumed on the first evening after Mr. Gaskell's term of confinement was expired. After they had performed several suites of Graziani, and finished as usual with the "Areopagita," Mr. Gaskell sat for a time silent at the instrument, as though thinking with himself, and then said:

"I cannot say how deeply this old-fashioned music affects me. Some would try to persuade us that these suites, of which the airs bear the names of different dances, were always written rather as a musical essay and for purposes of performance than for persons to dance to, as their names would more naturally imply. But I think these critics are wrong at least in some instances. It is to me impossible to believe that such a melody, for instance, as the Giga of Corelli which we have played, was not written for actual purposes of dancing. One can almost hear the beat of feet upon the floor, and I imagine that in the time of Corelli the practice of dancing, while not a whit inferior in grace, had more of the tripudistic or beating character than is now esteemed consistent with a correct ball-room performance. The Gagliarda too, which we play now so constantly, possesses a singular power of assisting the imagination to picture or reproduce such scenes as those which it no doubt formerly enlivened. I know not why, but it is constantly identified in my mind with some revel which I have perhaps seen in a picture, where several couples are dancing a licentious measure in a long room lit by a number of silver sconces of the debased model common at the end of the seventeenth century. It is probably a reminiscence of my late excursion that gives to these dancers in my fancy the olive skin, dark hair, and bright eyes of the Italian type; and they wear dresses of exceedingly rich fabric and elaborate design. Imagination is whimsical enough to paint for me the character of the room itself, as having an arcade of arches running down one side alone, of the fantastic and paganised Gothic of the Renaissance. At the end is a gallery or balcony for the musicians, which on its coved front has a florid coat of arms of foreign heraldry. The shield bears, on a field or, a cherub's head blowing on three lilies - a blazon I have no doubt seen somewhere in my travels, though I cannot recollect where. This scene, I say, is so nearly connected in my brain with the Gagliarda, that scarcely are its first notes sounded ere it presents itself to my eyes with a vividness which increases every day. The couples advance, set, and recede, using free and licentious gestures which my imagination should be ashamed to recall. Amongst so many foreigners, fancy pictures, I know not in the least why, the presence of a young man of an English type of face, whose features, however, always elude my mind's attempt to fix them. I think that the opening subject of this Gagliarda is a superior composition to the rest of it, for it is only during the first sixteen bars that the vision of bygone revelry presents itself to me. With the last note of the sixteenth bar a veil is drawn suddenly across the scene, and with a sense almost of some catastrophe it vanishes. This I attribute to the fact that the second subject must be inferior in conception to the first, and by some sense of incongruity destroys the fabric which the fascination of the preceding one built up."

My brother, though he had listened with interest to what Mr. Gaskell had said, did not reply, and the subject was allowed to drop.

CHAPTER III

It was in the same summer of 1842, and near the middle of June, that my brother John wrote inviting me to come to Oxford for the Commemoration festivities. I had been spending some weeks with Mrs. Temple, a distant cousin of ours, at their house of Royston in Derbyshire, and John was desirous that Mrs. Temple should come up to Oxford and chaperone her daughter Constance and myself at the balls and various other entertainments which take place at the close of the summer term. Owing to Royston being some two hundred miles from Worth Maltravers, our families had hitherto seen little of one another, but during my present visit I had learned to love Mrs. Temple, a lady of singular sweetness of disposition, and had contracted a devoted attachment to her daughter Constance. Constance Temple was then eighteen years of age, and to great beauty united such mental graces and excellent traits of character as must ever appear to reasoning persons more enduringly valuable than even the highest personal attractions. She was well read and witty, and had been trained in those principles of true religion which she afterwards followed with devoted consistency in the self-sacrifice and resigned piety of her too short life. In person, I may remind you, my dear Edward, since death removed her ere you were of years to appreciate either her appearance or her qualities, she was tall, with a somewhat long and oval face, with brown hair and eyes.

Mrs. Temple readily accepted Sir John Maltravers' invitation. She had never seen Oxford herself, and was pleased to afford us the pleasure of so delightful an excursion. John had secured convenient rooms for us above the shop of a well-known printseller in High Street, and we arrived in Oxford on Friday evening, June 18, 1842. I shall not dilate to you on the various Commemoration festivities, which have probably altered little since those days, and with which you are familiar. Suffice it to say that my brother had secured us admission to every entertainment, and that we enjoyed our visit as only youth with its keen sensibilities and uncloyed pleasures can. I could not help observing that John was very much struck by the attractions of Miss Constance Temple, and that she for her part, while exhibiting no unbecoming forwardness, certainly betrayed no aversion to him. I was greatly pleased both with my own powers of observation which had enabled me to discover so important a fact, and also with the circumstance itself. To a romantic girl of nineteen it appeared high time that a brother of twenty-two should be at least preparing some matrimonial project; and my friend was so good and beautiful that it seemed impossible that I should ever obtain a more lovable sister or my brother a better wife. Mrs. Temple could not refuse her sanction to such a scheme; for while their mental qualities seemed eminently compatible, John was in his own right master of Worth Maltravers, and her daughter sole heiress of the Royston estates.

The Commemoration festivities terminated on Wednesday night with a grand ball at the Music-Room in Holywell Street. This was given by a Lodge of University Freemasons, and John was there with Mr. Gaskell - whose acquaintance we had made with much gratification - both wearing blue silk scarves and small white aprons. They introduced us to many other of their friends similarly adorned, and these important and mysterious insignia sat not amiss with their youthful figures and boyish faces. After a long and pleasurable programme, it was decided that we should prolong our visit till the next evening, leaving Oxford at half-past ten o'clock at night and driving to Didcot, there to join the mail for the west. We rose late the next morning and spent the day rambling among the old colleges and gardens of the most beautiful of English cities. At seven o'clock we dined together for the last time at our lodgings in High Street, and my brother proposed that before parting we should enjoy the fine evening in the gardens of St. John's College. This was at once agreed to, and we proceeded thither, John walking on in front with Constance and Mrs. Temple, and I following with Mr. Gaskell. My companion explained that these gardens were esteemed the most beautiful in the University, but that under ordinary circumstances it was not permitted to strangers to walk there of an evening. Here he quoted some Latin about "aurum per medios ire satellites," which I smilingly made as if I understood, and did indeed gather from it that John had bribed the porter to admit us. It was a warm and very still night, without a moon, but with enough of fading light to show the outlines of the garden front. This long low line of buildings built in Charles I's reign looked so exquisitely beautiful that I shall never forget it, though I have not since seen its oriel windows and creeper-covered walls. There was a very heavy dew on the broad lawn, and we walked at first only on the paths. No one spoke, for we were oppressed by the very beauty of the scene, and by the sadness which an imminent parting from friends and from so sweet a place combined to cause. John had been silent and depressed the whole day, nor did Mr. Gaskell himself seem inclined to conversation. Constance and my brother fell a little way behind, and Mr. Gaskell asked me to cross the lawn if I was not afraid of the dew, that I might see the garden front to better advantage from the corner. Mrs. Temple waited for us on the path, not wishing to wet her feet. Mr. Gaskell pointed out the beauties of the perspective as seen from his vantage-point, and we were fortunate in hearing the sweet descant of nightingales for which this garden has ever been famous. As we stood silent and listening, a candle was lit in a small oriel at the end, and the light showing the tracery of the window added to the picturesqueness of the scene.

Within an hour we were in a landau driving through the still warm lanes to Didcot. I had seen that Constance's parting with my brother had been tender, and I am not sure that she was not in tears during some part at least of our drive; but I did not observe her closely, having my thoughts elsewhere.

Though we were thus being carried every moment further from the sleeping city, where I believe that both our hearts were busy, I feel as if I had been a personal witness of the incidents I am about to narrate, so often have I heard them from my brother's lips. The two young men, after parting with us in the High Street, returned to their respective colleges. John reached his rooms shortly before eleven o'clock. He was at once sad and happy - sad at our departure, but happy in a new-found world of delight which his admiration for Constance Temple opened to him. He was, in fact, deeply in love with her, and the full flood of a hitherto unknown passion filled him with an emotion so overwhelming that his ordinary life seemed transfigured. He moved, as it were, in an ether superior to our mortal atmosphere, and a new region of high resolves and noble possibilities spread itself before his eyes. He slammed his heavy outside door (called an "oak") to prevent anyone entering and flung himself into the window-seat. Here he sat for a long time, the sash thrown up and his head outside, for he was excited and feverish. His mental exaltation was so great and his thoughts of so absorbing an interest that he took no notice of time, and only remembered afterwards that the scent of a syringa-bush was borne up to him from a little garden-patch opposite, and that a bat had circled slowly up and down the lane, until he heard the clocks striking three. At the same time the faint light of dawn made itself felt almost imperceptibly; the classic statues on the roof of the schools began to stand out against the white sky, and a faint glimmer to penetrate the darkened room. It glistened on the varnished top of his violin-case lying on the table, and on a jug of toast-and-water placed there by his college servant or scout every night before he left. He drank a glass of this mixture, and was moving towards his bedroom door when a sudden thought struck him. He turned back, took the violin from its case, tuned it, and began to play the "Areopagita" suite. He was conscious of that mental clearness and vigour which not infrequently comes with the dawn to those who have sat watching or reading through the night: and his thoughts were exalted by the effect which the first consciousness of a deep passion causes in imaginative minds. He had never played the suite with more power; and the airs, even without the piano part, seemed fraught with a meaning hitherto unrealised. As he began the Gagliarda he heard the wicker chair creak; but he had his back towards it, and the sound was now too familiar to him to cause him even to look round. It was not till he was playing the repeat that he became aware of a new and overpowering sensation. At first it was a vague feeling, so often experienced by us all, of not being alone. He did not stop playing, and in a few seconds the impression of a presence in the room other than his own became so strong that he was actually afraid to look round. But in another moment he felt that at all hazards he must see what or who this presence was. Without stopping he partly turned and partly looked over his shoulder. The silver light of early morning was filling the room, making the various objects appear of less bright colour than usual, and giving to everything a pearl-grey neutral tint. In this cold but clear light he saw seated in the wicker chair the figure of a man.

In the first violent shock of so terrifying a discovery, he could not appreciate such details as those of features, dress, or appearance. He was merely conscious that with him, in a locked room of which he knew himself to be the only human inmate, there sat something which bore a human form. He looked at it for a moment with a hope, which he felt to be vain, that it might vanish and prove a phantom of his excited imagination, but still it sat there. Then my brother put down his violin, and he used to assure me that a horror overwhelmed him of an intensity which he had previously believed impossible. Whether the image which he saw was subjective or objective, I cannot pretend to say: you will be in a position to judge for yourself when you have finished this narrative. Our limited experience would lead us to believe that it was a phantom conjured up by some unusual condition of his own brain; but we are fain to confess that there certainly do exist in nature phenomena such as baffle human reason; and it is possible that, for some hidden purposes of Providence, permission may occasionally be granted to those who have passed from this life to assume again for a time the form of their earthly tabernacle. We must, I say, be content to suspend our judgment on such matters; but in this instance the subsequent course of events is very difficult to explain, except on the supposition that there was then presented to my brother's view the actual bodily form of one long deceased. The dread which took possession of him was due, he has more than once told me when analysing his feelings long afterwards, to two predominant causes. Firstly, he felt that mental dislocation which accompanies the sudden subversion of preconceived theories, the sudden alteration of long habit, or even the occurrence of any circumstance beyond the walk of our daily experience. This I have observed myself in the perturbing effect which a sudden death, a grievous accident, or in recent years the declaration of war, has exercised upon all except the most lethargic or the most determined minds. Secondly, he experienced the profound self-abasement or mental annihilation caused by the near conception of a being of a superior order. In the presence of an existence wearing, indeed, the human form, but of attributes widely different from and superior to his own, he felt the combined reverence and revulsion which even the noblest wild animals exhibit when brought for the first time face to face with man. The shock was so great that I feel persuaded it exerted an effect on him from which he never wholly recovered.

After an interval which seemed to him interminable, though it was only of a second's duration, he turned his eyes again to the occupant of the wicker chair. His faculties had so far recovered from the first shock as to enable him to see that the figure was that of a man perhaps thirty-five years of age and still youthful in appearance. The face was long and oval, the hair brown, and brushed straight off an exceptionally high forehead. His complexion was very pale or bloodless. He was clean shaven, and his finely cut mouth, with compressed lips, wore something of a sneering smile. His general expression was unpleasing, and from the first my brother felt as by intuition that there was present some malign and wicked influence. His eyes were not visible, as he kept them cast down, resting his head on his hand in the attitude of one listening. His face and even his dress were impressed so vividly upon John's mind, that he never had any difficulty in recalling them to his imagination; and he and I had afterwards an opportunity of verifying them in a remarkable manner. He wore a long cut-away coat of green cloth with an edge of gold embroidery, and a white satin waistcoat figured with rose-sprigs, a full cravat of rich lace, knee-breeches of buff silk, and stockings of the same. His shoes were of polished black leather with heavy silver buckles, and his costume in general recalled that worn a century ago. As my brother gazed at him, he got up, putting his hands on the arms of the chair to raise himself, and causing the creaking so often heard before. The hands forced themselves on my brother's notice: they were very white, with the long delicate fingers of a musician. He showed a considerable height; and still keeping his eyes on the floor, walked with an ordinary gait towards the end of the bookcase at the side of the room farthest from the window. He reached the bookcase, and then John suddenly lost sight of him. The figure did not fade gradually, but went out, as it were, like the flame of a suddenly extinguished candle.

The room was now filled with the clear light of the summer morning: the whole vision had lasted but a few seconds, but my brother knew that there was no possibility of his having been mistaken, that the mystery of the creaking chair was solved, that he had seen the man who had come evening by evening for a month past to listen to the rhythm of the Gagliarda. Terribly disturbed, he sat for some time half dreading and half expecting a return of the figure; but all remained unchanged: he saw nothing, nor did he dare to challenge its reappearance by playing again the Gagliarda, which seemed to have so strange an attraction for it. At last, in the full sunlight of a late June morning at Oxford, he heard the steps of early pedestrians on the pavement below his windows, the cry of a milkman, and other sounds which showed the world was awake. It was after six o'clock, and going to his bedroom he flung himself on the outside of the bed for an hour's troubled slumber.

CHAPTER IV

When his servant called him about eight o'clock my brother sent a note to Mr. Gaskell at New College, begging him to come round to Magdalen Hall as soon as might be in the course of the morning. His summons was at once obeyed, and Mr. Gaskell was with him before he had finished breakfast. My brother was still much agitated, and at once told him what had happened the night before, detailing the various circumstances with minuteness, and not even concealing from him the sentiments which he entertained towards Miss Constance Temple. In narrating the appearance which he had seen in the chair, his agitation was still so excessive that he had difficulty in controlling his voice.

Mr. Gaskell heard him with much attention, and did not at once reply when John had finished his narration. At length he said, "I suppose many friends would think it right to affect, even if they did not feel, an incredulity as to what you have just told me. They might consider it more prudent to attempt to allay your distress by persuading you that what you have seen has no objective reality, but is merely the phantasm of an excited imagination; that if you had not been in love, had not sat up all night, and had not thus overtaxed your physical powers, you would have seen no vision. I shall not argue thus, for I am as certainly convinced as of the fact that we sit here, that on all the nights when we have played this suite called the 'Areopagita,' there has been some one listening to us, and that you have at length been fortunate or unfortunate enough to see him."

"Do not say fortunate," said my brother; "for I feel as though I shall never recover from last night's shock."

"That is likely enough," Mr. Gaskell answered, coolly; "for as in the history of the race or individual, increased culture and a finer mental susceptibility necessarily impair the brute courage and powers of endurance which we note in savages, so any supernatural vision such as you have seen must be purchased at the cost of physical reaction. From the first evening that we played this music, and heard the noises mimicking so closely the sitting down and rising up of some person, I have felt convinced that causes other than those which we usually call natural were at work, and that we were very near the manifestation of some extraordinary phenomenon."

"I do not quite apprehend your meaning."

"I mean this," he continued, "that this man or spirit of a man has been sitting here night after night, and that we have not been able to see him, because our minds are dull and obtuse. Last night the elevating force of a strong passion, such as that which you have confided to me, combined with the power of fine music, so exalted your mind that you became endowed, as it were, with a sixth sense, and suddenly were enabled to see that which had previously been invisible. To this sixth sense music gives, I believe, the key. We are at present only on the threshold of such a knowledge of that art as will enable us to use it eventually as the greatest of all humanising and educational agents. Music will prove a ladder to the loftier regions of thought; indeed I have long found for myself that I cannot attain to the highest range of my intellectual power except when hearing good music. All poets, and most writers of prose, will say that their thought is never so exalted, their sense of beauty and proportion never so just, as when they are listening either to the artificial music made by man, or to some of the grander tones of nature, such as the roar of a western ocean, or the sighing of wind in a clump of firs. Though I have often felt on such occasions on the very verge of some high mental discovery, and though a hand has been stretched forward as it were to rend the veil, yet it has never been vouchsafed me to see behind it. This you no doubt were allowed in a measure to do last night. You probably played the music with a deeper intuition than usual, and this, combined with the excitement under which you were already labouring, raised you for a moment to the required pitch of mental exaltation."

"It is true," John said, "that I never felt the melody so deeply as when I played it last night."

"Just so," answered his friend; "and there is probably some link between this air and the history of the man whom you saw last night; some fatal power in it which enables it to exert an attraction on him even after death. For we must remember that the influence of music, though always powerful, is not always for good. We can scarcely doubt that as certain forms of music tend to raise us above the sensuality of the animal, or the more degrading passion of material gain, and to transport us into the ether of higher thought, so other forms are directly calculated to awaken in us luxurious emotions, and to whet those sensual appetites which it is the business of a philosopher not indeed to annihilate or to be ashamed of, but to keep rigidly in check. This possibility of music to effect evil as well as good I have seen recognised, and very aptly expressed in some beautiful verses by Mr. Keble which I have just read:

"'Cease, stranger, cease those witching notes,
The art of syren choirs;
Hush the seductive voice that floats
Across the trembling wires.

"'Music's ethereal power was given
Not to dissolve our clay,
But draw Promethean beams from heaven
To purge the dross away.'"

"They are fine lines," said my brother, "but I do not see how you apply your argument to the present instance."

"I mean," Mr. Gaskell answered, "that I have little doubt that the melody of this Gagliarda has been connected in some manner with the life of the man you saw last night. It is not unlikely, either, that it was a favourite air of his whilst in the flesh, or even that it was played by himself or others at the moment of some crisis in his history. It is possible that such connection may be due merely to the innocent pleasure the melody gave him in life; but the nature of the music itself, and a peculiar effect it has upon my own thoughts, induce me to believe that it was associated with some occasion when he either fell into great sin or when some evil fate, perhaps even death itself, overtook him. You will remember I have told you that this air calls up to my mind a certain scene of Italian revelry in which an Englishman takes part. It is true that I have never been able to fix his features in my mind, nor even to say exactly how he was dressed. Yet now some instinct tells me that it is this very man whom you saw last night. It is not for us to attempt to pierce the mystery which veils from our eyes the secrets of an after-death existence; but I can scarcely suppose that a spirit entirely at rest would feel so deeply the power of a certain melody as to be called back by it to his old haunts like a dog by his master's whistle. It is more probable that there is some evil history connected with the matter, and this, I think, we ought to consider if it be possible to unravel."

My brother assenting, he continued, "When this man left you, Johnnie, did he walk to the door?"

"No; he made for the side wall, and when he reached the end of the bookcase I lost sight of him."

Mr. Gaskell went to the bookcase and looked for a moment at the titles of the books, as though expecting to see something in them to assist his inquiries; but finding apparently no clue, he said:

"This is the last time we shall meet for three months or more; let us play the Gagliarda and see if there be any response."

My brother at first would not hear of this, showing a lively dread of challenging any reappearance of the figure he had seen: indeed he felt that such an event would probably fling him into a state of serious physical disorder. Mr. Gaskell, however, continued to press him, assuring him that the fact of his now being no longer alone should largely allay any fear on his part, and urging that this would be the last opportunity they would have of playing together for some months.

At last, being overborne, my brother took his violin, and Mr. Gaskell seated himself at the pianoforte. John was very agitated, and as he commenced the Gagliarda his hands trembled so that he could scarcely play the air. Mr. Gaskell also exhibited some nervousness, not performing with his customary correctness. But for the first time the charm failed: no noise accompanied the music, nor did anything of an unusual character occur. They repeated the whole suite, but with a similar result.

Both were surprised, but neither, had any explanation to offer. My brother, who at first dreaded intensely a repetition of the vision, was now almost disappointed that nothing had occurred; so quickly does the mood of man change.

After some further conversation the young men parted for the Long Vacation - John returning to Worth Maltravers and Mr. Gaskell going to London, where he was to pass a few days before he proceeded to his home in Westmorland.

CHAPTER V

John spent nearly the whole of this summer vacation at Worth Maltravers. He had been anxious to pay a visit to Royston; but the continued and serious illness of Mrs. Temple's sister had called her and Constance to Scotland, where they remained until the death of their relative allowed them to return to Derbyshire in the late autumn. John and I had been brought up together from childhood. When he was at Eton we had always spent the holidays at Worth, and after my dear mother's death, when we were left quite alone, the bonds of our love were naturally drawn still closer. Even after my brother went to Oxford, at a time when most young men are anxious to enjoy a new-found liberty, and to travel or to visit friends in their vacation, John's ardent affection for me and for Worth Maltravers kept him at home; and he was pleased on most occasions to make me the partner of his thoughts and of his pleasures. This long vacation of 1842 was, I think, the happiest of our lives. In my case I know it was so, and I think it was happy also for him; for none could guess that the small cloud seen in the distance like a man's hand was afterwards to rise and darken all his later days. It was a summer of brilliant and continued sunshine; many of the old people said that they could never recollect so fine a season, and both fruit and crops were alike abundant. John hired a small cutter-yacht, the Palestine, which he kept in our little harbour of Encombe, and in which he and I made many excursions, visiting Weymouth, Lyme Regis, and other places of interest on the south coast.

In this summer my brother confided to me two secrets - his love for Constance Temple, which indeed was after all no secret, and the history of the apparition which he had seen. This last filled me with inexpressible dread and distress. It seemed cruel and unnatural that any influence so dark and mysterious should thus intrude on our bright life, and from the first I had an impression which I could not entirely shake off, that any such appearance or converse of a disembodied spirit must portend misfortune, if not worse, to him who saw or heard it. It never occurred to me to combat or to doubt the reality of the vision; he believed that he had seen it, and his conviction was enough to convince me. He had meant, he said, to tell no one, and had given a promise to Mr. Gaskell to that effect; but I think that he could not bear to keep such a matter in his own breast, and within the first week of his return he made me his confidant. I remember, my dear Edward, the look everything wore on that sad night when he first told me what afterwards proved so terrible a secret. We had dined quite alone, and he had been moody and depressed all the evening. It was a chilly night, with some fret blowing up from the sea. The moon showed that blunted and deformed appearance which she assumes a day or two past the full, and the moisture in the air encircled her with a stormy-looking halo. We had stepped out of the dining-room windows on to the little terrace looking down towards Smedmore and Encombe. The glaucous shrubs that grow in between the balusters were wet and dripping with the salt breath of the sea, and we could hear the waves coming into the cove from the west. After standing a minute I felt chill, and proposed that we should go back to the billiard-room, where a fire was lit on all except the warmest nights. "No," John said, "I want to tell you something, Sophy," and then we walked on to the old boat summer-house. There he told me everything. I cannot describe to you my feelings of anguish and horror when he told me of the appearance of the man. The interest of the tale was so absorbing to me that I took no note of time, nor of the cold night air, and it was only when it was all finished that I felt how deadly chill it had become. "Let us go in, John," I said; "I am cold and feel benumbed."

But youth is hopeful and strong, and in another week the impression had faded from our minds, and we were enjoying the full glory of midsummer weather, which I think only those know who have watched the blue sea come rippling in at the foot of the white chalk cliffs of Dorset.

I had felt a reluctance even so much as to hear the air of the Gagliarda, and though he had spoken to me of the subject on more than one occasion, my brother had never offered to play it to me. I knew that he had the copy of Graziani's suites with him at Worth Maltravers, because he had told me that he had brought it from Oxford; but I had never seen the book, and fancied that he kept it intentionally locked up. He did not, however, neglect the violin, and during the summer mornings, as I sat reading or working on the terrace, I often heard him playing to himself in the library. Though he had never even given me any description of the melody of the Gagliarda, yet I felt certain that he not infrequently played it. I cannot say how it was; but from the moment that I heard him one morning in the library performing an air set in a curiously low key, it forced itself upon my attention, and I knew, as it were by instinct, that it must be the Gagliarda of the "Areopagita." He was using a sordino and playing it very softly; but I was not mistaken. One wet afternoon in October, only a week before the time of his leaving us to return to Oxford for the autumn term, he walked into the drawing-room where I was sitting, and proposed that we should play some music together. To this I readily agreed. Though but a mediocre performer, I have always taken much pleasure in the use of the pianoforte, and esteemed it an honour whenever he asked me to play with him, since my powers as a musician were so very much inferior to his. After we had played several pieces, he took up an oblong music-book bound in white vellum, placed it upon the desk of the pianoforte, and proposed that we should play a suite by Graziani. I knew that he meant the "Areopagita," and begged him at once not to ask me to play it. He rallied me lightly on my fears, and said it would much please him to play it, as he had not heard the pianoforte part since he had left Oxford three months ago. I saw that he was eager to perform it, and being loath to disoblige so kind a brother during the last week of his stay at home, I at length overcame my scruples and set out to play it. But I was so alarmed at the possibility of any evil consequences ensuing, that when we commenced the Gagliarda I could scarcely find my notes. Nothing in any way unusual, however, occurred; and being reassured by this, and feeling an irresistible charm in the music, I finished the suite with more appearance of ease. My brother, however, was, I fear, not satisfied with my performance, and compared it, very possibly, with that of Mr. Gaskell, to which it was necessarily much inferior, both through weakness of execution and from my insufficient knowledge of the principles of the basso continuo. We stopped playing, and John stood looking out of the window across the sea, where the sky was clearing low down under the clouds. The sun went down behind Portland in a fiery glow which cheered us after a long day's rain. I had taken the copy of Graziani's suites off the desk, and was holding it on my lap turning over the old foxed and yellow pages. As I closed it a streak of evening sunlight fell across the room and lighted up a coat of arms stamped in gilt on the cover. It was much faded and would ordinarily have been hard to make out; but the ray of strong light illumined it, and in an instant I recognised the same shield which Mr. Gaskell had pictured to himself as hanging on the musicians' gallery of his phantasmal dancing-room. My brother had often recounted to me this effort of his friend's imagination, and here I saw before me the same florid foreign blazon, a cherub's head blowing on three lilies on a gold field. This discovery was not only of interest, but afforded me much actual relief; for it accounted rationally for at least one item of the strange story. Mr. Gaskell had no doubt noticed at some time this shield stamped on the outside of the book, and bearing the impression of it unconsciously in his mind, had reproduced it in his imagined revels. I said as much to my brother, and he was greatly interested, and after examining the shield agreed that this was certainly a probable solution of that part of the mystery. On the 12th of October John returned to Oxford.

CHAPTER VI

My brother told me afterwards that more than once during the summer vacation he had seriously considered with himself the propriety of changing his rooms at Magdalen Hall. He had thought that it might thus be possible for him to get rid at once of the memory of the apparition, and of the fear of any reappearance of it. He could either have moved into another set of rooms in the Hall itself, or else gone into lodgings in the town - a usual proceeding, I am told, for gentlemen near the end of their course at Oxford. Would to God that he had indeed done so! but with the supineness which has, I fear, my dear Edward, been too frequently a characteristic of our family, he shrank from the trouble such a course would involve, and the opening of the autumn term found him still in his old rooms. You will forgive me for entering here on a very brief description of your father's sitting-room. It is, I think, necessary for the proper understanding of the incidents that follow. It was not a large room, though probably the finest in the small buildings of Magdalen Hall, and panelled from floor to ceiling with oak which successive generations had obscured by numerous coats of paint. On one side were two windows having an aspect on to New College Lane, and fitted with deep cushioned seats in the recesses. Outside these windows there were boxes of flowers, the brightness of which formed in the summer term a pretty contrast to the grey and crumbling stone, and afforded pleasure at once to the inmate and to passers-by. Along nearly the whole length of the wall opposite to the windows, some tenant in years long past had had mahogany book-shelves placed, reaching to a height of perhaps five feet from the floor. They were handsomely made in the style of the eighteenth century and pleased my brother's taste. He had always exhibited a partiality for books, and the fine library at Worth Maltravers had no doubt contributed to foster his tastes in that direction. At the time of which I write he had formed a small collection for himself at Oxford, paying particular attention to the bindings, and acquiring many excellent specimens of that art, principally I think, from Messrs. Payne & Foss, the celebrated London booksellers.

Towards the end of the autumn term, having occasion one cold day to take down a volume of Plato from its shelf, he found to his surprise that the book was quite warm. A closer examination easily explained to him the reason - namely, that the flue of a chimney, passing behind one end of the bookcase, sensibly heated not only the wall itself, but also the books in the shelves. Although he had been in his rooms now near three years, he had never before observed this fact; partly, no doubt, because the books in these shelves were seldom handled, being more for show as specimens of bindings than for practical use. He was somewhat annoyed at this discovery, fearing lest such a heat, which in moderation is beneficial to books, might through its excess warp the leather or otherwise injure the bindings. Mr. Gaskell was sitting with him at the time of the discovery, and indeed it was for his use that my brother had taken down the volume of Plato. He strongly advised that the bookcase should be moved, and suggested that it would be better to place it across that end of the room where the pianoforte then stood. They examined it and found that it would easily admit of removal, being, in fact, only the frame of a bookcase, and showing at the back the painted panelling of the wall. Mr. Gaskell noted it as curious that all the shelves were fixed and immovable except one at the end, which had been fitted with the ordinary arrangement allowing its position to be altered at will. My brother thought that the change would improve the appearance of his rooms, besides being advantageous for the books, and gave instructions to the college upholsterer to have the necessary work carried out at once.

The two young men had resumed their musical studies, and had often played the "Areopagita" and other music of Graziani since their return to Oxford in the Autumn. They remarked, however, that the chair no longer creaked during the Gagliarda - and, in fact, that no unusual occurrence whatever attended its performance. At times they were almost tempted to doubt the accuracy of their own remembrances, and to consider as entirely mythical the mystery which had so much disturbed them in the summer term. My brother had also pointed out to Mr. Gaskell my discovery that the coat of arms on the outside of the music-book was identical with that which his fancy portrayed on the musicians' gallery. He readily admitted that he must at some time have noticed and afterwards forgotten the blazon on the book, and that an unconscious reminiscence of it had no doubt inspired his imagination in this instance. He rebuked my brother for having agitated me unnecessarily by telling me at all of so idle a tale; and was pleased to write a few lines to me at Worth Maltravers, felicitating me on my shrewdness of perception, but speaking banteringly of the whole matter.

On the evening of the 14th of November my brother and his friend were sitting talking in the former's room. The position of the bookcase had been changed on the morning of that day, and Mr. Gaskell had come round to see how the books looked when placed at the end instead of at the side of the room. He had applauded the new arrangement, and the young men sat long over the fire, with a bottle of college port and a dish of medlars which I had sent my brother from our famous tree in the Upper Croft at Worth Maltravers. Later on they fell to music, and played a variety of pieces, performing also the "Areopagita" suite. Mr. Gaskell before he left complimented John on the improvement which the alteration in the place of the bookcase had made in his room, saying, "Not only do the books in their present place very much enhance the general appearance of the room, but the change seems to me to have affected also a marked acoustical improvement. The oak panelling now exposed on the side of the room has given a resonant property to the wall which is peculiarly responsive to the tones of your violin. While you were playing the Gagliarda to-night, I could almost have imagined that someone in an adjacent room was playing the same air with a sordino, so distinct was the echo."

Shortly after this he left.

My brother partly undressed himself in his bedroom, which adjoined, and then returning to his sitting-room, pulled the large wicker chair in front of the fire, and sat there looking at the glowing coals, and thinking perhaps of Miss Constance Temple. The night promised to be very cold, and the wind whistled down the chimney, increasing the comfortable sensation of the clear fire. He sat watching the ruddy reflection of the firelight dancing on the panelled wall, when he noticed that a picture placed where the end of the bookcase formerly stood was not truly hung, and needed adjustment. A picture hung askew was particularly offensive to his eyes, and he got up at once to alter it.

He remembered as he went up to it that at this precise spot four months ago he had lost sight of the man's figure which he saw rise from the wicker chair, and at the memory felt an involuntary shudder. This reminiscence probably influenced his fancy also in another direction; for it seemed to him that very faintly, as though played far off, and with the sordino, he could hear the air of the Gagliarda. He put one hand behind the picture to steady it, and as he did so his finger struck a very slight projection in the wall. He pulled the picture a little to one side, and saw that what he had touched was the back of a small hinge sunk in the wall, and almost obliterated with many coats of paint. His curiosity was excited, and he took a candle from the table and examined the wall carefully. Inspection soon showed him another hinge a little further up, and by degrees he perceived that one of the panels had been made at some time in the past to open, and serve probably as the door of a cupboard. At this point he assured me that a feverish anxiety to re-open this cupboard door took possession of him, and that the intense excitement filled his mind which we experience on the eve of a discovery which we fancy may produce important results. He loosened the paint in the cracks with a penknife, and attempted to press open the door; but his instrument was not adequate to such a purpose, and all his efforts remained ineffective. His excitement had now reached an overmastering pitch; for he anticipated, though he knew not why, some strange discovery to be made in this sealed cupboard. He looked round the room for some weapon with which to force the door, and at length with his penknife cut away sufficient wood at the joint to enable him to insert the end of the poker in the hole. The clock in the New College Tower struck one at the exact moment when with a sharp effort he thus forced open the door. It appeared never to have had a fastening, but merely to have been stuck fast by the accumulation of paint. As he bent it slowly back upon the rusted hinges his heart beat so fast that he could scarcely catch his breath, though he was conscious all the while of a ludicrous aspect of his position, knowing that it was most probable that the cavity within would be found empty. The cupboard was small but very deep, and in the obscure light seemed at first to contain nothing except a small heap of dust and cobwebs. His sense of disappointment was keen as he thrust his hand into it, but changed again in a moment to breathless interest on feeling something solid in what he had imagined to be only an accumulation of mould and dirt. He snatched up a candle, and holding this in one hand, with the other pulled out an object from the cupboard and put it on the table, covered as it was with the curious drapery of black and clinging cobwebs which I have seen adhering to bottles of old wine. It lay there between the dish of medlars and the decanter, veiled indeed with thick dust as with a mantle, but revealing beneath it the shape and contour of a violin.

CHAPTER VII

John was excited at his discovery, and felt his thoughts confused in a manner that I have often experienced myself on the unexpected receipt of news interesting me deeply, whether for pleasure or pain. Yet at the same time he was half amused at his own excitement, feeling that it was childish to be moved over an event so simple as the finding of a violin in an old cupboard. He soon collected himself and took up the instrument, using great care, as he feared lest age should have rendered the wood brittle or rotten. With some vigorous puffs of breath and a little dusting with a handkerchief he removed the heavy outer coating of cobwebs, and began to see more clearly the delicate curves of the body and of the scroll. A few minutes' more gentle handling left the instrument sufficiently clean to enable him to appreciate its chief points. Its seclusion from the outer world, which the heavy accumulation of dust proved to have been for many years, did not seem to have damaged it in the least; and the fact of a chimney-flue passing through the wall at no great distance had no doubt conduced to maintain the air in the cupboard at an equable temperature. So far as he was able to judge, the wood was as sound as when it left the maker's hands; but the strings were of course broken, and curled up in little tangled knots. The body was of a light-red colour, with a varnish of peculiar lustre and softness. The neck seemed rather longer than ordinary, and the scroll was remarkably bold and free.

The violin which my brother was in the habit of using was a fine Pressenda, given to him on his fifteenth birthday by Mr. Thoresby, his guardian. It was of that maker's later and best period, and a copy of the Stradivarius model. John took this from its case and laid it side by side with his new discovery, meaning to compare them for size and form. He perceived at once that while the model of both was identical, the superiority of the older violin in every detail was so marked as to convince him that it was undoubtedly an instrument of exceptional value. The extreme beauty of its varnish impressed him vividly, and though he had never seen a genuine Stradivarius, he felt a conviction gradually gaining on him that he stood in the presence of a masterpiece of that great maker. On looking into the interior he found that surprisingly little dust had penetrated into it, and by blowing through the sound-holes he soon cleared it sufficiently to enable him to discern a label. He put the candle close to him, and held the violin up so that a little patch of light fell through the sound-hole on to the label. His heart leapt with a violent pulsation as he read the characters, "Antonius Stradiuarius Cremonensis faciebat, 1704." Under ordinary circumstances it would naturally be concluded that such a label was a forgery, but the conditions were entirely altered in the case of a violin found in a forgotten cupboard, with proof so evident of its having remained there for a very long period.

He was not at that time as familiar with the history of the fiddles of the great maker as he, and indeed I also, afterwards became. Thus he was unable to decide how far the exact year of its manufacture would determine its value as compared with other specimens of Stradivarius. But although the Pressenda he had been used to play on was always considered a very fine instrument both in make and varnish, his new discovery so far excelled it in both points as to assure him that it must be one of the Cremonese master's greatest productions.

He examined the violin minutely, scrutinising each separate feature, and finding each in turn to be of the utmost perfection, so far as his knowledge of the instrument would enable him to judge. He lit more candles that he might be able better to see it, and holding it on his knees, sat still admiring it until the dying fire and increasing cold warned him that the night was now far advanced. At last, carrying it to his bedroom, he locked it carefully into a drawer and retired for the night.

He woke next morning with that pleasurable consciousness of there being some reason for gladness, which we feel on waking in seasons of happiness, even before our reason, locating it, reminds us what the actual source of our joy may be. He was at first afraid lest his excitement, working on the imagination, should have led him on the previous night to overestimate the fineness of the instrument, and he took it from the drawer half expecting to be disappointed with its daylight appearance. But a glance sufficed to convince him of the unfounded nature of his suspicions. The various beauties which he had before observed were enhanced a hundredfold by the light of day, and he realised more fully than ever that the instrument was one of altogether exceptional value.

And now, my dear Edward, I shall ask your forgiveness if in the history I have to relate any observation of mine should seem to reflect on the character of your late father, Sir John Maltravers. And I beg you to consider that your father was also my dear and only brother, and that it is inexpressibly painful to me to recount any actions of his which may not seem becoming to a noble gentleman, as he surely was. I only now proceed because, when very near his end, he most strictly enjoined me to narrate these circumstances to you fully when you should come of age. We must humbly remember that to God alone belongs judgment, and that it is not for poor mortals to decide what is right or wrong in certain instances for their fellows, but that each should strive most earnestly to do his own duty.

Your father entirely concealed from me the discovery he had made. It was not till long afterwards that I had it narrated to me, and I only obtained a knowledge of this and many other of the facts which I am now telling you at a date much subsequent to their actual occurrence.

He explained to his servant that he had discovered and opened an old cupboard in the panelling, without mentioning the fact of his having found anything in it, but merely asking him to give instructions for the paint to be mended and the cupboard put into a usable state. Before he had finished a very late breakfast Mr. Gaskell was with him, and it has been a source of lasting regret to me that my brother concealed also from his most intimate and trusted friend the discovery of the previous night. He did, indeed, tell him that he had found and opened an old cupboard in the panelling, but made no mention of there having been anything within. I cannot say what prompted him to this action; for the two young men had for long been on such intimate terms that the one shared almost as a matter of course with the other any pleasure or pain which might fall to his lot. Mr. Gaskell looked at the cupboard with some interest, saying afterwards, "I know now, Johnnie, why the one shelf of the bookcase which stood there was made movable when all the others were fixed. Some former occupant used the cupboard, no doubt, as a secret receptacle for his treasures, and masked it with the book-shelves in front. Who knows what he kept in here, or who he was! I should not be surprised if he were that very man who used to come here so often to hear us play the 'Areopagita,' and whom you saw that night last June. He had the one shelf made, you see, to move so as to give him access to this cavity on occasion: then when he left Oxford, or perhaps died, the mystery was forgotten, and with a few times of painting the cracks closed up."

Mr. Gaskell shortly afterwards took his leave as he had a lecture to attend, and my brother was left alone to the contemplation of his new-found treasure. After some consideration he determined that he would take the instrument to London, and obtain the opinion of an expert as to its authenticity and value. He was well acquainted with the late Mr. George Smart, the celebrated London dealer, from whom his guardian, Mr. Thoresby, had purchased the Pressenda violin which John commonly used. Besides being a dealer in valuable instruments, Mr. Smart was a famous collector of Stradivarius fiddles, esteemed one of the first authorities in Europe in that domain of art, and author of a valuable work of reference in connection with it. It was to him, therefore, that my brother decided to submit the violin, and he wrote a letter to Mr. Smart saying that he should give himself the pleasure of waiting on him the next day on a matter of business. He then called on his tutor, and with some excuse obtained leave to journey to London the next morning. He spent the rest of the day in very carefully cleaning the violin, and noon of the next saw him with it, securely packed, in Mr. Smart's establishment in Bond Street.

Mr. Smart received Sir John Maltravers with deference, demanded in what way he could serve him; and on hearing that his opinion was required on the authenticity of a violin, smiled somewhat dubiously and led the way into a back parlour.

"My dear Sir John," he said, "I hope you have not been led into buying any instrument by a faith in its antiquity. So many good copies of instruments by famous makers and bearing their labels are now afloat, that the chances of obtaining a genuine fiddle from an unrecognised source are quite remote; of hundreds of violins submitted to me for opinion, I find that scarce one in fifty is actually that which it represents itself to be. In fact the only safe rule," he added as a professional commentary, "is never to buy a violin unless you obtain it from a dealer with a reputation to lose, and are prepared to pay a reasonable price for it."

My brother had meanwhile unpacked the violin and laid it on the table. As he took from it the last leaf of silver paper he saw Mr. Smart's smile of condescension fade, and assuming a look of interest and excitement, he stepped forward, took the violin in his hands, and scrutinised it minutely. He turned it over in silence for some moments, looking narrowly at each feature, and even applying the test of a magnifying-glass. At last he said with an altered tone, "Sir John, I have had in my hands nearly all the finest productions of Stradivarius, and thought myself acquainted with every instrument of note that ever left his workshop; but I confess myself mistaken, and apologise to you for the doubt which I expressed as to the instrument you had brought me. This violin is of the great master's golden period, is incontestably genuine, and finer in some respects than any Stradivarius that I have ever seen, not even excepting the famous Dolphin itself. You need be under no apprehension as to its authenticity: no connoisseur could hold it in his hand for a second and entertain a doubt on the point."

My brother was greatly pleased at so favourable a verdict, and Mr. Smart continued:

"The varnish is of that rich red which Stradivarius used in his best period after he had abandoned the yellow tint copied by him at first from his master Amati. I have never seen a varnish thicker or more lustrous, and it shows on the back that peculiar shading to imitate wear which we term 'breaking up.' The purfling also is of an unsurpassable excellence. Its execution is so fine that I should recommend you to use a magnifying-glass for its examination."

So he ran on, finding from moment to moment some new beauties to admire.

My brother was at first anxious lest Mr. Smart should ask him whence so extraordinary an instrument came, but he saw that the expert had already jumped to a conclusion in the matter. He knew that John had recently come of age, and evidently supposed that he had found the violin among the heirlooms of Worth Maltravers. John allowed Mr. Smart to continue in this misconception, merely saying that he had discovered the instrument in an old cupboard, where he had reason to think it had remained hidden for many years.

"Are there no records attached to so splendid an instrument?" asked Mr. Smart. "I suppose it has been with your family a number of years. Do you not know how it came into their possession?"

I believe this was the first occasion on which it had occurred to John to consider what right he had to the possession of the instrument. He had been so excited by its discovery that the question of ownership had never hitherto crossed his mind. The unwelcome suggestion that it was not his after all, that the College might rightfully prefer a claim to it, presented itself to him for a moment; but he set it instantly aside, quieting his conscience with the reflection that this at least was not the moment to make such a disclosure.

He fenced with Mr. Smart's inquiry as best he could, saying that he was ignorant of the history of the instrument, but not contradicting the assumption that it had been a long time in his family's possession.

"It is indeed singular," Mr. Smart continued, "that so magnificent an instrument should have lain buried so long; that even those best acquainted with such matters should be in perfect ignorance of its existence. I shall have to revise the list of famous instruments in the next edition of my 'History of the Violin,' and to write," he added smiling, "a special paragraph on the 'Worth Maltravers Stradivarius.'"

After much more, which I need not narrate, Mr. Smart suggested that the violin should be left with him that he might examine it more at leisure, and that my brother should return in a week's time, when he would have the instrument opened, an operation which would be in any case advisable. "The interior," he added, "appears to be in a strictly original state, and this I shall be able to ascertain when opened. The label is perfect, but if I am not mistaken I can see something higher up on the back which appears like a second label. This excites my interest, as I know of no instance of an instrument bearing two labels."

To this proposal my brother readily assented, being anxious to enjoy alone the pleasure of so gratifying a discovery as that of the undoubted authenticity of the instrument.

As he thought over the matter more at leisure, he grew anxious as to what might be the import of the second label in the violin of which Mr. Smart had spoken. I blush to say that he feared lest it might bear some owner's name or other inscription proving that the instrument had not been so long in the Maltravers family as he had allowed Mr. Smart to suppose. So within so short a time it was possible that Sir John Maltravers of Worth should dread being detected, if not in an absolute falsehood, at least in having by his silence assented to one.

During the ensuing week John remained in an excited and anxious condition. He did little work, and neglected his friends, having his thoughts continually occupied with the strange discovery he had made. I know also that his sense of honour troubled him, and that he was not satisfied with the course he was pursuing. The evening of his return from London he went to Mr. Gaskell's rooms at New College, and spent an hour conversing with him on indifferent subjects. In the course of their talk he proposed to his friend as a moral problem the question of the course of action to be taken were one to find some article of value concealed in his room. Mr. Gaskell answered unhesitatingly that he should feel bound to disclose it to the authorities. He saw that my brother was ill at ease, and with a clearness of judgment which he always exhibited, guessed that he had actually made some discovery of this sort in the old cupboard in his rooms. He could not divine, of course, the exact nature of the object found, and thought it might probably relate to a hoard of gold; but insisted with much urgency on the obligation to at once disclose anything of this kind. My brother, however, misled, I fear, by that feeling of inalienable right which the treasure-hunter experiences over the treasure, paid no more attention to the advice of his friend than to the promptings of his own conscience, and went his way.

From that day, my dear Edward, he began to exhibit a spirit of secretiveness and reserve entirely alien to his own open and honourable disposition, and also saw less of Mr. Gaskell. His friend tried, indeed, to win his confidence and affection in every way in his power; but in spite of this the rift between them widened insensibly, and my brother lost the fellowship and counsel of a true friend at a time when he could ill afford to be without them.

He returned to London the ensuing week, and met Mr. George Smart by appointment in Bond Street. If the expert had been enthusiastic on a former occasion, he was ten times more so on this. He spoke in terms almost of rapture about the violin. He had compared it with two magnificent instruments in the collection of the late Mr. James Loding, then the finest in Europe; and it was admittedly superior to either, both in the delicate markings of its wood and singularly fine varnish. "Of its tone," he said, "we cannot, of course, yet pronounce with certainty, but I am very sure that its voice will not belie its splendid exterior. It has been carefully opened, and is in a strangely perfect condition. Several persons eminently qualified to judge unite with me in considering that it has been exceedingly little played upon, and admit that never has so intact an interior been seen. The scroll is exceptionally bold and original. Although undoubtedly from the hand of the great master, this is of a pattern entirely different and distinct from any that have ever come under my observation."

He then pointed out to my brother that the side lines of the scroll were unusually deeply cut, and that the front of it projected far more than is common with such instruments.

"The most remarkable feature," he concluded, "is that the instrument bears a double label. Besides the label which you have already seen bearing 'Antonius Stradiuarius Cremonensis faciebat,' with the date of his most splendid period, 1704, so clearly that the ink seems scarcely dry, there is another smaller one higher up on the back which I will show you."

He took the violin apart and showed him a small label with characters written in faded ink. "That is the writing of Antonio Stradivarius himself, and is easily recognisable, though it is much firmer than a specimen which I once saw, written in extreme old age, and giving his name and the date 1736. He was then ninety-two, and died in the following year. But this, as you will see, does not give his name, but merely the two words 'Porphyrius philosophus.' What this may refer to I cannot say: it is beyond my experience. My friend Mr. Calvert has suggested that Stradivarius may have dedicated this violin to the pagan philosopher, or named it after him; but this seems improbable. I have, indeed, heard of two famous violins being called 'Peter' and 'Paul,' but the instances of such naming are very rare; and I believe it to be altogether without precedent to find a name attached thus on a label.

"In any case, I must leave this matter to your ingenuity to decipher. Neither the sound-post nor the bass-bar have ever been moved, and you see here a Stradivarius violin wearing exactly the same appearance as it once wore in the great master's workshop, and in exactly the same condition; yet I think the belly is sufficiently strong to stand modern stringing. I should advise you to leave the instrument with me for some little while, that I may give it due care and attention and ensure its being properly strung."

My brother thanked him and left the violin with him, saying that he would instruct him later by letter to what address he wished it sent.

CHAPTER VIII

Within a few days after this the autumn term came to an end, and in the second week of December John returned to Worth Maltravers for the Christmas vacation. His advent was always a very great pleasure to me, and on this occasion I had looked forward to his company with anticipation keener than usual, as I had been disappointed of the visit of a friend and had spent the last month alone. After the joy of our first meeting had somewhat sobered, it was not long before I remarked a change in his manner, which puzzled me. It was not that he was less kind to me, for I think he was even more tenderly forbearing and gentle than I had ever known him, but I had an uneasy feeling that some shadow had crept in between us. It was the small cloud rising in the distance that afterwards darkened his horizon and mine. I missed the old candour and open-hearted frankness that he had always shown; and there seemed to be always something in the background which he was trying to keep from me. It was obvious that his thoughts were constantly elsewhere, so much so that on more than one occasion he returned vague and incoherent answers to my questions. At times I was content to believe that he was in love, and that his thoughts were with Miss Constance Temple; but even so, I could not persuade myself that his altered manner was to be thus entirely accounted for. At other times a dazed air, entirely foreign to his bright disposition, which I observed particularly in the morning, raised in my mind the terrible suspicion that he was in the habit of taking some secret narcotic or other deleterious drug.

We had never spent a Christmas away from Worth Maltravers, and it had always been a season of quiet joy for both of us. But under these altered circumstances it was a great relief and cause of thankfulness to me to receive a letter from Mrs. Temple inviting us both to spend Christmas and New Year at Royston. This invitation had upon my brother precisely the effect that I had hoped for. It roused him from his moody condition, and he professed much pleasure in accepting it, especially as he had never hitherto been in Derbyshire.

There was a small but very agreeable party at Royston, and we passed a most enjoyable fortnight. My brother seemed thoroughly to have shaken off his indisposition; and I saw my fondest hopes realised in the warm attachment which was evidently springing up between him and Miss Constance Temple.

Our visit drew near its close, and it was within a week of John's return to Oxford. Mrs. Temple celebrated the termination of the Christmas festivities by giving a ball on Twelfth-night, at which a large party were present, including most of the county families. Royston was admirably adapted for such entertainments, from the number and great size of its reception-rooms. Though Elizabethan in date and external appearance, succeeding generations had much modified and enlarged the house; and an ancestor in the middle of the last century had built at the back an enormous hall after the classic model, and covered it with a dome or cupola. In this room the dancing went forward. Supper was served in the older hall in the front, and it was while this was in progress that a thunderstorm began. The rarity of such a phenomenon in the depth of winter formed the subject of general remark; but though the lightning was extremely brilliant, being seen distinctly through the curtained windows, the storm appeared to be at some distance, and, except for one peal, the thunder was not loud. After supper dancing was resumed, and I was taking part in a polka (called, I remember, the "King Pippin"), when my partner pointed out that one of the footmen wished to speak with me. I begged him to lead me to one side, and the servant then informed me that my brother was ill. Sir John, he said, had been seized with a fainting fit, but had been got to bed, and was being attended by Dr. Empson, a physician who chanced to be present among the visitors.

I at once left the hall and hurried to my brother's room. On the way I met Mrs. Temple and Constance, the latter much agitated and in tears. Mrs. Temple assured me that Dr. Empson reported favourably of my brother's condition, attributing his faintness to over-exertion in the dancing-room. The medical man had got him to bed with the assistance of Sir John's valet, had given him a quieting draught, and ordered that he should not be disturbed for the present. It was better that I should not enter the room; she begged that I would kindly comfort and reassure Constance, who was much upset, while she herself returned to her guests.

I led Constance to my bedroom, where there was a bright fire burning, and calmed her as best I could. Her interest in my brother was evidently very real and unaffected, and while not admitting her partiality for him in words, she made no effort to conceal her sentiments from me. I kissed her tenderly, and bade her narrate the circumstances of John's attack.

It seemed that after supper they had gone upstairs into the music-room, and he had himself proposed that they should walk thence into the picture-gallery, where they would better be able to see the lightning, which was then particularly vivid. The picture-gallery at Royston is a very long, narrow, and rather low room, running the whole length of the south wing, and terminating in a large Tudor oriel or flat bay window looking east. In this oriel they had sat for some time watching the flashes, and the wintry landscape revealed for an instant and then plunged into outer blackness. The gallery itself was not illuminated, and the effect of the lightning was very fine.

There had been an unusually bright flash accompanied by that single reverberating peal of thunder which I had previously noticed. Constance had spoken to my brother, but he had not replied, and in a moment she saw that he had swooned. She summoned aid without delay, but it was some short time before consciousness had been restored to him.

She had concluded this narrative, and sat holding my hand in hers. We were speculating on the cause of my brother's illness, thinking it might be due to over-exertion, or to sitting in a chilly atmosphere as the picture-gallery was not warmed, when Mrs. Temple knocked at the door and said that John was now more composed and desired earnestly to see me.

On entering my brother's bedroom I found him sitting up in bed wearing a dressing-gown. Parnham, his valet, who was arranging the fire, left the room as I came in. A chair stood at the head of the bed and I sat down by him. He took my hand in his and without a word burst into tears. "Sophy," he said, "I am so unhappy, and I have sent for you to tell you of my trouble, because I know you will be forbearing to me. An hour ago all seemed so bright. I was sitting in the picture-gallery with Constance, whom I love dearly. We had been watching the lightning, till the thunder had grown fainter and the storm seemed past. I was just about to ask her to become my wife when a brighter flash than all the rest burst on us, and I saw - I saw, Sophy, standing in the gallery as close to me as you are now - I saw - that man I told you about at Oxford; and then this faintness came on me."

"Whom do you mean?" I said, not understanding what he spoke of, and thinking for a moment he referred to someone else. "Did you see Mr. Gaskell?"

"No, it was not he; but that dead man whom I saw rising from my wicker chair the night you went away from Oxford."

You will perhaps smile at my weakness, my dear Edward, and indeed I had at that time no justification for it; but I assure you that I have not yet forgotten, and never shall forget, the impression of overwhelming horror which his words produced upon me. It seemed as though a fear which had hitherto stood vague and shadowy in the background, began now to advance towards me, gathering more distinctness as it approached. There was to me something morbidly terrible about the apparition of this man at such a momentous crisis in my brother's life, and I at once recognised that unknown form as being the shadow which was gradually stealing between John and myself. Though I feigned incredulity as best I might, and employed those arguments or platitudes which will always be used on such occasions, urging that such a phantom could only exist in a mind disordered by physical weakness, my brother was not deceived by my words, and perceived in a moment that I did not even believe in them myself.

"Dearest Sophy," he said, with a much calmer air, "let us put aside all dissimulation. I know that what I have to-night seen, and that what I saw last summer at Oxford, are not phantoms of my brain; and I believe that you too in your inmost soul are convinced of this truth. Do not, therefore, endeavour to persuade me to the contrary. If I am not to believe the evidence of my senses, it were better at once to admit my madness - and I know that I am not mad. Let us rather consider what such an appearance can portend, and who the man is who is thus presented. I cannot explain to you why this appearance inspires me with so great a revulsion. I can only say that in its presence I seem to be brought face to face with some abysmal and repellent wickedness. It is not that the form he wears is hideous. Last night I saw him exactly as I saw him at Oxford - his face waxen pale, with a sneering mouth, the same lofty forehead, and hair brushed straight up so as almost to appear standing on end. He wore the same long coat of green cloth and white waistcoat. He seemed as if he had been standing listening to what we said, though we had not seen him till this bright flash of lightning made him manifest. You will remember that when I saw him at Oxford his eyes were always cast down, so that I never knew their colour. This time they were wide open; indeed he was looking full at us, and they were a light brown and very brilliant."

I saw that my brother was exciting himself, and was still weak from his recent swoon. I knew, too, that any ordinary person of strong mind would say at once that his brain wandered, and yet I had a dreadful conviction all the while that what he told me was the truth. All I could do was to beg him to calm himself, and to reflect how vain such fancies must be. "We must trust, dear John," I said, "in God. I am sure that so long as we are not living in conscious sin, we shall never be given over to any evil power; and I know my brother too well to think that he is doing anything he knows to be evil. If there be evil spirits, as we are taught there are, we are taught also that there are good spirits stronger than they, who will protect us."

So I spoke with him a little while, until he grew calmer; and then we talked of Constance and of his love for her. He was deeply pleased to hear from me how she had shown such obvious, signs of interest in his illness, and sincere affection for him. In any case, he made me promise that I would never mention to her either what he had seen this night or last summer at Oxford.

It had grown late, and the undulating beat of the dances, which had been distinctly sensible in his room - even though we could not hear any definite noise - had now ceased. Mrs. Temple knocked at the door as she went to bed and inquired how he did, giving him at the same time a kind message of sympathy from Constance, which afforded him much gratification. After she had left I prepared also to retire; but before going he begged me to take a prayer-book lying on the table, and to read aloud a collect which he pointed out. It was that for the second Sunday in Lent, and evidently well known to him. As I read it the words seemed to bear a new and deeper significance, and my heart repeated with fervour the petition for protection from those "evil thoughts which may assault and hurt the soul." I bade him good night and went away very sorrowful. Parnham, at John's request, had arranged to sleep on a sofa in his master's bedroom.

I rose betimes the next morning and inquired at my brother's room how he was. Parnham reported that he had passed a restless night, and on entering a little later I found him in a high fever, slightly delirious, and evidently not so well as when I saw him last. Mrs. Temple, with much kindness and forethought, had begged Dr. Empson to remain at Royston for the night, and he was soon in attendance on his patient. His verdict was sufficiently grave: John was suffering from a sharp access of brain-fever; his condition afforded cause for alarm; he could not answer for any turn his sickness might take. You will easily imagine how much this intelligence affected me; and Mrs. Temple and Constance shared my anxiety and solicitude. Constance and I talked much with one another that morning.

Unaffected anxiety had largely removed her reserve, and she spoke openly of her feelings towards my brother, not concealing her partiality for him. I on my part let her understand how welcome to me would be any union between her and John, and how sincerely I should value her as a sister.

It was a wild winter's morning, with some snow falling and a high wind. The house was in the disordered condition which is generally observable on the day following a ball or other important festivity. I roamed restlessly about, and at last found my way to the picture-gallery, which had formed the scene of John's adventure on the previous night. I had never been in this part of the house before, as it contained no facilities for heating, and so often remained shut in the winter months. I found a listless pleasure in admiring the pictures which lined the walls, most of them being portraits of former members of the family, including the famous picture of Sir Ralph Temple and his family, attributed to Holbein. I had reached the end of the gallery and sat down in the oriel watching the snow-flakes falling sparsely, and the evergreens below me waving wildly in the sudden rushes of the wind. My thoughts were busy with the events of the previous evening - with John's illness, with the ball - and I found myself humming the air of a waltz that had caught my fancy. At last I turned away from the garden scene towards the gallery, and as I did so my eyes fell on a remarkable picture just opposite to me.

It was a full-length portrait of a young man, life-size, and I had barely time to appreciate even its main features when I knew that I had before me the painted counterfeit of my brother's vision. The discovery caused me a violent shock, and it was with an infinite repulsion that I recognised at once the features and dress of the man whom John had seen rising from the chair at Oxford. So accurately had my brother's imagination described him to me, that it seemed as if I had myself seen him often before. I noted each feature, comparing them with my brother's description, and finding them all familiar and corresponding exactly. He was a man still in the prime of life. His features were regular and beautifully modelled; yet there was something in his face that inspired me with a deep aversion, though his brown eyes were open and brilliant. His mouth was sharply cut, with a slight sneer on the lips, and his complexion of that extreme pallor which had impressed itself deeply on my brother's imagination and my own.

After the first intense surprise had somewhat subsided, I experienced a feeling of great relief, for here was an extraordinary explanation of my brother's vision of last night. It was certain that the flash of lightning had lit up this ill-starred picture, and that to his predisposed fancy the painted figure had stood forth as an actual embodiment. That such an incident, however startling, should have been able to fling John into a brain-fever, showed that he must already have been in a very low and reduced state, on which excitement would act much more powerfully than on a more robust condition of health. A similar state of weakness, perturbed by the excitement of his passion for Constance Temple, might surely also have conjured up the vision which he thought he saw the night of our leaving Oxford in the summer. These thoughts, my dear Edward, gave me great relief; for it seemed a comparatively trivial matter that my brother should be ill, even seriously ill, if only his physical indisposition could explain away the supernatural dread which had haunted us for the past six months. The clouds were breaking up. It was evident that John had been seriously unwell for some months; his physical weakness had acted on his brain; and I had lent colour to his wandering fancies by being alarmed by them, instead of rejecting them at once or gently laughing them away as I should have done. But these glad thoughts took me too far, and I was suddenly brought up by a reflection that did not admit of so simple an explanation. If the man's form my brother saw at Oxford were merely an effort of disordered imagination, how was it that he had been able to describe it exactly like that represented in this picture? He had never in his life been to Royston, therefore he could have no image of the picture impressed unconsciously on or hidden away in his mind. Yet his description had never varied. It had been so close as to enable me to produce in my fancy a vivid representation of the man he had seen; and here I had before me the features and dress exactly reproduced. In the presence of a coincidence so extraordinary reason stood confounded, and I knew not what to think. I walked nearer to the picture and scrutinised it closely.

The dress corresponded in every detail with that which my brother had described the figure as wearing at Oxford: a long cut-away coat of green cloth with an edge of gold embroidery, a white satin waistcoat with sprigs of embroidered roses, gold-lace at the pocket-holes, buff silk knee-breeches, and low down on the finely modelled neck a full cravat of rich lace. The figure was posed negligently against a fluted stone pedestal or short column on which the left elbow leant, and the right foot was crossed lightly over the left. His shoes were of polished black leather with heavy silver buckles, and the whole costume was very old-fashioned, and such as I had only seen worn at fancy dress balls. On the foot of the pedestal was the painter's name, "BATTONI pinxit, Romæ, 1750." On the top of the pedestal, and under his left elbow, was a long roll apparently of music, of which one end, unfolded, hung over the edge.

For some minutes I stood still gazing at this portrait which so much astonished me, but turned on hearing footsteps in the gallery, and saw Constance, who had come to seek for me.

"Constance," I said, "whose portrait is this? It is a very striking picture, is it not?"

"Yes, it is a splendid painting, though of a very bad man. His name was Adrian Temple, and he once owned Royston. I do not know much about him, but I believe he was very wicked and very clever. My mother would be able to tell you more. It is a picture we none of us like, although so finely painted; and perhaps because he was always pointed out to me from childhood as a bad man, I have myself an aversion to it. It is singular that when the very bright flash of lightning came last night while your brother John and I were sitting here, it lit this picture with a dazzling glare that made the figure stand out so strangely as to seem almost alive. It was just after that I found that John had fainted."

The memory was not a pleasant one for either of us and we changed the subject. "Come," I said, "let us leave the gallery, it is very cold here."

Though I said nothing more at the time, her words had made a great impression on me. It was so strange that, even with the little she knew of this Adrian Temple, she should speak at once of his notoriously evil life, and of her personal dislike to the picture. Remembering what my brother had said on the previous night, that in the presence of this man he felt himself brought face to face with some indescribable wickedness, I could not but be surprised at the coincidence. The whole story seemed to me now to resemble one of those puzzle pictures or maps which I have played with as a child, where each bit fits into some other until the outline is complete. It was as if I were finding the pieces one by one of a bygone history, and fitting them to one another until some terrible whole should be gradually built up and stand out in its complete deformity.

Dr. Empson spoke gravely of John's illness, and entertained without reluctance the proposal of Mrs. Temple, that Dr. Dobie, a celebrated physician in Derby, should be summoned to a consultation. Dr. Dobie came more than once, and was at last able to report an amendment in John's condition, though both the doctors absolutely forbade anyone to visit him, and said that under the most favourable circumstances a period of some weeks must elapse before he could be moved.

Mrs. Temple invited me to remain at Royston until my brother should be sufficiently convalescent to be moved; and both she and Constance, while regretting the cause, were good enough to express themselves pleased that accident should detain me so long with them.

As the reports of the doctors became gradually more favourable, and our minds were in consequence more free to turn to other subjects, I spoke to Mrs. Temple one day about the picture, saying that it interested me, and asking for some particulars as to the life of Adrian Temple.

"My dear child," she said, "I had rather that you should not exhibit any curiosity as to this man, whom I wish that we had not to call an ancestor. I know little of him myself, and indeed his life was of such a nature as no woman, much less a young girl, would desire to be well acquainted with. He was, I believe, a man of remarkable talent, and spent most of his time between Oxford and Italy, though he visited Royston occasionally, and built the large hall here, which we use as a dancing-room. Before he was twenty wild stories were prevalent as to his licentious life, and by thirty his name was a by-word among sober and upright people. He had constantly with him at Oxford and on his travels a boon companion called Jocelyn, who aided him in his wickednesses, until on one of their Italian tours Jocelyn left him suddenly and became a Trappist monk. It was currently reported that some wild deed of Adrian Temple had shocked even him, and so outraged his surviving instincts of common humanity that he was snatched as a brand from the burning and enabled to turn back even in the full tide of his wickedness. However that may be, Adrian went on in his evil course without him, and about four years after disappeared. He was last heard of in Naples, and it is believed that he succumbed during a violent outbreak of the plague which took place in Italy in the autumn of 1752. That is all I shall tell you of him, and indeed I know little more myself. The only good trait that has been handed down concerning him is that he was a masterly musician, performing admirably upon the violin, which he had studied under the illustrious Tartini himself. Yet even his art of music, if tradition speaks the truth, was put by him to the basest of uses."

I apologised for my indiscretion in asking her about an unpleasant subject, and at the same time thanked her for what she had seen fit to tell me, professing myself much interested, as indeed I really was.

"Was he a handsome man?"

"That is a girl's question," she answered, smiling. "He is said to have been very handsome; and indeed his picture, painted after his first youth was past, would still lead one to suppose so. But his complexion was spoiled, it is said, and turned to deadly white by certain experiments, which it is neither possible nor seemly for us to understand. His face is of that long oval shape of which all the Temples are proud, and he had brown eyes: we sometimes tease Constance, saying she is like Adrian."

It was indeed true, as I remembered after Mrs. Temple had pointed it out, that Constance had a peculiarly long and oval face. It gave her, I think, an air of staid and placid beauty, which formed in my eyes, and perhaps in John's also, one of her greatest attractions.

"I do not like even his picture," Mrs. Temple continued, "and strange tales have been narrated of it by idle servants which are not worth repeating. I have sometimes thought of destroying it; but my late husband, being a Temple, would never hear of this, or even of removing it from its present place in the gallery; and I should be loath to do anything now contrary to his wishes, once so strongly expressed. It is, besides, very perfect from an artistic point of view, being painted by Battoni, and in his happiest manner."

I could never glean more from Mrs. Temple; but what she told me interested me deeply. It seemed another link in the chain, though I could scarcely tell why, that Adrian Temple should be so great a musician and violinist. I had, I fancy, a dim idea of that malign and outlawed spirit sitting alone in darkness for a hundred years, until he was called back by the sweet tones of the Italian music, and the lilt of the "Areopagita" that he had loved so long ago.

CHAPTER IX

John's recovery, though continuous and satisfactory, was but slow; and it was not until Easter, which fell early, that his health was pronounced to be entirely re-established. The last few weeks of his convalescence had proved to all of us a time of thankful and tranquil enjoyment. If I may judge from my own experience, there are few epochs in our life more favourable to the growth of sentiments of affection and piety, or more full of pleasurable content, than is the period of gradual recovery from serious illness. The chastening effect of our recent sickness has not yet passed away, and we are at once grateful to our Creator for preserving us, and to our friends for the countless acts of watchful kindness which it is the peculiar property of illness to evoke.

No mother ever nursed a son more tenderly than did Mrs. Temple nurse my brother, and before his restoration to health was complete the attachment between him and Constance had ripened into a formal betrothal. Such an alliance was, as I have before explained, particularly suitable, and its prospect afforded the most lively pleasure to all those concerned. The month of March had been unusually mild, and Royston being situated in a valley, as is the case with most houses of that date, was well sheltered from cold winds. It had, moreover, a south aspect, and as my brother gradually gathered strength, Constance and he and I would often sit out of doors in the soft spring mornings. We put an easy-chair with many cushions for him on the gravel by the front door, where the warmth of the sun was reflected from the red brick walls, and he would at times read aloud to us while we were engaged with our crochet-work. Mr. Tennyson had just published anonymously a first volume of poems, and the sober dignity of his verse well suited our frame of mind at that time. The memory of those pleasant spring mornings, my dear Edward, has not yet passed away, and I can still smell the sweet moist scent of the violets, and see the bright colours of the crocus-flowers in the parterres in front of us.

John's mind seemed to be gathering strength with his body. He had apparently flung off the cloud which had overshadowed him before his illness, and avoided entirely any reference to those unpleasant events which had been previously so constantly in his thoughts. I had, indeed, taken an early opportunity of telling him of my discovery of the picture of Adrian Temple, as I thought it would tend to show him that at least the last appearance of this ghostly form admitted of a rational explanation. He seemed glad to hear of this, but did not exhibit the same interest in the matter that I had expected, and allowed it at once to drop. Whether through lack of interest, or from a lingering dislike to revisit the spot where he was seized with illness, he did not, I believe, once enter the picture-gallery before he left Royston.

I cannot say as much for myself. The picture of Adrian Temple exerted a curious fascination over me, and I constantly took an opportunity of studying it. It was, indeed, a beautiful work; and perhaps because John's recovery gave a more cheerful tone to my thoughts, or perhaps from the power of custom to dull even the keenest antipathies, I gradually got to lose much of the feeling of aversion which it had at first inspired. In time the unpleasant look grew less unpleasing, and I noticed more the beautiful oval of the face, the brown eyes, and the fine chiselling of the features. Sometimes, too, I felt a deep pity for so clever a gentleman who had died young, and whose life, were it ever so wicked, must often have been also lonely and bitter. More than once I had been discovered by Mrs. Temple or Constance sitting looking at the picture, and they had gently laughed at me, saying that I had fallen in love with Adrian Temple.

One morning in early April, when the sun was streaming brightly through the oriel, and the picture received a fuller light than usual, it occurred to me to examine closely the scroll of music painted as hanging over the top of the pedestal on which the figure leant. I had hitherto thought that the signs depicted on it were merely such as painters might conventionally use to represent a piece of musical notation. This has generally been the case, I think, in such pictures as I have ever seen in which a piece of music has been introduced. I mean that while the painting gives a general representation of the musical staves, no attempt is ever made to paint any definite notes such as would enable an actual piece to be identified. Though, as I write this, I do remember that on the monument to Handel in Westminster Abbey there is represented a musical scroll similar to that in Adrian Temple's picture, but actually sculptured with the opening phrase of the majestic melody, "I know that my Redeemer liveth."

On this morning, then, at Royston I thought I perceived that there were painted on the scroll actual musical staves, bars, and notes; and my interest being excited, I stood upon a chair so as better to examine them. Though time had somewhat obscured this portion of the picture as with a veil or film, yet I made out that the painter had intended to depict some definite piece of music. In another moment I saw that the air represented consisted of the opening bars of the Gagliarda in the suite by Graziani with which my brother and I were so well acquainted. Though I believe that I had not seen the volume of music in which that piece was contained more than twice, yet the melody was very familiar to me, and I had no difficulty whatever in making myself sure that I had here before me the air of the Gagliarda and none other. It was true that it was only roughly painted, but to one who knew the tune there was no room left for doubt.

Here was a new cause, I will not say for surprise, but for reflection. It might, of course, have been merely a coincidence that the artist should have chosen to paint in this picture this particular piece of music; but it seemed more probable that it had actually been a favourite air of Adrian Temple, and that he had chosen deliberately to have it represented with him. This discovery I kept entirely to myself, not thinking it wise to communicate it to my brother, lest by doing so I might reawaken his interest in a subject which I hoped he had finally dismissed from his thoughts.

In the second week of April the happy party at Royston was dispersed, John returning to Oxford for the summer term, Mrs.

Temple making a short visit to Scotland, and Constance coming to Worth Maltravers to keep me company for a time.

It was John's last term at Oxford. He expected to take his degree in June, and his marriage with Constance Temple had been provisionally arranged for the September following. He returned to Magdalen Hall in the best of spirits, and found his rooms looking cheerful with well-filled flower-boxes in the windows. I shall not detain you with any long narration of the events of the term, as they have no relation to the present history. I will only say that I believe my brother applied himself diligently to his studies, and took his amusement mostly on horseback, riding two horses which he had had sent to him from Worth Maltravers.

About the second week after his return he received a letter from Mr. George Smart to the effect that the Stradivarius violin was now in complete order. Subsequent examination, Mr. Smart wrote, and the unanimous verdict of connoisseurs whom he had consulted, had merely confirmed the views he had at first expressed - namely, that the violin was of the finest quality, and that my brother had in his possession a unique and intact example of Stradivarius's best period. He had had it properly strung; and as the bass-bar had never been moved, and was of a stronger nature than that usual at the period of its manufacture, he had considered it unnecessary to replace it. If any signs should become visible of its being inadequate to support the tension of modern stringing, another could be easily substituted for it at a later date. He had allowed a young German virtuoso to play on it, and though this gentleman was one of the first living performers, and had had an opportunity of handling many splendid instruments, he assured Mr. Smart that he had never performed on one that could in any way compare with this. My brother wrote in reply thanking him, and begging that the violin might be sent to Magdalen Hall.

The pleasant musical evenings, however, which John had formerly been used to spend in the company of Mr. Gaskell were now entirely pretermitted. For though there was no cause for any diminution of friendship between them, and though on Mr. Gaskell's part there was an ardent desire to maintain their former intimacy, yet the two young men saw less and less of one another, until their intercourse was confined to an accidental greeting in the street. I believe that during all this time my brother played very frequently on the Stradivarius violin, but always alone. Its very possession seemed to have engendered from the first in his mind a secretive tendency which, as I have already observed, was entirely alien to his real disposition. As he had concealed its discovery from his sister, so he had also from his friend, and Mr. Gaskell remained in complete ignorance of the existence of such an instrument.

On the evening of its arrival from London, John seems to have carefully unpacked the violin and tried it with a new bow of Tourte's make which he had purchased of Mr. Smart. He had shut the heavy outside door of his room before beginning to play, so that no one might enter unawares; and he told me afterwards that though he had naturally expected from the instrument a very fine tone, yet its actual merits so far exceeded his anticipations as entirely to overwhelm him. The sound issued from it in a volume of such depth and purity as to give an impression of the passages being chorded, or even of another violin being played at the same time. He had had, of course, no opportunity of practising during his illness, and so expected to find his skill with the bow somewhat diminished; but he perceived, on the contrary, that his performance was greatly improved, and that he was playing with a mastery and feeling of which he had never before been conscious. While attributing this improvement very largely to the beauty of the instrument on which he was performing, yet he could not but believe that by his illness, or in some other unexplained way, he had actually acquired a greater freedom of wrist and fluency of expression, with which reflection he was not a little elated. He had had a lock fixed on the cupboard in which he had originally found the violin, and here he carefully deposited it on each occasion after playing, before he opened the outer door of his room.

So the summer term passed away. The examinations had come in their due time, and were now over. Both the young men had submitted themselves to the ordeal, and while neither would of course have admitted as much to anyone else, both felt secretly that they had no reason to be dissatisfied with their performance. The results would not be published for some weeks to come. The last night of the term had arrived, the last night too of John's Oxford career. It was near nine o'clock, but still quite light, and the rich orange glow of sunset had not yet left the sky. The air was warm and sultry, as on that eventful evening when just a year ago he had for the first time seen the figure or the illusion of the figure of Adrian Temple. Since that time he had played the "Areopagita" many, many times; but there had never been any reappearance of that form, nor even had the once familiar creaking of the wicker chair ever made itself heard. As he sat alone in his room, thinking with a natural melancholy that he had seen the sun set for the last time on his student life, and reflecting on the possibilities of the future and perhaps on opportunities wasted in the past, the memory of that evening last June recurred strongly to his imagination, and he felt an irresistible impulse to play once more the "Areopagita." He unlocked the now familiar cupboard and took out the violin, and never had the exquisite gradations of colour in its varnish appeared to greater advantage than in the soft mellow light of the fading day. As he began the Gagliarda he looked at the wicker chair, half expecting to see a form he well knew seated in it; but nothing of the kind ensued, and he concluded the "Areopagita" without the occurrence of any unusual phenomenon.

It was just at its close that he heard some one knocking at the outer door. He hurriedly locked away the violin and opened the "oak." It was Mr. Gaskell. He came in rather awkwardly, as though not sure whether he would be welcomed.

"Johnnie," he began, and stopped.

The force of ancient habit sometimes, dear nephew, leads us unwittingly to accost those who were once our friends by a familiar or nick-name long after the intimacy that formerly justified it has vanished. But sometimes we intentionally revert to the use of such a name, not wishing to proclaim openly, as it were, by a more formal address that we are no longer the friends we once were. I think this latter was the case with Mr. Gaskell as he repeated the familiar name.

"Johnnie, I was passing down New College Lane, and heard the violin from your open windows. You were playing the 'Areopagita,' and it all sounded so familiar to me that I thought I must come up. I am not interrupting you, am I?"

"No, not at all," John answered.

"It is the last night of our undergraduate life, the last night we shall meet in Oxford as students. To-morrow we make our bow to youth and become men. We have not seen much of each other this term at any rate, and I daresay that is my fault. But at least let us part as friends. Surely our friends are not so many that we can afford to fling them lightly away."

He held out his hand frankly, and his voice trembled a little as he spoke - partly perhaps from real emotion, but more probably from the feeling of reluctance which I have noticed men always exhibit to discovering any sentiment deeper than those usually deemed conventional in correct society. My brother was moved by his obvious wish to renew their former friendship, and grasped the proffered hand.

There was a minute's pause, and then the conversation was resumed, a little stiffly at first, but more freely afterwards. They spoke on many indifferent subjects, and Mr. Gaskell congratulated John on the prospect of his marriage, of which he had heard. As he at length rose up to take his departure, he said, "You must have practised the violin diligently of late, for I never knew anyone make so rapid progress with it as you have done. As I came along I was spellbound by your music. I never before heard you bring from the instrument so exquisite a tone: the chorded passages were so powerful that I believed there had been another person playing with you. Your Pressenda is certainly a finer instrument than I ever imagined."

My brother was pleased with Mr. Gaskell's compliment, and the latter continued, "Let me enjoy the pleasure of playing with you once more in Oxford; let us play the 'Areopagita.'"

And so saying he opened the pianoforte and sat down.

John was turning to take out the Stradivarius when he remembered that he had never even revealed its existence to Mr. Gaskell, and that if he now produced it an explanation must follow. In a moment his mood changed, and with less geniality he excused himself, somewhat awkwardly, from complying with the request, saying that he was fatigued.

Mr. Gaskell was evidently hurt at his friend's altered manner, and without renewing his petition rose at once from the pianoforte, and after a little forced conversation took his departure. On leaving he shook my brother by the hand, wished him all prosperity in his marriage and after-life, and said, "Do not entirely forget your old comrade, and remember that if at any time you should stand in need of a true friend, you know where to find him!"

John heard his footsteps echoing down the passage and made a half-involuntary motion towards the door as if to call him back, but did not do so, though he thought over his last words then and on a subsequent occasion.

CHAPTER X

The summer was spent by us in the company of Mrs. Temple and Constance, partly at Royston and partly at Worth Maltravers. John had again hired the cutter-yacht Palestine, and the whole party made several expeditions in her. Constance was entirely devoted to her lover; her life seemed wrapped up in his; she appeared to have no existence except in his presence.

I can scarcely enumerate the reasons which prompted such thoughts, but during these months I sometimes found myself wondering if John still returned her affection as ardently as I knew had once been the case. I can certainly call to mind no single circumstance which could justify me in such a suspicion. He performed punctiliously all those thousand little acts of devotion which are expected of an accepted lover; he seemed to take pleasure in perfecting any scheme of enjoyment to amuse her; and yet the impression grew in my mind that he no longer felt the same heart-whole love to her that she bore him, and that he had himself shown six months earlier. I cannot say, my dear Edward, how lively was the grief that even the suspicion of such a fact caused me, and I continually rebuked myself for entertaining for a moment a thought so unworthy, and dismissed it from my mind with reprobation. Alas! ere long it was sure again to make itself felt. We had all seen the Stradivarius violin; indeed it was impossible for my brother longer to conceal it from us, as he now played continually on it. He did not recount to us the story of its discovery, contenting himself with saying that he had become possessed of it at Oxford. We imagined naturally that he had purchased it; and for this I was sorry, as I feared Mr. Thoresby, his guardian, who had given him some years previously an excellent violin by Pressenda, might feel hurt at seeing his present so unceremoniously laid aside. None of us were at all intimately acquainted with the fancies of fiddle-collectors, and were consequently quite ignorant of the enormous value that fashion attached to so splendid an instrument. Even had we known, I do not think that we should have been surprised at John purchasing it; for he had recently come of age, and was in possession of so large a fortune as would amply justify him in such an indulgence had he wished to gratify it. No one, however, could remain unaware of the wonderful musical qualities of the instrument. Its rich and melodious tones would commend themselves even to the most unmusical ear, and formed a subject of constant remark. I noticed also that my brother's knowledge of the violin had improved in a very perceptible manner, for it was impossible to attribute the great beauty and power of his present performance entirely to the excellence of the instrument he was using. He appeared more than ever devoted to the art, and would shut himself up in his room alone for two or more hours together for the purpose of playing the violin - a habit which was a source of sorrow to Constance, for he would never allow her to sit with him on such occasions, as she naturally wished to do.

So the summer fled. I should have mentioned that in July, after going up to complete the viva-voce part of their examination, both Mr. Gaskell and John received information that they had obtained "first-classes." The young men had, it appears, done excellently well, and both had secured a place in that envied division of the first-class which was called "above the line." John's success proved a source of much pleasure to us all, and mutual congratulations were freely exchanged. We were pleased also at Mr. Gaskell's high place, remembering the kindness which he had shown us at Oxford in the previous year. I desired to send him my compliments and felicitations when he should next be writing to him. I did not doubt that my brother would return Mr. Gaskell's congratulations, which he had already received: he said, however, that his friend had given no address to which he could write, and so the matter dropped.

On the 1st of September John and Constance Temple were married. The wedding took place at Royston, and by John's special desire (with which Constance fully agreed) the ceremony was of a strictly private and unpretentious nature. The newly married pair had determined to spend their honeymoon in Italy, and left for the Continent in the forenoon.

Mrs. Temple invited me to remain with her for the present at Royston, which I was very glad to do, feeling deeply the loss of a favourite brother, and looking forward with dismay to six weeks of loneliness which must elapse before I should again see him and my dearest Constance.

We received news of our travellers about a fortnight afterwards, and then heard from them at frequent intervals. Constance wrote in the best of spirits, and with the keenest appreciation. She had never travelled in Switzerland or Italy before and all was enchantingly novel to her. They had journeyed through Basle to Lucerne, spending a few days in that delightful spot, and thence proceeding by the Simplon Pass to Lugano and the Italian lakes. Then we heard that they had gone further south than had been at first contemplated; they had reached Rome, and were intending to go on to Naples.

After the first few weeks we neither of us received any more letters from John. It was always Constance who wrote, and even her letters grew very much less frequent than had at first been the case. This was perhaps natural, as the business of travel no doubt engrossed their thoughts. But ere long we both perceived that the letters of our dear girl were more constrained and formal than before. It was as if she was writing now rather to comply with a sense of duty than to give vent to the light-hearted gaiety and naïve enjoyment which breathed in every line of her earlier communications. So at least it seemed to us, and again the old suspicion presented itself to my mind, and I feared that all was not as it should be.

Naples was to be the turning-point of their travels, and we expected them to return to England by the end of October. November had arrived, however, and we still had no intimation that their return journey had commenced or was even decided on. From John there was no word, and Constance wrote less often than ever. John, she said, was enraptured with Naples and its surroundings; he devoted himself much to the violin, and though she did not say so, this meant, I knew, that she was often left alone. For her own part, she did not think that a continued residence in Italy would suit her health; the sudden changes of temperature tried her, and people said that the airs rising in the evening from the bay were unwholesome.

Then we received a letter from her which much alarmed us. It was written from Naples and dated October 25. John, she said, had been ailing of late with nervousness and insomnia. On Wednesday, two days before the date of her letter, he had suffered all day from a strange restlessness, which increased after they had retired for the evening. He could not sleep and had dressed again, telling her he would walk a little in the night air to compose himself. He had not returned till near six in the morning, and then was so deadly pale and seemed so exhausted that she insisted on his keeping to his bed till she could get medical advice. The doctors feared that he had been attacked by some strange form of malarial fever, and said he needed much care. Our anxiety was, however, at least temporarily relieved by the receipt of later tidings which spoke of John's recovery; but November drew to a close without any definite mention of their return having reached us.

That month is always, I think, a dreary one in the country. It has neither the brilliant tints of October, nor the cosy jollity of mid-winter with its Christmas joys to alleviate it. This year it was more gloomy than usual. Incessant rain had marked its close, and the Roy, a little brook which skirted the gardens not far from the house, had swollen to unusual proportions. At last one wild night the flood rose so high as to completely cover the garden terraces, working havoc in the parterres, and covering the lawns with a thick coat of mud. Perhaps this gloominess of nature's outer face impressed itself in a sense of apprehension on our spirits, and it was with a feeling of more than ordinary pleasure and relief that early in December we received a letter dated from Laon, saying that our travellers were already well advanced on their return journey, and expected to be in England a week after the receipt by us of this advice. It was, as usual, Constance who wrote. John begged, she said, that Christmas might be spent at Worth Maltravers, and that we would at once proceed thither to see that all was in order against their return. They reached Worth about the middle of the month, and were, I need not say, received with the utmost affection by Mrs. Temple and myself.

In reply to our inquiries John professed that his health was completely restored; but though we could indeed discern no other signs of any special weakness, we were much shocked by his changed appearance. He had completely lost his old healthy and sunburnt complexion, and his face, though not thin or sunken, was strangely pale. Constance assured us that though in other respects he had apparently recovered, he had never regained his old colour from the night of his attack of fever at Naples.

I soon perceived that her own spirits were not so bright as was ordinarily the case with her; and she exhibited none of the eagerness to narrate to others the incidents of travel which is generally observable in those who have recently returned from a journey. The cause of this depression was, alas! not difficult to discover, for John's former abstraction and moodiness seemed to have returned with an increased force. It was a source of infinite pain to Mrs. Temple, and perhaps even more so to me, to observe this sad state of things. Constance never complained, and her affection towards her husband seemed only to increase in the face of difficulties. Yet the matter was one which could not be hid from the anxious eyes of loving kinswomen, and I believe that it was the consciousness that these altered circumstances could not but force themselves upon our notice that added poignancy to my poor sister's grief. While not markedly neglecting her, my brother had evidently ceased to take that pleasure in her company which might reasonably have been expected in any case under the circumstances of a recent marriage, and a thousand times more so when his wife was so loving and beautiful a creature as Constance Temple. He appeared little except at meals, and not even always at lunch, shutting himself up for the most part in his morning-room or study and playing continually on the violin. It was in vain that we attempted even by means of his music to win him back to a sweeter mood. Again and again I begged him to allow me to accompany him on the pianoforte, but he would never do so, always putting me off with some excuse. Even when he sat with us in the evening, he spoke little, devoting himself for the most part to reading. His books were almost always Greek or Latin, so that I am ignorant of the subjects of his study; but he was content that either Constance or I should play on the pianoforte, saying that the melody, so far from distracting his attention, helped him rather to appreciate what he was reading. Constance always begged me to allow her to take her place at the instrument on these occasions, and would play to him sometimes for hours without receiving a word of thanks, being eager even in this unreciprocated manner to testify her love and devotion to him.

Christmas Day, usually so happy a season, brought no alleviation of our gloom. My brother's reserve continually increased, and even his longest-established habits appeared changed. He had been always most observant of his religious duties, attending divine service with the utmost regularity whatever the weather might be, and saying that it was a duty a landed proprietor owed as much to his tenantry as himself to set a good example in such matters. Ever since our earliest years he and I had gone morning and afternoon on Sundays to the little church of Worth, and there sat together in the Maltravers chapel where so many of our name had sat before us. Here their monuments and achievements stood about us on every side, and it had always seemed to me that with their name and property we had inherited also the obligation to continue those acts of piety, in the practice of which so many of them had lived and died. It was, therefore, a source of surprise and great grief to me when on the Sunday after his return my brother omitted all religious observances, and did not once attend the parish church. He was not present with us at breakfast, ordering coffee and a roll to be taken to his private sitting-room. At the hour at which we usually set out for church I went to his room to tell him that we were all dressed and waiting for him. I tapped at the door, but on trying to enter found it locked. In reply to my message he did not open the door, but merely begged us to go on to church, saying he would possibly follow us later. We went alone, and I sat anxiously in our seat with my eyes fixed on the door, hoping against hope that each late comer might be John, but he never came. Perhaps this will appear to you, Edward, a comparatively trivial circumstance (though I hope it may not), but I assure you that it brought tears to my eyes. When I sat in the Maltravers chapel and thought that for the first time my dear brother had preferred in an open way his convenience or his whim to his duty, and had of set purpose neglected to come to the house of God, I felt a bitter grief that seemed to rise up in my throat and choke me. I could not think of the meaning of the prayers nor join in the singing: and all the time that Mr. Butler, our clergyman, was preaching, a verse of a little piece of poetry which I learnt as a girl was running in my head:

"How easy are the paths of ill;
How steep and hard the upward ways;
A child can roll the stone down hill
That breaks a giant's arm to raise."

It seemed to me that our loved one had set his foot upon the downward slope, and that not all the efforts of those who would have given their lives to save him could now hold him back.

It was even worse on Christmas Day. Ever since we had been confirmed John and I had always taken the Sacrament on that happy morning, and after service he had distributed the Maltravers dole in our chapel. There are given, as you know, on that day to each of twelve old men £5 and a green coat, and a like sum of money with a blue cloth dress to as many old women. These articles of dress are placed on the altar-tomb of Sir Esmoun de Maltravers, and have been thence distributed from days immemorial by the head of our house. Ever since he was twelve years old it had been my pride to watch my handsome brother doing this deed of noble charity, and to hear the kindly words he added with each gift.

Alas! alas! it was all different this Christmas. Even on this holy day my brother did not approach either the altar or the house of God. Till then Christmas had always seemed to me to be a day given us from above, that we might see even while on earth a faint glimpse of that serenity and peaceful love which will hereafter gild all days in heaven. Then covetous men lay aside their greed and enemies their rancour, then warm hearts grow warmer, and Christians feel their common brotherhood. I can scarcely imagine any man so lost or guilty as not to experience on that day some desire to turn back to the good once more, as not to recognise some far-off possibility of better things. It was thoughts free and happy such as these that had previously come into my heart in the service of Christmas Day, and been particularly associated with the familiar words that we all love so much. But that morning the harmonies were all jangled: it seemed as though some evil spirit was pouring wicked thoughts into my ear; and even while children sang "Hark the herald angels," I thought I could hear through it all a melody which I had learnt to loathe, the Gagliarda of the "Areopagita."

Poor Constance! Though her veil was down, I could see her tears, and knew her thoughts must be sadder even than mine: I drew her hand towards me, and held it as I would a child's. After the service was over a new trial awaited us. John had made no arrangement for the distribution of the dole. The coats and dresses were all piled ready on Sir Esmoun's tomb, and there lay the little leather pouches of money, but there was no one to give them away. Mr. Butler looked puzzled, and approaching us, said he feared Sir John was ill - had he made no provision for the distribution? Pride kept back the tears which were rising fast, and I said my brother was indeed unwell, that it would be better for Mr. Butler to give away the dole, and that Sir John would himself visit the recipients during the week. Then we hurried away, not daring to watch the distribution of the dole, lest we should no longer be able to master our feelings, and should openly betray our agitation.

From one another we no longer attempted to conceal our grief. It seemed as though we had all at once resolved to abandon the farce of pretending not to notice John's estrangement from his wife, or of explaining away his neglectful and unaccountable treatment of her.

I do not think that three poor women were ever so sad on Christmas Day before as were we on our return from church that morning. None of us had seen my brother, but about five in the afternoon Constance went to his room, and through the locked door begged piteously to see him. After a few minutes he complied with her request and opened the door. The exact circumstances of that interview she never revealed to me, but I knew from her manner when she returned that something she had seen or heard had both grieved and frightened her. She told me only that she had flung herself in an agony of tears at his feet, and kneeling there, weary and broken-hearted, had begged him to tell her if she had done aught amiss, had prayed him to give her back his love. To all this he answered little, but her entreaties had at least such an effect as to induce him to take his dinner with us that evening. At that meal we tried to put aside our gloom, and with feigned smiles and cheerful voices, from which the tears were hardly banished, sustained a weary show of conversation and tried to wile away his evil mood. But he spoke little; and when Foster, my father's butler, put on the table the three-handled Maltravers' loving-cup that he had brought up Christmas by Christmas for thirty years, my brother merely passed it by without a taste. I saw by Foster's face that the master's malady was no longer a secret even from the servants.

I shall not harass my own feelings nor yours, my dear Edward, by entering into further details of your father's illness, for such it was obvious his indisposition had become. It was the only consolation, and that was a sorry one, that we could use with Constance, to persuade her that John's estrangement from her was merely the result or manifestation of some physical infirmity. He obviously grew worse from week to week, and his treatment of his wife became colder and more callous. We had used all efforts to persuade him to take a change of air - to go to Royston for a month, and place himself under the care of Dr. Dobie. Mrs. Temple had even gone so far as to write privately to this physician, telling him as much of the case as was prudent, and asking his advice. Not being aware of the darker sides of my brother's ailment, Dr. Dobie replied in a less serious strain than seemed to us convenient, but recommended in any case a complete change of air and scene.

It was, therefore, with no ordinary pleasure and relief that we heard my brother announce quite unexpectedly one morning in March that he had made up his mind to seek change, and was going to leave almost immediately for the Continent. He took his valet Parnham with him, and quitted Worth one morning before lunch, bidding us an unceremonious adieu, though he kissed Constance with some apparent tenderness. It was the first time for three months, she confessed to me afterwards, that he had shown her even so ordinary a mark of affection; and her wounded heart treasured up what she hoped would prove a token of returning love. He had not proposed to take her with him, and even had he done so, we should have been reluctant to assent, as signs were not wanting that it might have been imprudent for her to undertake foreign travel at that period.

For nearly a month we had no word of him. Then he wrote a short note to Constance from Naples, giving no news, and indeed, scarce speaking of himself at all, but mentioning as an address to which she might write if she wished, the Villa de Angelis at Posilipo. Though his letter was cold and empty, yet Constance was delighted to get it, and wrote henceforth herself nearly every day, pouring out her heart to him, and retailing such news as she thought would cheer him.

CHAPTER XI

A month later Mrs. Temple wrote to John warning him of the state in which Constance now found herself, and begging him to return at least for a few weeks in order that he might be present at the time of her confinement. Though it would have been in the last degree unkind, or even inhuman, that a request of this sort should have been refused, yet I will confess to you that my brother's recent strangeness had prepared me for behaviour on his part however wild; and it was with a feeling of extreme relief that I heard from Mrs. Temple a little later that she had received a short note from John to say that he was already on his return journey. I believe Mrs. Temple herself felt as I did in the matter, though she said nothing.

When he returned we were all at Royston, whither Mrs. Temple had taken Constance to be under Dr. Dobie's care. We found John's physical appearance changed for the worse. His pallor was as remarkable as before, but he was visibly thinner; and his strange mental abstraction and moodiness seemed little if any abated. At first, indeed, he greeted Constance kindly or even affectionately. She had been in a terrible state of anxiety as to the attitude he would assume towards her, and this mental strain affected prejudicially her very delicate bodily condition. His kindness, of an ordinary enough nature indeed, seemed to her yearning heart a miracle of condescending love, and she was transported with the idea that his affection to her, once so sincere, was indeed returning. But I grieve to say that his manner thawed only for a very short time, and ere long he relapsed into an attitude of complete indifference. It was as if his real, true, honest, and loving character had made one more vigorous effort to assert itself - as though it had for a moment broken through the hard and selfish crust that was forming around him; but the blighting influence which was at work proved seemingly too strong for him to struggle against, and riveted its chains again upon him with a weight heavier than before. That there was some malefic influence, mental or physical, thus working on him, no one who had known him before could for a moment doubt. But while Mrs. Temple and I readily admitted this much, we were entirely unable even to form a conjecture as to its nature. It is true that Mrs. Temple's fancy suggested that Constance had some rival in his affections; but we rejected such a theory almost before it was proposed, feeling that it was inherently improbable, and that, had it been true, we could not have remained entirely unaware of the circumstances which had conduced to such a state of things. It was this inexplicable nature of my brother's affliction that added immeasurably to our grief. If we could only have ascertained its cause we might have combated it; but as it was, we were fighting in the dark, as against some enemy who was assaulting us from an obscurity so thick that we could not see his form. Of any mental trouble we thus knew nothing, nor could we say that my brother was suffering from any definite physical ailment, except that he was certainly growing thinner.

Your birth, my dear Edward, followed very shortly. Your poor mother rallied in an unusually short time, and was filled with rapture at the new treasure which was thus given as a solace to her afflictions. Your father exhibited little interest at the event, though he sat nearly half an hour with her one evening, and allowed her even to stroke his hair and caress him as in time long past. Although it was now the height of summer he seldom left the house, sitting much and sleeping in his own room, where he had a field-bed provided for him, and continually devoting himself to the violin.

One evening near the end of July we were sitting after dinner in the drawing-room at Royston, having the French windows looking on to the lawn open, as the air was still oppressively warm. Though things were proceeding as indifferently as before, we were perhaps less cast down than usual, for John had taken his dinner with us that evening. This was a circumstance now, alas! sufficiently uncommon, for he had nearly all his meals served for him in his own rooms. Constance, who was once more downstairs, sat playing at the pianoforte, performing chiefly melodies by Scarlatti or Bach, of which old-fashioned music she knew her husband to be most fond. A later fashion, as you know, has revived the cultivation of these composers, but at the time of which I write their works were much less commonly known. Though she was more than a passable musician, he would not allow her to accompany him; indeed he never now performed at all on the violin before us, reserving his practice entirely for his own chamber. There was a pause in the music while coffee was served. My brother had been sitting in an easy-chair apart reading some classical work during his wife's performance, and taking little notice of us. But after a while he put down his book and said, "Constance, if you will accompany me, I will get my violin and play a little while." I cannot say how much his words astonished us. It was so simple a matter for him to say, and yet it filled us all with an unspeakable joy. We concealed our emotion till he had left the room to get his instrument, then Constance showed how deeply she was gratified by kissing first her mother and then me, squeezing my hand but saying nothing. In a minute he returned, bringing his violin and a music-book. By the soiled vellum cover and the shape I perceived instantly that it was the book containing the "Areopagita." I had not seen it for near two years, and was not even aware that it was in the house, but I knew at once that he intended to play that suite. I entertained an unreasoning but profound aversion to its melodies, but at that moment I would have welcomed warmly that or any other music, so that he would only choose once more to show some thought for his neglected wife. He put the book open at the "Areopagita" on the desk of the pianoforte, and asked her to play it with him. She had never seen the music before, though I believe she was not unacquainted with the melody, as she had heard him playing it by himself, and once heard, it was not easily forgotten.

They began the "Areopagita" suite, and at first all went well. The tone of the violin, and also, I may say with no undue partiality, my brother's performance, were so marvellously fine that though our thoughts were elsewhere when, the music commenced, in a few seconds they were wholly engrossed in the melody, and we sat spellbound. It was as if the violin had become suddenly endowed with life, and was singing to us in a mystical language more deep and awful than any human words. Constance was comparatively unused to the figuring of the basso continuo, and found some trouble in reading it accurately, especially in manuscript; but she was able to mask any difficulty she may have had until she came to the Gagliarda. Here she confessed to me her thoughts seemed against her will to wander, and her attention became too deeply riveted on her husband's performance to allow her to watch her own. She made first one slight fault, and then growing nervous, another, and another. Suddenly John stopped and said brusquely, "Let Sophy play, I cannot keep time with you." Poor Constance! The tears came swiftly to my own eyes when I heard him speak so thoughtlessly to her, and I was almost provoked to rebuke him openly. She was still weak from her recent illness; her nerves were excited by the unusual pleasure she felt in playing once more with her husband, and this sudden shattering of her hopes of a renewed tenderness proved more than she could bear: she put her head between her hands upon the keyboard and broke into a paroxysm of tears.

We both ran to her; but while we were attempting to assuage her grief, John shut his violin into its case, took the music-book under his arm, and left the room without saying a word to any of us, not even to the weeping girl, whose sobs seemed as though they would break her heart.

We got her put to bed at once, but it was some hours before her convulsive sobbing ceased. Mrs. Temple had administered to her a soothing draught of proved efficacy, and after sitting with her till after one o'clock, I left her at last dozing off to sleep, and myself sought repose. I was quite wearied out with the weight of my anxiety, and with the crushing bitterness of seeing my dearest Constance's feelings so wounded. Yet in spite, or rather perhaps on account of my trouble, my head had scarcely touched my pillow ere I fell into a deep sleep.

A room in the south wing had been converted for the nonce into a nursery, and for the convenience of being near her infant Constance now slept in a room adjoining. As this portion of the house was somewhat isolated, Mrs. Temple had suggested that I should keep her daughter company, and occupy a room in the same passage, only removed a few doors, and this I had accordingly done. I was aroused from my sleep that night by some one knocking gently on the door of my bedroom; but it was some seconds before my thoughts became sufficiently awake to allow me to remember where I was. There was some moonlight, but I lighted a candle, and looking at my watch saw that it was two o'clock. I concluded that either Constance or her baby was unwell, and that the nurse needed my assistance. So I left my bed, and moving to the door, asked softly who was there. It was, to my surprise, the voice of Constance that replied, "O Sophy, let me in."

In a second I had opened the door, and found my poor sister wearing only her night-dress, and standing in the moonlight before me.

She looked frightened and unusually pale in her white dress and with the cold gleam of the moon upon her. At first I thought she was walking in her sleep, and perhaps rehearsing again in her dreams the troubles which dogged her waking footsteps. I took her gently by the arm, saying, "Dearest Constance, come back at once to bed; you will take cold."

She was not asleep, however, but made a motion of silence, and said in a terrified whisper, "Hush; do you hear nothing?" There was something so vague and yet so mysterious in the question and in her evident perturbation that I was infected too by her alarm. I felt myself shiver, as I strained my ear to catch if possible the slightest sound. But a complete silence pervaded everything: I could hear nothing.

"Can you hear it?" she said again. All sorts of images of ill presented themselves to my imagination: I thought the baby must be ill with croup, and that she was listening for some stertorous breath of anguish; and then the dread came over me that perhaps her sorrows had been too much for her, and that reason had left her seat. At that thought the marrow froze in my bones.

"Hush," she said again; and just at that moment, as I strained my ears, I thought I caught upon the sleeping air a distant and very faint murmur.

"Oh, what is it, Constance?" I said. "You will drive me mad;" and while I spoke the murmur seemed to resolve itself into the vibration, felt almost rather than heard, of some distant musical instrument. I stepped past her into the passage. All was deadly still, but I could perceive that music was being played somewhere far away; and almost at the same minute my ears recognised faintly but unmistakably the Gagliarda of the "Areopagita."

I have already mentioned that for some reason which I can scarcely explain, this melody was very repugnant to me. It seemed associated in some strange and intimate way with my brother's indisposition and moral decline. Almost at the moment that I had heard it first two years ago, peace seemed to have risen up and left our house, gathering her skirts about her, as we read that the angels left the Temple at the siege of Jerusalem. And now it was even more detestable to my ears, recalling as it did too vividly the cruel events of the preceding evening.

"John must be sitting up playing," I said.

"Yes," she answered; "but why is he in this part of the house, and why does he always play that tune?"

It was as if some irresistible attraction drew us towards the music. Constance took my hand in hers and we moved together slowly down the passage. The wind had risen, and though there was a bright moon, her beams were constantly eclipsed by driving clouds. Still there was light enough to guide us, and I extinguished the candle. As we reached the end of the passage the air of the Gagliarda grew more and more distinct.

Our passage opened on to a broad landing with a balustrade, and from one side of it ran out the picture-gallery which you know.

I looked at Constance significantly. It was evident that John was playing in this gallery. We crossed the landing, treading carefully and making no noise with our naked feet, for both of us had been too excited even to think of putting on shoes.

We could now see the whole length of the gallery. My poor brother sat in the oriel window of which I have before spoken. He was sitting so as to face the picture of Adrian Temple, and the great windows of the oriel flung a strong light on him. At times a cloud hid the moon, and all was plunged in darkness; but in a moment the cold light fell full on him, and we could trace every feature as in a picture. He had evidently not been to bed, for he was fully dressed, exactly as he had left us in the drawing-room five hours earlier when Constance was weeping over his thoughtless words. He was playing the violin, playing with a passion and reckless energy which I had never seen, and hope never to see again. Perhaps he remembered that this spot was far removed from the rest of the house, or perhaps he was careless whether any were awake and listening to him or not; but it seemed to me that he was playing with a sonorous strength greater than I had thought possible for a single violin. There came from his instrument such a volume and torrent of melody as to fill the gallery so full, as it were, of sound that it throbbed and vibrated again. He kept his eyes fixed on something at the opposite side of the gallery; we could not indeed see on what, but I have no doubt at all that it was the portrait of Adrian Temple. His gaze was eager and expectant, as though he were waiting for something to occur which did not.

I knew that he had been growing thin of late, but this was the first time I had realised how sunk were the hollows of his eyes and how haggard his features had become. It may have been some effect of moonlight which I do not well understand, but his fine-cut face, once so handsome, looked on this night worn and thin like that of an old man. He never for a moment ceased playing. It was always one same dreadful melody, the Gagliarda of the "Areopagita," and he repeated it time after time with the perseverance and apparent aimlessness of an automaton.

He did not see us, and we made no sign, standing afar off in silent horror at that nocturnal sight. Constance clutched me by the arm: she was so pale that I perceived it even in the moonlight. "Sophy," she said, "he is sitting in the same place as on the first night when he told me how he loved me." I could answer nothing, my voice was frozen in me. I could only stare at my brother's poor withered face, realising then for the first time that he must be mad, and that it was the haunting of the Gagliarda that had made him so.

We stood there I believe for half an hour without speech or motion, and all the time that sad figure at the end of the gallery continued its performance. Suddenly he stopped, and an expression of frantic despair came over his face as he laid down the violin and buried his head in his hands. I could bear it no longer. "Constance," I said, "come back to bed. We can do nothing." So we turned and crept away silently as we had come. Only as we crossed the landing Constance stopped, and looked back for a minute with a heart-broken yearning at the man she loved. He had taken his hands from his head, and she saw the profile of his face clear cut and hard in the white moonlight.

It was the last time her eyes ever looked upon it.

She made for a moment as if she would turn back and go to him, but her courage failed her, and we went on. Before we reached her room we heard in the distance, faintly but distinctly, the burden of the Gagliarda.

CHAPTER XII

The next morning, my maid brought me a hurried note written in pencil by my brother. It contained only a few lines, saying that he found that his continued sojourn at Royston was not beneficial to his health, and had determined to return to Italy. If we wished to write, letters would reach him at the Villa de Angelis: his valet Parnham was to follow him thither with his baggage as soon as it could be got together. This was all; there was no word of adieu even to his wife.

We found that he had never gone to bed that night. But in the early morning he had himself saddled his horse Sentinel and ridden in to Derby, taking the early mail thence to London. His resolve to leave Royston had apparently been arrived at very suddenly, for so far as we could discover, he had carried no luggage of any kind. I could not help looking somewhat carefully round his room to see if he had taken the Stradivarius violin. No trace of it or even of its case was to be seen, though it was difficult to imagine how he could have carried it with him on horseback. There was, indeed, a locked travelling-trunk which Parnham was to bring with him later, and the instrument might, of course, have been in that; but I felt convinced that he had actually taken it with him in some way or other, and this proved afterwards to have been the case.

I shall draw a veil, my dear Edward, over the events which immediately followed your father's departure. Even at this distance of time the memory is too inexpressibly bitter to allow me to do more than briefly allude to them.

A fortnight after John's departure, we left Royston and removed to Worth, wishing to get some sea-air, and to enjoy the late summer of the south coast. Your mother seemed entirely to have recovered from her confinement, and to be enjoying as good health as could be reasonably expected under the circumstances of her husband's indisposition. But suddenly one of those insidious maladies which are incidental to women in her condition seized upon her. We had hoped and believed that all such period of danger was already happily past; but, alas! it was not so, and within a few hours of her first seizure all realised how serious was her case. Everything that human skill can do under such conditions was done, but without avail. Symptoms of blood-poisoning showed themselves, accompanied with high fever, and within a week she was in her coffin.

Though her delirium was terrible to watch, yet I thank God to this day, that if she was to die, it pleased Him to take her while in an unconscious condition. For two days before her death she recognised no one, and was thus spared at least the sadness of passing from life without one word of kindness or even of reconciliation from her unhappy husband.

The communication with a place so distant as Naples was not then to be made under fifteen or twenty days, and all was over before we could hope that the intelligence even of his wife's illness had reached John. Both Mrs. Temple and I remained at Worth in a state of complete prostration, awaiting his return. When more than a month had passed without his arrival, or even a letter to say that he was on his way, our anxiety took a new turn, as we feared that some accident had befallen him, or that the news of his wife's death, which would then be in his hands, had so seriously affected him as to render him incapable of taking any action. To repeated subsequent communications we received no answer; but at last, to a letter which I wrote to Parnham, the servant replied, stating that his master was still at the Villa de Angelis, and in a condition of health little differing from that in which he left Royston, except that he was now slightly paler if possible and thinner. It was not till the end of November that any word came from him, and then he wrote only one page of a sheet of note-paper to me in pencil, making no reference whatever to his wife's death, but saying that he should not return for Christmas, and instructing me to draw on his bankers for any moneys that I might require for household purposes at Worth.

I need not tell you the effect that such conduct produced on Mrs. Temple and myself; you can easily imagine what would have been your own feelings in such a case. Nor will I relate any other circumstances which occurred at this period, as they would have no direct bearing upon my narrative. Though I still wrote to my brother at frequent intervals, as not wishing to neglect a duty, no word from him ever came in reply.

About the end of March, indeed, Parnham returned to Worth Maltravers, saying that his master had paid him a half-year's wages in advance, and then dispensed with his services. He had always been an excellent servant, and attached to the family, and I was glad to be able to offer him a suitable position with us at Worth until his master should return. He brought disquieting reports of John's health, saying that he was growing visibly weaker. Though I was sorely tempted to ask him many questions as to his master's habits and way of life, my pride forbade me to do so. But I heard incidentally from my maid that Parnham had told her Sir John was spending money freely in alterations at the Villa de Angelis, and had engaged Italians to attend him, with which his English valet was naturally much dissatisfied.

So the spring passed and the summer was well advanced.

On the last morning of July I found waiting for me on the breakfast-table an envelope addressed in my brother's hand. I opened it hastily. It only contained a few words, which I have before me as I write now. The ink is a little faded and yellow, but the impression it made is yet vivid as on that summer morning.

"MY DEAREST SOPHY," it began. "Come to me here at once, if possible, or it may be too late. I want to see you. They say that I am ill, and too weak to travel to England.

"Your loving brother,

"JOHN."

There was a great change in the style, from the cold and conventional notes that he had hitherto sent at such long intervals; from the stiff "Dear Sophia" and "Sincerely yours" to which, I grieve to say, I had grown accustomed. Even the writing itself was altered. It was more the bold boyish hand he wrote when first he went to Oxford, than the smaller cramped and classic character of his later years. Though it was a little matter enough, God knows, in comparison with his grievous conduct, yet it touched me much that he should use again the once familiar "Dearest Sophy," and sign himself "my loving brother." I felt my heart go out towards him; and so strong is woman's affection for her own kin, that I had already forgotten any resentment and reprobation in my great pity for the poor wanderer, lying sick perhaps unto death and alone in a foreign land.

I took his note at once to Mrs. Temple. She read it twice or thrice, trying to take in the meaning of it. Then she drew me to her and, kissing me, said, "Go to him at once, Sophy. Bring him back to Worth; try to bring him back to the right way."

I ordered my things to be packed, determining to drive to Southampton and take train thence to London; and at the same time Mrs. Temple gave instructions that all should be prepared for her own return to Royston within a few days. I knew she did not dare to see John after her daughter's death.

I took my maid with me, and Parnham to act as courier. At London we hired a carriage for the whole journey, and from Calais posted direct to Naples. We took the short route by Marseilles and Genoa, and travelled for seventeen days without intermission, as my brother's note made me desirous of losing no time on the way. I had never been in Italy before; but my anxiety was such that my mind was unable to appreciate either the beauty of the scenery or the incidents of travel. I can, in fact, remember nothing of our journey now, except the wearisome and interminable jolting over bad roads and the insufferable heat. It was the middle of August in an exceptionally warm summer, and after passing Genoa the heat became almost tropical. There was no relief even at night, for the warm air hung stagnant and suffocating, and the inside of my travelling coach was often like a furnace.

We were at last approaching the conclusion of our journey, and had left Rome behind us. The day that we set out from Aversa was the hottest that I have ever felt, the sun beating down with an astonishing power even in the early hours, and the road being thick with a white and blinding dust. It was soon after midnight that our carriage began rattling over the great stone blocks with which the streets of Naples are paved. The suburbs that we at first passed through were, I remember, in darkness and perfect quiet; but after traversing the heart of the city and reaching the western side, we suddenly found ourselves in the midst of an enormous and very dense crowd. There were lanterns everywhere, and interminable lanes of booths, whose proprietors were praising their wares with loud shouts; and here acrobats, jugglers, minstrels, black-vested priests, and blue-coated soldiers mingled with a vast crowd whose numbers at once arrested the progress of the carriage. Though it was so late of a Sunday night, all seemed here awake and busy as at noonday. Oil-lamps with reeking fumes of black smoke flung a glare over the scene, and the discordant cries and chattering conversation united in so deafening a noise as to make me turn faint and giddy, wearied as I already was with long travelling. Though I felt that intense eagerness and expectation which the approaching termination of a tedious journey inspires, and was desirous of pushing forward with all imaginable despatch, yet here our course was sadly delayed. The horses could only proceed at the slowest of foot-paces, and we were constantly brought to a complete stop for some minutes before the post-boy could force a passage through the unwilling crowd. This produced a feeling of irritation, and despair of ever reaching my destination; and the mirth and careless hilarity of the people round us chafed with bitter contrast on my depressed spirits. I inquired from the post-boy what was the origin of so great a commotion, and understood him to say in reply that it was a religious festival held annually in honour of "Our Lady of the Grotto." I cannot, however, conceive of any truly religious person countenancing such a gathering, which seemed to me rather like the unclean orgies of a heathen deity than an act of faith of Christian people. This disturbance occasioned us so serious a delay that as we were climbing the steep slope leading up to Posilipo it was already three in the morning and the dawn was at hand.

After mounting steadily for a long time we began to rapidly descend, and just as the sun came up over the sea we arrived at the Villa de Angelis. I sprang from the carriage, and passing through a trellis of vines, reached the house. A man-servant was in waiting, and held the door open for me; but he was an Italian, and did not understand me when I asked in English where Sir John Maltravers was. He had evidently, however, received instructions to take me at once to my brother, and led the way to an inner part of the house. As we proceeded I heard the sound of a rich alto voice singing very sweetly to a mandolin some soothing or religious melody. The servant pulled aside a heavy curtain and I found myself in my brother's room. An Italian youth sat on a stool near the door, and it was he who had been singing. At a few words from John, addressed to him in his own language, he set down his mandolin and left the room, pulling to the curtain and shutting a door behind it.

The room looked directly on to the sea: the villa was, in fact, built upon rocks at the foot of which the waves lapped. Through two folding windows which opened on to a balcony the early light of the summer morning streamed in with a rosy flush. My brother sat on a low couch or sofa, propped up against a heap of pillows, with a rug of brilliant colours flung across his feet and legs. He held out his arms to me, and I ran to him; but even in so brief an interval I had perceived that he was terribly weak and wasted.

All my memories of his past faults had vanished and were dead in that sad aspect of his worn features, and in the conviction which I felt, even from the first moment, that he had but little time longer to remain with us. I knelt by him on the floor, and with my arms round his neck, embraced him tenderly, not finding any place for words, but only sobbing in great anguish. Neither of us spoke, and my weariness from long travel and the strangeness of the situation caused me to feel that paralysing sensation of doubt as to the reality of the scene, and even of my own existence, which all, I believe, have experienced at times of severe mental tension. That I, a plain English girl, should be kneeling here beside my brother in the Italian dawn; that I should read, as I believed, on his young face the unmistakable image and superscription of death; and reflect that within so few months he had married, had wrecked his home, that my poor Constance was no more - these things seemed so unrealisable that for a minute I felt that it must all be a nightmare, that I should immediately wake with the fresh salt air of the Channel blowing through my bedroom window at Worth, and find I had been dreaming. But it was not so; the light of day grew stronger and brighter, and even in my sorrow the panorama of the most beautiful spot on earth, the Bay of Naples, with Vesuvius lying on the far side, as seen then from these windows, stamped itself for ever on my mind. It was unreal as a scene in some brilliant dramatic spectacle, but, alas! no unreality was here. The flames of the candles in their silver sconces waxed paler and paler, the lines and shadows on my brother's face grew darker, and the pallor of his wasted features showed more striking in the bright rays of the morning sun.

CHAPTER XIII

I had spent near a week at the Villa de Angelis. John's manner to me was most tender and affectionate; but he showed no wish to refer to the tragedy of his wife's death and the sad events which had preceded it, or to attempt to explain in any way his own conduct in the past. Nor did I ever lead the conversation to these topics; for I felt that even if there were no other reason, his great weakness rendered it inadvisable to introduce such subjects at present, or even to lead him to speak at all more than was actually necessary. I was content to minister to him in quiet, and infinitely happy in his restored affection. He seemed desirous of banishing from his mind all thoughts of the last few months, but spoke much of the years before he had gone to Oxford, and of happy days which we had spent together in our childhood at Worth Maltravers. His weakness was extreme, but he complained of no particular malady except a short cough which troubled him at night.

I had spoken to him of his health, for I could see that his state was such as to inspire anxiety, and begged that he would allow me to see if there was an English doctor at Naples who could visit him. This he would not assent to, saying that he was quite content with the care of an Italian doctor who visited him almost daily, and that he hoped to be able, under my escort, to return within a very short time to England.

"I shall never be much better, dear Sophy," he said one day. "The doctor tells me that I am suffering from some sort of consumption, and that I must not expect to live long. Yet I yearn to see Worth once more, and to feel again the west winds blowing in the evening across from Portland, and smell the thyme on the Dorset downs. In a few days I hope perhaps to be a little stronger, and I then wish to show you a discovery which I have made in Naples. After that you may order them to harness the horses, and carry me back to Worth Maltravers."

I endeavoured to ascertain from Signor Baravelli, the doctor, something as to the actual state of his patient; but my knowledge of Italian was so slight that I could neither make him understand what I would be at, nor comprehend in turn what he replied, so that this attempt was relinquished. From my brother himself I gathered that he had begun to feel his health much impaired as far back as the early spring, but though his strength had since then gradually failed him, he had not been confined to the house until a month past. He spent the day and often the night reclining on his sofa and speaking little. He had apparently lost the taste for the violin which had once absorbed so much of his attention; indeed I think the bodily strength necessary for its performance had probably now failed him. The Stradivarius instrument lay near his couch in its case; but I only saw the latter open on one occasion, I think, and was deeply thankful that John no longer took the same delight as heretofore in the practice of this art - not only because the mere sound of his violin was now fraught to me with such bitter memories, but also because I felt sure that its performance had in some way which I could not explain a deleterious effect upon himself. He exhibited that absence of vitality which is so often noticeable in those who have not long to live, and on some days lay in a state of semi-lethargy from which it was difficult to rouse him. But at other times he suffered from a distressing restlessness which forbade him to sit still even for a few minutes, and which was more painful to watch than his lethargic stupor. The Italian boy, of whom I have already spoken, exhibited an untiring devotion to his master which won my heart. His name was Raffaelle Carotenuto, and he often sang to us in the evening, accompanying himself on the mandolin. At nights, too, when John could not sleep, Raffaelle would read for hours till at last his master dozed off. He was well educated, and though I could not understand the subject he read, I often sat by and listened, being charmed with his evident attachment to my brother and with the melodious intonation of a sweet voice.

My brother was nervous apparently in some respects, and would never be left alone even for a few minutes; but in the intervals while Raffaelle was with him I had ample opportunity to examine and appreciate the beauties of the Villa de Angelis. It was built, as I have said, on some rocks jutting into the sea, just before coming to the Capo di Posilipo as you proceed from Naples. The earlier foundations were, I believe, originally Roman, and upon them a modern villa had been constructed in the eighteenth century, and to this again John had made important additions in the past two years. Looking down upon the sea from the windows of the villa, one could on calm days easily discern the remains of Roman piers and moles lying below the surface of the transparent water; and the tufa-rock on which the house was built was burrowed with those unintelligible excavations of a classic date so common in the neighbourhood.

These subterraneous rooms and passages, while they aroused my curiosity, seemed at the same time so gloomy and repellent that I never explored them. But on one sunny morning, as I walked at the foot of the rocks by the sea, I ventured into one of the larger of these chambers, and saw that it had at the far end an opening leading apparently to an inner room. I had walking with me an old Italian female servant who took a motherly interest in my proceedings, and who, relying principally upon a very slight knowledge of English, had constituted herself my body-guard. Encouraged by her presence, I penetrated this inner room and found that it again opened in turn into another, and so on until we had passed through no less than four chambers.

They were all lighted after a fashion through vent-holes which somewhere or other reached the outer air, but the fourth room opened into a fifth which was unlighted. My companion, who had been showing signs of alarm and an evident reluctance to proceed further, now stopped abruptly and begged me to return. It may have been that her fear communicated itself to me also, for on attempting to cross the threshold and explore the darkness of the fifth cell, I was seized by an unreasoning panic and by the feeling of undefined horror experienced in a nightmare. I hesitated for an instant, but my fear became suddenly more intense, and springing back, I followed my companion, who had set out to run back to the outer air. We never paused until we stood panting in the full sunlight by the sea. As soon as the maid had found her breath, she begged me never to go there again, explaining in broken English that the caves were known in the neighbourhood as the "Cells of Isis," and were reputed to be haunted by demons. This episode, trifling as it may appear, had so great an effect upon me that I never again ventured on to the lower walk which ran at the foot of the rocks by the sea.

In the house above, my brother had built a large hall after the ancient Roman style, and this, with a dining-room and many other chambers, were decorated in the fashion of those discovered at Pompeii. They had been furnished with the utmost luxury, and the beauty of the paintings, furniture, carpets, and hangings was enhanced by statues in bronze and marble. The villa, indeed, and its fittings were of a kind to which I was little used, and at the same time of such beauty that I never ceased to regard all as a creation of an enchanter's wand, or as the drop-scene to some drama which might suddenly be raised and disappear from my sight. The house, in short, together with its furniture, was, I believe, intended to be a reproduction of an ancient Roman villa, and had something about it repellent to my rustic and insular ideas. In the contemplation of its perfection I experienced a curious mental sensation, which I can only compare to the physical oppression produced on some persons by the heavy and cloying perfume of a bouquet of gardenias or other too highly scented exotics.

In my brother's room was a medieval reproduction in mellow alabaster of a classic group of a dolphin encircling a Cupid. It was, I think, the fairest work of art I ever saw, but it jarred upon my sense of propriety that close by it should hang an ivory crucifix. I would rather, I think, have seen all things material and pagan entirely, with every view of the future life shut out, than have found a medley of things sacred and profane, where the emblems of our highest hopes and aspirations were placed in insulting indifference side by side with the embodied forms of sensuality. Here, in this scene of magical beauty, it seemed to me for a moment that the years had rolled back, that Christianity had still to fight with a living Paganism, and that the battle was not yet won. It was the same all through the house; and there were many other matters which filled me with regret, mingled with vague and apprehensive surmises which I shall not here repeat.

At one end of the house was a small library, but it contained few works except Latin and Greek classics. I had gone thither one day to look for a book that John had asked for, when in turning out some drawers I found a number of letters written from Worth by my lost Constance to her husband. The shock of being brought suddenly face to face with a handwriting that evoked memories at once so dear and sad was in itself a sharp one; but its bitterness was immeasurably increased by the discovery that not one of these envelopes had ever been opened. While that dear heart, now at rest, was pouring forth her love and sorrow to the ears that should have been above all others ready to receive them, her letters, as they arrived, were flung uncared for, unread, even unopened, into any haphazard receptacle.

The days passed one by one at the Villa de Angelis with but little incident, nor did my brother's health either visibly improve or decline. Though the weather was still more than usually warm, a grateful breeze came morning and evening from the sea and tempered the heat so much as to render it always supportable. John would sometimes in the evening sit propped up with cushions on the trellised balcony looking towards Baia, and watch the fishermen setting their nets. We could hear the melody of their deep-voiced songs carried up on the night air. "It was here, Sophy," my brother said, as we sat one evening looking on a scene like this. "It was here that the great epicure Pollio built himself a famous house, and called it by two Greek words meaning a 'truce to care,' from which our name of Posilipo is derived. It was his sans-souci, and here he cast aside his vexations; but they were lighter than mine. Posilipo has brought no cessation of care to me. I do not think I shall find any truce this side the grave; and beyond, who knows?"

This was the first time John had spoken in this strain, and he seemed stirred to an unusual activity, as though his own words had suddenly reminded him how frail was his state. He called Raffaelle to him and despatched him on an errand to Naples. The next morning he sent for me earlier than usual, and begged that a carriage might be ready by six in the evening, as he desired to drive into the city. I tried at first to dissuade him from his project, urging him to consider his weak state of health. He replied that he felt somewhat stronger, and had something that he particularly wished me to see in Naples. This done, it would be better to return at once to England: he could, he thought, bear the journey if we travelled by very short stages.

CHAPTER XIV

Shortly after six o'clock in the evening we left the Villa de Angelis. The day had been as usual cloudlessly serene; but a gentle sea-breeze, of which I have spoken, rose in the afternoon and brought with it a refreshing coolness. We had arranged a sort of couch in the landau with many cushions for my brother, and he mounted into the carriage with more ease than I had expected. I sat beside him, with Raffaelle facing me on the opposite seat. We drove down the hill of Posilipo through the ilex-trees and tamarisk-bushes that then skirted the sea, and so into the town. John spoke little except to remark that the carriage was an easy one. As we were passing through one of the principal streets he bent over to me and said, "You must not be alarmed if I show you to-day a strange sight. Some women might perhaps be frightened at what we are going to see; but my poor sister has known already so much of trouble that a light thing like this will not affect her." In spite of his encomiums upon my supposed courage, I felt alarmed and agitated by his words. There was a vagueness in them which frightened me, and bred that indefinite apprehension which is often infinitely more terrifying than the actual object which inspires it. To my inquiries he would give no further response than to say that he had whilst at Posilipo made some investigations in Naples leading to a strange discovery, which he was anxious to communicate to me. After traversing a considerable distance, we had penetrated apparently into the heart of the town. The streets grew narrower and more densely thronged; the houses were more dirty and tumbledown, and the appearance of the people themselves suggested that we had reached some of the lower quarters of the city. Here we passed through a further network of small streets of the name of which I took no note, and found ourselves at last in a very dark and narrow lane called the Via del Giardino. Although my brother had, so far as I had observed, given no orders to the coachman, the latter seemed to have no difficulty in finding his way, driving rapidly in the Neapolitan fashion, and proceeding direct as to a place with which he was already familiar.

In the Via del Giardino the houses were of great height, and overhung the street so as nearly to touch one another. It seemed that this quarter had been formerly inhabited, if not by the aristocracy, at least by a class very much superior to that which now lived there; and many of the houses were large and dignified, though long since parcelled out into smaller tenements. It was before such a house that we at last brought up. Here must have been at one time a house or palace of some person of distinction, having a long and fine façade adorned with delicate pilasters, and much florid ornamentation of the Renaissance period. The ground-floor was divided into a series of small shops, and its upper storeys were evidently peopled by sordid families of the lowest class. Before one of these little shops, now closed and having its windows carefully blocked with boards, our carriage stopped. Raffaelle alighted, and taking a key from his pocket unlocked the door, and assisted John to leave the carriage. I followed, and directly we had crossed the threshold, the boy locked the door behind us, and I heard the carriage drive away.

We found ourselves in a narrow and dark passage, and as soon as my eyes grew accustomed to the gloom I perceived there was at the end of it a low staircase leading to some upper room, and on the right a door which opened into the closed shop. My brother moved slowly along the passage, and began to ascend the stairs. He leant with one hand on Raffaelle's arm, taking hold of the balusters with the other. But I could see that to mount the stairs cost him considerable effort, and he paused frequently to cough and get his breath again. So we reached a landing at the top, and found ourselves in a small chamber or magazine directly over the shop. It was quite empty except for a few broken chairs, and appeared to be a small loft formed by dividing what had once been a high room into two storeys, of which the shop formed the lower. A long window, which had no doubt once formed one of several in the walls of this large room, was now divided across its width by the flooring, and with its upper part served to light the loft, while its lower panes opened into the shop. The ceiling was, in consequence of these alterations, comparatively low, but though much mutilated, retained evident traces of having been at one time richly decorated, with the raised mouldings and pendants common in the sixteenth century. At one end of the loft was a species of coved and elaborately carved dado, of which the former use was not obvious; but the large original room had without doubt been divided in length as Well as in height, as the lath-and-plaster walls at either end of the loft had evidently been no part of the ancient structure.

My brother sat down in one of the old chairs, and seemed to be collecting his strength before speaking. My anxiety was momentarily increasing, and it was a great relief when he began, talking in a low voice as one that had much to say and wished to husband his strength.

"I do not know whether you will recollect my having told you of something Mr. Gaskell once said about the music of Graziani's 'Areopagita' suite. It had always, he used to say, a curious effect upon his imagination, and the melody of the Gagliarda especially called up to his thoughts in some strange way a picture of a certain hall where people were dancing. He even went so far as to describe the general appearance of the room itself, and of the persons who were dancing there."

"Yes," I answered, "I remember your telling me of this;" and indeed my memory had in times past so often rehearsed Mr. Gaskell's description that, although I had not recently thought of it, its chief features immediately returned to my mind.

"He described it," my brother continued, "as a long hall with an arcade of arches running down one side, of the fantastic Gothic of the Renaissance. At the end was a gallery or balcony for the musicians, which on its front carried a coat of arms."

I remembered this perfectly and told John so, adding that the shield bore a cherub's head fanning three lilies on a golden field.

"It is strange," John went on, "that the description of a scene which our friend thought a mere effort of his own imagination has impressed itself so deeply on both our minds. But the picture which he drew was more than a fancy, for we are at this minute in the very hall of his dream."

I could not gather what my brother meant, and thought his reason was failing him; but he continued, "This miserable floor on which we stand has of course been afterwards built in; but you see above you the old ceiling, and here at the end was the musicians' gallery with the shield upon its front."

He pointed to the carved and whitewashed dado which had hitherto so puzzled me. I stepped up to it, and although the lath-and-plaster partition wall was now built around it, it was clear that its curved outline might very easily, as John said, have formed part of the front of a coved gallery. I looked closer at the relief-work which had adorned it. Though the edges were all rubbed off, and the mouldings in some cases entirely removed, I could trace without difficulty a shield in the midst; and a more narrow inspection revealed underneath the whitewash, which had partly peeled away, enough remnants of colour to show that it had certainly been once painted gold and borne a cherub's head with three lilies.

"That is the shield of the old Neapolitan house of Doma-Cavalli," my brother continued; "they bore a cherub's head fanning three lilies on a shield or. It was in the balcony behind this shield, long since blocked up as you see, that the musicians sat on that ball night of which Gaskell dreamt. From it they looked down on the hall below where dancing was going forward, and I will now take you downstairs that you may see if the description tallies."

So saying, he raised himself, and descending the stairs with much less difficulty than he had shown in mounting them, flung open the door which I had seen in the passage and ushered us into the shop on the ground-floor. The evening light had now faded so much that we could scarcely see even in the passage, and the shop having its windows barricaded with shutters, was in complete darkness. Raffaelle, however, struck a match and lit three half-burnt candles in a tarnished sconce upon the wall.

The shop had evidently been lately in the occupation of a wine-seller, and there were still several empty wooden wine-butts, and some broken flasks on shelves. In one corner I noticed that the earth which formed the floor had been turned up with spades. There was a small heap of mould, and a large flat stone was thus exposed below the surface. This stone had an iron ring attached to it, and seemed to cover the aperture of a well, or perhaps a vault. At the back of the shop, and furthest from the street, were two lofty arches separated by a column in the middle, from which the outside casing had been stripped.

To these arches John pointed and said, "That is a part of the arcade which once ran down the whole length of the hall. Only these two arches are now left, and the fine marbles which doubtless coated the outside of this dividing pillar have been stripped off. On a summer's night about one hundred years ago dancing was going on in this hall. There were a dozen couples dancing a wild step such as is never seen now. The tune that the musicians were playing in the gallery above was taken from the 'Areopagita' suite of Graziani. Gaskell has often told me that when he played it the music brought with it to his mind a sense of some impending catastrophe, which culminated at the end of the first movement of the Gagliarda. It was just at that moment, Sophy, that an Englishman who was dancing here was stabbed in the back and foully murdered."

I had scarcely heard all that John had said, and had certainly not been able to take in its import; but without waiting to hear if I should say anything, he moved across to the uncovered stone with the ring in it. Exerting a strength which I should have believed entirely impossible in his weak condition, he applied to the stone a lever which lay ready at hand. Raffaelle at the same time seized the ring, and so they were able between them to move the covering to one side sufficiently to allow access to a small staircase which thus appeared to view. The stair was a winding one, and once led no doubt to some vaults below the ground-floor. Raffaelle descended first, taking in his hand the sconce of three candles, which he held above his head so as to fling a light down the steps. John went next, and then I followed, trying to support my brother if possible with my hand. The stairs were very dry, and on the walls there was none of the damp or mould which fancy usually associates with a subterraneous vault. I do not know what it was I expected to see, but I had an uneasy feeling that I was on the brink of some evil and distressing discovery. After we had descended about twenty steps we could see the entry to some vault or underground room, and it was just at the foot of the stairs that I saw something lying, as the light from the candles fell on it from above. At first I thought it was a heap of dust or refuse, but on looking closer it seemed rather a bundle of rags. As my eyes penetrated the gloom, I saw there was about it some tattered cloth of a faded green tint, and almost at the same minute I seemed to trace under the clothes the lines or dimensions of a human figure. For a moment I imagined it was some poor man lying face downwards and bent up against the wall. The idea of a man or of a dead body being there shocked me violently, and I cried to my brother, "Tell me, what is it?" At that instant the light from. Raffaelle's candles fell in a somewhat different direction. It lighted up the white bowl of a human skull, and I saw that what I had taken for a man's form was instead that of a clothed skeleton. I turned faint and sick for an instant, and should have fallen had it not been for John, who put his arm about me and sustained me with an unexpected strength.

"God help us!" I exclaimed, "let us go. I cannot bear this; there are foul vapours here; let us get back to the outer air."

He took me by the arm, and pointing at the huddled heap, said, "Do you know whose bones those are? That is Adrian Temple. After it was all over, they flung his body down the steps, dressed in the clothes he wore."

At that name, uttered in so ill-omened a place, I felt a fresh access of terror. It seemed as though the soul of that wicked man must be still hovering over his unburied remains, and boding evil to us all. A chill crept over me, the light, the walls, my brother, and Raffaelle all swam round, and I sank swooning on the stairs.

When I returned fully to my senses we were in the landau again making our way back to the Villa de Angelis.

CHAPTER XV

The next morning my health and strength were entirely restored to me, but my brother, on the contrary, seemed weak and exhausted from his efforts of the previous night. Our return journey to the Villa de Angelis had passed in complete silence. I had been too much perturbed to question him on the many points relating to the strange events as to which I was still completely in the dark, and he on his side had shown no desire to afford me any further information. When I saw him the next morning he exhibited signs of great weakness, and in response to an effort on my part to obtain some explanation of the discovery of Adrian Temple's body, avoided an immediate reply, promising to tell me all he knew after our return to Worth Maltravers.

I pondered over the last terrifying episode very frequently in my own mind, and as I thought more deeply of it all, it seemed to me that the outlines of some evil history were piece by piece developing themselves, that I had almost within my grasp the clue that would make all plain, and that had eluded me so long. In that dim story Adrian Temple, the music of the Gagliarda, my brother's fatal passion for the violin, all seemed to have some mysterious connection, and to have conspired in working John's mental and physical ruin. Even the Stradivarius violin bore a part in the tragedy, becoming, as it were, an actively malignant spirit, though I could not explain how, and was yet entirely unaware of the manner in which it had come into my brother's possession.

I found that John was still resolved on an immediate return to England. His weakness, it is true, led me to entertain doubts as to how he would support so long a journey; but at the same time I did not feel justified in using any strong efforts to dissuade him from his purpose. I reflected that the more wholesome air and associations of England would certainly re-invigorate both body and mind, and that any extra strain brought about by the journey would soon be repaired by the comforts and watchful care with which we could surround him at Worth Maltravers.

So the first week in October saw us once more with our faces set towards England. A very comfortable swinging-bed or hammock had been arranged for John in the travelling carriage, and we determined to avoid fatigue as much as possible by dividing our journey into very short stages. My brother seemed to have no intention of giving up the Villa de Angelis. It was left complete with its luxurious furniture, and with all his servants, under the care of an Italian maggior-duomo. I felt that as John's state of health forbade his entertaining any hope of an immediate return thither, it would have been much better to close entirely his Italian house. But his great weakness made it impossible for him to undertake the effort such a course would involve, and even if my own ignorance of the Italian tongue had not stood in the way, I was far too eager to get my invalid back to Worth to feel inclined to import any further delay, while I should myself adjust matters which were after all comparatively trifling. As Parnham was now ready to discharge his usual duties of valet, and as my brother seemed quite content that he should do so, Raffaelle was of course to be left behind. The boy had quite won my heart by his sweet manners, combined with his evident affection to his master, and in making him understand that he was now to leave us, I offered him a present of a few pounds as a token of my esteem. He refused, however, to touch this money, and shed tears when he learnt that he was to be left in Italy, and begged with many protestations of devotion that he might be allowed to accompany us to England. My heart was not proof against his entreaties, supported by so many signs of attachment, and it was agreed, therefore, that he should at least attend us as far as Worth Maltravers. John showed no surprise at the boy being with us; indeed I never thought it necessary to explain that I had originally purposed to leave him behind.

Our journey, though necessarily prolonged by the shortness of its stages, was safely accomplished. John bore it as well as I could have hoped, and though his body showed no signs of increased vigour, his mind, I think, improved in tone, at any rate for a time. From the evening on which he had shown me the terrible discovery in the Via del Giardino he seemed to have laid aside something of his care and depression. He now exhibited little trace of the moroseness and selfishness which had of late so marred his character; and though he naturally felt severely at times the fatigue of travel, yet we had no longer to dread any relapse into that state of lethargy or stupor which had so often baffled every effort to counteract it at Posilipo. Some feeling of superstitious aversion had prompted me to give orders that the Stradivarius violin should be left behind at Posilipo. But before parting my brother asked for it, and insisted that it should be brought with him, though I had never heard him play a note on it for many weeks. He took an interest in all the petty episodes of travel, and certainly appeared to derive more entertainment from the journey than was to have been anticipated in his feeble state of health.

To the incidents of the evening spent in the Via del Giardino he made no allusion of any kind, nor did I for my part wish to renew memories of so unpleasant a nature. His only reference occurred one Sunday evening as we were passing a small graveyard near Genoa. The scene apparently turned his thoughts to that subject, and he told me that he had taken measures before leaving Naples to ensure that the remains of Adrian Temple should be decently interred in the cemetery of Santa Bibiana. His words set me thinking again, and unsatisfied curiosity prompted me strongly to inquire of him how he had convinced himself that the skeleton at the foot of the stairs was indeed that of Adrian Temple. But I restrained myself, partly from a reliance on his promise that he would one day explain the whole story to me, and partly being very reluctant to mar the enjoyment of the peaceful scenes through which we were passing, by the introduction of any subjects so jarring and painful as those to which I have alluded.

We reached London at last, and here we stopped a few days to make some necessary arrangements before going down to Worth Maltravers. I had urged upon John during the journey that immediately on his arrival in London he should obtain the best English medical advice as to his own health. Though he at first demurred, saying that nothing more was to be done, and that he was perfectly satisfied with the medicine given him by Dr. Baravelli, which he continued to take, yet by constant entreaty I prevailed upon him to accede to so reasonable a request. Dr. Frobisher, considered at that time the first living authority on diseases of the brain and nerves, saw him on the morning after our arrival. He was good enough to speak with me at some length after seeing my brother, and to give me many hints and recipes whereby I might be better enabled to nurse the invalid.

Sir John's condition, he said, was such as to excite serious anxiety. There was, indeed, no brain mischief of any kind to be discovered, but his lungs were in a state of advanced disease, and there were signs of grave heart affection. Yet he did not bid me to despair, but said that with careful nursing life might certainly be prolonged, and even some measure of health in time restored. He asked me more than once if I knew of any trouble or worry that preyed upon Sir John's mind. Were there financial difficulties; had he been subjected to any mental shock; had he received any severe fright? To all this I could only reply in the negative. At the same time I told Dr. Frobisher as much of John's history as I considered pertinent to the question. He shook his head gravely, and recommended that Sir John should remain for the present in London, under his own constant supervision. To this course my brother would by no means consent. He was eager to proceed at once to his own house, saying that if necessary we could return again to London for Christmas. It was therefore agreed that we should go down to Worth Maltravers at the end of the week.

Parnham had already left us for Worth in order that he might have everything ready against his master's return, and when we arrived we found all in perfect order for our reception. A small morning-room next to the library, with a pleasant south aspect and opening on to the terrace, had been prepared for my brother's use, so that he might avoid the fatigue of mounting stairs, which Dr. Frobisher considered very prejudicial in his present condition. We had also purchased in London a chair fitted with wheels, which enabled him to be moved, or, if he were feeling equal to the exertion, to move himself, without difficulty, from room to room.

His health, I think, improved; very gradually, it is true, but still sufficiently to inspire me with hope that he might yet be spared to us. Of the state of his mind or thoughts I knew little, but I could see that he was at times a prey to nervous anxiety. This showed itself in the harassed look which his pale face often wore, and in his marked dislike to being left alone. He derived, I think, a certain pleasure from the quietude and monotony of his life at Worth, and perhaps also from the consciousness that he had about him loving and devoted hearts. I say hearts, for every servant at Worth was attached to him, remembering the great consideration and courtesy of his earlier years, and grieving to see his youthful and once vigorous frame reduced to so sad a strait. Books he never read himself, and even the charm of Raffaelle's reading seemed to have lost its power; though he never tired of hearing the boy sing, and liked to have him sit by his chair even when his eyes were shut and he was apparently asleep. His general health seemed to me to change but little either for better or worse. Dr. Frobisher had led me to expect some such a sequel. I had not concealed from him that I had at times entertained suspicions as to my brother's sanity; but he had assured me that they were totally unfounded, that Sir John's brain was as clear as his own. At the same time he confessed that he could not account for the exhausted vitality of his patient - a condition which he would under ordinary circumstances have attributed to excessive study or severe trouble. He had urged upon me the pressing necessity for complete rest, and for much sleep. My brother never even incidentally referred to his wife, his child, or to Mrs. Temple, who constantly wrote to me from Royston, sending kind messages to John, and asking how he did. These messages I never dared to give him, fearing to agitate him, or retard his recovery by diverting his thoughts into channels which must necessarily be of a painful character. That he should never even mention her name, or that of Lady Maltravers, led me to wonder sometimes if one of those curious freaks of memory which occasionally accompany a severe illness had not entirely blotted out from his mind the recollection of his marriage and of his wife's death. He was unable to consider any affairs of business, and the management of the estate remained as it had done for the last two years in the hands of our excellent agent, Mr. Baker.

But one evening in the early part of December he sent Raffaelle about nine o'clock, saying he wished to speak to me. I went to his room, and without any warning he began at once, "You never show me my boy now, Sophy; he must be grown a big child, and I should like to see him." Much startled by so unexpected a remark, I replied that the child was at Royston under the care of Mrs. Temple, but that I knew that if it pleased him to see Edward she would be glad to bring him down to Worth. He seemed gratified with this idea, and begged me to ask her to do so, desiring that his respects should be at the same time conveyed to her. I almost ventured at that moment to recall his lost wife to his thoughts, by saying that his child resembled her strongly; for your likeness at that time, and even now, my dear Edward, to your poor mother was very marked. But my courage failed me, and his talk soon reverted to an earlier period, comparing the mildness of the month to that of the first winter which he spent at Eton. His thoughts, however, must, I fancy, have returned for a moment to the days when he first met your mother, for he suddenly asked, "Where is Gaskell? Why does he never come to see me?" This brought quite a new idea to my mind. I fancied it might do my brother much good to have by him so sensible and true a friend as I knew Mr. Gaskell to be. The latter's address had fortunately not slipped from my memory, and I put all scruples aside and wrote by the next mail to him, setting forth my brother's sad condition, saying that I had heard John mention his name, and begging him on my own account to be so good as to help us if possible and come to us in this hour of trial. Though he was so far off as Westmorland, Mr. Gaskell's generosity brought him at once to our aid, and within a week he was installed at Worth Maltravers, sleeping in the library, where we had arranged a bed at his own desire, so that he might be near his sick friend.

His presence was of the utmost assistance to us all. He treated John at once with the tenderness of a woman and the firmness of a clever and strong man. They sat constantly together in the mornings, and Mr. Gaskell told me John had not shown with him the same reluctance to talk freely of his married life as he had discovered with me. The tenor of his communications I cannot guess, nor did I ever ask; but I knew that Mr. Gaskell was much affected by them.

John even amused himself now at times by having Mr. Baker into his rooms of a morning, that the management of the estate might be discussed with his friend; and he also expressed his wish to see the family solicitor, as he desired to draw his will. Thinking that any diversion of this nature could not but be beneficial to him, we sent to Dorchester for our solicitor, Mr. Jeffreys, who together with his clerk spent three nights at Worth, and drew up a testament for my brother.

So time went on, and the year was drawing to a close.

It was Christmas Eve, and I had gone to bed shortly after twelve o'clock, having an hour earlier bid good night to John and Mr. Gaskell. The long habit of watching with, or being in charge of an invalid at night, had made my ears extraordinarily quick to apprehend even the slightest murmur. It must have been, I think, near three in the morning when I found myself awake and conscious of some unusual sound. It was low and far off, but I knew instantly what it was, and felt a choking sensation of fear and horror, as if an icy hand had gripped my throat, on recognising the air of the Gagliarda. It was being played on the violin, and a long way off, but I knew that tune too well to permit of my having any doubt on the subject.

Any trouble or fear becomes, as you will some day learn, my dear nephew, immensely intensified and exaggerated at night. It is so, I suppose, because our nerves are in an excited condition, and our brain not sufficiently awake to give a due account of our foolish imaginations. I have myself many times lain awake wrestling in thought with difficulties which in the hours of darkness seemed insurmountable, but with the dawn resolved themselves into merely trivial inconveniences. So on this night, as I sat up in bed looking into the dark, with the sound of that melody in my ears, it seemed as if something too terrible for words had happened; as though the evil spirit, which we had hoped was exorcised, had returned with others sevenfold more wicked than himself, and taken up his abode again with my lost brother. The memory of another night rushed to my mind when

Constance had called me from my bed at Royston, and we had stolen together down the moonlit passages with the lilt of that wicked music vibrating on the still summer air. Poor Constance! She was in her grave now; yet her troubles at least were over, but here, as by some bitter irony, instead of carol or sweet symphony, it was the Gagliarda that woke me from my sleep on Christmas morning.

I flung my dressing-gown about me, and hurried through the corridor and down the stairs which led to the lower storey and my brother's room. As I opened my bedroom door the violin ceased suddenly in the middle of a bar. Its last sound was not a musical note, but rather a horrible scream, such as I pray I may never hear again. It was a sound such as a wounded beast might utter. There is a picture I have seen of Blake's, showing the soul of a strong wicked man leaving his body at death. The spirit is flying out through the window with awful staring eyes, aghast at the desolation into which it is going. If in the agony of dissolution such a lost soul could utter a cry, it would, I think, sound like the wail which I heard from the violin that night.

Instantly all was in absolute stillness. The passages were silent and ghostly in the faint light of my candle; but as I reached the bottom of the stairs I heard the sound of other footsteps, and Mr. Gaskell met me. He was fully dressed, and had evidently not been to bed. He took me kindly by the hand and said, "I feared you might be alarmed by the sound of music. John has been walking in his sleep; he had taken out his violin and was playing on it in a trance. Just as I reached him something in it gave way, and the discord caused by the slackened strings roused him at once. He is awake now and has returned to bed. Control your alarm for his sake and your own. It is better that he should not know you have been awakened."

He pressed my hand and spoke a few more reassuring words, and I went back to my room still much agitated, and yet feeling half ashamed for having shown so much anxiety with so little reason.

That Christmas morning was one of the most beautiful that I ever remember. It seemed as though summer was so loath to leave our sunny Dorset coast that she came back on this day to bid us adieu before her final departure. I had risen early and had partaken of the Sacrament at our little church. Dr. Butler had recently introduced this early service, and though any alteration of time-honoured customs in such matters might not otherwise have met with my approval, I was glad to avail myself of the privilege on this occasion, as I wished in any case to spend the later morning with my brother. The singular beauty of the early hours, and the tranquillising effect of the solemn service brought back serenity to my mind, and effectually banished from it all memories of the preceding night. Mr. Gaskell met me in the hall on my return, and after greeting me kindly with the established compliments of the day, inquired after my health, and hoped that the disturbance of my slumber on the previous night had not affected me injuriously. He had good news for me: John seemed decidedly better, was already dressed, and desired, as it was Christmas morning, that we would take our breakfast with him in his room.

To this, as you may imagine, I readily assented. Our breakfast party passed off with much content, and even with some quiet humour, John sitting in his easy-chair at the head of the table and wishing us the compliments of the season. I found laid in my place a letter from Mrs. Temple greeting us all (for she knew Mr. Gaskell was at Worth), and saying that she hoped to bring little Edward to us at the New Year. My brother seemed much pleased at the prospect of seeing his son, and though perhaps it was only imagination, I fancied he was particularly gratified that Mrs. Temple herself was to pay us a visit. She had not been to Worth since the death of Lady Maltravers.

Before we had finished breakfast the sun beat on the panes with an unusual strength and brightness. His rays cheered us all, and it was so warm that John first opened the windows, and then wheeled his chair on to the walk outside. Mr. Gaskell brought him a hat and mufflers, and we sat with him on the terrace basking in the sun. The sea was still and glassy as a mirror, and the Channel lay stretched before us like a floor of moving gold. A rose or two still hung against the house, and the sun's rays reflected from the red sandstone gave us a December morning more mild and genial than many June days that I have known in the north. We sat for some minutes without speaking, immersed in our own reflections and in the exquisite beauty of the scene.

The stillness was broken by the bells of the parish church ringing for the morning service. There were two of them, and their sound, familiar to us from childhood, seemed like the voices of old friends. John looked at me and said with a sigh, "I should like to go to church. It is long since I was there. You and I have always been on Christmas mornings, Sophy, and Constance would have wished it had she been with us."

His words, so unexpected and tender, filled my eyes with tears; not tears of grief, but of deep thankfulness to see my loved one turning once more to the old ways. It was the first time I had heard him speak of Constance, and that sweet name, with the infinite pathos of her death, and of the spectacle of my brother's weakness, so overcame me that I could not speak. I only pressed his hand and nodded. Mr. Gaskell, who had turned away for a minute, said he thought John would take no harm in attending the morning service provided the church were warm. On this point I could reassure him, having found it properly heated even in the early morning.

Mr. Gaskell was to push John's chair, and I ran off to put on my cloak, with my heart full of profound thankfulness for the signs of returning grace so mercifully vouchsafed to our dear sufferer on this happy day. I was ready dressed and had just entered the library when Mr. Gaskell stepped hurriedly through the window from the terrace. "John has fainted!" he said. "Run for some smelling salts and call Parnham!"

There was a scene of hurried alarm, giving place ere long to terrified despair. Parnham mounted a horse and set off at a wild gallop to Swanage to fetch Dr. Bruton; but an hour before he returned we knew the worst. My brother was beyond the aid of the physician: his wrecked life had reached a sudden term!

*

I have now, dear Edward, completed the brief narrative of some of the facts attending the latter years of your father's life. The motive which has induced me to commit them to writing has been a double one. I am anxious to give effect as far as may be to the desire expressed most strongly to Mr. Gaskell by your father, that you should be put in possession of these facts on your coming of age. And for my own part I think it better that you should thus hear the plain truth from me, lest you should be at the mercy of haphazard reports, which might at any time reach you from ignorant or interested sources. Some of the circumstances were so remarkable that it is scarcely possible to suppose that they were not known, and most probably frequently discussed, in so large an establishment as that of Worth Maltravers. I even have reason to believe that exaggerated and absurd stories were current at the time of Sir John's death, and I should be grieved to think that such foolish tales might by any chance reach your ear without your having any sure means of discovering where the truth lay. God knows how grievous it has been to me to set down on paper some of the facts that I have here narrated. You as a dutiful son will reverence the name even of a father whom you never knew; but you must remember that his sister did more; she loved him with a single-hearted devotion, and it still grieves her to the quick to write anything which may seem to detract from his memory. Only, above all things, let us speak the truth. Much of what I have told you needs, I feel, further explanation, but this I cannot give, for I do not understand the circumstances. Mr. Gaskell, your guardian, will, I believe, add to this account a few notes of his own, which may tend to elucidate some points, as he is in possession of certain facts of which I am still ignorant.

MR. GASKELL'S NOTE

I have read what Miss Maltravers has written, and have but little to add to it. I can give no explanation that will tally with all the facts or meet all the difficulties involved in her narrative. The most obvious solution of some points would be, of course, to suppose that Sir John Maltravers was insane. But to anyone who knew him as intimately as I did, such a hypothesis is untenable; nor, if admitted, would it explain some of the strangest incidents. Moreover, it was strongly negatived by Dr. Frobisher, from whose verdict in such matters there was at the time no appeal, by Dr. Dobie, and by Dr. Bruton, who had known Sir John from his infancy. It is possible that towards the close of his life he suffered occasionally from hallucination, though I could not positively affirm even so much; but this was only when his health had been completely undermined by causes which are very difficult to analyse.

When I first knew him at Oxford he was a strong man physically as well as mentally; open-hearted, and of a merry and genial temperament. At the same time he was, like most cultured persons - and especially musicians - highly strung and excitable. But at a certain point in his career his very nature seemed to change; he became reserved, secretive, and saturnine. On this moral metamorphosis followed an equally startling physical change. His robust health began to fail him, and although there was no definite malady which doctors could combat, he went gradually from bad to worse until the end came.

The commencement of this extraordinary change coincided, I believe, almost exactly with his discovery of the Stradivarius violin; and whether this was, after all, a mere coincidence or something more it is not easy to say. Until a very short time before his death neither Miss Maltravers nor I had any idea how that instrument had come into his possession, or I think something might perhaps have been done to save him.

Though towards the end of his life he spoke freely to his sister of the finding of the violin, he only told her half the story, for he concealed from her entirely that there was anything else in the hidden cupboard at Oxford. But as a matter of fact, he had found there also two manuscript books containing an elaborate diary of some years of a man's life. That man was Adrian Temple, and I believe that in the perusal of this diary must be sought the origin of John Maltravers's ruin. The manuscript was beautifully written in a clear but cramped eighteenth century hand, and gave the idea of a man writing with deliberation, and wishing to transcribe his impressions with accuracy for further reference. The style was excellent, and the minute details given were often of high antiquarian interest; but the record throughout was marred by gross licence. Adrian Temple's life had undoubtedly so definite an influence on Sir John's that a brief outline of it, as gathered from his diaries, is necessary for the understanding of what followed.

Temple went up to Oxford in 1737. He was seventeen years old, without parents, brothers, or sisters; and he possessed the Royston estates in Derbyshire, which were then, as now, a most valuable property. With the year 1738 his diaries begin, and though then little more than a boy, he had tasted every illicit pleasure that Oxford had to offer. His temptations were no doubt great; for besides being wealthy he was handsome, and had probably never known any proper control, as both his parents had died when he was still very young. But in spite of other failings, he was a brilliant scholar, and on taking his degree, was made at once a fellow of St. John's. He took up his abode in that College in a fine set of rooms looking on to the gardens, and from this period seems to have used Royston but little, living always either at Oxford or on the Continent. He formed at this time the acquaintance of one Jocelyn, whom he engaged as companion and amanuensis. Jocelyn was a man of talent, but of irregular life, and was no doubt an accomplice in many of Temple's excesses. In 1743 they both undertook the so-called "grand tour," and though it was not his first visit, it was then probably that Temple first felt the fascination of pagan Italy - a fascination which increased with every year of his after-life.

On his return from foreign travel he found himself among the stirring events of 1745. He was an ardent supporter of the Pretender, and made no attempt to conceal his views. Jacobite tendencies were indeed generally prevalent in the College at the time, and had this been the sum of his offending, it is probable that little notice would have been taken by the College authorities. But his notoriously wild life told against the young man, and certain dark suspicions were not easily passed over. After the fiasco of the Rebellion Dr. Holmes, then President of the College, seems to have made a scapegoat of Temple. He was deprived of his fellowship, and though not formally expelled, such pressure was put upon him as resulted in his leaving St. John's and removing to Magdalen Hall. There his great wealth evidently secured him consideration, and he was given the best rooms in the Hall, that very set looking on to New College Lane which Sir John Maltravers afterwards occupied.

In the first half of the eighteenth century the romance of the Middle Ages, though dying, was not dead, and the occult sciences still found followers among the Oxford towers. From his early years Temple's mind seems to have been set strongly towards mysticism of all kinds, and he and Jocelyn were versed in the jargon of the alchemist and astrologer, and practised according to the ancient rules. It was his reputation as a necromancer, and the stories current of illicit rites performed in the garden-rooms at St. John's, that contributed largely to his being dismissed from that College. He had also become acquainted with Francis Dashwood, the notorious Lord le Despencer, and many a winter's night saw him riding through the misty Thames meadows to the door of the sham Franciscan abbey. In his diaries were more notices than one of the "Franciscans" and the nameless orgies of Medmenham.

He was devoted to music. It was a rare enough accomplishment then, and a rarer thing still to find a wealthy landowner performing on the violin. Yet so he did, though he kept his passion very much to himself, as fiddling was thought lightly of in those days. His musical skill was altogether exceptional, and he was the first possessor of the Stradivarius violin which afterwards fell so unfortunately into Sir John's hands. This violin Temple bought in the autumn of 1738, on the occasion of a first visit to Italy. In that year died the nonagenarian Antonius Stradivarius, the greatest violin-maker the world has ever seen. After Stradivarius's death the stock of fiddles in his shop was sold by auction. Temple happened to be travelling in Cremona at the time with a tutor, and at the auction he bought that very instrument which we afterwards had cause to know so well. A note in his diary gave its cost at four louis, and said that a curious history attached to it. Though it was of his golden period, and probably the finest instrument he ever made, Stradivarius would never sell it, and it had hung for more than thirty years in his shop. It was said that from some whim as he lay dying he had given orders that it should be burnt; but if that were so, the instructions were neglected, and after his death it came under the hammer. Adrian Temple from the first recognised the great value of the instrument. His notes show that he only used it on certain special occasions, and it was no doubt for its better protection that he devised the hidden cupboard where Sir John eventually found it.

The later years of Temple's life were spent for the most part in Italy. On the Scoglio di Venere, near Naples, he built the Villa de Angelis, and there henceforth passed all except the hottest months of the year. Shortly after the completion of the villa Jocelyn left him suddenly, and became a Carthusian monk. A caustic note in his diary hinted that even this foul parasite was shocked into the austerest form of religion by something he had seen going forward. At Naples Temple's dark life became still darker. He dallied, it is true, with Neo-Platonism, and boasts that he, like Plotinus, had twice passed the circle of the nous and enjoyed the fruition of the deity; but the ideals of even that easy doctrine grew in his evil life still more miserably debased. More than once in the manuscript he made mention by name of the Gagliarda of Graziani as having been played at pagan mysteries which these enthusiasts revived at Naples, and the air had evidently impressed itself deeply on his memory. The last entry in his diary is made on the 16th of December, 1752. He was then in Oxford for a few days, but shortly afterwards returned to Naples. The accident of his having just completed a second volume, induced him, no doubt, to leave it behind him in the secret cupboard. It is probable that he commenced a third, but if so it was never found.

In reading the manuscript I was struck with the author's clear and easy style, and found the interest of the narrative increase rather than diminish. At the same time its study was inexpressibly painful to me. Nothing could have supported me in my determination to thoroughly master it but the conviction that if I was to be of any real assistance to my poor friend Maltravers, I must know as far as possible every circumstance connected with his malady. As it was, I felt myself breathing an atmosphere of moral contagion during the perusal of the manuscript, and certain passages have since returned at times to haunt me in spite of all efforts to dislodge them from my memory. When I came to Worth at Miss Maltravers's urgent invitation, I found my friend Sir John terribly altered. It was not only that he was ill and physically weak, but he had entirely lost the manner of youth, which, though indefinable, is yet so appreciable, and draws so sharp a distinction between the first period of life and middle age. But the most striking feature of his illness was the extraordinary pallor of his complexion, which made his face resemble a subtle counterfeit of white wax rather than that of a living man. He welcomed me undemonstratively, but with evident sincerity; and there was an entire absence of the constraint which often accompanies the meeting again of friends whose cordial relations have suffered interruption. From the time of my arrival at Worth until his death we were constantly together; indeed I was much struck by the almost childish dislike which he showed to be left alone even for a few moments. As night approached this feeling became intensified. Parnham slept always in his master's room; but if anything called the servant away even for a minute, he would send for Carotenuto or myself to be with him until his return. His nerves were weak; he started violently at any unexpected noise, and above all, he dreaded being in the dark. When night fell he had additional lamps brought into his room, and even when he composed himself to sleep, insisted on a strong light being kept by his bedside.

I had often read in books of people wearing a "hunted" expression, and had laughed at the phrase as conventional and unmeaning. But when I came to Worth I knew its truth; for if any face ever wore a hunted - I had almost written a haunted - look, it was the white face of Sir John Maltravers. His air seemed that of a man who was constantly expecting the arrival of some evil tidings, and at times reminded me painfully of the guilty expectation of a felon who knows that a warrant is issued for his arrest.

During my visit he spoke to me frequently about his past life, and instead of showing any reluctance to discuss the subject, seemed glad of the opportunity of disburdening his mind. I gathered from him that the reading of Adrian Temple's memoirs had made a deep impression on his mind, which was no doubt intensified by the vision which he thought he saw in his rooms at Oxford, and by the discovery of the portrait at Royston. Of those singular phenomena I have no explanation to offer.

The romantic element in his disposition rendered him peculiarly susceptible to the fascination of that mysticism which breathed through Temple's narrative. He told me that almost from the first time he read it he was filled with a longing to visit the places and to revive the strange life of which it spoke. This inclination he kept at first in check, but by degrees it gathered strength enough to master him.

There is no doubt in my mind that the music of the Gagliarda of Graziani helped materially in this process of mental degradation. It is curious that Michael Prætorius in the "Syntagma musicum" should speak of the Galliard generally as an "invention of the devil, full of shameful and licentious gestures and immodest movements," and the singular melody of the Gagliarda in the "Areopagita" suite certainly exercised from the first a strange influence over me. I shall not do more than touch on the question here, because I see Miss Maltravers has spoken of it at length, and will only say, that though since the day of Sir John's death I have never heard a note of it, the air is still fresh in my mind, and has at times presented itself to me unexpectedly, and always with an unwholesome effect. This I have found happen generally in times of physical depression, and the same air no doubt exerted a similar influence on Sir John, which his impressionable nature rendered from the first more deleterious to him.

I say this advisedly, because I am sure that if some music is good for man and elevates him, other melodies are equally bad and enervating. An experience far wider than any we yet possess is necessary to enable us to say how far this influence is capable of extension. How far, that is, the mind may be directed on the one hand to ascetic abnegation by the systematic use of certain music, or on the other to illicit and dangerous pleasures by melodies of an opposite tendency. But this much is, I think, certain, that after a comparatively advanced standard of culture has once been attained, music is the readiest if not the only key which admits to the yet narrower circle of the highest imaginative thought.

On the occasion for travel afforded him by his honeymoon, an impulse which he could not at the time explain, but which after-events have convinced me was the haunting suggestion of the Gagliarda, drove him to visit the scenes mentioned so often in Temple's diary. He had always been an excellent scholar, and a classic of more than ordinary ability. Rome and Southern Italy filled him with a strange delight. His education enabled him to appreciate to the full what he saw; he peopled the stage with the figures of the original actors, and tried to assimilate his thought to theirs. He began reading classical literature widely, no longer from the scholarly but the literary standpoint. In Rome he spent much time in the librarians' shops, and there met with copies of the numerous authors of the later empire and of those Alexandrine philosophers which are rarely seen in England. In these he found a new delight and fresh food for his mysticism.

Such study, if carried to any extent, is probably dangerous to the English character, and certainly was to a man of Maltravers's romantic sympathies. This reading produced in time so real an effect upon his mind that if he did not definitely abandon Christianity, as I fear he did, he at least adulterated it with other doctrines till it became to him Neo-Platonism. That most seductive of philosophies, which has enthralled so many minds from Proclus and Julian to Augustine and the Renaissancists, found an easy convert in John Maltravers. Its passionate longing for the vague and undefined good, its tolerance of æsthetic impressions, the pleasant superstitions of its dynamic pantheism, all touched responsive chords in his nature. His mind, he told me, became filled with a measureless yearning for the old culture of pagan philosophy, and as the past became clearer and more real, so the present grew dimmer, and his thoughts were gradually weaned entirely from all the natural objects of affection and interest which should otherwise have occupied them. To what a terrible extent this process went on, Miss Maltravers's narrative shows. Soon after reaching Naples he visited the Villa de Angelis, which Temple had built on the ruins of a sea-house of Pomponius. The later building had in its turn become dismantled and ruinous, and Sir John found no difficulty in buying the site outright. He afterwards rebuilt it on an elaborate scale, endeavouring to reproduce in its equipment the luxury of the later empire. I had occasion to visit the house more than once in my capacity of executor, and found it full of priceless works of art, which, though neither so difficult to procure at that time nor so costly as they would be now, were yet sufficiently valuable to have necessitated an unjustifiable outlay.

The situation of the building fostered his infatuation for the past. It lay between the Bay of Naples and the Bay of Baia, and from its windows commanded the same exquisite view which had charmed Cicero and Lucullus, Severus and the Antonines. Hard by stood Baia, the princely seaside resort of the empire. That most luxurious and wanton of all cities of antiquity survived the cataclysms of ages, and only lost its civic continuity and became the ruined village of to-day in the sack of the fifteenth century. But a continuity of wickedness is not so easily broken, and those who know the spot best say that it is still instinct with memories of a shameful past.

For miles along that haunted coast the foot cannot be put down except on the ruins of some splendid villa, and over all there broods a spirit of corruption and debasement actually sensible and oppressive. Of the dawns and sunsets, of the noonday sun tempered by the sea-breeze and the shade of scented groves, those who have been there know the charm, and to those who have not no words can describe it. But there are malefic vapours rising from the corpse of a past not altogether buried, and most cultivated Englishmen who tarry there long feel their influence as did John Maltravers. Like so many decepti deceptores of the Neo-Platonic school, he did not practise the abnegation enjoined by the very cult he professed to follow. Though his nature was far too refined, I believe, ever to sink into the sensualism revealed in Temple's diaries, yet it was through the gratification of corporeal tastes that he endeavoured to achieve the divine extasis; and there were constantly lavish and sumptuous entertainments at the villa, at which strange guests were present.

In such a nightmare of a life it was not to be expected that any mind would find repose, and Maltravers certainly found none. All those cares which usually occupy men's minds, all thoughts of wife, child, and home were, it is true, abandoned; but a wild unrest had hold of him, and never suffered him to be at ease. Though he never told me as much, yet I believe he was under the impression that the form which he had seen at Oxford and Royston had reappeared to him on more than one subsequent occasion. It must have been, I fancy, with a vague hope of "laying" this spectre that he now set himself with eagerness to discover where or how Temple had died. He remembered that Royston tradition said he had succumbed at Naples in the plague of 1752, but an idea seized him that this was not the case; indeed I half suspect his fancy unconsciously pictured that evil man as still alive. The methods by which he eventually discovered the skeleton, or learnt the episodes which preceded Temple's death, I do not know. He promised to tell me some day at length, but a sudden death prevented his ever doing so. The facts as he narrated them, and as I have little doubt they actually occurred, were these: Adrian Temple, after Jocelyn's departure, had made a confidant of one Palamede Domacavalli, a scion of a splendid Parthenopean family of that name.

Palamede had a palace in the heart of Naples, and was Temple's equal in age and also in his great wealth. The two men became boon companions, associated in all kinds of wickedness and excess. At length Palamede married a beautiful girl named Olimpia Aldobrandini, who was also of the noblest lineage; but the intimacy between him and Temple was not interrupted. About a year subsequent to this marriage dancing was going on after a splendid banquet in the great hall of the Palazzo Domacavalli. Adrian, who was a favoured guest, called to the musicians in the gallery to play the "Areopagita" suite, and danced it with Olimpia, the wife of his host. The Gagliarda was reached but never finished, for near the end of the second movement Palamede from behind drove a stiletto into his friend's heart. He had found out that day that Adrian had not spared even Olimpia's honour.

I have endeavoured to condense into a connected story the facts learnt piecemeal from Sir John in conversation. To a certain extent they supplied, if not an explanation, at least an account of the change that had come over my friend. But only to a certain extent; there the explanation broke down and I was left baffled. I could imagine that a life of unwholesome surroundings and disordered studies might in time produce such a loss of mental tone as would lead in turn to moral acolasia, sensual excess, and physical ruin. But in Sir John's case the cause was not adequate; he had, so far as I know, never wholly given the reins to sensuality, and the change was too abrupt and the breakdown of body and mind too complete to be accounted for by such events as those of which he had spoken.

I had, too, an uneasy feeling, which grew upon me the more I saw of him, that while he spoke freely enough on certain topics, and obviously meant to give a complete history of his past life, there was in reality something in the background which he always kept from my view. He was, it seemed, like a young man asked by an indulgent father to disclose his debts in order that they may be discharged, who, although he knows his parent's leniency, and that any debt not now disclosed will be afterwards but a weight upon his own neck, yet hesitates for very shame to tell the full amount, and keeps some items back. So poor Sir John kept something back from me his friend, whose only aim was to afford him consolation and relief, and whose compassion would have made me listen without rebuke to the narration of the blackest crimes. I cannot say how much this conviction grieved me. I would most willingly have given my all, my very life, to save my friend and Miss Maltravers's brother; but my efforts were paralysed by the feeling that I did not know what I had to combat, that some evil influence was at work on him which continually evaded my grasp. Once or twice it seemed as though he were within an ace of telling me all; once or twice, I believe, he had definitely made up his mind to do so; but then the mood changed, or more probably his courage failed him.

It was on one of these occasions that he asked me, somewhat suddenly, whether I thought that a man could by any conscious act committed in the flesh take away from himself all possibility of repentance and ultimate salvation. Though, I trust, a sincere Christian, I am nothing of a theologian, and the question touching on a topic which had not occurred to my mind since childhood, and which seemed to savour rather of medieval romance than of practical religion, took me for a moment aback. I hesitated for an instant, and then replied that the means of salvation offered man were undoubtedly so sufficient as to remove from one truly penitent the guilt of any crime however dark. My hesitation had been but momentary; but Sir John seemed to have noticed it, and sealed his lips to any confession, if he had indeed intended to make any, by changing the subject abruptly. This question naturally gave me food for serious reflection and anxiety. It was the first occasion on which he appeared to me to be undoubtedly suffering from definite hallucination, and I was aware that any illusions connected with religion are generally most difficult to remove. At the same time, anything of this sort was the more remarkable in Sir John's case, as he had, so far as I knew, for a considerable time entirely abandoned the Christian belief.

Unable to elicit any further information from him, and being thus thrown entirely upon my own resources, I determined that I would read through again the whole of Temple's diaries. The task was a very distasteful one, as I have already explained, but I hoped that a second reading might perhaps throw some light on the dark misgiving that was troubling Sir John. I read the manuscript again with the closest attention. Nothing, however, of any importance seemed to have escaped me on the former occasions, and I had reached nearly the end of the second volume when a comparatively slight matter arrested my attention. I have said that the pages were all carefully numbered, and the events of each day recorded separately; even where Temple had found nothing of moment to notice on a given day, he had still inserted the date with the word nil written against it. But as I sat one evening in the library at Worth after Sir John had gone to bed, and was finally glancing through the days of the months in Temple's diary to make sure that all were complete, I found one day was missing. It was towards the end of the second volume, and the day was the 23d of October in the year 1752. A glance at the numbering of the pages revealed the fact that three leaves had been entirely removed, and that the pages numbered 349 to 354 were not to be found. Again I ran through the diaries to see whether there were any leaves removed in other places, but found no other single page missing. All was complete except at this one place, the manuscript beautifully written, with scarcely an error or erasure throughout. A closer examination showed that these leaves had been cut out close to the back, and the cut edges of the paper appeared too fresh to admit of this being done a century ago. A very short reflection convinced me, in fact, that the excision was not likely to have been Temple's, and that it must have been made by Sir John.

My first intention was to ask him at once what the lost pages had contained, and why they had been cut out. The matter might be a mere triviality which he could explain in a moment. But on softly opening his bedroom door I found him sleeping, and Parnham (whom the strong light always burnt in the room rendered more wakeful) informed me that his master had been in a deep sleep for more than an hour. I knew how sorely his wasted energies needed such repose, and stepped back to the library without awaking him. A few minutes before, I had been feeling sleepy at the conclusion of my task, but now all wish for sleep was suddenly banished and a painful wakefulness took its place. I was under a species of mental excitement which reminded me of my feelings some years before at Oxford on the first occasion of our ever playing the Gagliarda together, and an idea struck me with the force of intuition that in these three lost leaves lay the secret of my friend's ruin.

I turned to the context to see whether there was anything in the entries preceding or following the lacuna that would afford a clue to the missing passage. The record of the few days immediately preceding the 23d of October was short and contained nothing of any moment whatever. Adrian and Jocelyn were alone together at the Villa de Angelis. The entry on the 22d was very unimportant and apparently quite complete, ending at the bottom of page 348. Of the 23d there was, as I have said, no record at all, and the entry for the 24th began at the top of page 355. This last memorandum was also brief, and written when the author was annoyed by Jocelyn leaving him.

The defection of his companion had been apparently entirely unexpected. There was at least no previous hint of any such intention. Temple wrote that Jocelyn had left the Villa de Angelis that day and taken up his abode with the Carthusians of San Martino. No reason for such an extraordinary change was given; but there was a hint that Jocelyn had professed himself shocked at something that had happened. The entry concluded with a few bitter remarks: "So farewell to my holy anchoret; and if I cannot speed him with a leprosie as one Elisha did his servant, yet at least he went out from my presence with a face as white as snow."

I had read this sentence more than once before without its attracting other than a passing attention. The curious expression, that Jocelyn had gone out from his presence with a face as white as snow, had hitherto seemed to me to mean nothing more than that the two men had parted in violent anger, and that Temple had abused or bullied his companion. But as I sat alone that night in the library the words seemed to assume an entirely new force, and a strange suspicion began to creep over me.

I have said that one of the most remarkable features of Sir John's illness was his deadly pallor. Though I had now spent some time at Worth, and had been daily struck by this lack of colour, I had never before remembered in this connection that a strange paleness had also been an attribute of Adrian Temple, and was indeed very clearly marked in the picture painted of him by Battoni. In Sir John's account, moreover, of the vision which he thought he had seen in his rooms at Oxford, he had always spoken of the white and waxen face of his spectral visitant. The family tradition of Royston said that Temple had lost his colour in some deadly magical experiment, and a conviction now flashed upon me that Jocelyn's face "as white as snow" could refer only to this same unnatural pallor, and that he too had been smitten with it as with the mark of the beast.

In a drawer of my despatch-box, I kept by me all the letters which the late Lady Maltravers had written home during her ill-fated honeymoon. Miss Maltravers had placed them in my hands in order that I might be acquainted with every fact that could at all elucidate the progress of Sir John's malady. I remembered that in one of these letters mention was made of a sharp attack of fever in Naples, and of her noticing in him for the first time this singular pallor. I found the letter again without difficulty and read it with a new light. Every line breathed of surprise and alarm. Lady Maltravers feared that her husband was very seriously ill. On the Wednesday, two days before she wrote, he had suffered all day from a strange restlessness, which had increased after they had retired in the evening. He could not sleep and had dressed again, saying he would walk a little in the night air to compose himself. He had not returned till near six in the morning, and then seemed so exhausted that he had since been confined to his bed. He was terribly pale, and the doctors feared he had been attacked by some strange fever.

The date of the letter was the 25th of October, fixing the night of the 23d as the time of Sir John's first attack. The coincidence of the date with that of the day missing in Temple's diary was significant, but it was not needed now to convince me that Sir John's ruin was due to something that occurred on that fatal night at Naples.

The question that Dr. Frobisher had asked Miss Maltravers when he was first called to see her brother in London returned to my memory with an overwhelming force. "Had Sir John been subjected to any mental shock; had he received any severe fright?" I knew now that the question should have been answered in the affirmative, for I felt as certain as if Sir John had told me himself that he had received a violent shock, probably some terrible fright, on the night of the 23d of October. What the nature of that shock could have been my imagination was powerless to conceive, only I knew that whatever Sir John had done or seen, Adrian Temple and Jocelyn had done or seen also a century before and at the same place. That horror which had blanched the face of all three men for life had fallen perhaps with a less overwhelming force on Temple's seasoned wickedness, but had driven the worthless Jocelyn to the cloister, and was driving Sir John to the grave.

These thoughts as they passed through my mind filled me with a vague alarm. The lateness of the hour, the stillness and the subdued light, made the library in which I sat seem so vast and lonely that I began to feel the same dread of being alone that I had observed so often in my friend. Though only a door separated me from his bedroom, and I could hear his deep and regular breathing, I felt as though I must go in and waken him or Parnham to keep me company and save me from my own reflections. By a strong effort I restrained myself, and sat down to think the matter over and endeavour to frame some hypothesis that might explain the mystery. But it was all to no purpose. I merely wearied myself without being able to arrive at even a plausible conjecture, except that it seemed as though the strange coincidence of date might point to some ghastly charm or incantation which could only be carried out on one certain night of the year.

It must have been near morning when, quite exhausted, I fell into an uneasy slumber in the arm-chair where I sat. My sleep, however brief, was peopled with a succession of fantastic visions, in which I continually saw Sir John, not ill and wasted as now, but vigorous and handsome as I had known him at Oxford, standing beside a glowing brazier and reciting words I could not understand, while another man with a sneering white face sat in a corner playing the air of the Gagliarda on a violin. Parnham woke me in my chair at seven o'clock; his master, he said, was still sleeping easily.

I had made up my mind that as soon as he awoke I would inquire of Sir John as to the pages missing from the diary; but though my expectation and excitement were at a high pitch, I was forced to restrain my curiosity, for Sir John's slumber continued late into the day. Dr. Bruton called in the morning, and said that this sleep was what the patient's condition most required, and was a distinctly favourable symptom; he was on no account to be disturbed. Sir John did not leave his bed, but continued dozing all day till the evening. When at last he shook off his drowsiness, the hour was already so late that, in spite of my anxiety, I hesitated to talk with him about the diaries, lest I should unduly excite him before the night.

As the evening advanced he became very uneasy, and rose more than once from his bed. This restlessness, following on the repose of the day, ought perhaps to have made me anxious, for I have since observed that when death is very near an apprehensive unrest often sets in both with men and animals. It seems as if they dreaded to resign themselves to sleep, lest as they slumber the last enemy should seize them unawares. They try to fling off the bedclothes, they sometimes must leave their beds and walk. So it was with poor John Maltravers on his last Christmas Eve. I had sat with him grieving for his disquiet until he seemed to grow more tranquil, and at length fell asleep. I was sleeping that night in his room instead of Parnham, and tired with sitting up through the previous night, I flung myself, dressed as I was, upon the bed. I had scarcely dozed off, I think, before the sound of his violin awoke me. I found he had risen from his bed, had taken his favourite instrument, and was playing in his sleep. The air was the Gagliarda of the "Areopagita" suite, which I had not heard since we had played it last together at Oxford, and it brought back with it a crowd of far-off memories and infinite regrets. I cursed the sleepiness which had overcome me at my watchman's post, and allowed Sir John to play once more that melody which had always been fraught with such evil for him; and I was about to wake him gently when he was startled from sleep by a strange accident. As I walked towards him the violin seemed entirely to collapse in his hands, and, as a matter of fact, the belly then gave way and broke under the strain of the strings. As the strings slackened, the last note became an unearthly discord. If I were superstitious I should say that some evil spirit then went out of the violin, and broke in his parting throes the wooden tabernacle which had so long sheltered him. It was the last time the instrument was ever used, and that hideous chord was the last that Maltravers ever played.

I had feared that the shock of waking thus suddenly from sleep would have a very prejudicial effect upon the sleep-walker, but this seemed not to be the case. I persuaded him to go back at once to bed, and in a few minutes he fell asleep again. In the morning he seemed for the first time distinctly better; there was indeed something of his old self in his manner. It seemed as though the breaking of the violin had been an actual relief to him; and I believe that on that Christmas morning his better instincts woke, and that his old religious training and the associations of his boyhood then made their last appeal. I was pleased at such a change, however temporary it might prove. He wished to go to church, and I determined that again I would subdue my curiosity and defer the questions I was burning to put till after our return from the morning service. Miss Maltravers had gone indoors to make some preparation, Sir John was in his wheel-chair on the terrace, and I was sitting by him in the sun. For a few moments he appeared immersed in silent thought, and then bent over towards me till his head was close to mine, and said, "Dear William, there is something I must tell you. I feel I cannot even go to church till I have told you all." His manner shocked me beyond expression. I knew that he was going to tell me the secret of the lost pages, but instead of wishing any longer to have my curiosity satisfied, I felt a horrible dread of what he might say next. He took my hand in his and held it tightly, as a man who was about to undergo severe physical pain and sought the consolation of a friend's support. Then he went on: "You will be shocked at what I am going to tell you; but listen, and do not give me up: You must stand by me and comfort me and help me to turn again." He paused for a moment and continued: "It was one night in October, when Constance and I were at Naples. I took that violin and went by myself to the ruined villa on the Scoglio di Venere." He had been speaking with difficulty. His hand clutched mine convulsively, but still I felt it trembling, and I could see the moisture standing thick on his forehead. At this point the effort seemed too much for him and he broke off. "I cannot go on, I cannot tell you, but you can read it for yourself. In that diary which I gave you there are some pages missing." The suspense was becoming intolerable to me, and I broke in, "Yes, yes, I know; you cut them out. Tell me where they are," He went on: "Yes, I cut them out lest they should possibly fall into anyone's hands unaware. But before you read them you must swear, as you hope for salvation, that you will never try to do what is written in them. Swear this to me now, or I never can let you see them." My eagerness was too great to stop now to discuss trifles, and to humour him I swore as desired. He had been speaking with a continual increasing effort; he cast a hurried and fearful glance round as though he expected to see someone listening, and it was almost in a whisper that he went on, "You will find them in -" His agitation had become most painful to watch, and as he spoke the last words a convulsion passed over his face, and speech failing him, he sank back on his pillow. A strange fear took hold of me. For a moment I thought there were others on the terrace beside myself, and turned round expecting to see Miss Maltravers returned; but we were still alone. I even fancied that just as Sir John spoke his last words I felt something brush swiftly by me. He put up his hands, beating the air with a most painful gesture, as though he were trying to keep off an antagonist who had gripped him by the throat, and made a final struggle to speak. But the spasm was too strong for him; a dreadful stillness followed, and he was gone.

There is little more to add; for Sir John's guilty secret perished with him. Though I was sure from his manner that the missing leaves were concealed somewhere at Worth, and though as executor I caused the most diligent search to be made, no trace of them was afterwards found; nor did any circumstance ever transpire to fling further light upon the matter. I must confess that I should have felt the discovery of these pages as a relief; for though I dreaded what I might have had to read, yet I was more anxious lest, being found at a later period and falling into other hands, they should cause a recrudescence of that plague which had blighted Sir John's life.

Of the nature of the events which took place on that night at Naples I can form no conjecture. But as certain physical sights have ere now proved so revolting as to unhinge the intellect, so I can imagine that the mind may in a state of extreme tension conjure up to itself some form of moral evil so hideous as metaphysically to sear it: and this, I believe, happened in the case both of Adrian Temple and of Sir John Maltravers.

It is difficult to imagine the accessories used to produce the mental excitation in which alone such a presentment of evil could become imaginable. Fancy and legend, which have combined to represent as possible appearances of the supernatural, agree also in considering them as more likely to occur at certain times and places than at others; and it is possible that the missing pages of the diary contained an account of the time, place, and other conditions chosen by Temple for some deadly experiment. Sir John most probably re-enacted the scene under precisely similar conditions, and the effect on his overwrought imagination was so vivid as to upset the balance of his mind. The time chosen was no doubt the night of the 23d of October, and I cannot help thinking that the place was one of those evil-looking and ruinous sea-rooms which had so terrifying an effect on Miss Maltravers. Temple may have used on that night one of the medieval incantations, or possibly the more ancient invocation of the Isiac rite with which a man of his knowledge and proclivities would certainly be familiar. The accessories of either are sufficiently hideous to weaken the mind by terror, and so prepare it for a belief in some frightful apparition. But whatever was done, I feel sure that the music of the Gagliarda formed part of the ceremonial.

Medieval philosophers and theologians held that evil is in its essence so horrible that the human mind, if it could realise it, must perish at its contemplation. Such realisation was by mercy ordinarily withheld, but its possibility was hinted in the legend of the Visio Malefica. The Visio Beatifica was, as is well known, that vision of the Deity or realisation of the perfect Good which was to form the happiness of heaven, and the reward of the sanctified in the next world. Tradition says that this vision was accorded also to some specially elect spirits even in this life, as to Enoch, Elijah, Stephen, and Jerome. But there was a converse to the Beatific Vision in the Visio Malefica, or presentation of absolute Evil, which was to be the chief torture of the damned, and which, like the Beatific Vision, had been made visible in life to certain desperate men. It visited Esau, as was said, when he found no place for repentance, and Judas, whom it drove to suicide. Cain saw it when he murdered his brother, and legend relates that in his case, and in that of others, it left a physical brand to be borne by the body to the grave. It was supposed that the Malefic Vision, besides being thus spontaneously presented to typically abandoned men, had actually been purposely called up by some few great adepts, and used by them to blast their enemies. But to do so was considered equivalent to a conscious surrender to the powers of evil, as the vision once seen took away all hope of final salvation.

Adrian Temple would undoubtedly be cognisant of this legend, and the lost experiment may have been an attempt to call up the Malefic Vision. It is but a vague conjecture at the best, for the tree of the knowledge of Evil bears many sorts of poisonous fruit, and no one can give full account of the extravagances of a wayward fancy.

Conjointly with Miss Sophia, Sir John appointed me his executor and guardian of his only son. Two months later we had lit a great fire in the library at Worth. In it, after the servants were gone to bed, we burnt the book containing the "Areopagita" of Graziani, and the Stradivarius fiddle. The diaries of Temple I had already destroyed, and wish that I could as easily blot out their foul and debasing memories from my mind. I shall probably be blamed by those who would exalt art at the expense of everything else, for burning a unique violin. This reproach I am content to bear. Though I am not unreasonably superstitious, and have no sympathy for that potential pantheism to which Sir John Maltravers surrendered his intellect, yet I felt so great an aversion to this violin that I would neither suffer it to remain at Worth, nor pass into other hands. Miss Sophia was entirely at one with me on this point. It was the same feeling which restrains any except fools or braggarts from wishing to sleep in "haunted" rooms, or to live in houses polluted with the memory of a revolting crime. No sane mind believes in foolish apparitions, but fancy may at times bewitch the best of us. So the Stradivarius was burnt. It was, after all, perhaps not so serious a matter, for, as I have said, the bass-bar had given way. There had always been a question whether it was strong enough to resist the strain of modern stringing. Experience showed at last that it was not. With the failure of the bass-bar the belly collapsed, and the wood broke across the grain in so extraordinary a manner as to put the fiddle beyond repair, except as a curiosity. Its loss, therefore, is not to be so much regretted. Sir Edward has been brought up to think more of a cricket-bat than of a violin-bow; but if he wishes at any time to buy a Stradivarius, the fortunes of Worth and Royston, nursed through two long minorities, will certainly justify his doing so.

Miss Sophia and I stood by and watched the holocaust. My heart misgave me for a moment when I saw the mellow red varnish blistering off the back, but I put my regret resolutely aside. As the bright flames jumped up and lapped it round, they flung a red glow on the scroll. It was wonderfully wrought, and differed, as I think Miss Maltravers has already said, from any known example of Stradivarius. As we watched it, the scroll took form, and we saw what we had never seen before, that it was cut so that the deep lines in a certain light showed as the profile of a man. It was a wizened little paganish face, with sharp-cut features and a bald head. As I looked at it I knew at once (and a cameo has since confirmed the fact) that it was a head of Porphyry. Thus the second label found in the violin was explained and Sir John's view confirmed, that Stradivarius had made the instrument for some Neo-Platonist enthusiast who had dedicated it to his master Porphyrius.

*

A year after Sir John's death I went with Miss Maltravers to Worth church to see a plain slab of slate which we had placed over her brother's grave. We stood in bright sunlight in the Maltravers chapel, with the monuments of that splendid family about us. Among them were the altar-tomb of Sir Esmoun, and the effigies of more than one Crusader. As I looked on their knightly forms, with their heads resting on their tilting helms, their faces set firm, and their hands joined in prayer, I could not help envying them that full and unwavering faith for which they had fought and died. It seemed to stand out in such sharp contrast with our latter-day sciolism and half-believed creeds, and to be flung into higher relief by the dark shadow of John Maltravers's ruined life. At our feet was the great brass of one Sir Roger de Maltravers. I pointed out the end of the inscription to my companion:

"CVIVS ANIMÆ, ATQVE ANIMABVS OMNIVM FIDELIVM DEFVNCTORVM, ATQVE NOSTRIS ANIMABVS QVVM EX HAC LVCE TRANSIVERIMVS, PROPITIETVR DEVS." Though no Catholic, I could not refuse to add a sincere Amen. Miss Sophia, who is not ignorant of Latin, read the inscription after me. "Ex hac luce," she said, as though speaking to herself, "out of this light; alas! alas! for some the light is darkness."

THE HOUSE OF THE DEAD HAND
By Edith Wharton

I

"Above all," the letter ended, "don't leave Siena without seeing Doctor Lombard's Leonardo. Lombard is a queer old Englishman, a mystic or a madman (if the two are not synonymous), and a devout student of the Italian Renaissance. He has lived for years in Italy, exploring its remotest corners, and has lately picked up an undoubted Leonardo, which came to light in a farmhouse near Bergamo. It is believed to be one of the missing pictures mentioned by Vasari, and is at any rate, according to the most competent authorities, a genuine and almost untouched example of the best period.

"Lombard is a queer stick, and jealous of showing his treasures; but we struck up a friendship when I was working on the Sodomas in Siena three years ago, and if you will give him the enclosed line you may get a peep at the Leonardo. Probably not more than a peep, though, for I hear he refuses to have it reproduced. I want badly to use it in my monograph on the Windsor drawings, so please see what you can do for me, and if you can't persuade him to let you take a photograph or make a sketch, at least jot down a detailed description of the picture and get from him all the facts you can. I hear that the French and Italian governments have offered him a large advance on his purchase, but that he refuses to sell at any price, though he certainly can't afford such luxuries; in fact, I don't see where he got enough money to buy the picture. He lives in the Via Papa Giulio."

Wyant sat at the table d'hote of his hotel, re-reading his friend's letter over a late luncheon. He had been five days in Siena without having found time to call on Doctor Lombard, not from any indifference to the opportunity presented, but because it was his first visit to the strange red city and he was still under the spell of its more conspicuous wonders - the brick palaces flinging out their wrought-iron torch-holders with a gesture of arrogant suzerainty; the great council-chamber emblazoned with civic allegories; the pageant of Pope Julius on the Library walls; the Sodomas smiling balefully through the dusk of mouldering chapels - and it was only when his first hunger was appeased that he remembered that one course in the banquet was still untasted.

He put the letter in his pocket and turned to leave the room, with a nod to its only other occupant, an olive-skinned young man with lustrous eyes and a low collar, who sat on the other side of the table, perusing the Fanfulla di Domenica. This gentleman, his daily vis-a-vis, returned the nod with a Latin eloquence of gesture, and Wyant passed on to the ante-chamber, where he paused to light a cigarette. He was just restoring the case to his pocket when he heard a hurried step behind him, and the lustrous-eyed young man advanced through the glass doors of the dining-room.

"Pardon me, sir," he said in measured English, and with an intonation of exquisite politeness; "you have let this letter fall."

Wyant, recognizing his friend's note of introduction to Doctor Lombard, took it with a word of thanks, and was about to turn away when he perceived that the eyes of his fellow diner remained fixed on him with a gaze of melancholy interrogation.

"Again pardon me," the young man at length ventured, "but are you by chance the friend of the illustrious Doctor Lombard?"

"No," returned Wyant, with the instinctive Anglo-Saxon distrust of foreign advances. Then, fearing to appear rude, he said with a guarded politeness: "Perhaps, by the way, you can tell me the number of his house. I see it is not given here."

The young man brightened perceptibly. "The number of the house is thirteen; but any one can indicate it to you - it is well known in Siena. It is called," he continued after a moment, "the House of the Dead Hand."

Wyant stared. "What a queer name!" he said.

"The name comes from an antique hand of marble which for many hundred years has been above the door."

Wyant was turning away with a gesture of thanks, when the other added: "If you would have the kindness to ring twice."

"To ring twice?"

"At the doctor's." The young man smiled. "It is the custom."

It was a dazzling March afternoon, with a shower of sun from the mid-blue, and a marshalling of slaty clouds behind the umber-coloured hills. For nearly an hour Wyant loitered on the Lizza, watching the shadows race across the naked landscape and the thunder blacken in the west; then he decided to set out for the House of the Dead Hand. The map in his guidebook showed him that the Via Papa Giulio was one of the streets which radiate from the Piazza, and thither he bent his course, pausing at every other step to fill his eye with some fresh image of weather-beaten beauty. The clouds had rolled upward, obscuring the sunshine and hanging like a funereal baldachin above the projecting cornices of Doctor Lombard's street, and Wyant walked for some distance in the shade of the beetling palace fronts before his eye fell on a doorway surmounted by a sallow marble hand. He stood for a moment staring up at the strange emblem. The hand was a woman's - a dead drooping hand, which hung there convulsed and helpless, as though it had been thrust forth in denunciation of some evil mystery within the house, and had sunk struggling into death.

A girl who was drawing water from the well in the court said that the English doctor lived on the first floor, and Wyant, passing through a glazed door, mounted the damp degrees of a vaulted stairway with a plaster AEsculapius mouldering in a niche on the landing. Facing the AEsculapius was another door, and as Wyant put his hand on the bell-rope he remembered his unknown friend's injunction, and rang twice.

His ring was answered by a peasant woman with a low forehead and small close-set eyes, who, after a prolonged scrutiny of himself, his card, and his letter of introduction, left him standing in a high, cold ante-chamber floored with brick. He heard her wooden pattens click down an interminable corridor, and after some delay she returned and told him to follow her.

They passed through a long saloon, bare as the ante-chamber, but loftily vaulted, and frescoed with a seventeenth-century Triumph of Scipio or Alexander - martial figures following Wyant with the filmed melancholy gaze of shades in limbo. At the end of this apartment he was admitted to a smaller room, with the same atmosphere of mortal cold, but showing more obvious signs of occupancy. The walls were covered with tapestry which had faded to the grey-brown tints of decaying vegetation, so that the young man felt as though he were entering a sunless autumn wood. Against these hangings stood a few tall cabinets on heavy gilt feet, and at a table in the window three persons were seated: an elderly lady who was warming her hands over a brazier, a girl bent above a strip of needle-work, and an old man.

As the latter advanced toward Wyant, the young man was conscious of staring with unseemly intentness at his small round-backed figure, dressed with shabby disorder and surmounted by a wonderful head, lean, vulpine, eagle-beaked as that of some art-loving despot of the Renaissance: a head combining the venerable hair and large prominent eyes of the humanist with the greedy profile of the adventurer. Wyant, in musing on the Italian portrait-medals of the fifteenth century, had often fancied that only in that period of fierce individualism could types so paradoxical have been produced; yet the subtle craftsmen who committed them to the bronze had never drawn a face more strangely stamped with contradictory passions than that of Doctor Lombard.

"I am glad to see you," he said to Wyant, extending a hand which seemed a mere framework held together by knotted veins. "We lead a quiet life here and receive few visitors, but any friend of Professor Clyde's is welcome." Then, with a gesture which included the two women, he added dryly: "My wife and daughter often talk of Professor Clyde."

"Oh yes - he used to make me such nice toast; they don't understand toast in Italy," said Mrs. Lombard in a high plaintive voice.

It would have been difficult, from Doctor Lombard's manner and appearance to guess his nationality; but his wife was so inconsciently and ineradicably English that even the silhouette of her cap seemed a protest against Continental laxities. She was a stout fair woman, with pale cheeks netted with red lines. A brooch with a miniature portrait sustained a bogwood watch-chain upon her bosom, and at her elbow lay a heap of knitting and an old copy of *The Queen*.

The young girl, who had remained standing, was a slim replica of her mother, with an apple-cheeked face and opaque blue eyes. Her small head was prodigally laden with braids of dull fair hair, and she might have had a kind of transient prettiness but for the sullen droop of her round mouth. It was hard to say whether her expression implied ill-temper or apathy; but Wyant was struck by the contrast between the fierce vitality of the doctor's age and the inanimateness of his daughter's youth.

Seating himself in the chair which his host advanced, the young man tried to open the conversation by addressing to Mrs. Lombard some random remark on the beauties of Siena. The lady murmured a resigned assent, and Doctor Lombard interposed with a smile: "My dear sir, my wife considers Siena a most salubrious spot, and is favourably impressed by the cheapness of the marketing; but she deplores the total absence of muffins and cannel coal, and cannot resign herself to the Italian method of dusting furniture."

"But they don't, you know - they don't dust it!" Mrs. Lombard protested, without showing any resentment of her husband's manner.

"Precisely - they don't dust it. Since we have lived in Siena we have not once seen the cobwebs removed from the battlements of the Mangia. Can you conceive of such housekeeping? My wife has never yet dared to write it home to her aunts at Bonchurch."

Mrs. Lombard accepted in silence this remarkable statement of her views, and her husband, with a malicious smile at Wyant's embarrassment, planted himself suddenly before the young man.

"And now," said he, "do you want to see my Leonardo?"

"DO I?" cried Wyant, on his feet in a flash.

The doctor chuckled. "Ah," he said, with a kind of crooning deliberation, "that's the way they all behave - that's what they all come for." He turned to his daughter with another variation of mockery in his smile. "Don't fancy it's for your beaux yeux, my dear; or for the mature charms of Mrs. Lombard," he added, glaring suddenly at his wife, who had taken up her knitting and was softly murmuring over the number of her stitches

Neither lady appeared to notice his pleasantries, and he continued, addressing himself to Wyant: "They all come - they all come; but many are called and few are chosen." His voice sank to solemnity. "While I live," he said, "no unworthy eye shall desecrate that picture. But I will not do my friend Clyde the injustice to suppose that he would send an unworthy representative. He tells me he wishes a description of the picture for his book; and you shall describe it to him - if you can."

Wyant hesitated, not knowing whether it was a propitious moment to put in his appeal for a photograph.

"Well, sir," he said, "you know Clyde wants me to take away all I can of it."

Doctor Lombard eyed him sardonically. "You're welcome to take away all you can carry," he replied; adding, as he turned to his daughter: "That is, if he has your permission, Sybilla."

The girl rose without a word, and laying aside her work, took a key from a secret drawer in one of the cabinets, while the doctor continued in the same note of grim jocularity: "For you must know that the picture is not mine - it is my daughter's."

He followed with evident amusement the surprised glance which Wyant turned on the young girl's impassive figure.

"Sybilla," he pursued, "is a votary of the arts; she has inherited her fond father's passion for the unattainable. Luckily, however, she also recently inherited a tidy legacy from her grandmother; and having seen the Leonardo, on which its discoverer had placed a price far beyond my reach, she took a step which deserves to go down to history: she invested her whole inheritance in the purchase of the picture, thus enabling me to spend my closing years in communion with one of the world's masterpieces. My dear sir, could Antigone do more?"

The object of this strange eulogy had meanwhile drawn aside one of the tapestry hangings, and fitted her key into a concealed door.

"Come," said Doctor Lombard, "let us go before the light fails us."

Wyant glanced at Mrs. Lombard, who continued to knit impassively.

"No, no," said his host, "my wife will not come with us. You might not suspect it from her conversation, but my wife has no feeling for art - Italian art, that is; for no one is fonder of our early Victorian school."

"Frith's Railway Station, you know," said Mrs. Lombard, smiling. "I like an animated picture."

Miss Lombard, who had unlocked the door, held back the tapestry to let her father and Wyant pass out; then she followed them down a narrow stone passage with another door at its end. This door was iron-barred, and Wyant noticed that it had a complicated patent lock. The girl fitted another key into the lock, and Doctor Lombard led the way into a small room. The dark panelling of this apartment was irradiated by streams of yellow light slanting through the disbanded thunder clouds, and in the central brightness hung a picture concealed by a curtain of faded velvet.

"A little too bright, Sybilla," said Doctor Lombard. His face had grown solemn, and his mouth twitched nervously as his daughter drew a linen drapery across the upper part of the window.

"That will do - that will do." He turned impressively to Wyant. "Do you see the pomegranate bud in this rug? Place yourself there - keep your left foot on it, please. And now, Sybilla, draw the cord."

Miss Lombard advanced and placed her hand on a cord hidden behind the velvet curtain.

"Ah," said the doctor, "one moment: I should like you, while looking at the picture, to have in mind a few lines of verse. Sybilla -"

Without the slightest change of countenance, and with a promptness which proved her to be prepared for the request, Miss Lombard began to recite, in a full round voice like her mother's, St. Bernard's invocation to the Virgin, in the thirty-third canto of the Paradise.

"Thank you, my dear," said her father, drawing a deep breath as she ended. "That unapproachable combination of vowel sounds prepares one better than anything I know for the contemplation of the picture."

As he spoke the folds of velvet slowly parted, and the Leonardo appeared in its frame of tarnished gold:

From the nature of Miss Lombard's recitation Wyant had expected a sacred subject, and his surprise was therefore great as the composition was gradually revealed by the widening division of the curtain.

In the background a steel-coloured river wound through a pale calcareous landscape; while to the left, on a lonely peak, a crucified Christ hung livid against indigo clouds. The central figure of the foreground, however, was that of a woman seated in an antique chair of marble with bas-reliefs of dancing maenads. Her feet rested on a meadow sprinkled with minute wild-flowers, and her attitude of smiling majesty recalled that of Dosso Dossi's Circe. She wore a red robe, flowing in closely fluted lines from under a fancifully embroidered cloak. Above her high forehead the crinkled golden hair flowed sideways beneath a veil; one hand drooped on the arm of her chair; the other held up an inverted human skull, into which a young Dionysus, smooth, brown and sidelong as the St. John of the Louvre, poured a stream of wine from a high-poised flagon. At the lady's feet lay the symbols of art and luxury: a flute and a roll of music, a platter heaped with grapes and roses, the torso of a Greek statuette, and a bowl overflowing with coins and jewels; behind her, on the chalky hilltop, hung the crucified Christ. A scroll in a corner of the foreground bore the legend: Lux Mundi.

Wyant, emerging from the first plunge of wonder, turned inquiringly toward his companions. Neither had moved. Miss Lombard stood with her hand on the cord, her lids lowered, her mouth drooping; the doctor, his strange Thoth-like profile turned toward his guest, was still lost in rapt contemplation of his treasure.

Wyant addressed the young girl.

"You are fortunate," he said, "to be the possessor of anything so perfect."

"It is considered very beautiful," she said coldly.

"Beautiful - BEAUTIFUL!" the doctor burst out. "Ah, the poor, worn out, over-worked word! There are no adjectives in the language fresh enough to describe such pristine brilliancy; all their brightness has been worn off by misuse. Think of the things that have been called beautiful, and then look at THAT!"

"It is worthy of a new vocabulary," Wyant agreed.

"Yes," Doctor Lombard continued, "my daughter is indeed fortunate. She has chosen what Catholics call the higher life - the counsel of perfection. What other private person enjoys the same opportunity of understanding the master? Who else lives under the same roof with an untouched masterpiece of Leonardo's? Think of the happiness of being always under the influence of such a creation; of living INTO it; of partaking of it in daily and hourly communion! This room is a chapel; the sight of that picture is a sacrament. What an atmosphere for a young life to unfold itself in! My daughter is singularly blessed. Sybilla, point out some of the details to Mr. Wyant; I see that he will appreciate them."

The girl turned her dense blue eyes toward Wyant; then, glancing away from him, she pointed to the canvas.

"Notice the modelling of the left hand," she began in a monotonous voice; "it recalls the hand of the Mona Lisa. The head of the naked genius will remind you of that of the St. John of the Louvre, but it is more purely pagan and is turned a little less to the right. The embroidery on the cloak is symbolic: you will see that the roots of this plant have burst through the vase. This recalls the famous definition of Hamlet's character in Wilhelm Meister. Here are the mystic rose, the flame, and the serpent, emblem of eternity. Some of the other symbols we have not yet been able to decipher."

Wyant watched her curiously; she seemed to be reciting a lesson.

"And the picture itself?" he said. "How do you explain that? Lux Mundi - what a curious device to connect with such a subject! What can it mean?"

Miss Lombard dropped her eyes: the answer was evidently not included in her lesson.

"What, indeed?" the doctor interposed. "What does life mean? As one may define it in a hundred different ways, so one may find a hundred different meanings in this picture. Its symbolism is as many-faceted as a well-cut diamond. Who, for instance, is that divine lady? Is it she who is the true Lux Mundi - the light reflected from jewels and young eyes, from polished marble and clear waters and statues of bronze? Or is that the Light of the World, extinguished on yonder stormy hill, and is this lady the Pride of Life, feasting blindly on the wine of iniquity, with her back turned to the light which has shone for her in vain? Something of both these meanings may be traced in the picture; but to me it symbolizes rather the central truth of existence: that all that is raised in incorruption is sown in corruption; art, beauty, love, religion; that all our wine is drunk out of skulls, and poured for us by the mysterious genius of a remote and cruel past."

The doctor's face blazed: his bent figure seemed to straighten itself and become taller.

"Ah," he cried, growing more dithyrambic, "how lightly you ask what it means! How confidently you expect an answer! Yet here am I who have given my life to the study of the Renaissance; who have violated its tomb, laid open its dead body, and traced the course of every muscle, bone, and artery; who have sucked its very soul from the pages of poets and humanists; who have wept and believed with Joachim of Flora, smiled and doubted with AEneas Sylvius Piccolomini; who have patiently followed to its source the least inspiration of the masters, and groped in neolithic caverns and Babylonian ruins for the first unfolding tendrils of the arabesques of Mantegna and Crivelli; and I tell you that I stand abashed and ignorant before the mystery of this picture. It means nothing - it means all things. It may represent the period which saw its creation; it may represent all ages past and to come. There are volumes of meaning in the tiniest emblem on the lady's cloak; the blossoms of its border are rooted in the deepest soil of myth and tradition. Don't ask what it means, young man, but bow your head in thankfulness for having seen it!"

Miss Lombard laid her hand on his arm.

"Don't excite yourself, father," she said in the detached tone of a professional nurse.

He answered with a despairing gesture. "Ah, it's easy for you to talk. You have years and years to spend with it; I am an old man, and every moment counts!"

"It's bad for you," she repeated with gentle obstinacy.

The doctor's sacred fury had in fact burnt itself out. He dropped into a seat with dull eyes and slackening lips, and his daughter drew the curtain across the picture.

Wyant turned away reluctantly. He felt that his opportunity was slipping from him, yet he dared not refer to Clyde's wish for a photograph. He now understood the meaning of the laugh with which Doctor Lombard had given him leave to carry away all the details he could remember. The picture was so dazzling, so unexpected, so crossed with elusive and contradictory suggestions, that the most alert observer, when placed suddenly before it, must lose his coordinating faculty in a sense of confused wonder. Yet how valuable to Clyde the record of such a work would be! In some ways it seemed to be the summing up of the master's thought, the key to his enigmatic philosophy.

The doctor had risen and was walking slowly toward the door. His daughter unlocked it, and Wyant followed them back in silence to the room in which they had left Mrs. Lombard. That lady was no longer there, and he could think of no excuse for lingering.

He thanked the doctor, and turned to Miss Lombard, who stood in the middle of the room as though awaiting farther orders.

"It is very good of you," he said, "to allow one even a glimpse of such a treasure."

She looked at him with her odd directness. "You will come again?" she said quickly; and turning to her father she added: "You know what Professor Clyde asked. This gentleman cannot give him any account of the picture without seeing it again."

Doctor Lombard glanced at her vaguely; he was still like a person in a trance.

"Eh?" he said, rousing himself with an effort.

"I said, father, that Mr. Wyant must see the picture again if he is to tell Professor Clyde about it," Miss Lombard repeated with extraordinary precision of tone.

Wyant was silent. He had the puzzled sense that his wishes were being divined and gratified for reasons with which he was in no way connected.

"Well, well," the doctor muttered, "I don't say no - I don't say no. I know what Clyde wants - I don't refuse to help him." He turned to Wyant. "You may come again - you may make notes," he added with a sudden effort. "Jot down what occurs to you. I'm willing to concede that."

Wyant again caught the girl's eye, but its emphatic message perplexed him.

"You're very good," he said tentatively, "but the fact is the picture is so mysterious - so full of complicated detail - that I'm afraid no notes I could make would serve Clyde's purpose as well as - as a photograph, say. If you would allow me -"

Miss Lombard's brow darkened, and her father raised his head furiously.

"A photograph? A photograph, did you say? Good God, man, not ten people have been allowed to set foot in that room! A PHOTOGRAPH?"

Wyant saw his mistake, but saw also that he had gone too far to retreat.

"I know, sir, from what Clyde has told me, that you object to having any reproduction of the picture published; but he hoped you might let me take a photograph for his personal use - not to be reproduced in his book, but simply to give him something to work by. I should take the photograph myself, and the negative would of course be yours. If you wished it, only one impression would be struck off, and that one Clyde could return to you when he had done with it."

Doctor Lombard interrupted him with a snarl. "When he had done with it? Just so: I thank thee for that word! When it had been re-photographed, drawn, traced, autotyped, passed about from hand to hand, defiled by every ignorant eye in England, vulgarised by the blundering praise of every art-scribbler in Europe! Bah! I'd as soon give you the picture itself: why don't you ask for that?"

"Well, sir," said Wyant calmly, "if you will trust me with it, I'll engage to take it safely to England and back, and to let no eye but Clyde's see it while it is out of your keeping."

The doctor received this remarkable proposal in silence; then he burst into a laugh.

"Upon my soul!" he said with sardonic good humour.

It was Miss Lombard's turn to look perplexedly at Wyant. His last words and her father's unexpected reply had evidently carried her beyond her depth.

"Well, sir, am I to take the picture?" Wyant smilingly pursued.

"No, young man; nor a photograph of it. Nor a sketch, either; mind that - nothing that can be reproduced. Sybilla," he cried with sudden passion, "swear to me that the picture shall never be reproduced! No photograph, no sketch - now or afterward. Do you hear me?"

"Yes, father," said the girl quietly.

"The vandals," he muttered, "the desecrators of beauty; if I thought it would ever get into their hands I'd burn it first, by God!" He turned to Wyant, speaking more quietly. "I said you might come back - I never retract what I say. But you must give me your word that no one but Clyde shall see the notes you make."

Wyant was growing warm.

"If you won't trust me with a photograph I wonder you trust me not to show my notes!" he exclaimed.

The doctor looked at him with a malicious smile.

"Humph!" he said; "would they be of much use to anybody?"

Wyant saw that he was losing ground and controlled his impatience.

"To Clyde, I hope, at any rate," he answered, holding out his hand. The doctor shook it without a trace of resentment, and Wyant added: "When shall I come, sir?"

"To-morrow - to-morrow morning," cried Miss Lombard, speaking suddenly.

She looked fixedly at her father, and he shrugged his shoulders.

"The picture is hers," he said to Wyant.

In the ante-chamber the young man was met by the woman who had admitted him. She handed him his hat and stick, and turned to unbar the door. As the bolt slipped back he felt a touch on his arm.

"You have a letter?" she said in a low tone.

"A letter?" He stared. "What letter?"

She shrugged her shoulders, and drew back to let him pass.

II

As Wyant emerged from the house he paused once more to glance up at its scarred brick facade. The marble hand drooped tragically above the entrance: in the waning light it seemed to have relaxed into the passiveness of despair, and Wyant stood musing on its hidden meaning. But the Dead Hand was not the only mysterious thing about Doctor Lombard's house. What were the relations between Miss Lombard and her father? Above all, between Miss Lombard and her picture? She did not look like a person capable of a disinterested passion for the arts; and there had been moments when it struck Wyant that she hated the picture.

The sky at the end of the street was flooded with turbulent yellow light, and the young man turned his steps toward the church of San Domenico, in the hope of catching the lingering brightness on Sodoma's St. Catherine.

The great bare aisles were almost dark when he entered, and he had to grope his way to the chapel steps. Under the momentary evocation of the sunset, the saint's figure emerged pale and swooning from the dusk, and the warm light gave a sensual tinge to her ecstasy. The flesh seemed to glow and heave, the eyelids to tremble; Wyant stood fascinated by the accidental collaboration of light and colour.

Suddenly he noticed that something white had fluttered to the ground at his feet. He stooped and picked up a small thin sheet of note-paper, folded and sealed like an old-fashioned letter, and bearing the superscription:

To the Count Ottaviano Celsi.

Wyant stared at this mysterious document. Where had it come from? He was distinctly conscious of having seen it fall through the air, close to his feet. He glanced up at the dark ceiling of the chapel; then he turned and looked about the church. There was only one figure in it, that of a man who knelt near the high altar.

Suddenly Wyant recalled the question of Doctor Lombard's maid-servant. Was this the letter she had asked for? Had he been unconsciously carrying it about with him all the afternoon? Who was Count Ottaviano Celsi, and how came Wyant to have been chosen to act as that nobleman's ambulant letter-box?

Wyant laid his hat and stick on the chapel steps and began to explore his pockets, in the irrational hope of finding there some clue to the mystery; but they held nothing which he had not himself put there, and he was reduced to wondering how the letter, supposing some unknown hand to have bestowed it on him, had happened to fall out while he stood motionless before the picture.

At this point he was disturbed by a step on the floor of the aisle, and turning, he saw his lustrous-eyed neighbour of the table d'hote.

The young man bowed and waved an apologetic hand.

"I do not intrude?" he inquired suavely.

Without waiting for a reply, he mounted the steps of the chapel, glancing about him with the affable air of an afternoon caller.

"I see," he remarked with a smile, "that you know the hour at which our saint should be visited."

Wyant agreed that the hour was indeed felicitous.

The stranger stood beamingly before the picture.

"What grace! What poetry!" he murmured, apostrophising the St. Catherine, but letting his glance slip rapidly about the chapel as he spoke.

Wyant, detecting the manoeuvre, murmured a brief assent.

"But it is cold here - mortally cold; you do not find it so?" The intruder put on his hat. "It is permitted at this hour - when the church is empty. And you, my dear sir - do you not feel the dampness? You are an artist, are you not? And to artists it is permitted to cover the head when they are engaged in the study of the paintings."

He darted suddenly toward the steps and bent over Wyant's hat.

"Permit me - cover yourself!" he said a moment later, holding out the hat with an ingratiating gesture.

A light flashed on Wyant.

"Perhaps," he said, looking straight at the young man, "you will tell me your name. My own is Wyant."

The stranger, surprised, but not disconcerted, drew forth a coroneted card, which he offered with a low bow. On the card was engraved:

Il Conte Ottaviano Celsi.

"I am much obliged to you," said Wyant; "and I may as well tell you that the letter which you apparently expected to find in the lining of my hat is not there, but in my pocket."

He drew it out and handed it to its owner, who had grown very pale.

"And now," Wyant continued, "you will perhaps be good enough to tell me what all this means."

There was no mistaking the effect produced on Count Ottaviano by this request. His lips moved, but he achieved only an ineffectual smile.

"I suppose you know," Wyant went on, his anger rising at the sight of the other's discomfiture, "that you have taken an unwarrantable liberty. I don't yet understand what part I have been made to play, but it's evident that you have made use of me to serve some purpose of your own, and I propose to know the reason why."

Count Ottaviano advanced with an imploring gesture.

"Sir," he pleaded, "you permit me to speak?"

"I expect you to," cried Wyant. "But not here," he added, hearing the clank of the verger's keys. "It is growing dark, and we shall be turned out in a few minutes."

He walked across the church, and Count Ottaviano followed him out into the deserted square.

"Now," said Wyant, pausing on the steps.

The Count, who had regained some measure of self-possession, began to speak in a high key, with an accompaniment of conciliatory gesture.

"My dear sir - my dear Mr. Wyant - you find me in an abominable position - that, as a man of honour, I immediately confess. I have taken advantage of you - yes! I have counted on your amiability, your chivalry - too far, perhaps? I confess it! But what could I do? It was to oblige a lady" - he laid a hand on his heart - "a lady whom I would die to serve!" He went on with increasing volubility, his deliberate English swept away by a torrent of Italian, through which Wyant, with some difficulty, struggled to a comprehension of the case.

Count Ottaviano, according to his own statement, had come to Siena some months previously, on business connected with his mother's property; the paternal estate being near Orvieto, of which ancient city his father was syndic. Soon after his arrival in Siena the young Count had met the incomparable daughter of Doctor Lombard, and falling deeply in love with her, had prevailed on his parents to ask her hand in marriage. Doctor Lombard had not opposed his suit, but when the question of settlements arose it became known that Miss Lombard, who was possessed of a small property in her own right, had a short time before invested the whole amount in the purchase of the Bergamo Leonardo. Thereupon Count Ottaviano's parents had politely suggested that she should sell the picture and thus recover her independence; and this proposal being met by a curt refusal from Doctor Lombard, they had withdrawn their consent to their son's marriage. The young lady's attitude had hitherto been one of passive submission; she was horribly afraid of her father, and would never venture openly to oppose him; but she had made known to Ottaviano her intention of not giving him up, of waiting patiently till events should take a more favourable turn. She seemed hardly aware, the Count said with a sigh, that the means of escape lay in her own hands; that she was of age, and had a right to sell the picture, and to marry without asking her father's consent. Meanwhile her suitor spared no pains to keep himself before her, to remind her that he, too, was waiting and would never give her up.

Doctor Lombard, who suspected the young man of trying to persuade Sybilla to sell the picture, had forbidden the lovers to meet or to correspond; they were thus driven to clandestine communication, and had several times, the Count ingenuously avowed, made use of the doctor's visitors as a means of exchanging letters.

"And you told the visitors to ring twice?" Wyant interposed.

The young man extended his hands in a deprecating gesture. Could Mr. Wyant blame him? He was young, he was ardent, he was enamoured! The young lady had done him the supreme honour of avowing her attachment, of pledging her unalterable fidelity; should he suffer his devotion to be outdone? But his purpose in writing to her, he admitted, was not merely to reiterate his fidelity; he was trying by every means in his power to induce her to sell the picture. He had organized a plan of action; every detail was complete; if she would but have the courage to carry out his instructions he would answer for the result. His idea was that she should secretly retire to a convent of which his aunt was the Mother Superior, and from that stronghold should transact the sale of the Leonardo. He had a purchaser ready, who was willing to pay a large sum; a sum, Count Ottaviano whispered, considerably in excess of the young lady's original inheritance; once the picture sold, it could, if necessary, be removed by force from Doctor Lombard's house, and his daughter, being safely in the convent, would be spared the painful scenes incidental to the removal. Finally, if Doctor Lombard were vindictive enough to refuse his consent to her marriage, she had only to make a *sommation respectueuse*, and at the end of the prescribed delay no power on earth could prevent her becoming the wife of Count Ottaviano.

Wyant's anger had fallen at the recital of this simple romance. It was absurd to be angry with a young man who confided his secrets to the first stranger he met in the streets, and placed his hand on his heart whenever he mentioned the name of his betrothed. The easiest way out of the business was to take it as a joke. Wyant had played the wall to this new Pyramus and Thisbe, and was philosophic enough to laugh at the part he had unwittingly performed.

He held out his hand with a smile to Count Ottaviano.

"I won't deprive you any longer," he said, "of the pleasure of reading your letter."

"Oh, sir, a thousand thanks! And when you return to the casa Lombard, you will take a message from me - the letter she expected this afternoon?"

"The letter she expected?" Wyant paused. "No, thank you. I thought you understood that where I come from we don't do that kind of thing - knowingly."

"But, sir, to serve a young lady!"

"I'm sorry for the young lady, if what you tell me is true" - the Count's expressive hands resented the doubt - "but remember that if I am under obligations to any one in this matter, it is to her father, who has admitted me to his house and has allowed me to see his picture."

"HIS picture? Hers!"

"Well, the house is his, at all events."

"Unhappily - since to her it is a dungeon!"

"Why doesn't she leave it, then?" exclaimed Wyant impatiently.

The Count clasped his hands. "Ah, how you say that - with what force, with what virility! If you would but say it to HER in that tone - you, her countryman! She has no one to advise her; the mother is an idiot; the father is terrible; she is in his power; it is my belief that he would kill her if she resisted him. Mr. Wyant, I tremble for her life while she remains in that house!"

"Oh, come," said Wyant lightly, "they seem to understand each other well enough. But in any case, you must see that I can't interfere - at least you would if you were an Englishman," he added with an escape of contempt.

III

Wyant's affiliations in Siena being restricted to an acquaintance with his land-lady, he was forced to apply to her for the verification of Count Ottaviano's story.

The young nobleman had, it appeared, given a perfectly correct account of his situation. His father, Count Celsi-Mongirone, was a man of distinguished family and some wealth. He was syndic of Orvieto, and lived either in that town or on his neighbouring estate of Mongirone. His wife owned a large property near Siena, and Count Ottaviano, who was the second son, came there from time to time to look into its management. The eldest son was in the army, the youngest in the Church; and an aunt of Count Ottaviano's was Mother Superior of the Visitandine convent in Siena. At one time it had been said that Count Ottaviano, who was a most amiable and accomplished young man, was to marry the daughter of the strange Englishman, Doctor Lombard, but difficulties having arisen as to the adjustment of the young lady's dower, Count Celsi-Mongirone had very properly broken off the match. It was sad for the young man, however, who was said to be deeply in love, and to find frequent excuses for coming to Siena to inspect his mother's estate.

Viewed in the light of Count Ottaviano's personality the story had a tinge of opera bouffe; but the next morning, as Wyant mounted the stairs of the House of the Dead Hand, the situation insensibly assumed another aspect. It was impossible to take Doctor Lombard lightly; and there was a suggestion of fatality in the appearance of his gaunt dwelling. Who could tell amid what tragic records of domestic tyranny and fluttering broken purposes the little drama of Miss Lombard's fate was being played out? Might not the accumulated influences of such a house modify the lives within it in a manner unguessed by the inmates of a suburban villa with sanitary plumbing and a telephone?

One person, at least, remained unperturbed by such fanciful problems; and that was Mrs. Lombard, who, at Wyant's entrance, raised a placidly wrinkled brow from her knitting. The morning was mild, and her chair had been wheeled into a bar of sunshine near the window, so that she made a cheerful spot of prose in the poetic gloom of her surroundings.

"What a nice morning!" she said; "it must be delightful weather at Bonchurch."

Her dull blue glance wandered across the narrow street with its threatening house fronts, and fluttered back baffled, like a bird with clipped wings. It was evident, poor lady, that she had never seen beyond the opposite houses.

Wyant was not sorry to find her alone. Seeing that she was surprised at his reappearance he said at once: "I have come back to study Miss Lombard's picture."

"Oh, the picture -" Mrs. Lombard's face expressed a gentle disappointment, which might have been boredom in a person of acuter sensibilities. "It's an original Leonardo, you know," she said mechanically.

"And Miss Lombard is very proud of it, I suppose? She seems to have inherited her father's love for art."

Mrs. Lombard counted her stitches, and he went on: "It's unusual in so young a girl. Such tastes generally develop later."

Mrs. Lombard looked up eagerly. "That's what I say! I was quite different at her age, you know. I liked dancing, and doing a pretty bit of fancy-work. Not that I couldn't sketch, too; I had a master down from London. My aunts have some of my crayons hung up in their drawing-room now - I did a view of Kenilworth which was thought pleasing. But I liked a picnic, too, or a pretty walk through the woods with young people of my own age. I say it's more natural, Mr. Wyant; one may have a feeling for art, and do crayons that are worth framing, and yet not give up everything else. I was taught that there were other things."

Wyant, half-ashamed of provoking these innocent confidences, could not resist another question. "And Miss Lombard cares for nothing else?"

Her mother looked troubled.

"Sybilla is so clever - she says I don't understand. You know how self-confident young people are! My husband never said that of me, now - he knows I had an excellent education. My aunts were very particular; I was brought up to have opinions, and my husband has always respected them. He says himself that he wouldn't for the world miss hearing my opinion on any subject; you may have noticed that he often refers to my tastes.

He has always respected my preference for living in England; he likes to hear me give my reasons for it. He is so much interested in my ideas that he often says he knows just what I am going to say before I speak. But Sybilla does not care for what I think -"

At this point Doctor Lombard entered. He glanced sharply at Wyant. "The servant is a fool; she didn't tell me you were here." His eye turned to his wife. "Well, my dear, what have you been telling Mr. Wyant? About the aunts at Bonchurch, I'll be bound!"

Mrs. Lombard looked triumphantly at Wyant, and her husband rubbed his hooked fingers, with a smile.

"Mrs. Lombard's aunts are very superior women. They subscribe to the circulating library, and borrow Good Words and the Monthly Packet from the curate's wife across the way. They have the rector to tea twice a year, and keep a page-boy, and are visited by two baronets' wives. They devoted themselves to the education of their orphan niece, and I think I may say without boasting that Mrs. Lombard's conversation shows marked traces of the advantages she enjoyed."

Mrs. Lombard coloured with pleasure.

"I was telling Mr. Wyant that my aunts were very particular."

"Quite so, my dear; and did you mention that they never sleep in anything but linen, and that Miss Sophia puts away the furs and blankets every spring with her own hands? Both those facts are interesting to the student of human nature." Doctor Lombard glanced at his watch. "But we are missing an incomparable moment; the light is perfect at this hour."

Wyant rose, and the doctor led him through the tapestried door and down the passageway.

The light was, in fact, perfect, and the picture shone with an inner radiancy, as though a lamp burned behind the soft screen of the lady's flesh. Every detail of the foreground detached itself with jewel-like precision. Wyant noticed a dozen accessories which had escaped him on the previous day.

He drew out his note-book, and the doctor, who had dropped his sardonic grin for a look of devout contemplation, pushed a chair forward, and seated himself on a carved settle against the wall.

"Now, then," he said, "tell Clyde what you can; but the letter killeth."

He sank down, his hands hanging on the arm of the settle like the claws of a dead bird, his eyes fixed on Wyant's notebook with the obvious intention of detecting any attempt at a surreptitious sketch.

Wyant, nettled at this surveillance, and disturbed by the speculations which Doctor Lombard's strange household excited, sat motionless for a few minutes, staring first at the picture and then at the blank pages of the note-book. The thought that Doctor Lombard was enjoying his discomfiture at length roused him, and he began to write.

He was interrupted by a knock on the iron door. Doctor Lombard rose to unlock it, and his daughter entered.

She bowed hurriedly to Wyant, without looking at him.

"Father, had you forgotten that the man from Monte Amiato was to come back this morning with an answer about the bas-relief? He is here now; he says he can't wait."

"The devil!" cried her father impatiently. "Didn't you tell him -"

"Yes; but he says he can't come back. If you want to see him you must come now."

"Then you think there's a chance?"

She nodded.

He turned and looked at Wyant, who was writing assiduously.

"You will stay here, Sybilla; I shall be back in a moment."

He hurried out, locking the door behind him.

Wyant had looked up, wondering if Miss Lombard would show any surprise at being locked in with him; but it was his turn to be surprised, for hardly had they heard the key withdrawn when she moved close to him, her small face pale and tumultuous.

"I arranged it - I must speak to you," she gasped. "He'll be back in five minutes."

Her courage seemed to fail, and she looked at him helplessly.

Wyant had a sense of stepping among explosives. He glanced about him at the dusky vaulted room, at the haunting smile of the strange picture overhead, and at the pink-and-white girl whispering of conspiracies in a voice meant to exchange platitudes with a curate.

"How can I help you?" he said with a rush of compassion.

"Oh, if you would! I never have a chance to speak to any one; it's so difficult - he watches me - he'll be back immediately."

"Try to tell me what I can do."

"I don't dare; I feel as if he were behind me." She turned away, fixing her eyes on the picture. A sound startled her. "There he comes, and I haven't spoken! It was my only chance; but it bewilders me so to be hurried."

"I don't hear any one," said Wyant, listening. "Try to tell me."

"How can I make you understand? It would take so long to explain." She drew a deep breath, and then with a plunge - "Will you come here again this afternoon - at about five?" she whispered.

"Come here again?"

"Yes - you can ask to see the picture - make some excuse. He will come with you, of course; I will open the door for you – and - and lock you both in," she gasped.

"Lock us in?"

"You see? You understand? It's the only way for me to leave the house - if I am ever to do it." She drew another difficult breath. "The key will be returned - by a safe person - in half an hour - perhaps sooner -"

She trembled so much that she was obliged to lean against the settle for support.

Wyant looked at her steadily; he was very sorry for her.

"I can't, Miss Lombard," he said at length.

"You can't?"

"I'm sorry; I must seem cruel; but consider -"

He was stopped by the futility of the word: as well ask a hunted rabbit to pause in its dash for a hole!

Wyant took her hand; it was cold and nerveless.

"I will serve you in any way I can; but you must see that this way is impossible. Can't I talk to you again? Perhaps -"

"Oh," she cried, starting up, "there he comes!"

Doctor Lombard's step sounded in the passage.

Wyant held her fast. "Tell me one thing: he won't let you sell the picture?"

"No - hush!"

"Make no pledges for the future, then; promise me that."

"The future?"

"In case he should die: your father is an old man. You haven't promised?"

She shook her head.

"Don't, then; remember that."

She made no answer, and the key turned in the lock.

As he passed out of the house, its scowling cornice and facade of ravaged brick looked down on him with the startlingness of a strange face, seen momentarily in a crowd, and impressing itself on the brain as part of an inevitable future. Above the doorway, the marble hand reached out like the cry of an imprisoned anguish.

Wyant turned away impatiently.

"Rubbish!" he said to himself. "SHE isn't walled in; she can get out if she wants to."

IV

Wyant had any number of plans for coming to Miss Lombard's aid: he was elaborating the twentieth when, on the same afternoon, he stepped into the express train for Florence. By the time the train reached Certaldo he was convinced that, in thus hastening his departure, he had followed the only reasonable course; at Empoli, he began to reflect that the priest and the Levite had probably justified themselves in much the same manner.

A month later, after his return to England, he was unexpectedly relieved from these alternatives of extenuation and approval. A paragraph in the morning paper announced the sudden death of Doctor Lombard, the distinguished English dilettante who had long resided in Siena. Wyant's justification was complete. Our blindest impulses become evidence of perspicacity when they fall in with the course of events.

Wyant could now comfortably speculate on the particular complications from which his foresight had probably saved him. The climax was unexpectedly dramatic. Miss Lombard, on the brink of a step which, whatever its issue, would have burdened her with retrospective compunction, had been set free before her suitor's ardour could have had time to cool, and was now doubtless planning a life of domestic felicity on the proceeds of the Leonardo. One thing, however, struck Wyant as odd - he saw no mention of the sale of the picture. He had scanned the papers for an immediate announcement of its transfer to one of the great museums; but presently concluding that Miss Lombard, out of filial piety, had wished to avoid an appearance of unseemly haste in the disposal of her treasure, he dismissed the matter from his mind. Other affairs happened to engage him; the months slipped by, and gradually the lady and the picture dwelt less vividly in his mind.

It was not till five or six years later, when chance took him again to Siena, that the recollection started from some inner fold of memory. He found himself, as it happened, at the head of Doctor Lombard's street, and glancing down that grim thoroughfare, caught an oblique glimpse of the doctor's house front, with the Dead Hand projecting above its threshold. The sight revived his interest, and that evening, over an admirable frittata, he questioned his landlady about Miss Lombard's marriage.

"The daughter of the English doctor? But she has never married, signore."

"Never married? What, then, became of Count Ottaviano?"

"For a long time he waited; but last year he married a noble lady of the Maremma."

"But what happened - why was the marriage broken?"

The landlady enacted a pantomime of baffled interrogation.

"And Miss Lombard still lives in her father's house?"

"Yes, signore; she is still there."

"And the Leonardo -"

"The Leonardo, also, is still there."

The next day, as Wyant entered the House of the Dead Hand, he remembered Count Ottaviano's injunction to ring twice, and smiled mournfully to think that so much subtlety had been vain. But what could have prevented the marriage? If Doctor Lombard's death had been long delayed, time might have acted as a dissolvent, or the young lady's resolve have failed; but it seemed impossible that the white heat of ardour in which Wyant had left the lovers should have cooled in a few short weeks.

As he ascended the vaulted stairway the atmosphere of the place seemed a reply to his conjectures. The same numbing air fell on him, like an emanation from some persistent will-power, a something fierce and imminent which might reduce to impotence every impulse within its range. Wyant could almost fancy a hand on his shoulder, guiding him upward with the ironical intent of confronting him with the evidence of its work.

A strange servant opened the door, and he was presently introduced to the tapestried room, where, from their usual seats in the window, Mrs. Lombard and her daughter advanced to welcome him with faint ejaculations of surprise.

Both had grown oddly old, but in a dry, smooth way, as fruits might shrivel on a shelf instead of ripening on the tree. Mrs. Lombard was still knitting, and pausing now and then to warm her swollen hands above the brazier; and Miss Lombard, in rising, had laid aside a strip of needle-work which might have been the same on which Wyant had first seen her engaged.

Their visitor inquired discreetly how they had fared in the interval, and learned that they had thought of returning to England, but had somehow never done so.

"I am sorry not to see my aunts again," Mrs. Lombard said resignedly; "but Sybilla thinks it best that we should not go this year."

"Next year, perhaps," murmured Miss Lombard, in a voice which seemed to suggest that they had a great waste of time to fill.

She had returned to her seat, and sat bending over her work. Her hair enveloped her head in the same thick braids, but the rose colour of her cheeks had turned to blotches of dull red, like some pigment which has darkened in drying.

"And Professor Clyde - is he well?" Mrs. Lombard asked affably; continuing, as her daughter raised a startled eye: "Surely, Sybilla, Mr. Wyant was the gentleman who was sent by Professor Clyde to see the Leonardo?"

Miss Lombard was silent, but Wyant hastened to assure the elder lady of his friend's well-being.

"Ah - perhaps, then, he will come back some day to Siena," she said, sighing. Wyant declared that it was more than likely; and there ensued a pause, which he presently broke by saying to Miss Lombard: "And you still have the picture?"

She raised her eyes and looked at him. "Should you like to see it?" she asked.

On his assenting, she rose, and extracting the same key from the same secret drawer, unlocked the door beneath the tapestry.

They walked down the passage in silence, and she stood aside with a grave gesture, making Wyant pass before her into the room. Then she crossed over and drew the curtain back from the picture.

The light of the early afternoon poured full on it: its surface appeared to ripple and heave with a fluid splendour. The colours had lost none of their warmth, the outlines none of their pure precision; it seemed to Wyant like some magical flower which had burst suddenly from the mould of darkness and oblivion.

He turned to Miss Lombard with a movement of comprehension.

"Ah, I understand - you couldn't part with it, after all!" he cried.

"No - I couldn't part with it," she answered.

"It's too beautiful - too beautiful," he assented.

"Too beautiful?" She turned on him with a curious stare. "I have never thought it beautiful, you know."

He gave back the stare. "You have never -"

She shook her head. "It's not that. I hate it; I've always hated it. But he wouldn't let me - he will never let me now."

Wyant was startled by her use of the present tense. Her look surprised him, too: there was a strange fixity of resentment in her innocuous eye. Was it possible that she was labouring under some delusion? Or did the pronoun not refer to her father?

"You mean that Doctor Lombard did not wish you to part with the picture?"

"No - he prevented me; he will always prevent me."

There was another pause. "You promised him, then, before his death -"

"No; I promised nothing. He died too suddenly to make me." Her voice sank to a whisper. "I was free - perfectly free - or I thought I was till I tried."

"Till you tried?"

"To disobey him - to sell the picture. Then I found it was impossible. I tried again and again; but he was always in the room with me."

She glanced over her shoulder as though she had heard a step; and to Wyant, too, for a moment, the room seemed full of a third presence.

"And you can't," he faltered, unconsciously dropping his voice to the pitch of hers.

She shook her head, gazing at him mystically. "I can't lock him out; I can never lock him out now. I told you I should never have another chance."

Wyant felt the chill of her words like a cold breath in his hair.

"Oh," he groaned; but she cut him off with a grave gesture.

"It is too late," she said; "but you ought to have helped me that day."

A WICKED VOICE
By Vernon Lee

To M.W., IN REMEMBRANCE OF THE LAST SONG AT PALAZZO BARBARO, Chi ha inteso, intenda.

They have been congratulating me again today upon being the only composer of our days - of these days of deafening orchestral effects and poetical quackery - who has despised the new-fangled nonsense of Wagner, and returned boldly to the traditions of Handel and Gluck and the divine Mozart, to the supremacy of melody and the respect of the human voice.

O cursed human voice, violin of flesh and blood, fashioned with the subtle tools, the cunning hands, of Satan! O execrable art of singing, have you not wrought mischief enough in the past, degrading so much noble genius, corrupting the purity of Mozart, reducing Handel to a writer of high-class singing-exercises, and defrauding the world of the only inspiration worthy of Sophocles and Euripides, the poetry of the great poet Gluck? Is it not enough to have dishonoured a whole century in idolatry of that wicked and contemptible wretch the singer, without persecuting an obscure young composer of our days, whose only wealth is his love of nobility in art, and perhaps some few grains of genius?

And then they compliment me upon the perfection with which I imitate the style of the great dead masters; or ask me very seriously whether, even if I could gain over the modern public to this bygone style of music, I could hope to find singers to perform it. Sometimes, when people talk as they have been talking today, and laugh when I declare myself a follower of Wagner, I burst into a paroxysm of unintelligible, childish rage, and exclaim, "We shall see that some day!"

Yes; some day we shall see! For, after all, may I not recover from this strangest of maladies? It is still possible that the day may come when all these things shall seem but an incredible nightmare; the day when Ogier the Dane shall be completed, and men shall know whether I am a follower of the great master of the Future or the miserable singing-masters of the Past. I am but half-bewitched, since I am conscious of the spell that binds me. My old nurse, far off in Norway, used to tell me that were-wolves are ordinary men and women half their days, and that if, during that period, they become aware of their horrid transformation they may find the means to forestall it. May this not be the case with me? My reason, after all, is free, although my artistic inspiration be enslaved; and I can despise and loathe the music I am forced to compose, and the execrable power that forces me.

Nay, is it not because I have studied with the doggedness of hatred this corrupt and corrupting music of the Past, seeking for every little peculiarity of style and every biographical trifle merely to display its vileness, is it not for this presumptuous courage that I have been overtaken by such mysterious, incredible vengeance?

And meanwhile, my only relief consists in going over and over again in my mind the tale of my miseries. This time I will write it, writing only to tear up, to throw the manuscript unread into the fire. And yet, who knows? As the last charred pages shall crackle and slowly sink into the red embers, perhaps the spell may be broken, and I may possess once more my long-lost liberty, my vanished genius.

It was a breathless evening under the full moon, that implacable full moon beneath which, even more than beneath the dreamy splendour of noon-tide, Venice seemed to swelter in the midst of the waters, exhaling, like some great lily, mysterious influences, which make the brain swim and the heart faint - a moral malaria, distilled, as I thought, from those languishing melodies, those cooing vocalizations which I had found in the musty music-books of a century ago. I see that moonlight evening as if it were present. I see my fellow-lodgers of that little artists' boarding-house. The table on which they lean after supper is strewn with bits of bread, with napkins rolled in tapestry rollers, spots of wine here and there, and at regular intervals chipped pepper-pots, stands of toothpicks, and heaps of those huge hard peaches which nature imitates from the marble-shops of Pisa. The whole pension-full is assembled, and examining stupidly the engraving which the American etcher has just brought for me, knowing me to be mad about eighteenth century music and musicians, and having noticed, as he turned over the heaps of penny prints in the square of San Polo, that the portrait is that of a singer of those days.

Singer, thing of evil, stupid and wicked slave of the voice, of that instrument which was not invented by the human intellect, but begotten of the body, and which, instead of moving the soul, merely stirs up the dregs of our nature! For what is the voice but the Beast calling, awakening that other Beast sleeping in the depths of mankind, the Beast which all great art has ever sought to chain up, as the archangel chains up, in old pictures, the demon with his woman's face? How could the creature attached to this voice, its owner and its victim, the singer, the great, the real singer who once ruled over every heart, be otherwise than wicked and contemptible? But let me try and get on with my story.

I can see all my fellow-boarders, leaning on the table, contemplating the print, this effeminate beau, his hair curled into ailes de pigeon, his sword passed through his embroidered pocket, seated under a triumphal arch somewhere among the clouds, surrounded by puffy Cupids and crowned with laurels by a bouncing goddess of fame. I hear again all the insipid exclamations, the insipid questions about this singer: "When did he live? Was he very famous? Are you sure, Magnus, that this is really a portrait," &c. &c. And I hear my own voice, as if in the far distance, giving them all sorts of information, biographical and critical, out of a battered little volume called The Theatre of Musical Glory; or, Opinions upon the most Famous Chapel-masters and Virtuosi of this Century, by Father Prosdocimo Sabatelli, Barnalite, Professor of Eloquence at the College of Modena, and Member of the Arcadian Academy, under the pastoral name of Evander Lilybaean, Venice, 1785, with the approbation of the Superiors. I tell them all how this singer, this Balthasar Cesari, was nick-named Zaffirino because of a sapphire engraved with cabalistic signs presented to him one evening by a masked stranger, in whom wise folk recognized that great cultivator of the human voice, the devil; how much more wonderful had been this Zaffirino's vocal gifts than those of any singer of ancient or modern times; how his brief life had been but a series of triumphs, petted by the greatest kings, sung by the most famous poets, and finally, adds Father Prosdocimo, "courted (if the grave Muse of history may incline her ear to the gossip of gallantry) by the most charming nymphs, even of the very highest quality."

My friends glance once more at the engraving; more insipid remarks are made; I am requested - especially by the American young ladies - to play or sing one of this Zaffirino's favourite songs - "For of course you know them, dear Maestro Magnus, you who have such a passion for all old music. Do be good, and sit down to the piano." I refuse, rudely enough, rolling the print in my fingers. How fearfully this cursed heat, these cursed moonlight nights, must have unstrung me! This Venice would certainly kill me in the long-run! Why, the sight of this idiotic engraving, the mere name of that coxcomb of a singer, have made my heart beat and my limbs turn to water like a love-sick hobbledehoy.

After my gruff refusal, the company begins to disperse; they prepare to go out, some to have a row on the lagoon, others to saunter before the cafés at St. Mark's; family discussions arise, gruntings of fathers, murmurs of mothers, peals of laughing from young girls and young men. And the moon, pouring in by the wide-open windows, turns this old palace ballroom, nowadays an inn dining-room, into a lagoon, scintillating, undulating like the other lagoon, the real one, which stretches out yonder furrowed by invisible gondolas betrayed by the red prow-lights. At last the whole lot of them are on the move. I shall be able to get some quiet in my room, and to work a little at my opera of Ogier the Dane. But no! Conversation revives, and, of all things, about that singer, that Zaffirino, whose absurd portrait I am crunching in my fingers.

The principal speaker is Count Alvise, an old Venetian with dyed whiskers, a great check tie fastened with two pins and a chain; a threadbare patrician who is dying to secure for his lanky son that pretty American girl, whose mother is intoxicated by all his mooning anecdotes about the past glories of Venice in general, and of his illustrious family in particular. Why, in Heaven's name, must he pitch upon Zaffirino for his mooning, this old duffer of a patrician?

"Zaffirino - ah yes, to be sure! Balthasar Cesari, called Zaffirino," snuffles the voice of Count Alvise, who always repeats the last word of every sentence at least three times. "Yes,

Zaffirino, to be sure! A famous singer of the days of my forefathers; yes, of my forefathers, dear lady!" Then a lot of rubbish about the former greatness of Venice, the glories of old music, the former Conservatoires, all mixed up with anecdotes of Rossini and Donizetti, whom he pretends to have known intimately. Finally, a story, of course containing plenty about his illustrious family: "My great grand-aunt, the Procuratessa Vendramin, from whom we have inherited our estate of Mistrà, on the Brenta" - a hopelessly muddled story, apparently, fully of digressions, but of which that singer Zaffirino is the hero. The narrative, little by little, becomes more intelligible, or perhaps it is I who am giving it more attention.

"It seems," says the Count, "that there was one of his songs in particular which was called the 'Husbands' Air' - L'Aria dei Marit - because they didn't enjoy it quite as much as their better-halves... My grand-aunt, Pisana Renier, married to the Procuratore Vendramin, was a patrician of the old school, of the style that was getting rare a hundred years ago. Her virtue and her pride rendered her unapproachable. Zaffirino, on his part, was in the habit of boasting that no woman had ever been able to resist his singing, which, it appears, had its foundation in fact - the ideal changes, my dear lady, the ideal changes a good deal from one century to another! - and that his first song could make any woman turn pale and lower her eyes, the second make her madly in love, while the third song could kill her off on the spot, kill her for love, there under his very eyes, if he only felt inclined. My grandaunt Vendramin laughed when this story was told her, refused to go to hear this insolent dog, and added that it might be quite possible by the aid of spells and infernal pacts to kill a gentildonna, but as to making her fall in love with a lackey - never! This answer was naturally reported to Zaffirino, who piqued himself upon always getting the better of any one who was wanting in deference to his voice. Like the ancient Romans, *parcere subjectis et debellare superbos*. You American ladies, who are so learned, will appreciate this little quotation from the divine Virgil. While seeming to avoid the Procuratessa Vendramin, Zaffirino took the opportunity, one evening at a large assembly, to sing in her presence. He sang and sang and sang until the poor grand-aunt Pisana fell ill for love. The most skilful physicians were kept unable to explain the mysterious malady which was visibly killing the poor young lady; and the Procuratore Vendramin applied in vain to the most venerated Madonnas, and vainly promised an altar of silver, with massive gold candlesticks, to Saints Cosmas and Damian, patrons of the art of healing. At last the brother-in-law of the Procuratessa, Monsignor Almorò Vendramin, Patriarch of Aquileia, a prelate famous for the sanctity of his life, obtained in a vision of Saint Justina, for whom he entertained a particular devotion, the information that the only thing which could benefit the strange illness of his sister-in-law was the voice of Zaffirino. Take notice that my poor grand-aunt had never condescended to such a revelation.

"The Procuratore was enchanted at this happy solution; and his lordship the Patriarch went to seek Zaffirino in person, and carried him in his own coach to the Villa of Mistrà, where the Procuratessa was residing.

"On being told what was about to happen, my poor grand-aunt went into fits of rage, which were succeeded immediately by equally violent fits of joy. However, she never forgot what was due to her great position. Although sick almost unto death, she had herself arrayed with the greatest pomp, caused her face to be painted, and put on all her diamonds: it would seem as if she were anxious to affirm her full dignity before this singer. Accordingly she received Zaffirino reclining on a sofa which had been placed in the great ballroom of the Villa of Mistrà, and beneath the princely canopy; for the Vendramins, who had intermarried with the house of Mantua, possessed imperial fiefs and were princes of the Holy Roman Empire. Zaffirino saluted her with the most profound respect, but not a word passed between them. Only, the singer inquired from the Procuratore whether the illustrious lady had received the Sacraments of the Church. Being told that the Procuratessa had herself asked to be given extreme unction from the hands of her brother-in-law, he declared his readiness to obey the orders of His Excellency, and sat down at once to the harpsichord.

"Never had he sung so divinely. At the end of the first song the Procuratessa Vendramin had already revived most extraordinarily; by the end of the second she appeared entirely cured and beaming with beauty and happiness; but at the third air - the Aria dei Mariti, no doubt - she began to change frightfully; she gave a dreadful cry, and fell into the convulsions of death. In a quarter of an hour she was dead! Zaffirino did not wait to see her die. Having finished his song, he withdrew instantly, took post-horses, and travelled day and night as far as Munich. People remarked that he had presented himself at Mistrà dressed in mourning, although he had mentioned no death among his relatives; also that he had prepared everything for his departure, as if fearing the wrath of so powerful a family. Then there was also the extraordinary question he had asked before beginning to sing, about the Procuratessa having confessed and received extreme unction... No, thanks, my dear lady, no cigarettes for me. But if it does not distress you or your charming daughter, may I humbly beg permission to smoke a cigar?"

And Count Alvise, enchanted with his talent for narrative, and sure of having secured for his son the heart and the dollars of his fair audience, proceeds to light a candle, and at the candle one of those long black Italian cigars which require preliminary disinfection before smoking.

...If this state of things goes on I shall just have to ask the doctor for a bottle; this ridiculous beating of my heart and disgusting cold perspiration have increased steadily during Count Alvise's narrative. To keep myself in countenance among the various idiotic commentaries on this cock-and-bull story of a vocal coxcomb and a vaporing great lady, I begin to unroll the engraving, and to examine stupidly the portrait of Zaffirino, once so renowned, now so forgotten. A ridiculous ass, this singer, under his triumphal arch, with his stuffed Cupids and the great fat winged kitchenmaid crowning him with laurels. How flat and vapid and vulgar it is, to be sure, all this odious eighteenth century!

But he, personally, is not so utterly vapid as I had thought. That effeminate, fat face of his is almost beautiful, with an odd smile, brazen and cruel. I have seen faces like this, if not in real life, at least in my boyish romantic dreams, when I read Swinburne and Baudelaire, the faces of wicked, vindictive women. Oh yes! he is decidedly a beautiful creature, this Zaffirino, and his voice must have had the same sort of beauty and the same expression of wickedness...

"Come on, Magnus," sound the voices of my fellow-boarders,

"be a good fellow and sing us one of the old chap's songs; or at least something or other of that day, and we'll make believe it was the air with which he killed that poor lady."

"Oh yes! the Aria dei Mariti, the 'Husbands' Air,'" mumbles old Alvise, between the puffs at his impossible black cigar. "My poor grand-aunt, Pisana Vendramin; he went and killed her with those songs of his, with that Aria dei Mariti."

I feel senseless rage overcoming me. Is it that horrible palpitation (by the way, there is a Norwegian doctor, my fellow-countryman, at Venice just now) which is sending the blood to my brain and making me mad? The people round the piano, the furniture, everything together seems to get mixed and to turn into moving blobs of colour. I set to singing; the only thing which remains distinct before my eyes being the portrait of Zaffirino, on the edge of that boarding-house piano; the sensual, effeminate face, with its wicked, cynical smile, keeps appearing and disappearing as the print wavers about in the draught that makes the candles smoke and gutter. And I set to singing madly, singing I don't know what. Yes; I begin to identify it: 'tis the Biondina in Gondoleta, the only song of the eighteenth century which is still remembered by the Venetian people. I sing it, mimicking every old-school grace; shakes, cadences, languishingly swelled and diminished notes, and adding all manner of buffooneries, until the audience, recovering from its surprise, begins to shake with laughing; until I begin to laugh myself, madly, frantically, between the phrases of the melody, my voice finally smothered in this dull, brutal laughter... And then, to crown it all, I shake my fist at this long-dead singer, looking at me with his wicked woman's face, with his mocking, fatuous smile.

"Ah! you would like to be revenged on me also!" I exclaim. "You would like me to write you nice roulades and flourishes, another nice Aria dei Mariti, my fine Zaffirino!"

That night I dreamed a very strange dream. Even in the big half-furnished room the heat and closeness were stifling. The air seemed laden with the scent of all manner of white flowers, faint and heavy in their intolerable sweetness: tuberoses, gardenias, and jasmines drooping I know not where in neglected vases. The moonlight had transformed the marble floor around me into a shallow, shining, pool. On account of the heat I had exchanged my bed for a big old-fashioned sofa of light wood, painted with little nosegays and sprigs, like an old silk; and I lay there, not attempting to sleep, and letting my thoughts go vaguely to my opera of Ogier the Dane, of which I had long finished writing the words, and for whose music I had hoped to find some inspiration in this strange Venice, floating, as it were, in the stagnant lagoon of the past. But Venice had merely put all my ideas into hopeless confusion; it was as if there arose out of its shallow waters a miasma of long-dead melodies, which sickened but intoxicated my soul. I lay on my sofa watching that pool of whitish light, which rose higher and higher, little trickles of light meeting it here and there, wherever the moon's rays struck upon some polished surface; while huge shadows waved to and fro in the draught of the open balcony.

I went over and over that old Norse story: how the Paladin, Ogier, one of the knights of Charlemagne, was decoyed during his homeward wanderings from the Holy Land by the arts of an enchantress, the same who had once held in bondage the great Emperor Caesar and given him King Oberon for a son; how Ogier had tarried in that island only one day and one night, and yet, when he came home to his kingdom, he found all changed, his friends dead, his family dethroned, and not a man who knew his face; until at last, driven hither and thither like a beggar, a poor minstrel had taken compassion of his sufferings and given him all he could give - a song, the song of the prowess of a hero dead for hundreds of years, the Paladin Ogier the Dane.

The story of Ogier ran into a dream, as vivid as my waking thoughts had been vague. I was looking no longer at the pool of moonlight spreading round my couch, with its trickles of light and looming, waving shadows, but the frescoed walls of a great saloon. It was not, as I recognized in a second, the dining-room of that Venetian palace now turned into a boarding-house. It was a far larger room, a real ballroom, almost circular in its octagon shape, with eight huge white doors surrounded by stucco mouldings, and, high on the vault of the ceiling, eight little galleries or recesses like boxes at a theatre, intended no doubt for musicians and spectators. The place was imperfectly lighted by only one of the eight chandeliers, which revolved slowly, like huge spiders, each on its long cord. But the light struck upon the gilt stuccoes opposite me, and on a large expanse of fresco, the sacrifice of Iphigenia, with Agamemnon and Achilles in Roman helmets, lappets, and knee-breeches. It discovered also one of the oil panels let into the mouldings of the roof, a goddess in lemon and lilac draperies, foreshortened over a great green peacock. Round the room, where the light reached, I could make out big yellow satin sofas and heavy gilded consoles; in the shadow of a corner was what looked like a piano, and farther in the shade one of those big canopies which decorate the anterooms of Roman palaces. I looked about me, wondering where I was: a heavy, sweet smell, reminding me of the flavour of a peach, filled the place.

Little by little I began to perceive sounds; little, sharp, metallic, detached notes, like those of a mandolin; and there was united to them a voice, very low and sweet, almost a whisper, which grew and grew and grew, until the whole place was filled with that exquisite vibrating note, of a strange, exotic, unique quality. The note went on, swelling and swelling. Suddenly there was a horrible piercing shriek, and the thud of a body on the floor, and all manner of smothered exclamations. There, close by the canopy, a light suddenly appeared; and I could see, among the dark figures moving to and fro in the room, a woman lying on the ground, surrounded by other women. Her blond hair, tangled, full of diamond-sparkles which cut through the half-darkness, was hanging dishevelled; the laces of her bodice had been cut, and her white breast shone among the sheen of jewelled brocade; her face was bent forwards, and a thin white arm trailed, like a broken limb, across the knees of one of the women who were endeavouring to lift her. There was a sudden splash of water against the floor, more confused exclamations, a hoarse, broken moan, and a gurgling, dreadful sound… I awoke with a start and rushed to the window.

Outside, in the blue haze of the moon, the church and belfry of St. George loomed blue and hazy, with the black hull and rigging, the red lights, of a large steamer moored before them. From the lagoon rose a damp sea-breeze. What was it all? Ah! I began to understand: that story of old Count Alvise's, the death of his grand-aunt, Pisana Vendramin. Yes, it was about that I had been dreaming.

I returned to my room; I struck a light, and sat down to my writing-table. Sleep had become impossible. I tried to work at my opera. Once or twice I thought I had got hold of what I had looked for so long... But as soon as I tried to lay hold of my theme, there arose in my mind the distant echo of that voice, of that long note swelled slowly by insensible degrees, that long note whose tone was so strong and so subtle.

There are in the life of an artist moments when, still unable to seize his own inspiration, or even clearly to discern it, he becomes aware of the approach of that long-invoked idea. A mingled joy and terror warn him that before another day, another hour have passed, the inspiration shall have crossed the threshold of his soul and flooded it with its rapture. All day I had felt the need of isolation and quiet, and at nightfall I went for a row on the most solitary part of the lagoon. All things seemed to tell that I was going to meet my inspiration, and I awaited its coming as a lover awaits his beloved.

I had stopped my gondola for a moment, and as I gently swayed to and fro on the water, all paved with moonbeams, it seemed to me that I was on the confines of an imaginary world. It lay close at hand, enveloped in luminous, pale blue mist, through which the moon had cut a wide and glistening path; out to sea, the little islands, like moored black boats, only accentuated the solitude of this region of moonbeams and wavelets; while the hum of the insects in orchards hard by merely added to the impression of untroubled silence. On some such seas, I thought, must the Paladin Ogier, have sailed when about to discover that during that sleep at the enchantress's knees centuries had elapsed and the heroic world had set, and the kingdom of prose had come.

While my gondola rocked stationary on that sea of moonbeams, I pondered over that twilight of the heroic world. In the soft rattle of the water on the hull I seemed to hear the rattle of all that armour, of all those swords swinging rusty on the walls, neglected by the degenerate sons of the great champions of old. I had long been in search of a theme which I called the theme of the "Prowess of Ogier;" it was to appear from time to time in the course of my opera, to develop at last into that song of the Minstrel, which reveals to the hero that he is one of a long-dead world. And at this moment I seemed to feel the presence of that theme. Yet an instant, and my mind would be overwhelmed by that savage music, heroic, funereal.

Suddenly there came across the lagoon, cleaving, checkering, and fretting the silence with a lacework of sound even as the moon was fretting and cleaving the water, a ripple of music, a voice breaking itself in a shower of little scales and cadences and trills.

I sank back upon my cushions. The vision of heroic days had vanished, and before my closed eyes there seemed to dance multitudes of little stars of light, chasing and interlacing like those sudden vocalizations.

"To shore! Quick!" I cried to the gondolier.

But the sounds had ceased; and there came from the orchards, with their mulberry-trees glistening in the moonlight, and their black swaying cypress-plumes, nothing save the confused hum, the monotonous chirp, of the crickets.

I looked around me: on one side empty dunes, orchards, and meadows, without house or steeple; on the other, the blue and misty sea, empty to where distant islets were profiled black on the horizon.

A faintness overcame me, and I felt myself dissolve. For all of a sudden a second ripple of voice swept over the lagoon, a shower of little notes, which seemed to form a little mocking laugh.

Then again all was still. This silence lasted so long that I fell once more to meditating on my opera. I lay in wait once more for the half-caught theme. But no. It was not that theme for which I was waiting and watching with baited breath. I realized my delusion when, on rounding the point of the Giudecca, the murmur of a voice arose from the midst of the waters, a thread of sound slender as a moonbeam, scarce audible, but exquisite, which expanded slowly, insensibly, taking volume and body, taking flesh almost and fire, an ineffable quality, full, passionate, but veiled, as it were, in a subtle, downy wrapper. The note grew stronger and stronger, and warmer and more passionate, until it burst through that strange and charming veil, and emerged beaming, to break itself in the luminous facets of a wonderful shake, long, superb, triumphant.

There was a dead silence.

"Row to St. Mark's!" I exclaimed. "Quick!"

The gondola glided through the long, glittering track of moonbeams, and rent the great band of yellow, reflected light, mirroring the cupolas of St. Mark's, the lace-like pinnacles of the palace, and the slender pink belfry, which rose from the lit-up water to the pale and bluish evening sky.

In the larger of the two squares the military band was blaring through the last spirals of a crescendo of Rossini. The crowd was dispersing in this great open-air ballroom, and the sounds arose which invariably follow upon out-of-door music. A clatter of spoons and glasses, a rustle and grating of frocks and of chairs, and the click of scabbards on the pavement. I pushed my way among the fashionable youths contemplating the ladies while sucking the knob of their sticks; through the serried ranks of respectable families, marching arm in arm with their white frocked young ladies close in front. I took a seat before Florian's, among the customers stretching themselves before departing, and the waiters hurrying to and fro, clattering their empty cups and trays. Two imitation Neapolitans were slipping their guitar and violin under their arm, ready to leave the place.

"Stop!" I cried to them; "don't go yet. Sing me something - sing La Camesella or Funiculì, funicular - no matter what, provided you make a row;" and as they screamed and scraped their utmost, I added, "But can't you sing louder, d—n you! - sing louder, do you understand?"

I felt the need of noise, of yells and false notes, of something vulgar and hideous to drive away that ghost-voice which was haunting me.

Again and again I told myself that it had been some silly prank of a romantic amateur, hidden in the gardens of the shore or gliding unperceived on the lagoon; and that the sorcery of moonlight and sea-mist had transfigured for my excited brain mere humdrum roulades out of exercises of Bordogni or Crescentini.

But all the same I continued to be haunted by that voice. My work was interrupted ever and anon by the attempt to catch its imaginary echo; and the heroic harmonies of my Scandinavian legend were strangely interwoven with voluptuous phrases and florid cadences in which I seemed to hear again that same accursed voice.

To be haunted by singing-exercises! It seemed too ridiculous for a man who professedly despised the art of singing. And still, I preferred to believe in that childish amateur, amusing himself with warbling to the moon.

One day, while making these reflections the hundredth time over, my eyes chanced to light upon the portrait of Zaffirino, which my friend had pinned against the wall. I pulled it down and tore it into half a dozen shreds. Then, already ashamed of my folly, I watched the torn pieces float down from the window, wafted hither and thither by the sea-breeze. One scrap got caught in a yellow blind below me; the others fell into the canal, and were speedily lost to sight in the dark water. I was overcome with shame. My heart beat like bursting. What a miserable, unnerved worm I had become in this cursed Venice, with its languishing moonlights, its atmosphere as of some stuffy boudoir, long unused, full of old stuffs and potpourri!

That night, however, things seemed to be going better. I was able to settle down to my opera, and even to work at it. In the intervals my thoughts returned, not without a certain pleasure, to those scattered fragments of the torn engraving fluttering down to the water. I was disturbed at my piano by the hoarse voices and the scraping of violins which rose from one of those music-boats that station at night under the hotels of the Grand Canal. The moon had set. Under my balcony the water stretched black into the distance, its darkness cut by the still darker outlines of the flotilla of gondolas in attendance on the music-boat, where the faces of the singers, and the guitars and violins, gleamed reddish under the unsteady light of the Chinese-lanterns.

"Jammo, jammo; jammo, jammo jà," sang the loud, hoarse voices; then a tremendous scrape and twang, and the yelled-out burden, "Funiculi, funiculà; funiculi, funiculà; jammo, jammo, jammo, jammo, jammo jà."

Then came a few cries of "Bis, Bis!" from a neighbouring hotel, a brief clapping of hands, the sound of a handful of coppers rattling into the boat, and the oar-stroke of some gondolier making ready to turn away.

"Sing the Camesella," ordered some voice with a foreign accent.

"No, no! Santa Lucia."

"I want the Camesella."

"No! Santa Lucia. Hi! sing Santa Lucia - d'you hear?"

The musicians, under their green and yellow and red lamps,

held a whispered consultation on the manner of conciliating these contradictory demands. Then, after a minute's hesitation, the violins began the prelude of that once famous air, which has remained popular in Venice - the words written, some hundred years ago, by the patrician Gritti, the music by an unknown composer - La Biondina in Gondoleta.

That cursed eighteenth century! It seemed a malignant fatality that made these brutes choose just this piece to interrupt me.

At last the long prelude came to an end; and above the cracked guitars and squeaking fiddles there arose, not the expected nasal chorus, but a single voice singing below its breath.

My arteries throbbed. How well I knew that voice! It was singing, as I have said, below its breath, yet none the less it sufficed to fill all that reach of the canal with its strange quality of tone, exquisite, far-fetched.

They were long-drawn-out notes, of intense but peculiar sweetness, a man's voice which had much of a woman's, but more even of a chorister's, but a chorister's voice without its limpidity and innocence; its youthfulness was veiled, muffled, as it were, in a sort of downy vagueness, as if a passion of tears withheld.

There was a burst of applause, and the old palaces re-echoed with the clapping. "Bravo, bravo! Thank you, thank you! Sing again - please, sing again. Who can it be?"

And then a bumping of hulls, a splashing of oars, and the oaths of gondoliers trying to push each other away, as the red prow-lamps of the gondolas pressed round the gaily lit singing-boat.

But no one stirred on board. It was to none of them that this applause was due. And while every one pressed on, and clapped and vociferated, one little red prow-lamp dropped away from the fleet; for a moment a single gondola stood forth black upon the black water, and then was lost in the night.

For several days the mysterious singer was the universal topic. The people of the music-boat swore that no one besides themselves had been on board, and that they knew as little as ourselves about the owner of that voice. The gondoliers, despite their descent from the spies of the old Republic, were equally unable to furnish any clue. No musical celebrity was known or suspected to be at Venice; and every one agreed that such a singer must be a European celebrity. The strangest thing in this strange business was, that even among those learned in music there was no agreement on the subject of this voice: it was called by all sorts of names and described by all manner of incongruous adjectives; people went so far as to dispute whether the voice belonged to a man or to a woman: every one had some new definition.

In all these musical discussions I, alone, brought forward no opinion. I felt a repugnance, an impossibility almost, of speaking about that voice; and the more or less commonplace conjectures of my friend had the invariable effect of sending me out of the room.

Meanwhile my work was becoming daily more difficult, and I soon passed from utter impotence to a state of inexplicable agitation. Every morning I arose with fine resolutions and grand projects of work; only to go to bed that night without having accomplished anything. I spent hours leaning on my balcony, or wandering through the network of lanes with their ribbon of blue sky, endeavouring vainly to expel the thought of that voice, or endeavouring in reality to reproduce it in my memory; for the more I tried to banish it from my thoughts, the more I grew to thirst for that extraordinary tone, for those mysteriously downy, veiled notes; and no sooner did I make an effort to work at my opera than my head was full of scraps of forgotten eighteenth century airs, of frivolous or languishing little phrases; and I fell to wondering with a bitter-sweet longing how those songs would have sounded if sung by that voice.

At length it became necessary to see a doctor, from whom, however, I carefully hid away all the stranger symptoms of my malady. The air of the lagoons, the great heat, he answered cheerfully, had pulled me down a little; a tonic and a month in the country, with plenty of riding and no work, would make me myself again. That old idler, Count Alvise, who had insisted on accompanying me to the physician's, immediately suggested that I should go and stay with his son, who was boring himself to death superintending the maize harvest on the mainland: he could promise me excellent air, plenty of horses, and all the peaceful surroundings and the delightful occupations of a rural life. "Be sensible, my dear Magnus, and just go quietly to Mistrà."

Mistrà - the name sent a shiver all down me. I was about to decline the invitation, when a thought suddenly loomed vaguely in my mind.

"Yes, dear Count," I answered; "I accept your invitation with gratitude and pleasure. I will start tomorrow for Mistrà."

The next day found me at Padua, on my way to the Villa of Mistrà. It seemed as if I had left an intolerable burden behind me. I was, for the first time since how long, quite light of heart. The tortuous, rough-paved streets, with their empty, gloomy porticoes; the ill-plastered palaces, with closed, discoloured shutters; the little rambling square, with meagre trees and stubborn grass; the Venetian garden-houses reflecting their crumbling graces in the muddy canal; the gardens without gates and the gates without gardens, the avenues leading nowhere; and the population of blind and legless beggars, of whining sacristans, which issued as by magic from between the flag-stones and dust-heaps and weeds under the fierce August sun, all this dreariness merely amused and pleased me. My good spirits were heightened by a musical mass which I had the good fortune to hear at St. Anthony's.

Never in all my days had I heard anything comparable, although Italy affords many strange things in the way of sacred music. Into the deep nasal chanting of the priests there had suddenly burst a chorus of children, singing absolutely independent of all time and tune; grunting of priests answered by squealing of boys, slow Gregorian modulation interrupted by jaunty barrel-organ pipings, an insane, insanely merry jumble of bellowing and barking, mewing and cackling and braying, such as would have enlivened a witches' meeting, or rather some mediaeval Feast of Fools. And, to make the grotesqueness of such music still more fantastic and Hoffmannlike, there was, besides, the magnificence of the piles of sculptured marbles and gilded bronzes, the tradition of the musical splendour for which St. Anthony's had been famous in days gone by. I had read in old travellers, Lalande and Burney, that the Republic of St. Mark had squandered immense sums not merely on the monuments and decoration, but on the musical establishment of its great cathedral of Terra Firma. In the midst of this ineffable concert of impossible voices and instruments, I tried to imagine the voice of

Guadagni, the soprano for whom Gluck had written Che faru senza Euridice, and the fiddle of Tartini, that Tartini with whom the devil had once come and made music. And the delight in anything so absolutely, barbarously, grotesquely, fantastically incongruous as such a performance in such a place was heightened by a sense of profanation: such were the successors of those wonderful musicians of that hated eighteenth century!

The whole thing had delighted me so much, so very much more than the most faultless performance could have done, that I determined to enjoy it once more; and towards vesper-time, after a cheerful dinner with two bagmen at the inn of the Golden Star, and a pipe over the rough sketch of a possible cantata upon the music which the devil made for Tartini, I turned my steps once more towards St. Anthony's.

The bells were ringing for sunset, and a muffled sound of organs seemed to issue from the huge, solitary church; I pushed my way under the heavy leathern curtain, expecting to be greeted by the grotesque performance of that morning.

I proved mistaken. Vespers must long have been over. A smell of stale incense, a crypt-like damp filled my mouth; it was already night in that vast cathedral. Out of the darkness glimmered the votive-lamps of the chapels, throwing wavering lights upon the red polished marble, the gilded railing, and chandeliers, and plaqueing with yellow the muscles of some sculptured figure. In a corner a burning taper put a halo about the head of a priest, burnishing his shining bald skull, his white surplice, and the open book before him. "Amen" he chanted; the book was closed with a snap, the light moved up the apse, some dark figures of women rose from their knees and passed quickly towards the door; a man saying his prayers before a chapel also got up, making a great clatter in dropping his stick.

The church was empty, and I expected every minute to be turned out by the sacristan making his evening round to close the doors. I was leaning against a pillar, looking into the greyness of the great arches, when the organ suddenly burst out into a series of chords, rolling through the echoes of the church: it seemed to be the conclusion of some service. And above the organ rose the notes of a voice; high, soft, enveloped in a kind of downiness, like a cloud of incense, and which ran through the mazes of a long cadence. The voice dropped into silence; with two thundering chords the organ closed in. All was silent. For a moment I stood leaning against one of the pillars of the nave: my hair was clammy, my knees sank beneath me, an enervating heat spread through my body; I tried to breathe more largely, to suck in the sounds with the incense-laden air. I was supremely happy, and yet as if I were dying; then suddenly a chill ran through me, and with it a vague panic. I turned away and hurried out into the open.

The evening sky lay pure and blue along the jagged line of roofs; the bats and swallows were wheeling about; and from the belfries all around, half-drowned by the deep bell of St. Anthony's, jangled the peel of the Ave Maria.

"You really don't seem well," young Count Alvise had said the previous evening, as he welcomed me, in the light of a lantern held up by a peasant, in the weedy back-garden of the Villa of Mistrà. Everything had seemed to me like a dream: the jingle of the horse's bells driving in the dark from Padua, as the lantern swept the acacia-hedges with their wide yellow light; the grating of the wheels on the gravel; the supper-table, illumined by a single petroleum lamp for fear of attracting mosquitoes, where a broken old lackey, in an old stable jacket, handed round the dishes among the fumes of onion; Alvise's fat mother gabbling dialect in a shrill, benevolent voice behind the bullfights on her fan; the unshaven village priest, perpetually fidgeting with his glass and foot, and sticking one shoulder up above the other. And now, in the afternoon, I felt as if I had been in this long, rambling, tumble-down Villa of Mistrà - a villa three-quarters of which was given up to the storage of grain and garden tools, or to the exercise of rats, mice, scorpions, and centipedes - all my life; as if I had always sat there, in Count Alvise's study, among the pile of undusted books on agriculture, the sheaves of accounts, the samples of grain and silkworm seed, the ink-stains and the cigar-ends; as if I had never heard of anything save the cereal basis of Italian agriculture, the diseases of maize, the peronospora of the vine, the breeds of bullocks, and the iniquities of farm labourers; with the blue cones of the Euganean hills closing in the green shimmer of plain outside the window.

After an early dinner, again with the screaming gabble of the fat old Countess, the fidgeting and shoulder-raising of the unshaven priest, the smell of fried oil and stewed onions, Count Alvise made me get into the cart beside him, and whirled me along among clouds of dust, between the endless glister of poplars, acacias, and maples, to one of his farms.

In the burning sun some twenty or thirty girls, in coloured skirts, laced bodices, and big straw-hats, were threshing the maize on the big red brick threshing-floor, while others were winnowing the grain in great sieves. Young Alvise III. (the old one was Alvise II.: every one is Alvise, that is to say, Lewis, in that family; the name is on the house, the carts, the barrows, the very pails) picked up the maize, touched it, tasted it, said something to the girls that made them laugh, and something to the head farmer that made him look very glum; and then led me into a huge stable, where some twenty or thirty white bullocks were stamping, switching their tails, hitting their horns against the mangers in the dark. Alvise III. patted each, called him by his name, gave him some salt or a turnip, and explained which was the Mantuan breed, which the Apulian, which the Romagnolo, and so on. Then he bade me jump into the trap, and off we went again through the dust, among the hedges and ditches, till we came to some more brick farm buildings with pinkish roofs smoking against the blue sky. Here there were more young women threshing and winnowing the maize, which made a great golden Danaë cloud; more bullocks stamping and lowing in the cool darkness; more joking, fault-finding, explaining; and thus through five farms, until I seemed to see the rhythmical rising and falling of the flails against the hot sky, the shower of golden grains, the yellow dust from the winnowing-sieves on to the bricks, the switching of innumerable tails and plunging of innumerable horns, the glistening of huge white flanks and foreheads, whenever I closed my eyes.

"A good day's work!" cried Count Alvise, stretching out his long legs with the tight trousers riding up over the Wellington boots. "Mamma, give us some aniseed-syrup after dinner; it is an excellent restorative and precaution against the fevers of this country."

"Oh! you've got fever in this part of the world, have you? Why, your father said the air was so good!"

"Nothing, nothing," soothed the old Countess. "The only thing to be dreaded are mosquitoes; take care to fasten your shutters before lighting the candle."

"Well," rejoined young Alvise, with an effort of conscience, "of course there are fevers. But they needn't hurt you. Only, don't go out into the garden at night, if you don't want to catch them. Papa told me that you have fancies for moonlight rambles. It won't do in this climate, my dear fellow; it won't do. If you must stalk about at night, being a genius, take a turn inside the house; you can get quite exercise enough."

After dinner the aniseed-syrup was produced, together with brandy and cigars, and they all sat in the long, narrow, half-furnished room on the first floor; the old Countess knitting a garment of uncertain shape and destination, the priest reading out the newspaper; Count Alvise puffing at his long, crooked cigar, and pulling the ears of a long, lean dog with a suspicion of mange and a stiff eye. From the dark garden outside rose the hum and whirr of countless insects, and the smell of the grapes which hung black against the starlit blue sky, on the trellis. I went to the balcony. The garden lay dark beneath; against the twinkling horizon stood out the tall poplars. There was the sharp cry of an owl; the barking of a dog; a sudden whiff of warm, enervating perfume, a perfume that made me think of the taste of certain peaches, and suggested white, thick, wax-like petals. I seemed to have smelt that flower once before: it made me feel languid, almost faint.

"I am very tired," I said to Count Alvise. "See how feeble we city folk become!"

But, despite my fatigue, I found it quite impossible to sleep. The night seemed perfectly stifling. I had felt nothing like it at Venice. Despite the injunctions of the Countess I opened the solid wooden shutters, hermetically closed against mosquitoes, and looked out.

The moon had risen; and beneath it lay the big lawns, the rounded tree-tops, bathed in a blue, luminous mist, every leaf glistening and trembling in what seemed a heaving sea of light. Beneath the window was the long trellis, with the white shining piece of pavement under it. It was so bright that I could distinguish the green of the vine-leaves, the dull red of the catalpa-flowers. There was in the air a vague scent of cut grass, of ripe American grapes, of that white flower (it must be white) which made me think of the taste of peaches all melting into the delicious freshness of falling dew. From the village church came the stroke of one: Heaven knows how long I had been vainly attempting to sleep. A shiver ran through me, and my head suddenly filled as with the fumes of some subtle wine; I remembered all those weedy embankments, those canals full of stagnant water, the yellow faces of the peasants; the word malaria returned to my mind. No matter! I remained leaning on the window, with a thirsty longing to plunge myself into this blue moonmist, this dew and perfume and silence, which seemed to vibrate and quiver like the stars that strewed the depths of heaven... What music, even Wagner's, or of that great singer of starry nights, the divine Schumann, what music could ever compare with this great silence, with this great concert of voiceless things that sing within one's soul?

As I made this reflection, a note, high, vibrating, and sweet, rent the silence, which immediately closed around it. I leaned out of the window, my heart beating as though it must burst. After a brief space the silence was cloven once more by that note, as the darkness is cloven by a falling star or a firefly rising slowly like a rocket. But this time it was plain that the voice did not come, as I had imagined, from the garden, but from the house itself, from some corner of this rambling old villa of Mistrà.

Mistrà - Mistrà! The name rang in my ears, and I began at length to grasp its significance, which seems to have escaped me till then. "Yes," I said to myself, "it is quite natural." And with this odd impression of naturalness was mixed a feverish, impatient pleasure. It was as if I had come to Mistrà on purpose, and that I was about to meet the object of my long and weary hopes.

Grasping the lamp with its singed green shade, I gently opened the door and made my way through a series of long passages and of big, empty rooms, in which my steps re-echoed as in a church, and my light disturbed whole swarms of bats. I wandered at random, farther and farther from the inhabited part of the buildings.

This silence made me feel sick; I gasped as under a sudden disappointment.

All of a sudden there came a sound - chords, metallic, sharp, rather like the tone of a mandolin - close to my ear. Yes, quite close: I was separated from the sounds only by a partition. I fumbled for a door; the unsteady light of my lamp was insufficient for my eyes, which were swimming like those of a drunkard. At last I found a latch, and, after a moment's hesitation, I lifted it and gently pushed open the door. At first I could not understand what manner of place I was in. It was dark all round me, but a brilliant light blinded me, a light coming from below and striking the opposite wall. It was as if I had entered a dark box in a half-lighted theatre. I was, in fact, in something of the kind, a sort of dark hole with a high balustrade, half-hidden by an up-drawn curtain. I remembered those little galleries or recesses for the use of musicians or lookers-on - which exist under the ceiling of the ballrooms in certain old Italian palaces. Yes; it must have been one like that. Opposite me was a vaulted ceiling covered with gilt mouldings, which framed great time-blackened canvases; and lower down, in the light thrown up from below, stretched a wall covered with faded frescoes. Where had I seen that goddess in lilac and lemon draperies foreshortened over a big, green peacock? For she was familiar to me, and the stucco Tritons also who twisted their tails round her gilded frame. And that fresco, with warriors in Roman cuirasses and green and blue lappets, and knee-breeches - where could I have seen them before? I asked myself these questions without experiencing any surprise. Moreover, I was very calm, as one is calm sometimes in extraordinary dreams - could I be dreaming?

I advanced gently and leaned over the balustrade. My eyes were met at first by the darkness above me, where, like gigantic spiders, the big chandeliers rotated slowly, hanging from the ceiling. Only one of them was lit, and its Murano-glass pendants, its carnations and roses, shone opalescent in the light of the guttering wax. This chandelier lighted up the opposite wall and that piece of ceiling with the goddess and the green peacock; it illumined, but far less well, a corner of the huge room, where, in the shadow of a kind of canopy, a little group of people were crowding round a yellow satin sofa, of the same kind as those that lined the walls. On the sofa, half-screened from me by the surrounding persons, a woman was stretched out: the silver of her embroidered dress and the rays of her diamonds gleamed and shot forth as she moved uneasily. And immediately under the chandelier, in the full light, a man stooped over a harpsichord, his head bent slightly, as if collecting his thoughts before singing.

He struck a few chords and sang. Yes, sure enough, it was the voice, the voice that had so long been persecuting me! I recognized at once that delicate, voluptuous quality, strange, exquisite, sweet beyond words, but lacking all youth and clearness. That passion veiled in tears which had troubled my brain that night on the lagoon, and again on the Grand Canal singing the Biondina, and yet again, only two days since, in the deserted cathedral of Padua. But I recognized now what seemed to have been hidden from me till then, that this voice was what I cared most for in all the wide world.

The voice wound and unwound itself in long, languishing phrases, in rich, voluptuous rifiorituras, all fretted with tiny scales and exquisite, crisp shakes; it stopped ever and anon, swaying as if panting in languid delight. And I felt my body melt even as wax in the sunshine, and it seemed to me that I too was turning fluid and vaporous, in order to mingle with these sounds as the moonbeams mingle with the dew.

Suddenly, from the dimly lighted corner by the canopy, came a little piteous wail; then another followed, and was lost in the singer's voice. During a long phrase on the harpsichord, sharp and tinkling, the singer turned his head towards the dais, and there came a plaintive little sob. But he, instead of stopping, struck a sharp chord; and with a thread of voice so hushed as to be scarcely audible, slid softly into a long cadenza. At the same moment he threw his head backwards, and the light fell full upon the handsome, effeminate face, with its ashy pallor and big, black brows, of the singer Zaffirino. At the sight of that face, sensual and sullen, of that smile which was cruel and mocking like a bad woman's, I understood - I knew not why, by what process - that his singing must be cut short, that the accursed phrase must never be finished. I understood that I was before an assassin, that he was killing this woman, and killing me also, with his wicked voice.

I rushed down the narrow stair which led down from the box, pursued, as it were, by that exquisite voice, swelling, swelling by insensible degrees. I flung myself on the door which must be that of the big saloon. I could see its light between the panels. I bruised my hands in trying to wrench the latch. The door was fastened tight, and while I was struggling with that locked door I heard the voice swelling, swelling, rending asunder that downy veil which wrapped it, leaping forth clear, resplendent, like the sharp and glittering blade of a knife that seemed to enter deep into my breast. Then, once more, a wail, a death-groan, and that dreadful noise, that hideous gurgle of breath strangled by a rush of blood. And then a long shake, acute, brilliant, triumphant.

The door gave way beneath my weight, one half crashed in. I entered. I was blinded by a flood of blue moonlight. It poured in through four great windows, peaceful and diaphanous, a pale blue mist of moonlight, and turned the huge room into a kind of submarine cave, paved with moonbeams, full of shimmers, of pools of moonlight. It was as bright as at midday, but the brightness was cold, blue, vaporous, supernatural. The room was completely empty, like a great hayloft. Only, there hung from the ceiling the ropes which had once supported a chandelier; and in a corner, among stacks of wood and heaps of Indian-corn, whence spread a sickly smell of damp and mildew, there stood a long, thin harpsichord, with spindle-legs, and its cover cracked from end to end.

I felt, all of a sudden, very calm. The one thing that mattered was the phrase that kept moving in my head, the phrase of that unfinished cadence which I had heard but an instant before. I opened the harpsichord, and my fingers came down boldly upon its keys. A jingle-jangle of broken strings, laughable and dreadful, was the only answer.

Then an extraordinary fear overtook me. I clambered out of one of the windows; I rushed up the garden and wandered through the fields, among the canals and the embankments, until the moon had set and the dawn began to shiver, followed, pursued for ever by that jangle of broken strings.

People expressed much satisfaction at my recovery.

It seems that one dies of those fevers.

Recovery? But have I recovered? I walk, and eat and drink and talk; I can even sleep. I live the life of other living creatures. But I am wasted by a strange and deadly disease. I can never lay hold of my own inspiration. My head is filled with music which is certainly by me, since I have never heard it before, but which still is not my own, which I despise and abhor: little, tripping flourishes and languishing phrases, and long-drawn, echoing cadences.

O wicked, wicked voice, violin of flesh and blood made by the Evil One's hand, may I not even execrate thee in peace; but is it necessary that, at the moment when I curse, the longing to hear thee again should parch my soul like hell-thirst? And since I have satiated thy lust for revenge, since thou hast withered my life and withered my genius, is it not time for pity? May I not hear one note, only one note of thine, O singer, O wicked and contemptible wretch?

PHANTAS
By Oliver Onions

"For, barring all pother,
With this, or the other,
Still Britons are Lords of the Main."

THE CHAPTER OF ADMIRALS

I

As Abel Keeling lay on the galleon's deck, held from rolling down it only by his own weight and the sun-blackened hand that lay outstretched upon the planks, his gaze wandered, but ever returned to the bell that hung, jammed with the dangerous heel-over of the vessel, in the small ornamental belfry immediately abaft the mainmast. The bell was of cast bronze, with half-obliterated bosses upon it that had been the heads of cherubs; but wind and salt spray had given it a thick incrustation of bright, beautiful, lichenous green. It was this colour that Abel Keeling's eyes liked.

For wherever else on the galleon his eyes rested they found only whiteness - the whiteness of extreme eld. There were slightly varying degrees in her whiteness; here she was of a white that glistened like salt-granules, there of a greyish chalky white, and again her whiteness had the yellowish cast of decay; but everywhere it was the mild, disquieting whiteness of materials out of which the life had departed. Her cordage was bleached as old straw is bleached, and half her ropes kept their shape little more firmly than the ash of a string keeps its shape after the fire has passed; her pallid timbers were white and clean as bones found in sand; and even the wild frankincense with which (for lack of tar, at her last touching of land) she had been pitched, had dried to a pale hard gum that sparkled like quartz in her open seams. The sun was yet so pale a buckler of silver through the still white mists that not a cord or timber cast a shadow; and only Abel Keeling's face and hands were black, carked and cinder-black from exposure to his pitiless rays.

The galleon was the *Mary of the Tower*, and she had a frightful list to starboard. So canted was she that her mainyard dipped one of its steel sickles into the glassy water, and, had her foremast remained, or more than the broken stump of her bonaventure mizzen, she must have turned over completely. Many days ago they had stripped the mainyard of its course, and had passed the sail under the *Mary's* bottom, in the hope that it would stop the leak. This it had partly done as long as the galleon had continued to glide one way; then, without coming about, she had begun to glide the other, the ropes had parted, and she had dragged the sail after her, leaving a broad tarnish on the silver sea.

For it was broadside that the galleon glided, almost imperceptibly, ever sucking down. She glided as if a loadstone drew her, and, at first, Abel Keeling had thought it was a loadstone, pulling at her iron, drawing her through the pearly mists that lay like face-cloths to the water and hid at a short distance the tarnish left by the sail. But later he had known that it was no loadstone drawing at her iron. The motion was due - must be due - the absolute deadness of the calm in that silent, sinister, three-miles-broad waterway. With the eye of his mind he saw that loadstone now as he lay against a gun-truck, all but toppling down the deck. Soon that would happen again which had happened for five days past. He would hear again the chattering of monkeys and the screaming of parrots, the mat of green and yellow weeds would creep in towards the Mary over the quicksilver sea, once more the sheer wall of rock would rise, and the men would run...

But no; the men would not run this time to drop the fenders. There were no men left to do so, unless Bligh was still alive. Perhaps Bligh was still alive. He had walked half-way down the quarter-deck steps a little before the sudden nightfall of the day before, had then fallen and lain for a minute (dead, Abel Keeling had supposed, watching him from his place by the gun-truck), and had then got up again and tottered forward to the forecastle, his tall figure swaying and his long arms waving. Abel Keeling had not seen him since. Most likely, he had died in the forecastle during the night. If he had not been dead he would have come aft again for water...

At the remembrance of the water Abel Keeling lifted his head. The strands of lean muscle about his emaciated mouth worked, and he made a little pressure of his sun-blackened hand on the deck, as if to verify its steepness and his own balance. The mainmast was some seven or eight yards away... He put one stiff leg under him and began, seated as he was, to make shuffling movements down the slope.

To the mainmast, near the belfry, was affixed his contrivance for catching water. It consisted of a collar of rope set lower at one side than at the other (but that had been before the mast had steeved so many degrees away from the zenith), and tallowed beneath. The mists lingered later in that gully of a strait than they did on the open ocean, and the collar of rope served as a collector for the dews that condensed on the mast. The drops fell into a small earthen pipkin placed on the deck beneath it.

Abel Keeling reached the pipkin and looked into it. It was nearly a third full of fresh water. Good. If Bligh, the mate, was dead, so much the more water for Abel Keeling, master of the Mary of the Tower. He dipped two fingers into the pipkin and put them into his mouth. This he did several times. He did not dare to raise the pipkin to his black and broken lips for dread of a remembered agony, he could not have told how many days ago, when a devil had whispered to him, and he had gulped down the contents of the pipkin in the morning, and for the rest of the day had gone waterless... Again he moistened his fingers and sucked them; then he lay sprawling against the mast, idly watching the drops of water as they fell.

It was odd how the drops formed. Slowly they collected at the edge of the tallowed collar, trembled in their fullness for an instant, and fell, another beginning the process instantly. It amused Abel Keeling to watch them. Why (he wondered) were all the drops the same size? What cause and compulsion did they obey that they never varied, and what frail tenuity held the little globules intact? It must be due to some Cause... He remembered that the aromatic gum of the wild frankincense with which they had parcelled the seams had hung on the buckets in great sluggish gouts, obedient to a different compulsion; oil was different again, and so were juices and balsams. Only quicksilver (perhaps the heavy and motionless sea put him in mind of quicksilver) seemed obedient to no law... Why was it so?

Bligh, of course, would have had his explanation: it was the Hand of God. That sufficed for Bligh, who had gone forward the evening before, and whom Abel Keeling now seemed vaguely and as at a distance to remember as the deep-voiced fanatic who had sung his hymns as, man by man, he had committed the bodies of the ship's company to the deep. Bligh was that sort of man; accepted things without question; was content to take things as they were and be ready with the fenders when the wall of rock rose out of the opalescent mists. Bligh, too, like the waterdrops, had his Law, that was his and nobody else's...

There floated down from some rotten rope up aloft a flake of scurf, that settled in the pipkin. Abel Keeling watched it dully as it settled towards the pipkin's rim. When presently he again dipped his fingers into the vessel the water ran into a little vortex, drawing the flake with it. The water settled again; and again the minute flake determined towards the rim and adhered there, as if the rim had power to draw it...

It was exactly so that the galleon was gliding towards the wall of rock, the yellow and green weeds, and the monkeys and parrots. Put out into mid-water again (while there had been men to put her out) she had glided to the other wall. One force drew the chip in the pipkin and the ship over the tranced sea. It was the Hand of God, said Bligh...

Abel Keeling, his mind now noting minute things and now clouded with torpor, did not at first hear a voice that was quakingly lifted up over by the forecastle - a voice that drew nearer, to an accompaniment of swirling water.

"O Thou, that Jonas in the fish
Three days didst keep from pain,
Which was a figure of Thy death
And rising up again - "

It was Bligh, singing one of his hymns:

"O Thou, that Noah keptst from flood
And Abram, day by day,
As he along through Egypt passed
Didst guide him in the way - "

The voice ceased, leaving the pious period uncompleted. Bligh was alive, at any rate... Abel Keeling resumed his fitful musing.

Yes, that was the Law of Bligh's life, to call things the Hand of God; but Abel Keeling's Law was different; no better, no worse, only different. The Hand of God, that drew chips and galleons, must work by some method; and Abel Keeling's eyes were dully on the pipkin again as if he sought the method there...

Then conscious thought left him for a space, and when he resumed it was without obvious connection.

Oars, of course, were the thing. With oars, men could laugh at calms. Oars, that only pinnaces and galliasses now used, had had their advantages. But oars (which was to say a method, for you could say if you liked that the Hand of God grasped the oar-loom, as the Breath of God filled the sail) - oars were antiquated, belonged to the past, and meant a throwing-over of all that was good and new and a return to fine lines, a battle-formation abreast to give effect to the shock of the ram, and a day or two at sea and then to port again for provisions. Oars... no. Abel Keeling was one of the new men, the men who swore by the line-ahead, the broadside fire of sakers and demi-cannon, and weeks and months without a landfall. Perhaps one day the wits of such men as he would devise a craft, not oar-driven (because oars could not penetrate into the remote seas of the world) - not sail-driven (because men who trusted to sails found themselves in an airless, three-mile strait, suspended motionless between cloud and water, ever gliding to a wall of rock) - but a ship... a ship...

"To Noah and his sons with him
God spake, and thus said He:
A covenant set I up with you
And your posterity - "

It was Bligh again, wandering somewhere in the waist. Abel Keeling's mind was once more a blank. Then slowly, slowly, as the water drops collected on the collar of rope, his thought took shape again.

A galliasse? No, not a galliasse. The galliasse made shift to be two things, and was neither. This ship, that the hand of man should one day make for the Hand of God to manage, should be a ship that should take and conserve the force of the wind, take it and store it as she stored her victuals; at rest when she wished, going ahead when she wished; turning the forces both of calm and storm against themselves. For, of course, her force must be wind - stored wind - a bag of the winds, as the children's tale had it - wind probably directed upon the water astern, driving it away and urging forward the ship, acting by reaction. She would have a wind-chamber, into which wind would be pumped with pumps... Bligh would call that equally the Hand of God, this driving-force of the ship of the future that Abel Keeling dimly foreshadowed as he lay between the mainmast and the belfry, turning his eyes now and then from ashy white timbers to the vivid green bronze-rust of the bell above him...

Bligh's face, liver-coloured with the sun and ravaged from inwards by the faith that consumed him, appeared at the head of the quarter-deck steps. His voice beat uncontrolledly out.

"And in the earth here is no place
Of refuge to be found,
Nor in the deep and water-course
That passeth under ground - "

II

Bligh's eyes were lidded, as if in contemplation of his inner ecstasy. His head was thrown back, and his brows worked up and down tormentedly. His wide mouth remained open as his hymn was suddenly interrupted on the long-drawn note. From somewhere in the shimmering mists the note was taken up, and there drummed and rang and reverberated through the strait a windy, hoarse, and dismal bellow, alarming and sustained. A tremor rang through Bligh. Moving like a sightless man, he stumbled forward from the head of the quarter-deck steps, and Abel Keeling was aware of his gaunt figure behind him, taller for the steepness of the deck. As that vast empty sound died away, Bligh laughed in his mania.

"Lord, hath the grave's wide mouth a tongue to praise Thee? Lo, again - "

Again the cavernous sound possessed the air, louder and

nearer. Through it came another sound, a slow throb, throb - throb, throb - Again the sounds ceased.

"Even Leviathan lifteth up his voice in praise!" Bligh sobbed.

Abel Keeling did not raise his head. There had returned to him the memory of that day when, before the morning mists had lifted from the strait, he had emptied the pipkin of the water that was the allowance until night should fall again. During that agony of thirst he had seen shapes and heard sounds with other than his mortal eyes and ears, and even in the moments that had alternated with his lightness, when he had known these to be hallucinations, they had come again. He had heard the bells on a Sunday in his own Kentish home, the calling of children at play, the unconcerned singing of men at their daily labour, and the laughter and gossip of the women as they had spread the linen on the hedge or distributed bread upon the platters. These voices had rung in his brain, interrupted now and then by the groans of Bligh and of two other men who had been alive then. Some of the voices he had heard had been silent on earth this many a long year, but Abel Keeling, thirst-tortured, had heard them, even as he was now hearing that vacant moaning with the intermittent throbbing that filled the strait with alarm...

"Praise Him, praise Him, praise Him!" Bligh was calling deliriously.

Then a bell seemed to sound in Abel Keeling's ears, and, as if something in the mechanism of his brain had slipped, another picture rose in his fancy - the scene when the *Mary of the Tower* had put out, to a bravery of swinging bells and shrill fifes and valiant trumpets. She had not been a leper-white galleon then. The scroll-work on her prow had twinkled with gilding; her belfry and stern-galleries and elaborate lanterns had flashed in the sun with gold; and her fighting-tops and the war-pavesse about her waist had been gay with painted coats and escutcheons. To her sails had been stitched gaudy ramping lions of scarlet saye, and from her mainyard, now dipping in the water, had hung the broad two-tailed pennant with the Virgin and Child embroidered upon it...

Then suddenly a voice about him seemed to be saying, "And a half-seven - and a half-seven -" and in a twink the picture in Abel Keeling's brain changed again. He was at home again, instructing his son, young Abel, in the casting of the lead from the skiff they had pulled out of the harbour.

"And a half-seven!" the boy seemed to be calling.

Abel Keeling's blackened lips muttered: "Excellently well cast, Abel, excellently well cast!"

"And a half-seven - and a half-seven - seven - seven -"

"Ah," Abel Keeling murmured, "that last was not a clear cast - give me the line - thus it should go... ay, so... Soon you shall sail the seas with me in the *Mary of the Tower*. You are already perfect in the stars and the motions of the planets; to-morrow I will instruct you in the use of the backstaff..."

For a minute or two he continued to mutter; then he dozed. When again he came to semi-consciousness it was once more to the sound of bells, at first faint, then louder, and finally becoming a noisy clamour immediately above his head. It was Bligh. Bligh, in a fresh attack of delirium, had seized the bell-lanyard and was ringing the bell insanely. The cord broke in his fingers, but he thrust at the bell with his hand, and again called aloud.

"Upon an harp and an instrument of ten strings... let Heaven and Earth praise Thy Name!..."

He continued to call aloud, and to beat on the bronze-rusted bell.

"Ship ahoy! What ship's that?"

One would have said that a veritable hail had come out of the mists; but Abel Keeling knew those hails that came out of the mists. They came from ships which were not there. "Ay, ay, keep a good look-out, and have a care to your lodemanage," he muttered again to his son...

But, as sometimes a sleeper sits up in his dream, or rises from his couch and walks, so all of a sudden Abel Keeling found himself on his hands and knees on the deck, looking back over his shoulder. In some deep-seated region of his consciousness he was dimly aware that the cant of the deck had become more perilous, but his brain received the intelligence and forgot it again. He was looking out into the bright and baffling mists. The buckler of the sun was of a more ardent silver; the sea below it was lost in brilliant evaporation; and between them, suspended in the haze, no more substantial than the vague darknesses that float before dazzled eyes, a pyramidal phantom-shape hung. Abel Keeling passed his hand over his eyes, but when he removed it the shape was still there, gliding slowly towards the *Mary's* quarter. Its form changed as he watched it. The spirit-grey shape that had been a pyramid seemed to dissolve into four upright members, slightly graduated in tallness, that nearest the *Mary's* stern the tallest and that to the left the lowest. It might have been the shadow of the gigantic set of reed-pipes on which that vacant mournful note had been sounded.

And as he looked, with fooled eyes, again his ears became fooled:

"*Ahoy there!* What ship's that? Are you a ship?... Here, give me that trumpet -" Then a metallic barking. "*Ahoy there!* What the devil are you? Didn't you ring a bell? Ring it again, or blow a blast or something, and go dead slow!"

All this came, as it were, indistinctly, and through a sort of high singing in Abel Keeling's own ears. Then he fancied a short bewildered laugh, followed by a colloquy from somewhere between sea and sky.

"Here, Ward, just pinch me, will you? Tell me what you see there. I want to know if I'm awake."

"See where?"

"There, on the starboard bow. (Stop that ventilating fan; I can't hear myself think.) See anything? Don't tell me it's that damned Dutchman - don't pitch me that old Vanderdecken tale - give me an easy one first, something about a sea-serpent... You did hear that bell, didn't you?"

"Shut up a minute - listen -"

Again Bligh's voice was lifted up.

"This is the cov'nant that I make:
From henceforth nevermore
Will I again the world destroy
With water, as before."

Bligh's voice died away again in Abel Keeling's ears.

"Oh - my - fat - Aunt - Julia!" the voice that seemed to come from between sea and sky sounded again. Then it spoke more loudly. "I say," it began with careful politeness, "if you are a ship, do you mind telling us where the masquerade is to be? Our wireless is out of order, and we hadn't heard of it... Oh, you do see it, Ward, don't you?... Please, please tell us what the hell you are!"

Again Abel Keeling had moved as a sleepwalker moves. He had raised himself up by the belfry timbers, and Bligh had sunk in a heap on the deck. Abel Keeling's movement overturned the pipkin, which raced the little trickle of its contents down the deck and lodged where the still and brimming sea made, as it were, a chain with the carved balustrade of the quarter-deck - one link a still gleaming edge, then a dark baluster, and then another gleaming link. For one moment only Abel Keeling found himself noticing that that which had driven Bligh aft had been the rising of the water in the waist as the galleon settled by the head - the waist was now entirely submerged; then once more he was absorbed in his dream, its voices, and its shape in the mist, which had again taken the form of a pyramid before his eyeballs.

"Of course," a voice seemed to be complaining anew, and still through that confused dinning in Abel Keeling's ears, "we can't turn a four-inch on it... And, of course, Ward, I don't believe in 'em. D'you hear, Ward? I don't believe in 'em, I say... Shall we call down to old A. B.? This might interest His Scientific Skippership..."

"Oh, lower a boat and pull out to it - into it - over it - through it -"

"Look at our chaps crowded on the barbette yonder. They've seen it. Better not give an order you know won't be obeyed..."

Abel Keeling, cramped against the antique belfry, had begun to find his dream interesting. For, though he did not know her build, that mirage was the shape of a ship. No doubt it was projected from his brooding on ships of half an hour before; and that was odd... But perhaps, after all, it was not very odd. He knew that she did not really exist; only the appearance of her existed; but things had to exist like that before they really existed. Before the *Mary of the Tower* had existed she had been a shape in some man's imagination; before that, some dreamer had dreamed the form of a ship with oars; and before that, far away in the dawn and infancy of the world, some seer had seen in a vision the raft before man had ventured to push out over the water on his two planks. And since this shape that rode before Abel Keeling's eyes was a shape in his, Abel Keeling's dream, he, Abel Keeling, was the master of it. His own brooding brain had contrived her, and she was launched upon the illimitable ocean of his own mind...

"And I will not unmindful be
Of this, My covenant, passed
Twixt Me and you and every flesh
Whiles that the world should last,"

sang Bligh, rapt...

But as a dreamer, even in his dream, will scratch upon the wall by his couch some key or word to put him in mind of his vision on the morrow when it has left him, so Abel Keeling found himself seeking some sign to be a proof to those to whom no vision is vouchsafed. Even Bligh sought that - could not be silent in his bliss, but lay on the deck there, uttering great passionate Amens and praising his Maker, as he said, upon an harp and an instrument of ten strings. So with Abel Keeling. It would be the Amen of his life to have praised God, not upon a harp, but upon a ship that should carry her own power, that should store wind or its equivalent as she stored her victuals, that should be something wrested from the chaos of uninvention and ordered and disciplined and subordinated to Abel Keeling's will... And there she was, that ship-shaped thing of spirit-grey, with the four pipes that resembled a phantom organ now broadside and of equal length. And the ghost-crew of that ship were speaking again...

The interrupted silver chain by the quarterdeck balustrade had now become continuous, and the balusters made a herring-bone over their own motionless reflections. The spilt water from the pipkin had dried, and the pipkin was not to be seen. Abel Keeling stood beside the mast, erect as God made man to go. With his leathery hand he smote upon the bell. He waited for the space of a minute, and then cried:

"Ahoy!... Ship ahoy!... What ship's that?"

III

We are not conscious in a dream that we are playing a game the beginning and end of which are in ourselves. In this dream of Abel Keeling's a voice replied:

"Hallo, it's found its tongue... Ahoy there! What are you?"

Loudly and in a clear voice Abel Keeling called: "Are you a ship?"

With a nervous giggle the answer came:

"We are a ship, aren't we, Ward? I hardly feel sure... Yes, of course, we're a ship. No question about us. The question is what the dickens you are."

Not all the words these voices used were intelligible to Abel Keeling, and he knew not what it was in the tone of these last words that reminded him of the honour due to the *Mary of the Tower*. Blister-white and at the end of her life as she was, Abel Keeling was still jealous of her dignity; the voice had a youngish ring; and it was not fitting that young chins should be wagged about his galleon. He spoke curtly.

"You that spoke - are you the master of that ship?"

"Officer of the watch," the words floated back; "the captain's below."

"Then send for him. It is with masters that masters hold speech," Abel Keeling replied.

He could see the two shapes, flat and without relief, standing on a high narrow structure with rails. One of them gave a low whistle, and seemed to be fanning his face; but the other rumbled something into a sort of funnel. Presently the two shapes became three. There was a murmuring, as of a consultation, and then suddenly a new voice spoke. At its thrill and tone a sudden tremor ran through Abel Keeling's frame. He wondered what response it was that that voice found in the forgotten recesses of his memory...

"Ahoy!" seemed to call this new yet faintly remembered voice. "What's all this about? Listen. We're His Majesty's destroyer *Seapink*, out of Devonport last October, and nothing particular the matter with us. Now who are you?"

"The *Mary of the Tower*, out of the Port of Rye on the day of Saint Anne, and only two men -"

A gasp interrupted him.

"Out of WHERE?" that voice that so strangely moved Abel Keeling said unsteadily, while Bligh broke into groans of renewed rapture.

"Out of the Port of Rye, in the County of Sussex... nay, give ear, else I cannot make you hear me while this man's spirit and flesh wrestle so together!... Ahoy! Are you gone?" For the voices had become a low murmur, and the ship-shape had faded before Abel Keeling's eyes. Again and again he called. He wished to be informed of the disposition and economy of the wind-chamber...

"The wind-chamber!" he called, in an agony lest the knowledge almost within his grasp should be lost. "I would know about the wind-chamber..."

Like an echo, there came back the words, uncomprehendingly uttered, "The wind-chamber?..."

"... that driveth the vessel - perchance 'tis not wind - a steel bow that is bent also conserveth force - the force you store, to move at will through calm and storm..."

"Can you make out what it's driving at?"

"Oh, we shall all wake up in a minute..."

"Quiet, I have it; the engines; it wants to know about our engines. It'll be wanting to see our papers presently. Rye Port!... Well, no harm in humouring it; let's see what it can make of this. Ahoy there!" came the voice to Abel Keeling, a little more strongly, as if a shifting wind carried it, and speaking faster and faster as it went on. "Not wind, but steam; d'you hear? Steam, steam. Steam, in eight Yarrow water-tube boilers. S-t-e-a-m, steam. Got it? And we've twin-screw triple expansion engines, indicated horse-power four thousand, and we can do 430 revolutions per minute; savvy? Is there anything your phantomhood would like to know about our armament?..."

Abel Keeling was muttering fretfully to himself. It annoyed him that words in his own vision should have no meaning for him. How did words come to him in a dream that he had no knowledge of when wide awake? The *Seapink* - that was the name of this ship; but a pink was long and narrow, low-carged and square-built aft...

"And as for our armament," the voice with the tones that so profoundly troubled Abel Keeling's memory continued, "we've two revolving Whitehead torpedo-tubes, three six-pounders on the upper deck, and that's a twelve-pounder forward there by the conning-tower. I forgot to mention that we're nickel steel, with a coal capacity of sixty tons in most damnably placed bunkers, and that thirty and a quarter knots is about our top. Care to come aboard?"

But the voice was speaking still more rapidly and feverishly, as if to fill a silence with no matter what, and the shape that was uttering it was straining forward anxiously over the rail.

"Ugh! But I'm glad this happened in the daylight," another voice was muttering.

"I wish I was sure it was happening at all... Poor old spook!"

"I suppose it would keep its feet if her deck was quite vertical. Think she'll go down, or just melt?"

"Kind of go down... without wash...."

"Listen - here's the other one now -"

For Bligh was singing again:

"For, Lord, Thou know'st our nature such
If we great things obtain,
And in the getting of the same
Do feel no grief or pain,

"We little do esteem thereof;
But, hardly brought to pass,
A thousand times we do esteem
More than the other was."

"But oh, look - look - look at the other!... Oh, I say, wasn't he a grand old boy! Look!"

For, transfiguring Abel Reeling's form as a prophet's form is transfigured in the instant of his rapture, flooding his brain with the white eureka-light of perfect knowledge, that for which he and his dream had been at a standstill had come. He knew her, this ship of the future, as if God's Finger had bitten her lines into his brain. He knew her as those already sinking into the grave know things, miraculously, completely, accepting Life's impossibilities with a nodded "Of course." From the ardent mouths of her eight furnaces to the last drip from her lubricators, from her bed-plates to the breeches of her quick-firers, he knew her - read her gauges, thumbed her bearings, gave the ranges from her range-finders, and lived the life he lived who was in command of her. And he would not forget on the morrow, as he had forgotten on many morrows, for at last he had seen the water about his feet, and knew that there would be no morrow for him in this world...

And even in that moment, with but a sand or two to run in his glass, indomitable, insatiable, dreaming dream on dream, he could not die until he knew more. He had two questions to ask, and a master-question; and but a moment remained. Sharply his voice rang out.

"Ho, there!... This ancient ship, the *Mary of the Tower,* cannot steam thirty and a quarter knots, but yet she can sail the waters. What more does your ship? Can she soar above them, as the fowls of the air soar?"

"Lord, he thinks we're an aeroplane!... No, she can't..."

"And can you dive, even as the fishes of the deep?"

"No... Those are submarines... we aren't a submarine..."

But Abel Keeling waited for no more. He gave an exulting chuckle.

"Oho, oho - thirty knots, and but on the face of the waters - no more than that? Oho!... Now my ship, the ship I see as a mother sees full-grown the child she has but conceived - my ship, I say - oho! - my ship shall... Below there - trip that gun!"

The cry came suddenly and alertly, as a muffled sound came from below and an ominous tremor shook the galleon.

"By Jove, her guns are breaking loose below - that's her finish -"

"Trip that gun, and double-breech the others!" Abel Keeling's voice rang out, as if there had been any to obey him. He had braced himself within the belfry frame; and then in the middle of the next order his voice suddenly failed him. His ship-shape, that for the moment he had forgotten, rode once more before his eyes. This was the end, and his master-question, apprehension for the answer to which was now torturing his face and well-nigh bursting his heart, was still unasked.

"Ho - he that spoke with me - the master," he cried in a voice that ran high, "is he there?"

"Yes, yes!" came the other voice across the water, sick with suspense. "Oh, be quick!"

There was a moment in which hoarse cries from many voices, a heavy thud and rumble on wood, and a crash of timbers and a gurgle and a splash were indescribably mingled; the gun under which Abel Keeling had lain had snapped her rotten breechings and plunged down the deck, carrying Bligh's unconscious form with it. The deck came up vertical, and for one instant longer Abel Keeling clung to the belfry.

"I cannot see your face," he screamed, "but meseems your

voice is a voice I know. What is your name?"

In a torn sob the answer came across the water:

"Keeling - Abel Keeling… Oh, my God!"

And Abel Keeling's cry of triumph, that mounted to a victorious "Huzza!" was lost in the downward plunge of the *Mary of the Tower*, that left the strait empty save for the sun's fiery blaze and the last smoke-like evaporation of the mists.

Also available from
Parallel Universe Publications

COMING SOON

KITCHEN SINK GOTHIC
Selected by David and Linden Riley

AVAILABLE NOW

WILL ANYONE FIGURE OUT THAT THIS IS A REPACKAGED FIRST COLLECTION?
by Johnny Mains
ISBN: 978-0957453579

BLACK CEREMONIES
by Charles Black
ISBN-10: 0957453558

HIS OWN MAD DEMONS:
DARK TALES FROM DAVID A. RILEY
ISBN: 978-0-9574535-8-6

THEIR CRAMPED DARK WORLD AND OTHER TALES
by David A. Riley
ISBN: 978-0-9574535-9-3

THE HEAVEN MAKER AND OTHER GRUESOME TALES
by Craig Herbertson
ISBN-10: 0957453517

GOBLIN MIRE
by David A. Riley
ISBN-10: 095745354X

THINGS THAT GO BUMP IN THE NIGHT:
A TREASURY OF CLASSIC WEIRD
edited by Douglas Draa and David A. Riley
ISBN-10: 0957453566

Check our website:
http://paralleluniversepublications.blogspot.co.uk/

www.ingramcontent.com/pod-product-compliance
Lightning Source LLC
Chambersburg PA
CBHW070834250626
47159CB00003B/773
* 9 7 8 0 9 5 7 4 5 3 5 3 1 *